Purchased for Passion

A mistress bought and paid for...

Three exciting, sensual romances from three
favourite Mills & Boon authors!

In September 2009 Mills & Boon
bring you two classic collections, each
featuring three favourite romances
by our bestselling authors

TAKEN FOR REVENGE

Bedded for Revenge by Sharon Kendrick
Bought by a Billionaire by Kay Thorpe
The Bejewelled Bride by Lee Wilkinson

PURCHASED FOR PASSION

Shackled by Diamonds by Julia James
A Mistress for the Taking by Annie West
His Bought Mistress by Emma Darcy

Purchased for Passion

JULIA JAMES
ANNIE WEST
EMMA DARCY

MILLS & BOON

First published in Great Britain 2009
Harlequin Mills & Boon Limited,
Eton House, 18-24 Paradise Road, Richmond, Surrey TW9 1SR

PURCHASED FOR PASSION
© by Harlequin Enterprises II B.V./S.à.r.l 2009

Shackled by Diamonds, A Mistress for the Taking and *His Bought Mistress* were first published in Great Britain by Harlequin Mills & Boon Limited in separate, single volumes.

Shackled by Diamonds © Julia James 2006
A Mistress for the Taking © Annie West 2006
His Bought Mistress © Emma Darcy 2004

ISBN: 978 0 263 87139 5

05-0909

Printed and bound in Spain
by Litografia Rosés S.A., Barcelona

SHACKLED
BY DIAMONDS

BY
JULIA JAMES

Julia James lives in England with her family. Mills & Boon were the first 'grown up' books she read as a teenager, alongside Georgette Heyer and Daphne du Maurier, and she's been reading them ever since. Julia adores the English and Celtic countryside, in all its seasons, and is fascinated by all things historical, from castles to cottages. She also has a special love for the Mediterranean – 'The most perfect landscape after England'! – and she considers both ideal settings for romance stories. In between writing she enjoys walking, gardening, needlework, baking extremely gooey cakes and trying to stay fit!

CHAPTER ONE

LEO MAKARIOS paused in the shadows at the top of the flight of wide stairs leading down to the vast hall of Schloss Edelstein, one hand curved around the newel post of the massive carved wood banister, his powerful physique relaxing as he surveyed the arc-lit scene below with a sense of satisfaction.

Justin had chosen well. The four girls really were exquisite.

He stood a moment, looking them over.

The blonde caught his eye first, but despite her remarkable beauty she was too thin for his tastes, her pose too tense. He had no patience with neurotic women. The brunette beside her wasn't too thin, but for all her glorious swathe of chestnut hair her expression was vacant. Leo's gaze moved on. Unintelligent women irritated him.

The redhead's pre-Raphaelite looks were stunning indeed, but they had, Leo knew, already caught the attention of his cousin Markos, under whose protection the girl was living. His gaze moved on again to the final girl.

And stopped.

His eyes narrowed, taking in the picture she made.

The hair was sable. As black as night.

The skin was white. As pale as ivory.

And the eyes were green.

As green as the emeralds she was wearing.

Wearing with an air of such total boredom that a sudden shaft of anger went through him. What business had any female to look *bored* when wearing a Levantsky necklace? Did she not realise what a miracle of the jeweller's art the necklace was? And the earrings and the bracelets and the rings she was adorned with?

Evidently not. Even as he watched her lips pressed together

and she gave a conspicuously heavy sigh, placing one hand on her hip and very obviously shifting her weight from one leg to the other beneath her long skirts.

Leo stilled, the anger draining out of him. As she'd given that heavy sigh her breasts had lifted. Already lush from the tightly corseted black gown she was wearing, the movement had made their soft dove-white mounds swell delectably.

Through Leo's lean, powerful frame a familiar and pleasurable sensation started.

So the sable-haired, green-eyed beauty was bored, was she?

Well, he would be happy to remedy that.

Personally.

He started to walk down the stairs.

Anna felt her mood worsening. What was the hold-up now? Tonio Embrutti had gone into a huddle with his assistants, and she could hear the static hiss of vituperative Italian. She gave another sigh, feeling the low-cut décolletage digging in. She hated wearing it—it was far too revealing, and it invited the usual sleazy male attention she tried to avoid.

Her lips pressed together again. Mentally she forced herself to go through one of her karate *katas*. It both calmed her and reassured her, knowing she could fight off any physical harassment—even if she couldn't stop men leering over her.

She shifted her weight again minutely in the heavy dress. Modelling wasn't as easy as people thought it was, and she could tell that the two amateurs here—Kate and Vanessa— were finding it hard and tiring. Anna's eyes travelled to them. The brunette, Kate, looked vacant without her lenses in—but at least, thought Anna, it meant she couldn't see the lecherous looks aimed at her. The redhead, Vanessa, had other protection—word had gone round that her boyfriend was the cousin of the guy who'd set up this shindig and owned this medieval mansion. Though why, Anna mused, a Greek should own a castle in the Austrian Alps was beyond her. Maybe he just wanted to be close to the private Swiss bank he kept his loot in.

He certainly had a whole load of cash, that was for sure. Schloss Edelstein was vast, perched halfway up a mountain and surrounded by forests and snowfields.

Anna's bored expression lightened suddenly with remembered pleasure. The view from her bedroom was breathtaking: sunlight sparkling on the pristine snow, down to the frozen lake below, ringed by mountains. Very different from the view of the gasworks she'd had when she was growing up.

But then Anna had been lucky, she knew—spectacularly lucky.

Spotted in a shopping mall when she was eighteen by a scout for a modelling agency, she'd been incredibly suspicious at first. But the offer had proved genuine. Not that it hadn't taken non-stop hard work to succeed at modelling. Now, even though she was not in the supermodel bracket, and at twenty-six was already facing up to her limited remaining shelf-life, she made a living that was light-years away from what she'd been born to.

She'd learned a lot along the way. Not just how the other half lived—which had opened her eyes big-time—but about how to survive in one of the toughest careers around. And do it without letting the slime get to you.

Because slime, she had swiftly discovered, was a big, big feature of a fashion model's world. Some of the girls, she knew, did every drug they could, and slept with every man who could help their career. And a lot of the men in the fashion world weren't any better either.

Not that everyone was like that, she acknowledged. Some people in the fashion world were fine—there were designers she respected, photographers she trusted, models who were friends. Like Jenny, the blonde of the quartet, her best friend, draped now in white, with a diamond tiara and bracelets up to her elbows.

Anna's eyes narrowed.

Jenny didn't look well. She'd always been thin—what model wasn't?—but now she was on the point of looking emaciated. It wasn't drugs—Jenny didn't do drugs, or Anna would not have been friends with her. She hoped it wasn't just under-eating—especially not if some jerk of a photographer had been telling her to shift some non-existent weight. Illness? A shudder went through Anna. Life was uncertain enough, and you could die in your twenties all right. Hadn't her own mother not made it past twenty-five, leaving her fatherless baby daughter to be brought up by her widowed grandmother?

Whatever it was that was pulling Jenny down, Anna would try and catch some time with her, when today's shoot had finished. If it ever did. At least the huddle around Tonio Embrutti seemed to be ending. He was turning his attention back to the models. His little eyes flashed in his fleshy face, which a cultivated designer stubble did not enhance.

'You!' He pointed dramatically at Jenny. 'Off!'

Anna saw Jenny stare.

'Off?' she echoed dumbly.

The photographer waved his hands irritably.

'The dress. Off. Down to the hips. Peel it off. Then I need the hands crossed over in your cleavage. I want to shoot the bracelets. Hurry up!' He clicked impatiently at a hovering stylist and held out a hand for his camera from his assistant.

Jenny stood frozen.

'I can't.'

The photographer stared at her.

'Are you deaf? Remove your dress. Now!'

The stylist he'd pointed at was obediently undoing the fastenings down the back of Jenny's dress.

'I'm not taking the dress off!'

Jenny's voice sounded high-pitched with tension.

Anna saw Tonio Embrutti's face darken. She stepped forward to intervene.

'No strips,' she announced. 'It's in the contract.'

The photographer's face whipped round to hers.

'Shut up!' He turned back to Jenny.

Anna walked up to her, putting a hand out to stop the stylist. Jenny was looking as tense as a board.

Another voice spoke. A new voice.

'Do we have a problem?'

The voice was deep, and accented. It was also—and Anna could hear it like a low, subliminal tremor in her body—a warning.

A man had stepped out of the shadows consuming the rest of the vast hall beyond the brilliantly illuminated space they were being photographed in.

Anna felt the breath catch in her throat. The man who had stepped into the circle of light was like a leopard. Sleek, powerful, graceful—and dangerous.

Dangerous? She wondered why the word had come into her mind, but it had. And even as it formed it was replaced by another one.

Devastating.

The breath stayed caught in her throat as she stared, taking in everything about the man who had just appeared.

Tall. Very tall. Taller than her.

Dark hair, olive skin—and a face that could have stepped out of a Byzantine mosaic. Impassive, remote, assessing.

And incredibly sexy.

It was the eyes, she thought, as she slowly exhaled her breath. The eyes that did it. Almond-shaped, heavy-lidded, sensual.

Very dark.

He spoke again. Everyone seemed to have gone totally silent around him. He was the kind of man who'd have that effect on people, Anna found herself thinking.

'I repeat—do we have a problem?'

He doesn't like problems—he gets rid of them. They get in his way...

The words seemed to form in her mind of their own accord.

'And you are...?' Tonio Embrutti enquired aggressively.

Stupidly.

The man turned his impassive heavy-lidded eyes on him. For a moment he said nothing.

'Leo Makarios,' he said.

He didn't say it loudly, thought Anna. He didn't say it portentously. And he certainly didn't say it self-importantly.

Yet there was something about the way the man who owned Schloss Edelstein, whose company owned every jewel that she and the other three models were draped with, and who owned a whole heap more besides spoke. Something about the way he said his name that almost—almost—made her feel sorry for Tonio Embrutti.

Almost, but not quite. Because Tonio Embrutti was, without doubt, one of the biggest jerks she'd ever had the displeasure to be photographed by.

'Yes,' she announced clearly, before the photographer could get a word out. 'We do have a problem.'

The heavy-lidded eyes turned to her.

How, she found herself thinking, could eyes that were so impassive make her feel every muscle in her body tighten? As though she were an impala—caught out on a deserted African plain, with the sun going down.

When the big cats came out to hunt.

But she wasn't an impala, and this Leo Makarios was no leopard. He was just a rich man who was having a fun time getting his latest rich-man's toy some media attention. Starting with publicity photos, courtesy of four models specially hired for the purpose.

But *not* hired to strip.

'Your photographer,' she said sweetly, 'wants us to breach the contract.' Her voice changed. Hardened. 'No nude work. It's in the contract,' she informed him. 'I made sure it was. Check it out.'

She went on standing protectively beside Jenny. The other two girls—the amateurs—had, she noticed, instinctively closed in on each other as well. Both were looking uneasy.

Leo Makarios was still looking at her.

She was looking back.

Something was happening to her.

Something deep down. In her guts.

Something she didn't like.

Slime. Was that it? Was that what it was about the way Leo Makarios was looking at her that she didn't like?

No, she thought slowly. Definitely not slime. That she could handle. She'd had to learn how, and now she could.

But this was worse. What Leo Makarios was doing to her hit somewhere completely different.

She could feel it happening. Feel the slow, heavy slug of her heart rate. Feel the blood start to pulse.

As if for the very first time in her life.

Oh, no, she thought, with the kind of slow-motion thinking that came with great shock. Not this.

Not him.

But it was.

Leo let his eyes rest on her.

She wasn't looking bored now.

Two quite different emotions were animating her face, though she was, he could see, trying not to let the second one through.

The first emotion was anger. The girl was angry. Very angry.

It was an old anger too, one that was familiar to her.

But the second emotion was coming as a shock to her.

He felt a surge of satisfaction go through him.

She might be hiding it, but he'd seen it—seen the tell-tale minute flaring of her pupils as her eyes had impacted with his.

The satisfaction came again, but he put it to one side. He'd attend to it later—when the time was appropriate. Right now he had other matters to deal with.

He flicked his eyes to the blonde. Yes, definitely the neurotic type, he thought. Tense and jittery, and the type to give any man a headache. She was fantastically beautiful, of course, but he didn't envy the man who had the handling of her.

'Let me understand,' he said to her. 'You do not want this shot? The one Signor Embrutti desires?'

The girl was almost trembling she was so tense. She shook her head.

Tonio Embrutti burst into a fusillade of staccato Italian. Leo halted him with a peremptory hand.

'No breast shots. Not for her. Not for any of them. Their clothes stay on—all of them,' he spelt out, for good measure.

His eyes moved over the four girls, resting momentarily on the redhead. A smile almost flickered on his mouth. He could just imagine his cousin Markos's reaction to seeing his mistress's naked charms paraded in the publicity shots accompanying the launch of the rediscovered Levantsky collection—long-hidden in a secret Tsarist cache in the depths of Siberia and recently returned to the commercial world courtesy of a shrewd acquisition by Makarios Corp.

Markos would have beaten him to a pulp for allowing it!

If he could land a punch, that was, thought Leo, with dark humour.

Not that he would give him cause to—or any man who had an interest in the girls here.

His eyes flicked back to the sable-haired model. Was she taken? Just because she'd responded to him it didn't mean that another man didn't have his marker on her. She wouldn't be the first female to think she'd do better trading up to a Makarios.

Those that thought that way, however, he promptly lost interest in.

Such women made poor mistresses. Their minds were on his money—not on him.

And when he had a woman in bed with him he wanted her mind totally and utterly on him.

As the sable-haired model's would be when he bedded her. He would see to it.

He strolled to the side of the vast hall, nodding briefly to the senior security personnel hired to guard the Levantsky collection, leaned back against the edge of a heavy oak table, crossed one ankle over the other, folded his arms, and watched, wanting to see more of the girl he had selected for himself.

The shoot went on.

It was the turn of the sable-haired model next. Both to be shot and picked on.

Tonio Embrutti was clearly taking out his spleen on her. Nothing she did was right. He snapped and snarled and sneered at whatever she did, however she posed.

Leo felt an intense desire to stride across to the photographer and wring his scrawny neck. And he also felt a grudging admiration for the model.

She might be bored wearing a Levantsky *parure*, she might be the kind of troublemaker who quoted contractual conditions at the first sign of rough water, but when it came to putting up with what was being handed out to her she had the patience of a saint.

Which was curious, thought Leo, watching her assessingly, because she didn't look saint-like at all.

Not that she looked sexy.

Nothing that crass.

No, her intense sexual allure came from something quite different.

It came from her being supremely indifferent to it.

It really was, he mused, very powerful.

Very erotic.

His eyes swept over her. The black hair like a cloak, the milk-white shoulders and generous curve of her corseted breasts, her tiny waist and her accentuated hips, her slender but moulded arms—and then her face, of course. Almost square, with a defined jaw, and yet the high cheekbones, the straight nose, the wide, unconsciously voluptuous mouth—and the emerald eyes…

Oh, yes, she really was very, very erotic.

He felt his body stir, and he relaxed back to enjoy the view. And anticipate the night's entertainment to come.

Courtesy of the sable-haired model.

Idly, he wondered what her name was…

Anna sank her exhausted body into the hot, fragrant water. It felt blissful. God, she was tired. The shoot had been punishing.

Not just because of that jerk Embrutti—though keeping her cool with him had taken more effort than she enjoyed exerting—but simply because it had taken so long.

But in the end it had been a wrap. Every girl had been photographed wearing every different colour stone, with both matching and contrasting gowns. They would be wearing the jewels again tonight, at the grand reception Leo Makarios was holding to launch his revival of the Levantsky jewellery marque. Vanessa in emeralds, Kate in rubies, herself in diamonds and Jenny in sapphires.

Anna's eyes were troubled suddenly. She'd had her little chat with Jenny, following her into her room when they'd all finally been dismissed. She'd plonked her down on the bed, sat down beside her, and got the truth from her.

And it had shocked her totally.

'I'm pregnant!' Jenny had blurted out.

Anna had just stared. She hadn't needed to ask who by, or just why Jenny was so upset about it.

She'd warned her all along not to get involved with someone whose culture was so different from Western norms, that it could only end in trouble.

And it certainly had.

'He told me!' Jenny had rocked back and forth on the bed, clutching her abdomen where, scarcely visible, her baby was growing. 'He told me that if ever I got pregnant I faced two choices. Marrying him and living as his wife to raise the child. Or marrying him, giving him the child, and being divorced. But I can't. I can't do either! I can't!'

She'd started crying, and Anna had wrapped her up in her arms and let her cry.

'I can't marry him!' Jenny had sobbed. 'I can't live in some harem and never get out ever again. And as for giving up my baby…'

Her sobs had become even more anguished.

'I take it,' Anna had said, when they finally died away, 'that he doesn't know about the baby?'

'No! And he mustn't find out! Or he'll come and get me and

drag me back to his desert. Oh, God, Anna, he mustn't find out. Don't you see why I was so terrified when Tonio wanted me to strip down? In case it showed—the pregnancy. Supposing someone noticed—they would; you know they would—and it started circulating as a rumour. He'd pick up on it and he'd come storming down on me! Oh, God, I've got to get away. I've got to.'

Anna had frowned.

'Get away?'

'Yes. I've got to hide. Hide before anything starts really showing. And I mean hide for good, Anna. If he ever hears I've had a baby he'll know it's his. He'll have tests done and all that. So I've got to get away.'

She'd turned a stricken face to her friend.

'I've got to get really, really far away—and stay there. Totally resettle. Somewhere he'll never think of looking.' She bit her lip. 'I was planning on Australia. One of the obscure bits, round the northwest. Where the pearls come from. I can't remember what it's called, but it's the last place he'd look.'

Anna had looked sober.

'Can you afford to move out there, Jenny?'

She knew Jenny earned good money, but it was patchy. Neither of them were in the very top league of supermodels, and agency fees and other expenses ate into what they were paid. Besides, Jenny's ill-advised affair with the man she was now desperate to flee from had kept her out of circulation for too long—other, younger models were snapping up work she'd have now been grateful to get.

Jenny hadn't answered. Just bitten her lip.

'I can lend you—' Anna began, but Jenny had shaken her head.

'You need your money. I know how expensive that nursing home is for your gran. And I won't have you selling your flat. At our age we're both looking extinction in the face—you need your savings for when you quit modelling. So I'm not borrow-ing from you. I'll manage. Somehow.'

Anna hadn't bothered to press her offer. Somehow she

would make sure Jenny had at least enough to start running, start hiding—even if it meant mortgaging her flat to raise some cash.

Now she lay back in the water, letting the heat drain her tiredness. Poor Jenny—pregnant by a man who valued her only as a body, and who would part her from her baby with the click of his imperious fingers. Neither of the generous 'options' he'd given her was acceptable. No, Jenny had to get away, all right. As soon as this shoot was over.

But there was more to get through yet. Already guests had started to arrive. Driven up in chauffeured cars or deposited via helicopter. The rich, the famous, the influential—all invited by Leo Makarios.

She stared at the steam gently rising from the huge claw-footed bathtub.

Leo Makarios.

She was going to have to think about him.

She didn't want to.

Had been putting it off.

But now she had to think about him.

Cautiously she opened her mind to what had happened.

For the first time in four long, safe years she had seen a man who was dangerous to her.

And it was disturbing.

Because men weren't dangerous to her. Not any more. Not since Rupert Vane had told her that he was off to marry Caroline Finch-Carleton—a girl, unlike Anna, from his own upper-crust background.

Even now, four years on, she could still feel the burn of humiliation. Of hurt.

Rupert had been the first man—the only man—who had got past her defences. He'd had the lazily confident good-mannered charm of a scion of the landed classes, and he'd simply breezed through each and every one of her rigidly erected guards. He had been funny, and fun, and fond of her in his own shallow way.

'It's been a hoot, Anna,' he'd told her as he'd given her the news about his forthcoming marriage.

Since then she'd kept men—all men—at a safe distance. Thanking heaven, in a perverse way, that most of the ones she encountered held no attraction for her.

Into her mind, as the water lapped her breasts, an image stole. A picture of a man looking her over with dark heavy-lidded eyes.

Leo Makarios.

Deliberately she let herself think about him. I need to know, she thought. I need to know why he's dangerous to me.

So that I can guard against it.

Something had happened today that had got her worried. A man had looked her over and it had got to her. And she didn't know why.

It couldn't be because he was good looking—her world was awash with fantastic-looking men, and not all of them were gay. And it couldn't be because he was rich—because that had always been the biggest turn-off, accompanied as it usually was by an assumption that models were sexually available to rich men.

So what the hell was going on?

All she knew were two things.

That when it came to Leo Makarios she would have to be very, very careful.

And that she wanted to see him again.

CHAPTER TWO

EFFORTLESSLY, Leo switched from Italian to French, and then into German and English, as he greeted his guests. The vast hall had been cleared of all the photographic clutter, and was now thronged with women in evening dress and men in black tie, and waiters circulating with trays of champagne.

'Markos!' Leo switched to Greek and greeted his cousin. A couple of years younger than Leo's thirty-four, and of slightly slimmer build, his dark slate eyes revealed his portion of English ancestry. Markos was otherwise all Greek. They chatted a moment or two, and Leo cast a courteous smile at the pre-Raphaelite redhead at Markos's side.

She didn't return the smile. She didn't even see him. She was gazing at his cousin with a bemused, helpless expression in her eyes, as though Markos were the only person in the universe.

A strange ripple of emotion went through Leo.

No woman had ever looked at him like that...

Would you want them to?

The question thrust rhetorically, challengingly.

He answered promptly.

No, definitely not. Any woman who looked at him like that would be a nuisance.

Or faking it.

In the past there had been women who'd passionately declared their undying love for him, but he'd known better. The object of their devotion was not him, but his wealth. Now he never let any woman tell him she loved him.

He made the terms of his endearment crystal-clear from the outset. A temporary affair, exclusive while it lasted, with no emotional scenes to irritate him, no hysterical recriminations when it came to an end, and no post-affair harassment. When it was over, it was over—and could they please both move on? He would—she must too. They would inevitably cross paths again in the cosmopolitan world he moved in, and he didn't want any unwelcome scenes or unpleasant encounters.

He moved through the throng, meeting and greeting his myriad guests. His eyes were scanning the crowd, picking out the models circulating with their display of Levantsky jewels.

Where was the sable-haired one?

Suddenly he saw her, and he stopped dead.

She looked absolutely and totally stunning.

She was wearing a black dress so simple it was almost a sarong, wrapped tightly across her breasts and then falling in a single fluid line to her ankles. With it she wore black elbow-length evening gloves. Unlike earlier, her hair was up, in a soft, immensely flattering low pompadour on the back of her head, framing her face. She had far less make-up on than she'd had for the shoot; her mouth merely seemed to have lipgloss, and her eyes little more than mascara. Her skin was still ivory-white.

Against the whiteness the shimmer of diamonds circling her slender throat glittered iridescently, enhancing her already exquisite beauty.

For a full moment Leo did nothing but look, taking in the vision she presented. She really was quite exceptional…

Then, abruptly, a frown drew his brows together. He strode towards her.

She'd been standing on her own, a glass of champagne in one long black-satined hand, and she was gazing up at the snarling mask of a long-dead boar on one of the walls. There was an expression of strong disapproval on her face.

'Why are you not wearing the rest of the *parure*?' he demanded as he reached her.

Her head spun round.

There was that flaring of her pupils again, he could see it. But right now he wasn't interested. He was interested only in why she was not wearing the tiara, earrings and bracelets that matched the necklace, as she'd been instructed to do that evening.

'Well?' he prompted.

She seemed to collect herself minutely.

'One of the bulbs was on the blink,' she answered.

Leo frowned more deeply.

'What?' he snapped.

'As in Christmas lights. I mean,' she asked him, 'did you actually want me wandering around looking like a Christmas tree? It just looked ridiculously overdone wearing the whole lot together.'

'And that was your decision, was it?'

The tone was mild, but it raised the hairs on the back of Anna's neck.

There was no way she was backing down, though. She'd seen her reflection when she'd been wearing the whole lot, and she'd just looked like a glitterball.

'It would,' she riposted pointedly, 'be the decision of anyone who had any taste.'

His eyes narrowed at her tone. 'My instructions were quite clear.'

Anna knew exactly what she should say. Leo Makarios was paying her to model his jewellery, and he called the shots. She should say docilely, *Of course, Mr Makarios. Three bags full, Mr Makarios.*

But she didn't.

'Well, you were wrong,' she said instead. 'To wear any more jewellery than this necklace would be irredeemably vulgar.'

His face stilled. Something changed in the heavy-lidded eyes. She ought to back down; she knew she should. But she never backed down. If you did you got walked over.

For one long moment his eyes simply rested on her. She could feel the tension start to edge through her.

Then she realised what he was doing.

Out-psyching her.

So she took the battle into his corner.

'Surely, Mr Makarios,' she posed limpidly, 'a man with all your money would not wish to appear vulgar?'

For one timeless second it hung in the balance. And for that moment Anna found herself hoping for something—and she didn't even know why she was hoping for it.

But she got it all the same.

At the corner of his mouth, almost imperceptibly, she saw a quirk.

Something lightened inside her. She didn't know what, or why, but it did.

Then the quirk vanished and the mouth was a straight, tight line once more, the heavy-lidded eyes quelling.

'You live dangerously,' said Leo Makarios softly. 'Don't do it on my time.'

He gave a brief indication of his head. 'Go and put the jewels back on.'

He walked away. Cutting her out of existence.

For one intense moment an urge so strong almost overpowered her and she had to steel her whole body. She wanted to vault forward, lift her empty hand up and bring it slashing down. But, slowly, she stood, letting the aggressive urge drain out of her. Why on earth should she let a man like Leo Makarios get to her? He was just one more rich man who liked the world the way he paid it to be. And right now he was paying her to wear his jewels. All his jewels. However vulgar such an over-the-top display would be. She gave a shrug.

He wanted diamonds? She'd put on diamonds.

As she strode off, as fast as her narrow skirt would permit, she did not see a pair of heavy-lidded eyes flick past the shoulder of the chief executive Leo happened to be speaking to and rest narrowingly on her.

Then, as she disappeared from view, he went back seamlessly to discussing the implications of the latest G8 summit on world trade.

The chamber orchestra was tuning up, people were taking their seats in the ballroom. Unlike the medieval-style hall, the ball-

room was pure rococo, lined with mirrors and with an extrav-
agantly carved gilded ceiling. Set diagonally, like miniature
wings either side of the orchestra, were two pairs of gilt *fau-
teuils*. They were for the models, so the audience could admire
the Levantsky jewels in their massed splendour while they listened to Mozart. Three of the girls, noted Leo, as he entered,
had just taken their places. His eyes flicked over them again
as he made some conversational reply to the wife of one of the
Austrian government ministers sitting beside him.

The redhead was gazing into the audience, openly searching
for Markos. The brunette, Leo noted with mild surprise, had
lost her vacant look and was talking animatedly to the musician
closest to her.

His eyes flicked across to the two chairs on the other side
of the orchestra. The blonde was there, looking more uptight
than ever, but the chair beside her was empty.

Leo felt his mouth tightening again.

Definitely a troublemaker.

He'd had confirmation. He'd sent for his aide, Justin, who
was taking care of the publicity side of the Levantsky launch,
and told him to check that the black-haired girl was this time
obeying orders. Justin had looked nervous, and muttered something about her agency warning him that she had a bit of an
attitude issue.

Leo had just looked at Justin. 'Not while she's here,' he'd
said.

Justin had scurried off.

Leo took his place beside the minister's wife. The orchestra
went on tuning up.

The girl cut it fine. Very fine.

The audience were finally quietening; the conductor was at
his podium.

She came gliding in, whisking into her seat. Then she just
sat there, hands folded demurely in her lap.

She had the tiara in her hair, long drops in her ears, bracelets
on both arms, and the necklace of diamonds.

Looking exactly like an illuminated Christmas tree.

Leo's mouth tightened.

He hated being wrong. About anything.

Or anyone.

Anna's feet were killing her again. It was the worst aspect of modelling, she thought—apart from the boredom and the sleaze.

But she stood, politely attentive, while a stout German industrialist regaled her with the healing properties of spa waters. Across the room, Anna could see Leo Makarios talking to someone. She hoped he was happy with the Christmas lights.

They were certainly getting enough attention from the guests, that was for sure. She'd been on the receiving end of countless inspections by both men and women—though the male ones had been liberally blended with lecherous looks as well—speculating about the price. And not just of the jewels.

That was why she was sticking where she was. Spa cures might not be the most fascinating subject in the world, but the German industrialist was treating her with great courtesy. Better still, he was keeping other men away from her.

All except one.

'Hans, *wie gehts*?'

The deep, accented voice was unmistakable.

Anna felt herself tense automatically, vivid with awareness of who had just approached.

The industrialist's face lit into a warm smile and he launched into German. As Leo Makarios answered him in the same language, his voice rich and smooth, Anna could feel him looking at her, taking in the ostentatious display of diamonds she was showing off.

As he regarded her she kept her face expressionless, her eyes blank.

For a moment Leo thought of telling her that she'd been right, that wearing the entire *parure* was overkill, detracting from the exquisite beauty of the rainfall necklace.

Then Hans Federman was asking a question about his experience of doing business in the former Eastern Bloc, and comparing it with his own company's experiences.

Taking advantage of the diversion, Anna was about to drift off. But as she started to move, without pausing a beat in what he was saying, Leo Makarios snaked his hand out and fastened it round her wrist.

Anna froze. Entirely opposite reactions flashed through her. One was an instinct to yank her arm away from his restraining hold. The second was a bolt of hot electricity that shocked her to her core.

Then, abruptly, her wrist was dropped. Leo Makarios stopped talking and turned his head to her.

'Don't wander off, please, Ms…?' He cocked an eyebrow at her, pointedly waiting for her to supply her name.

'Anna Delane,' she said reluctantly. She wondered why she was so unwilling to let Leo Makarios know her name. All he had to do was ask one of his scores of minions, including that obsequious toady Justin Vennor, who'd lectured the four models for half an hour on how they must behave impeccably in such august and glittering surroundings.

'Anna.'

It was just her name, that was all. She'd heard it said all her life.

But not like this…

A shiver went down her spine. She could feel it. It started somewhere at the nape of her neck and shimmered down the length of her back.

For a second Leo's gaze just rested on her. She felt it like a tangible weight. Assessing her.

Then it was gone. Leo Makarios turned back and resumed his German conversation.

Mutely, Anna stayed at his side.

He kept her there for the rest of the evening.

It took all her professionalism to keep going. That and a dogged, grim determination that she was *not* going to let this get to her.

Let Leo Makarios get to her.

Because he was.

She could tell herself all she liked that to a man like Leo Makarios, surrounded as he was by chic, elegant, rich and aristocratic women from his own world, she was nothing but a walking jewellery display.

But why, then, was he keeping her at his side? And if her, then why not the other models in turn?

She said as much at one point. He had just disengaged himself gracefully from a Dutch banker and his wife, and had taken Anna's elbow to guide her towards the buffet tables.

'Isn't it time to show off the other stones now, Mr Makarios? There's Kate with the rubies—over there.'

She indicated where the brunette was gazing awestruck, or so it seemed to her, at one of the men in the group she was part of. He was, Anna recognised, the orchestra's conductor.

Leo Makarios's gaze flicked across to Kate.

'How could I deprive Antal Lukacs of his latest adoring fan?' he murmured sardonically. 'And such a young and beautiful one.'

Anna's eyes widened. 'That's Antal Lukacs?' Even she had heard of such a world-famous conductor.

The heavy-lidded eyes glanced down at her.

'Would you like to meet him?'

'I'm sure he's quite bored enough with people gushing all over him,' she said dismissively.

'Somehow,' Leo Makarios murmured, 'I can't see you *gushing* over anyone.' His voice became dryer suddenly, more critical. 'You are certainly quite unimpressed to be wearing jewels that every woman here envies you wearing.'

Anna looked up at him.

'They're just carbon crystals—valued only because they are rare. Lots of other common crystals are just as beautiful. Diamonds are only worth money—'

'They are the Levantsky diamonds! Works of art in their own right,' Leo said sharply.

She shrugged. 'So is Mozart's music—and that doesn't cost millions to enjoy!'

The dark eyes rested on her. She watched them narrow very slightly. She did not look away. Why should she?

'I was told,' he said softly—and it was that same softness that had raised the hair on the nape of her neck earlier '—that you have an attitude issue. Lose it.'

She smiled sweetly up at him. She could feel adrenaline start to run in her.

'Is that another of your instructions, Mr Makarios?'

For a long moment he looked at her. She felt the adrenaline curl around every cell in her body.

'What is your problem, Ms Delane?' he asked, in that same soft, deadly voice.

You, she wanted to say. *You're the problem.*

Then, even as she stared defiantly back at him, her false smile straightening to a thin, pressed line, something changed in his eyes.

He seemed to move minutely, as if closing her off from the rest of the room.

The lashes swept down over his eyes, and she felt the breath in her throat tighten.

'Don't fight me,' he said in a low voice. Then she could see it. Something else came into his eyes, something that made a hollow where her stomach usually was. 'You really are,' he added slowly, 'quite incredibly beautiful…'

Anna felt the hollow where her stomach had been turn slowly over.

No. She didn't want this happening. She didn't.

She opened her mouth to say so. Say something. Anything. But all she could do was stare. The room disappeared; the people disappeared; everything vanished. She was just standing, looking up at the man—letting him look at her. Look at her with those powerful heavy-lidded eyes, over which those long dark lashes were sweeping down.

The hollow where her stomach had been pooled with heat—

heat that was starting to spread out through the veins in her body, carried by her treacherous beating heart.

She saw him see it. See the way the heat was starting to flow through her body. The eyes, so dark, so lambent, narrowed. A smile curved along his wide, mobile mouth. It was a smile of acknowledgement, satisfaction.

Anticipation.

He murmured something to her. So quietly that in the buzz of noise and conversation all around Anna thought she must have imagined it.

Of course she had imagined it.

But for a moment she thought he had murmured, 'Later...'

Then, in an instant, his expression changed, becoming smooth and bland.

'Ah, Minister...'

The perambulation resumed. And Leo Makarios still kept Anna at his side.

Anna kicked off her shoes with a sense of relief. Then she peeled off the long black satin gloves, dropping them onto the dressing table stool in her room. Hooking her now bare fingers round her back, she started to undo the painstakingly fastened together dress. The diamonds had been handed back into the care of the security company, and finally the models had been free to go up to their rooms. Anna had hardly been able to wait.

God, the evening had been endless!

And more than that. Her nerves were shredded, stretched to breaking point.

Being touted around by Leo Makarios had been excruciating. She could feel the tension racking up in her.

He was getting to her, and she didn't like it. Not one bit.

Her lips pressed together. Spending time with the man the way she had should have *de*sensitised her to him. Should have made her get past that ridiculous disturbing rush she'd felt when he'd first walked in on the shoot and had such an impact on her. By now she should simply be able to see him abstractly, as a good-looking man. Exceptionally so, for a rich man—the combination was as rare as hen's teeth in her experience—but nothing more. Certainly not a man who should have the slightest effect on her.

Such as making her breath catch in her throat.

Heat flush through her.

Nerves quicken in awareness.

Electricity shoot through her.

No!

Grimly she stared at herself in the mirror over the dressing table.

Yes, she was slightly flushed; her eyes were a little wider than usual. But that was just because it had been a long day and a longer evening. She was tired, that was all.

She looked at her reflection defiantly.

Out of the glass stared back a familiar image. The black hair, the pale skin and the green eyes. Probably inherited from your dad—whoever he was—her gran had always told her. The dramatic, eye-catching features an accidental meshing of DNA that had just happened to produce a face that was beautiful.

But her beauty was just a commodity. She sold it, day after day, to anyone who paid the right price for it.

And that's all I sell.

Too many men thought otherwise. Thought she was also selling the right for them to look her up and down, strip her naked with their eyes, wonder what she was like in bed, offer to find out…

She turned away from the mirror sharply, continuing to undo, hook by hook, the simple but beautifully made dress.

At least she was free of the diamonds. The whole ridiculous glitter of them. Her eyes hardened again. Had Leo Makarios really not been able to see how overdone the whole lot was when worn together like that? That the sum was less than the individual pieces?

She shook her head in impatience. Who cared what Leo Makarios thought? About his wretched Levantsky diamonds or about her.

Or, she told herself doggedly, what she thought about him.

It's completely academic anyway. After this I'll never set eyes on him again. And then I'll be safe…

She stilled. Why had she used that word? She was safe from Leo Makarios right now! Yes, he'd cast his eye over her, and found her visually pleasing, but she'd obviously annoyed him with her attitude—and anyway, for heaven's sake, the man was in the middle of a glittering, glamorous party held to impress his rich pals—he wasn't going to take time out to chase around some clothes-horse he'd hired. And who said he wanted her in the first place? A man with his looks and money must have women queuing round the block for his attention. He could pick any woman he wanted from his glittering social circle. He was probably schmoozing some Austrian countess or Park Avenue princess right now.

So how come he clamped you to his side the whole evening?

She shrugged. Justin had probably warned him that her booker had called her 'difficult', and so Leo Makarios had just been keeping her in order—at his side.

A saying floated through her head.

Keep your friends close, but your enemies closer.

She frowned. Why had that come into her mind?

Leo Makarios was neither a friend nor an enemy.

He was a stranger. Nothing more.

And he was going to stay one.

That way, he'd never be dangerous to her.

CHAPTER THREE

LEO strolled down the long carpeted corridor, the two household staff in front of him loaded down with trays.

He wasn't sure he'd ever been to this floor before. It wasn't the old servants' quarters in the attic, but nor was it guest apartments. But even if the rooms up here lacked the opulent extravagance of the main floors of the Schloss they were still very comfortably appointed. Just right for office staff or other employees. He wondered idly if the three models were all housed in a row. The redhead, of course, would be with Markos, in one of the lavish suites below. Would the blonde and the brunette have found somewhere else to sleep tonight? he mused. Maybe the brunette was busy adoring Antal Lukacs from close quarters, he though cynically, knowing the conductor's penchant for females. The blonde, though, had looked far too tense to be receptive to the admiration she had received during the evening.

None of them were of any interest to him, however. There was only one woman who had caught his eye, and she, he knew, had been highly receptive to him. Oh, she might have an attitude issue, but that was immaterial. It wouldn't last. He would see to that. He'd have her purring like a cat before long.

Women always purred for him.

The two staff stopped outside one of the doors and glanced back at him. He gave a nod, and one of them knocked discreetly.

Inside the room, Anna paused, dropping her hands from her back. What on earth...? The knock came again. Hastily doing up her hooks again, for decency's sake, she crossed over and opened the door. Outside were two of the household staff, each bearing a huge tray covered with a linen cloth.

'I'm sorry,' she said, taken aback. 'I mean—um—*Entschuldigen Sie bitte, aber Ich habe nicht…*'

Her sketchy German failed her. She had no idea how to say she had not ordered anything.

The man merely bowed slightly and swept in, followed by the second man. They set both trays down on the low table in front of a pair of armchairs by the window, and removed the cloths.

An entire light supper was contained on the trays—including, she saw, a bottle of chilled white wine, a flagon of orange juice, a jug of mineral water and a coffee pot.

'I'm afraid I didn't ask for—' she began.

'But I, however, did.' A deep, familiar voice interrupted her.

She whipped round. There, in the doorway, stood Leo Makarios.

For a moment Anna just stared, unable to believe her eyes.

Let alone what was happening.

He strolled into her room.

He was still in evening dress, still looking impeccable, as only a man of his height, wealth and looks could look, but there was a faint shadow along his jaw that somehow suddenly made him look—

Sexy.

The word came out of nowhere into her brain, and the moment it formed she was horrified.

She opened her mouth to say something. Anything. But her mind was a maelstrom of conflicting emotions. Predominant was disbelief. Sheer disbelief that Leo Makarios was strolling into her bedroom, one hand in his trouser pocket, looking as though he had every right to be there.

The two members of his household staff evidently thought so. They were diligently laying out their wares on the low table, deftly and neatly, placing a large plate of thinly sliced smoked chicken, ham and salmon together with a bowl of salad and a basket of bread in the centre, with porcelain plates and silver cutlery nestling in white damask napkins. Crystal glasses followed suit, and then a coffee service and drinks and a plate of tiny chocolate truffles.

'Won't you sit down?' said Leo Makarios, indicating one of the armchairs. He simultaneously lowered his tall frame into the other one.

What the hell do you think you're doing? She wanted to scream at him.

But the presence of the two staff made it impossible. Good grief, the last thing she wanted was to make a public scene that would inevitably feed back into the gossip machine that was always at work around the rich and famous.

Every nerve screwed tight, she urged them mentally to clear out. Because the moment they were gone she would—

'*Gnadige Fraulein?*' One of the staff was indicating her chair, bowing politely. The other was busy opening the wine.

Oh, hell, she would have to sit down, pretend that—my goodness—no, of course there was nothing strange in the castle's multimillionaire owner turning up to have a little midnight supper with her!

Stiffly, she sat down, carefully ensuring the narrow skirts of her excruciatingly valuable dress were not catching on anything. Her face was a mask. But behind the mask her emotions were tumbling like a wash cycle set to crazy.

Skirts settled, and ignoring the fact that her back was imperfectly fastened, she looked up, ready to aim a killing glare at him.

Instead, she just stared, the breath stalling in her throat.

Leo Makarios was loosening his dress tie and slipping the top button on his shirt.

That, and the shadowed jawline, made her heart stop beating.

Oh, dear God, he is just so—

The word slipped straight into her mind—right out of her subconscious.

Sexy.

It was that word again, coming out of nowhere—refusing to go. She had heard it a million times—it was one of the most popular in the fashion world. But it had never meant anything at all to her. It was just people posing and pouting and putting it on for the camera or an audience.

With Leo Makarios it was real.

And it was, she realised, standing there as if someone had punched her in the solar plexus, incredibly powerful.

She tried desperately to analyse it away. It was just the juxtaposition of contrasting modes, that was all—the severe formality of the tuxedo with the raffish informality of a loosened tie and shirt, accentuated by the roughened jawline.

But the effect didn't diminish. Quite the reverse, it simply gained potency, aided and abetted by the way his lean frame lounged back in supreme ease, long legs stretched out, hands curved over the arms of the chair, head resting on the chairback, those dark heavy-lidded eyes resting on her.

Looking at her.

Letting her look back.

Suddenly she did not want the household staff to disappear. She didn't want to be alone with Leo Makarios.

Anna could feel a heat flaring out from somewhere deep inside her. She tried to douse it, extinguish it, but it wouldn't be cooled. Instead it curled and spread through her as she just sat there, drinking in the man sitting opposite her, now being offered a taste of the wine that had just been opened.

She saw him sample the wine, saw him nod, saw the member of staff turn to fill her glass and then his employer's, then be dismissed with his colleague, saw them both bowing briefly and then quitting the room, shutting the door behind them.

Leaving her alone with Leo Makarios.

With huge effort she quashed down the dangerous pooling heat inside her.

She opened her mouth to speak, protest his uninvited presence.

But Leo Makarios was before her.

'Well,' he said, *'Mahlzeit.'*

Anna's mouth snapped shut again.

'What?'

'Mahlzeit,' he repeated, in his accented voice. His eyes

gleamed slightly. 'Have you not heard that yet? Austrians invariably pronounce that to each other before eating. It means
mealtime. It appears to be their version of *bon appetit*. Now,
what may I help you to?'

He picked up the serving spoon and fork and let them hover
over the plate of meats and salmon.

She took a deep breath.

'Mr Makarios—' she began.

He looked up. 'Leo,' he said. 'I think we can dispense with
the formalities now. *Theos*, it's been a long evening! But,' he
went on, calmly selecting a slice of smoked chicken and placing it on her empty plate, 'a highly successful one. Ham and
salmon?'

'No, thank you,' she snapped. 'Mr Makarios, I—'

The dark eyes lifted to her.

'Leo,' he said softly. 'So, just chicken, then?' He placed
another slice on her plate. 'Salad?'

'No! I don't want any food. I don't want—'

He scooped up some salad and added it to her plate.

'I ate very little this evening, and you ate absolutely nothing.
You must be hungry.'

I'm always hungry, she wanted to snap. But if I eat I'll put
on weight and lose jobs. So I don't eat. And I ignore hunger!

But even as the words formed in her mind she felt a treacherous pang in her stomach. She didn't usually starve herself as
she had done this evening. That was just counter-productive.
But tonight had been so nerve-racking because of having to
stay glued to Leo's side that the very idea of eating some of
the buffet food, however delicious, had been impossible. She
had planned to have herbal tea and an orange—she never travelled without either—to see her through to breakfast in the
morning.

But the sight and smell of the beautifully prepared and presented food was so enticing. The hunger pang came again. The
scent of a freshly baked roll wafted to her. She felt her willpower weaken.

All right—she would eat a light supper, a very light supper, and then throw Leo Makarios out. It was perfectly obvious what he'd turned up here for—

Or was it?

Had she got it completely wrong?

He had started to speak again.

'Tell me,' he said, as he helped himself to food, 'have you known the other three models long?'

Anna paused in the middle of lifting her fork to start eating. Chicken and salad without dressing wouldn't be a crime—and she would, of course, ignore the rolls.

'I beg your pardon?' Her voice sounded surprised at his question.

He repeated it, shaking out a white damask napkin on his lap and lifting his plate.

She took a mouthful of chicken, which melted in her mouth. 'I've known Jenny for several years, but this is the first time I've worked with Kate and Vanessa.'

'Which one is the redhead?' Leo Makarios asked.

'That would be Vanessa,' Anna replied with exaggerated politeness. 'The one with the big boobs, in case you need another way of identifying her.' Her voice was acid.

Dark eyes flicked over her.

'You really do need to lose that attitude,' Leo Makarios murmured.

'So do you,' she bit back. 'Models do have names, as well as bodies.'

She forked up a large amount of salad with unnecessary vigour.

'You take offence where none is intended—I merely had not yet managed to distinguish the four of you by name, only hair colour,' he replied coolly. The eyes rested on her momentarily. She thought she saw irritation in them.

Was that supposed to be a reprimand? Anna wondered. If so, no sale.

She gave an indifferent shrug. 'Why do you ask about Vanessa?' she prompted. She was both relieved that he was not here for the reason she had assumed and warily curious as to why he was asking about his cousin's girlfriend. Maybe, she thought suddenly, Leo Makarios was in poaching mode. Not, however, that Vanessa had eyes for anyone other than this guy's cousin. Talk about stars in her eyes...the girl had it bad. Anna only hoped she wouldn't get hurt—but she wasn't taking bets on it.

He took a mouthful of wine.

'If you do not know her well, my enquiry will mean little,' he answered.

'Yes, well, what little I do know of her is that she's a nice girl.' Anna replied all the same—pointedly. 'Nice, if dumb,' she added.

Leo Makarios's eyebrows pulled together, making him look forbidding somehow.

'Dumb?' There was a bite in his voice she'd have been deaf not to hear.

'Dumb enough to fall for your cousin, I mean,' she elucidated.

The forbidding look suddenly became even more intense.

Anna gave him an old-fashioned look. 'Oh, come on—your fancy cousin hardly looks like a down-on-one-knee kind of guy! Vanessa's going to get burned—big-time. It's totally obvious.'

'My cousin is very generous to his mistresses,' Leo Makarios informed her. There was hauteur in his face now, and a repressive note in his voice.

A choking sound escaped Anna.

'Mistresses? Last time I looked, crinolines were definitely out of fashion!'

He frowned again.

'I do not understand your reference.'

'It means mistresses went out with Queen Victoria. Mistresses—kept women—rich protectors, you know.'

A cynical curve indented his mouth.

'You think women no longer like to take rich men as their lovers, and thereby live in a style that they could not afford for themselves?'

Her eyes hardened. He was right, damn it—her exposure to the realities of life in the fashion world had taught her that a long time ago.

'If they do, then 'mistress' is not the term I'd use for them,' she riposted.

'What would you use then?'

'One unfit for mixed company.' She gave her acid-sweet smile again. 'And, by the way, no—I do *not* count Vanessa as one of them!'

'You are so sure of that?' The cynical note was back in his voice.

Anna glared at him.

'Yes,' she said. 'I am. I just hope she's got a best friend to mop her up when your cousin gets bored with being adored and moves on to his next squeeze.'

The dark eyebrows drew together again.

'I have already told you that Markos has no reason not to be generous to her when he ends their affair.'

Anna gave up. There was clearly no point discussing the matter. Vanessa was going to get hurt, and if good old Markos was anything like his lovely cousin then it was going to be tears after bedtime for sure.

'You can't dry your eyes on diamonds,' she contented herself with answering dryly.

'She is a very beautiful woman—she will soon find another lover.'

The indifference in his voice raised her hackles.

'Oh, good—that's all right, then.' Anna bestowed another acid smile on him.

But Leo Makarios was frowning again—and then a different expression was on his face.

'What you say is disturbing,' he said slowly. 'You believe she has ambitions for marriage?'

'Ambitions?' Anna sat back. Her chicken and salad were gone, and she wasn't about to help herself to any more. The pangs had been stilled, and it was time to get rid of Mr Money-Bags Makarios—and his delightful views on female venality.

'I'd say she probably has some fairy-tale vision of wafting down an aisle to a heavenly choir towards your cousin suddenly transformed into Prince Charming with a halo, but she can't possibly be idiotic enough to think a man like your cousin is going to *marry* her!'

Leo Makarios's mouth tightened.

'Perhaps you could ensure,' he said, resting his eyes on her, 'that she understands that that is indeed the case. She must harbour no ambitions to entrap Markos into marriage.'

Anna reached for the water. 'I'll be sure to pass the message on,' she said dryly.

'A naïve woman can be even more dangerous than a clever one,' he rejoined darkly.

Dangerous. Suddenly Anna wished he hadn't used that particular word. It was the one that had been haunting her about *him* ever since she'd set eyes on him.

Of their own volition her eyes swept across to him.

He seemed to be lost in thought, heavy-lidded eyes inward-looking, a brooding expression on his face. Preoccupied as he was, she could not resist indulging in just gazing at him a moment.

Oh, dear God, he really was gorgeous! She just stared at him, as if he were a forbidden cream cake in a baker's shop. Then, forcing herself, she dragged her eyes away and finished pouring out her glass of water. She drank it down and set the glass back on the table.

She gave herself a mental shake. Whatever her first assumptions had been about why Leo Makarios had swanned in here at this time of night, it was clear she'd been completely wrong. He was simply here on an intelligence-gathering mission—the purpose of which was to protect his precious cousin from women who—shock, horror—fell in love with him.

Leo wasn't here to pounce. In fact he was probably just using up some rare spare time while a piece of posh totty slipped into her couture negligee and buffed her nails in his state apartment downstairs. Rich men, she knew, from her years in the fashion world, did odd things at odd times. Being eccentric, like turning up complete with a midnight supper just to get the gen on his cousin's squeeze, was one of the perks of being so loaded you could do what you liked and no one even blinked.

She watched him polish off the last of his meal. He definitely had a large frame to fill up. Not that there was the slightest sign of fat on him. All lean muscle. A lot of power and vigour at his disposal. Whoever was waiting for him was clearly in for an energetic night…

No—stop that! Her self-admonishment was instant and severe. The less she thought about Leo Makarios's sex life—which had *nothing* to do with her!—the better. In fact, the sooner he was out of here the better. The hooks at the back of her dress were digging into her, and she was dying to get her make-up off and have a shower.

Well, he wouldn't be long now, surely?

Leo set his plate down, picked up his wine glass, and leant back again.

'You are not drinking your wine,' he remarked.

'Empty calories,' she answered flippantly.

The frown came again.

'Why do you starve yourself?'

Anna shrugged. 'Some models have fast metabolisms and can eat a horse and not show it. Jenny's like that. Me, I'll just pile on the pounds if I eat.' She gave a twisted smile. 'I'll eat when I retire,' she said.

Why was she talking to him? She wanted him to finish his wine and go.

'Retire? But you are how old?'

She made a face. 'Long in the tooth for modelling. The cult is for youth—the younger the better.'

'Ridiculous! Who would want the bud instead of the full flower?'

'Modelling agencies,' she said succinctly. 'Young girls are a lot more malleable—controllable and exploitable. It's a nasty business, modelling.'

'And yet…' his eyes rested on her '…you thrive.'

'I survive,' she corrected him. 'But,' she went on, 'I'm not ungrateful. Modelling's been a well-paid career for me.'

There was a shuttered look on his face suddenly.

'Money is important to you?'

Anna looked at him. 'I'd be pretty stupid if it weren't! I've known models blowing the whole damn lot they earn—chucking it around on clothes and rich living—and they end up with nothing to show for it.'

'But you are more shrewd?' The heavy-lidded eyes were resting on her.

'I hope so.' She returned his look, keeping it level. His expression stayed shuttered.

Then suddenly, out of nowhere, it changed.

And Anna's breath stopped.

He was looking at her. Just looking at her.

How can a look stop me breathing? Breathe—for God's sake, breathe!

But she couldn't. The breathlessness was absolute, endless.

And as she just sat there, the breath frozen in her lungs, her stomach seemed to be doing a very long, slow motion flip inside her.

Anna felt her hands close over the arms of her chair. Felt, as if from a long, long distance away, her muscles tense as she levered herself to her feet. But, like a mirror image, Leo Makarios was doing the same—getting to his feet.

He was coming towards her.

It was obvious why. Totally, absolutely obvious. And it had been from the moment the expression in his eyes had changed.

Changed to one of intent.

An intent that should have been making her body react the way it always did when she saw that kind of look in a man's eyes.

But no man had ever looked like that at her before. With lust, yes; with speculation; with hot, hungry appetite; with eagerness and with expectation.

Never the way Leo Makarios was looking at her.

Anna's legs felt weak; her heart was hammering. A voice

seemed to be inside her head, shouting *Danger!* As if it was some kind of automated warning.

A warning she could do absolutely nothing about—was helpless to heed.

He was coming towards her.

Tall, so tall. Lean, with a clear purposefulness about him. The dark eyes never left her, the expression in them turning her insides to water.

She still couldn't breathe, couldn't move. Just stood there, like a statue, immobile, lips parted, gazing at the planes of his face, his wide, mobile mouth, the loosened tie, the open-necked shirt, with waves of weakness going through her.

Leo stopped. Reached out a hand for her. With a slow, controlled movement he drew a single forefinger down her cheek.

It melted her skin where it touched.

And went on melting.

'You really are,' he said, 'exquisitely lovely.'

The eyes changed again, becoming lambent.

'Exquisite,' he echoed softly.

And all Anna could do was just stand there, transfixed, as those heavy-lidded eyes rested on her, draining from her all will, all resistance.

Because in their lambent depths was something she had never seen before.

It was desire.

Not lust. Not slime. Not appetite.

Just—*desire*.

Desire—burning with a clear, ineluctable, irresistible flame…

Again that wave of weakness drowned through her, draining from her everything she had ever felt before about men looking at her…

Because nothing, *nothing* she had ever felt before, was anything like this.

She waited for the anger, the biting, aggressive anger that always came when some man looked at her with only one purpose, one intent in his mind.

But it didn't come.

Instead, a slow-dissolving honey seemed to be spreading out through her veins, warming and weakening her, making her almost sway with sudden debilitating bonelessness.

His eyes were half closed, it seemed, their heavy lids lowered in a sweep of long black lashes. Her breath caught again, another spoon of honey spilling slowly through her veins.

She felt her lips part. As if she did not even have the strength to hold her mouth closed. She felt her eyelids flicker heavily, her pupils dilate.

Her body swayed. Very, very slightly.

He was so close to her. So close. She could feel his presence in her body space, catch the scent of his musk mingled with the expensive notes of his aftershave, heady and spiced. She could see the roughened jawline, the wide, mobile mouth, the lean, tanned cheek—and those heavy, half-closed eyes with the clear, clear intent in them.

Slowly, her insides turned over again.

'Exquisite,' he murmured again.

One hand slid around her neck, the other to her waist, and he lowered his mouth to hers, tongue sliding effortlessly within the silken confines.

For a timeless, delicious moment Leo luxuriated in the feel of her mouth. Silky, sensual, and so very, very arousing.

Not that he needed to be aroused. True, he had taken the opportunity while he was eating to sound her out about the redhead who seemed to have captivated his cousin—in respect of which prudence alone dictated that he warn his cousin off the girl. Markos was no gullible fool—far from it—but still, who knew how stupid a man could be if he was subjected to enough adoring gazes like those Leo had been witnessing all evening? Maybe they were calculated and maybe not. But if they weren't—and they had, he acknowledged, looked genuine—then Markos might be at greater risk than he knew. At the very least the girl would be difficult to dislodge, and would probably cause a tearful scene when the inevitable end came, which he wouldn't wish on any man. At the worst—well, although tears and weeping wouldn't wash with himself—Markos might just be more vulnerable, and find himself in deeper water than he was comfortable with. A naïve woman, entertaining fantasies about marriage, Leo realised, could be far more dangerous than one who knew which way the world went round.

Like the woman he was enjoying now.

Anna was exactly what he wanted. There'd been a lot of tension surrounding the launch of the Levantsky marque, and he'd put a lot of personal effort into ensuring that tonight and tomorrow were being organised the way he wanted them to be. That, of course, was on top of his normal non-stop business schedule. It might annoy him, but it didn't surprise him, that something had had to give—and that something was his sex life. It had been nearly a month since he had parted company with the Italian divorcee with whom he had been more than happy to celebrate her new sexual freedom, and there had been no time to choose her successor.

So the sable-haired beauty in his arms had caught his attention at a timely moment. She was just what he needed. A sophisticated, independent, unattached woman who had made it more than clear that she was receptive to his attentions. The world she moved in was known for its liberal sexual habits, and she doubtless had her pick of lovers in her time. Her caustic tongue and attitude might well put some men off, but it didn't bother him. It could just be put on for effect, anyway, to make herself stand out from the competition—deliberately assumed to catch the attention of men like him, jaded by fawning women.

Whatever the cause, it certainly wasn't in evidence now. She was reacting just the way he'd known she would—letting him taste her to the full and taking her own pleasure in it.

Leisurely, Leo slid his hand over her hip. Though slender, it was not in the least bony—for which he was glad. There was a rounded softness there beneath the silk of her dress that was really very enticing.

He deepened the kiss, pulling her body closer against his.

He could feel his own body reacting very pleasurably to the contact. Rich anticipation filled him. A month's celibacy might have been unwelcome, but it had its compensations.

Tonight would be good, he knew.

She would be good.

Letting his tongue powerfully stroke hers, he felt her yield to him, and he liked that. Too many women these days started a competition when he was kissing them, presumably thinking he found it exciting. They did not appreciate—as this one did—just how very erotic it was for a man to feel a woman being pleasured by him...

He felt his arousal strengthen. A month's starvation had made him hungry.

Hungry for much more than a mere appetiser. Time to take their table for the main course.

He drew his mouth back a little, just enough to allow him to softly bite her swollen lower lip.

'Shall we?' he said, his mouth curving sensually, his lashes sweeping down over his eyes. He exerted the slightest pressure at her hip, loosening his hand from her neck to guide her towards the bed.

As he released her she swayed slightly, eyes dazed. A small frown started to form between his eyes.

Was she drunk? She'd nursed a single glass of champagne all evening, and it had still been almost as full at the end as at the beginning. And just now, over supper, she had stuck entirely to water. So why was she swaying? Looking dazed and dizzy?

Or was it merely sexual arousal? Her pupils were wide and dilated, lips swollen, parted. His eyes flickered downward, and then his mouth curved into a relaxing smile. Her breasts were straining against the confines of her dress, and even without the help of the laced corset, the soft mounds were swelling deliciously above her bodice.

He felt his own arousal surge through his body. Of its own volition his hand reached, curved around one lovely, tempting orb, thumb brushing the dark silk where the nipple strained against it.

He wanted her, badly. Now.

'You really are…' his voice was husky '…so very tempting.' His thumb brushed again, and he felt himself thicken at the contact. Unable to resist, he started to close in on her. He wanted that mouth once more, that silken lushness…

The crack of her palm against his cheek took him totally and completely by surprise.

Anna hauled herself back. Her heart was hammering in her chest, pounding as if she'd done a workout. Panic, horror and a whole storm of emotions she couldn't even identify poured through her like a deluge.

'What the *hell*—?'

Leo Makarios was staring at her, shock naked on his face. Where her hand had impacted was a red mark.

Anna jerked further back.

'Get out of here. Just get out!'

He was standing stock still. Every line of his body taut.

'You will tell me,' he bit out, '*exactly* what that was for!'

Her eyes flashed. Her breathing was ragged, tumultuous, her heart still pounding. Adrenaline was surging through her—and a whole lot more.

'How dare you? How dare you think you can help yourself to me? Get *out*!'

His face darkened, his eyes suddenly as hard as steel.

'It's a little late,' he spelt out, his voice harsh, contemptuous, 'to tell me that.' His eyes narrowed. 'I don't like teases. Don't say yes to me and then change your mind and blame me for it.'

Anna's eyes distended.

'Say yes? I never said yes!'

'You've been saying yes all evening,' he bit back. 'From the moment I first set eyes on you. You made it crystal-clear you wanted me. Right up to ten seconds ago. Don't pretend to be naïve.' The voice was still harsh, still contemptuous. Two lines of white were etched around his mouth, colour flaring along his cheekbones.

She took a thin, hissing breath, eyes aflame with fury.

'My God, you have a nerve. I don't have to take this from you. Go and find some other willing floozy for the night! How dare you think you can use me for a night's entertainment?'

'Forgive me, but you gave every impression that *you* were willing.' The sneer in his voice was open.

Anna's eyes spat fire. Oh, how she wanted to feel anger! She was feeling it now all right. Coruscating, burning, biting, furious, incandescent anger. She was shaking with it.

'Get *out*! I don't have to take this! I don't have to put up with men who think because I model clothes I'll take them off for them whenever they feel like it. Now get out of my room before I charge you for harassment!'

Leo's face was as if carved from marble.

'Be very careful,' he told her, his eyes like chips of rock, 'what you say to me.'

Her face contorted.

'Don't threaten me. I don't have to be treated like this by you or anyone else—however stinking rich they are!'

'Don't tell me—' the contemptuous note was back in his voice '—it's in your contract.'

'Well, it's just as bloody well it is, isn't it?' she spat back at him. 'Because with you around I need it!'

The eyes were like granite again.

'Enough. You have made your point of view very clear. But next time you want to play the outraged virtue card, Ms Delane, I suggest you do it *before* you entertain a man in your bedroom at midnight.'

He threw a last stony, contemptuously angry look at her, and walked out.

The door shut behind him with a violent reverberating thud.

Leo strode down the corridor in a cold rage such as he had seldom experienced.

Christos, where the hell had that come from?

From temptress to virago in ten seconds flat!

Deliberate?

His eyes narrowed. If there'd been the slightest indication that the whole thing was a put-on he'd—

He felt his hands clench as he walked rapidly away, and he had to force himself to release them.

No, she wasn't worth it. Whether or not she was putting it on—one of those women who enjoyed blowing hot then cold just to twist men up—he didn't care. Let her enjoy her virtue. *Theos*, it was all she was going to enjoy tonight.

Anna Delane could enjoy her precious celibacy, and he...he could have a cold shower.

How the hell was I supposed to know she didn't want it?

Indignation filled him—and a sense of unjustified ill usage.

Good God, he wasn't some callow teenager, unable to tell whether a woman was responding to him. Anna Delane had responded all right—clear and loud.

So why the outrage?

Roughly, he pushed the question aside. What the hell did he care what the answer was?

His interest in Anna Delane was over.

Permanently.

CHAPTER FOUR

ANNA lay in bed. Her heart was still pumping, adrenaline surging through her. She couldn't stop it. Her whole body was as tense as a board, every muscle rigid.

How had it come to this? How?

Disbelief kept flooding through her, cold and icy through her guts.

The cold emptied through her again, clutching at her with its icy fingers.

How, *how* had it happened?

The question went round and round, pounding ceaselessly, tormentingly.

How had she let Leo Makarios do that to her? Just walk up to her and start to touch her. And she'd done nothing—*nothing*! Pathetic. *Pathetic.*

A shudder went through her.

She had just let him stand there and kiss her, *fondle* her, as if she was some kind of…some kind of…

She felt anger excoriating her. Anger at Leo Makarios, who had just walked into her bedroom and decided to help himself to her. The anger wired through her nerves. Anger at Leo Makarios.

But a worse fury consumed her too.

Anger at herself.

How could she have succumbed to him like that? Letting him come into her room, kiss her, caress her, do what he wanted to her? How could he have just swept away all her defences, all her years of fighting men off?

And into her head stole a voice that chilled her to the bone.

Because you didn't want to fight him off. You wanted him…you wanted him badly…Wanted to feel his mouth on

48

yours, wanted his hands caressing you, wanted to feel him stroke you, arouse you…

She closed her eyes in anguish, her face contorting.

No, please—please. She mustn't want Leo Makarios.

Not a man like that, a man who's just proved himself to be everything you knew he was. Everything! The kind of man who wants instant cheap gratification and thinks you're going to roll over and let him get it from you!

Revulsion shuddered through her.

Then slowly, agonisingly slowly, piece by piece, she started to pull herself together.

Yes, she had been a fool, an idiot, but the worst had not happened—that was what she must hang on to. It might have been so close to the edge of the precipice that she must never, ever think of it again, but at least she had summoned the last of her sanity and sent him packing.

She opened her eyes again, staring into the dark.

Imagine if it were now after you'd given yourself totally to him. If you were lying here now and he'd gone back to his gilded state apartment, sleek and sated, leaving you here with nothing left but the bones…

Cold iced through her again.

She had had such a narrow escape…

But she *had* escaped—that was what she must remember. She had clawed back to sanity just in time.

And she was safe now. Safe.

Slowly, very slowly, she felt her heart-rate come down.

Never, ever again would Leo Makarios push her that close to the precipice.

Never.

Her mouth thinned.

Never.

'Plunge your hands in. Now lift them out—lift, lift, lift! Yes. Hold them up! Up!'

Anna held her hands the way she was being told to. So did the other three models. They were standing around the vast oak

table in the castle's echoing hall again, but this time none of
them was wearing any of the Levantsky jewels.

Their hands were all in a huge golden bowl into which had
been poured rivers of diamonds, emeralds, rubies and sapphires. And now the four models were plunging into this
golden cornucopia and lifting them out, their fingers dripping
necklaces and earrings and bracelets.

'*Basta!*' Tonio Embrutti called, simultaneously summoning
the stylist and her assistants. 'Now I want the jewels just draped
over their shoulders, in their hair, over their arms, their breasts.
Not fastened, just draped.'

His pudgy face took on a sulky look. 'Of course, their bodies
should be naked, but—'

He contented himself with merely making an Italian gesture
of exasperation with his hands, waving his camera around as
he did so.

Anna stood patiently as the stylist's assistants got to work.

Her mind was strangely numb. She'd got hardly any sleep
last night, and the disapproving make-up artist had commented
adversely on the effect thereof on her eyes and complexion.
Anna didn't care. She was, she knew, beyond caring. She had
only one overriding impulse.

To get out of here. Out and home.

But she still had today and tonight to get through before she
could run. At least today there was no sign of Leo Makarios.
He'd gone off with his guests—some whisked off to ski slopes,
some on horse-drawn sleigh rides, some on helicopter tours of
the Austrian Alps, or back to Vienna and Munich for shopping
trips.

Even so, today's shoot seemed longer than yesterday's, but
finally it was done. Released at last, changed back into her
normal clothes, Anna headed back up to her room. Vanessa
had disappeared instantly—presumably Markos was in the
wings somewhere—and Kate almost as quickly.

'There's an early concert in the town's Musikverein,' Kate
had explained to the others eagerly. 'Maestro Lukacs has given

me a ticket!' She'd said it as though he'd given her the keys to the kingdom, her eyes shining.

'Have fun,' Anna had said dryly. Preferably, she added silently, not in Antal Lukacs's bed. Kate was far too impressionable.

She headed off after Jenny, also making for her room. The other model had a head start on her up the vast stairs. Anna sprinted after her.

'Wait for me!' she called. But Jenny was ploughing on, reaching the set of stairs that led to the upper floors. She seemed to be walking faster and faster, as if the devil was driving her.

But then it was, Anna knew. Her face shadowed. God, she might have been an idiot the night before, letting Leo Makarios get to within a hair's breadth of tumbling her down into bed, but at least she'd found her sanity in time! Jenny had never found hers with the man who had got her into this mess. And now she was facing the complete disintegration of her life. Forced to cash in everything she had and flee.

Flee to keep her baby safe from the man who would take it from her.

Anna's eyes darkened. Well, whatever it took she would make sure she stood by Jenny! Money, support—someone there at the birth of her child—whatever Jenny needed, she'd stick by her.

But right now Jenny just needed reassurance. Someone to keep her spirits up, take away the edge of fear that was eating into her day by day at the thought of her pregnancy being discovered.

Anna hurried on, up the second flight of stairs and along the corridor to her bedroom. Jenny had rushed ahead and was out of sight. Anna paused outside her friend's door, wondering whether Jenny would like a cup of tea with her.

'Jen, do you want a cuppa? Rosehip or chamomile?'

There was no answer.

Anna opened the door and poked her head round. Maybe Jenny was in the bathroom.

She wasn't.

She was sitting on her bed. Like Anna, she was wearing trousers, but unlike Anna she had a large, fleecy long-sleeved pullover on.

And out of the sleeve she was sliding a long ruby bracelet.

For one long, timeless moment Anna did not believe what she was seeing. And then, with a rush of icy water in her stomach, she stepped into the room, closing the door behind her.

Jenny was staring at her. Staring at her with shock and fear naked on her face. She was as white as a sheet, every bone in her face starkly outlined.

Slowly, Anna came forward.

'Oh, my God, Jen, what have you done?'

Her voice was hollow.

Jenny just stared; she was beyond speech, Anna could see—wound up so tight she would break if stressed any further.

Carefully, Anna went and sat down beside her.

Jenny turned huge distended eyes on her.

'Do you know—' her voice sounded taut and strange '—Khalil wanted to give me a ruby bracelet? I said no. He wanted to give me lots of jewels, but I always said no. It made him angry, I know. He hid it, but it did.' Her eyes went down to the ruby bracelet lying across the palm of her hand, winking in the lamplight.

'It's ironic, isn't it?' she said, and her voice still had that strange breaking quality about it. 'If I'd just taken one, just one of all the jewels he wanted to give me, I'd be all right now. I could sell it and have enough…enough money to…to escape with. But I never took them. Not one. Even though he wanted to give them to me.'

She touched one of the stones with her finger.

Carefully, very carefully, Anna spoke.

'But these aren't Khalil's jewels, Jen. And he never gave them to you.' She paused. 'I'll take the bracelet back.'

She reached across to lift it from Jenny's palm. For a moment so brief it hardly happened she saw Jenny's fingers start to claw shut over the bracelet. Then, as if exerting a vast invisible effort, the fingers stilled.

'You can't keep it, Jen. You know you can't.'

Anna's voice was quiet, reassuring.

Slowly Jenny opened her palm completely, letting the glittering stones run red across her hand. She stared down at them.

Anna lifted them away. Her heart was beating fast, the icy water still in her stomach. Slowly she got to her feet. Her mind was racing, almost going into panic. But she mustn't panic— she mustn't.

What the hell am I going to do?

And, shooting right through her panicking brain, came one grim question.

How long have we got before it's discovered missing?

Claws pincered in her stomach. The security arrangements for the Levantsky jewels were draconian. They had to be, obviously. Every time they were brought out or put away—either for a shoot, or for her and the other models to wear the night before—security guards were all over the place. Every item was catalogued and signed in and out on a computerised check system personally entered by Leo Makarios's sidekick, Justin.

So how the hell had Jenny walked off with a bracelet?

There was no time to think about that—no time to do anything except hope and pray she could somehow, anyhow, get the bracelet back.

Back where, though?

She could hardly just swan up to Justin and calmly inform him he'd missed a piece! Everyone would go totally ballistic! There'd be a full-scale Spanish Inquisition, and that would end up with every damn finger in the Schloss pointing at Jenny!

And that was all Jenny needed! Police sirens and lawyers and the press—and a prison sentence for theft.

Because one thing was for sure. Leo Makarios was not the type to let anyone, *anyone* waltz off with a single Levantsky jewel!

She swallowed. She must not panic Jenny. Whatever happened, that was essential. Jenny was on the edge of a total breakdown, she could see. Well, already over the edge, actually, she realised, if she'd been driven to try and walk off with a priceless ruby bracelet...

Anna forced her voice to sound calm.

'Don't go anywhere, Jen. Just stay here. And don't answer the door unless it's me. Promise?'

The other girl still seemed to be in a state of shock. Anna wasn't surprised. God knew what state she must have been in to even think of taking any of the Levantsky jewels—and as for actually taking any...

Her stomach churning, panic nipping at her, Anna slipped out of Jenny's bedroom, hastily stuffing the bracelet inside the pocket of her trousers.

Its weight hung like a dead, accusing albatross.

She felt sick with fear.

Leo could hear his mobile vibrating deep beneath his skiing jacket as he slewed to a halt at the end of the run. With the light gone, his guests were discarding their skis and getting ready to board the waiting fleet of four-by-fours to take them back down to the Schloss.

Leo wished each and every one of them to perdition. He'd had to smile and converse and be a good host all damn day, and totally hide from them that inside he was in a worse mood than he could recall for a very long time. His temper was evil. He could feel it, lashing around inside him, not allowed an outlet.

But he knew exactly what outlet it wanted.

And it was one it wasn't going to get.

He wanted that damn girl, and he wasn't going to have her.

Anna Delane.

Sable-haired and breathtakingly desirable...

All through a night in which sleep had been persistently and exasperatingly scarce, all through a day which had tested his patience to the limit with its demanding and tedious social requirements, her image had kept intruding. He had banished it a hundred times, and it still came back.

And more than an image.

His memory was tactile.

Erotically, sensually tactile.

The feel of her silken mouth beneath his, the swelling round-ness of her breast in his hand, the straining peak rigid beneath his stroking thumb, his body hardening against hers...

With savage control he hammered down the pointless, treacherous thoughts that heated through him.

OK, so he was frustrated. That was all. He'd gone a month without sex, and for him that was a long time. Last night had been punishing because he'd been on the brink of sexual re-lease and then he'd been balked of it. No wonder his body was protesting!

But it was more than his body, he knew. If, say, he'd been interrupted by some kind of business emergency he'd have been a lot less angry than he was now. It wasn't just the ab-sence of sex that was winding him up tighter than a watch spring.

It was her—that black-haired, green-eyed witch, who'd given him every damn come-on in the book and then called time on him in an outburst of self-righteous outrage as if he were one down from some kind of lascivious groper!

Thee mou, but she had wanted it as much as he had. She'd been melting for him, soft and honeyed, aroused and respon-sive.

And then to turn on him like that. Make those accusations, those spitting, contemptible accusations of harassment, *harass-ment*—

He felt his anger bite viciously.

A *liar*—that was what she was. Saying no when her body said yes. Had been saying yes all evening to him. All the way until he'd been about to lower her down on her bed...

With monumental effort he slammed shut the lid on his snarling thoughts. He would simply put Anna Delane out of his head, and that was that. There were plenty of other women around—*willing* women—who didn't play infantile and hypo-critical games about sex.

Plenty who would be *happy* to be taken up as his mistress!
The trouble was, he couldn't think of any right now who held the slightest interest for him.

Damn Anna Delane. Turning him on—and then turfing him out! Well, she'd made her decision and so had he. He would *not* waste any more of his valuable time thinking about her.

With a rasp of irritation he realised his mobile had started to vibrate again. Hell, was he to have no peace at all? Impatiently he jabbed his ski-sticks into the snow and yanked out his phone.

'Yes?' he demanded icily, wanting only to dispose of the call and detach his skis.

But when he heard Justin's strained, panic-stricken voice, his body stilled completely.

Anna kept walking along the corridor. Her hands felt clammy, her heartbeat erratic, every muscle tense.

What am I going to do?

She still hadn't the faintest idea how she was to return the bracelet. She had to do something with it—anything—anything other than keep it on her person or in any way let its loss be linked back to Jenny.

She must have been mad to take it—

No! No time to think about that now! She'd cope with Jenny's breakdown later—her only priority now was to get rid of the bracelet.

She could just dump it somewhere. Somewhere it would be easily found by one of the household staff or something.

For a moment she thought of trying to tell someone that it had been taken completely by mistake, that its catch had got caught up in some material or something. But even as she ran it through her brain she knew it wouldn't wash. They hadn't been wearing their own clothes when the jewellery had been collected back in. They'd still been in their fashion shoot dresses. If any jewels had got caught they'd have been caught in them, not in the girls' mufti clothes.

How had she managed to take it?

Out of the blue, Anna suddenly knew. There'd been a shot with the four of them gathered around the table, their four pairs of hands buried wrist-deep in the golden bowl of priceless Levantsky jewels, spotlights blazing down at them to bring out every last glittering facet. Then Jenny had given a low moan. Anna had looked round at her immediately and realised that she was feeling nauseous.

She'd acted instinctively. Pulling back with deliberate clumsiness, she'd dragged on the edge of the bowl and it had tipped over, spilling jewels all over the table.

And some had slithered on to the floor.

She and Jenny—and half a dozen others—had scrambled around on the floor, mostly feeling with their fingers in the sharply delineated shadow under the table on the cold stone flags. While she was down there she'd managed to whisper to Jenny, 'Are you going to be sick? I'll call time and say I need the loo—come with me—'

All the other model had done was to shake her head vigorously and go on searching for bits of jewellery, almost head to head with three security personnel, a dresser, Kate, and one of the photographer's assistants.

Jenny had been the last to stand up, Anna recalled. She'd deposited an emerald ring, a ruby brooch and a sapphire bracelet back into the bowl, while Anna herself had contributed one ruby earring and a diamond choker. As Jenny had got to her feet, Anna, still watching her worriedly, had seen her wince.

I thought it was because she still felt nauseous, but it wasn't.
She slipped the ruby bracelet inside her shoe while she was getting to her feet…

That was how she'd done it. Kept it hidden inside her shoe for the rest of the shoot, and then somehow, in the crush of the changing room, she must have transferred it into her sleeve.

Dismay hollowed out again in her. How *could* Jenny have been so insane?

No—no time to think about what had driven her friend to such folly. All that was important now was getting rid of the bracelet in such a way that its temporary disappearance could not be linked to Jenny.

She gained the head of the staircase leading down to the guest level upper floor. From there, the huge main staircase flowed down to the hall. At the top, she paused a moment. Instinctively, she realised, she'd been heading back to the scene of the crime—the main hall, where the huge oaken table sat solidly in its splendour.

Her eyes blinked, even as her stomach flushed with icy water again.

Two of the security guards were systematically working their way along the length of the table on either side, feeling underneath the surface.

Anna watched, frozen with horror. Even as she stood there, unable to move, there was the sound of a vehicle approaching, drawing to a sudden halt, and then, moments later, the huge front door of the Schloss swung open and Leo Makarios walked in.

He was in skiing clothes, Anna registered absently. And he was also, she realised, fully cognisant of the fact that the ruby bracelet was missing.

He strode up to the security guards and barked something at them. Anna saw them shake their heads and then resume their painstaking search. Anna found herself wondering quite what they were doing. Then it came to her.

They must have realised that the only opportunity the thief had had was when the jewels had been spilt. Which meant—

Oh, God, she felt sick—if they thought that, then they could also severely limit the number of suspects.

For one long moment she stared down at Leo Makarios, standing hands on hips, thick skiing jacket pushed back, continuing to watch the guards. His face was expressionless, but his eyes—his eyes made a sick, cold punch go through her. Then, appearing out of the nether regions of the Schloss, she saw his gofer, Justin, come hurrying up to him. His face looked like curd-cheese, and Anna almost felt sorry for him.

But she couldn't think about him now, or the kind of tongue-lashing, and worse, he was about to get from his employer. She had to think of herself—and Jenny.

You can't just stand here—go—move! Clear off!

She jerked back from the balustrade.

It was a mistake.

The movement caught Leo Makarios's eye. His head whipped up from where he was on the receiving end of Justin's agitated discourse.

He saw her instantly.

And in that moment, Anna knew that she would rather die than have him discover the bracelet on her.

She just stood there, frozen. And then, from somewhere, she found a strength of mind she'd never even known she possessed. Slowly, she began to walk down the stairs. A model's walk—almost a saunter.

As she did so, she saw Leo Makarios's eyes narrow. Something leapt in them, and for a second she reeled from it. Then a flood of relief went through her.

She knew that look. And though at any other time she would have felt her hackles rise automatically, now, for the first time in her life, she could have gone down on her knees at being on the receiving end of such a look.

Casually, knowing she absolutely, totally and completely must not—*must not* behave in any way other than utterly ignorant—utterly *innocent*—she kept on walking downstairs.

Think—think! What would you do if you were seeing Leo Makarios for the first time after that scene last night?

But she was, of course. Seeing him for the first time since last night…

And it just so happens—the cold poured through her insides again —*that you currently happen to have his priceless Levantsky ruby bracelet in your pocket.*

For one overwhelming moment Anna felt the urge to just walk up to him, fish the bracelet out of her pocket, and hand it to him with some kind of smartass remark like, *Is this what you're looking for?*

But it was impossible—completely impossible. To reveal she

had it, however innocent she might be as to its original theft, would simply be to condemn Jenny. And she couldn't, *wouldn't* do that. She'd promised herself she would help Jenny get through this ruination of her life, and she would stick by that. Jenny's problems were far too great to have to cope with being accused of theft as well.

So, instead, she had to behave as she would have if she'd had no idea what was going on. As if her only concern was ignoring the man who had almost got her into bed last night.

She reached the bottom of the stairs. Leo was still looking at her, standing stock still. At his side, Justin stood, silenced and cowed. The two security guards were impassively continuing their search.

Anna glanced towards them, a slight frown on her face registering just the right amount of casual curiosity at what they were so inexplicably doing. Then her eyes drifted past them to the tall, threatening figure in the dark skiing jacket.

He was just looking at her. Quite expressionlessly.

Anna's face hardened. For an instant all knowledge of the fact she was walking past him with his stolen bracelet on her person disappeared. All she could see was him, Leo Makarios, who had had the audacity, the *nerve* to think he could turn up in her bedroom at midnight and tumble her over for a quick lay! Sating his carnal appetite on her conveniently available body.

Fury flashed in her eyes—and more than fury.

She kept walking past him.

It was like going through a forcefield, every step.

'One moment.'

Leo's voice was like iron.

She halted. She turned her head towards him. Saying nothing. Just letting that look of scornful anger sit in her eyes. Totally ignoring the sick fear inside her.

'Where are you going?'

Her lips pressed together. 'I'm off duty now, Mr Makarios. So I'm going to get some fresh air.'

Did she sound insolent? She didn't care.

His brows snapped together.

'Without a jacket or boots? In the dark?'

She gave a shrug. It cost her, but she did it.

'Five minutes won't kill me,' she returned indifferently.

She went on heading for the vast wooden doors.

It took every ounce of strength she possessed. Every nerve was screaming. Every muscle tearing. Every step was as if she were walking on glass.

The doors seemed a mile away. If she could just reach them and get outside she would be safe.

Safe outdoors. Safe from Leo Makarios's deadly, *dangerous* regard, with the bracelet safe in her pocket…

She didn't mean to. She really, really didn't mean to. But she could not stop herself. It was an instinct so overpowering that her hand moved of its own accord.

Her fingers brushed along her right thigh, feeling the hidden lumpiness of the rubies. Telling her they were still safe.

She was nearly at the doors. Behind her, she could hear Justin's voice agitatedly resume, presumably telling his employer all the things the security personnel were doing to recover the missing jewellery.

Her hand was reaching out for the iron ring, to turn it and open the door.

Ten more seconds and I'll be outside.

Just hold your nerve. Hold it!

'One moment, if you please, Ms Delane.'

Leo's command was like ice. Cold and very, very hard.

Anna froze.

She stood, quite immobile, her hand still reaching out to open the front door. She did not turn round. Had no power to do so. No power to do anything except stand there with her mind screaming at her.

She heard his heavy-booted footsteps ringing on the stone flags, walking up to her.

'I'd like a word with you.'

She twisted her head round slowly, disdainfully. Claws

crushed at her stomach, but she knew she had to keep her nerve.

What would she do if she were innocent?

She would be uncooperative, rejecting.

Her mouth tightened.

'Yes?' she said stonily.

'In private.' His voice was grim.

Deliberately, Anna stared at him. It was hard, punishingly hard, but she met his eyes. They were completely expressionless, and somehow that frightened her even more than if she had seen that look in them she hated.

'I have nothing to say to you, Mr Makarios,' she said, in a tight, low voice.

His expression did not change.

'I have some questions to ask you.' His voice twisted, and for a second she saw that look flash briefly. 'Be assured it has nothing to do with the subject you so clearly wish to avoid.' He gestured with his hand. 'This way.'

Should she refuse? What would look worse?

If she made too much objection would she draw attention to herself? Arouse suspicions? After all, there was nothing he could know—nothing he could *do*.

Except ask questions she would find—would *have* to find!—innocent answers to.

'Very well,' she said, in a clipped, tight voice.

She marched off in the direction he was indicating. It was to a door on the far side of the hall, and she had no idea where it led. Behind her she could hear Leo Makarios's heavy booted tread ringing on the flags. In her stomach acid pooled; her heart was racing.

Be glad about last night! It's giving you a cover for your obvious tension now!

Anna gritted her teeth. She just had to hold her nerve, that was all.

She stopped outside the room. Leo Makarios opened the door and ushered her in.

It was an office, she saw instantly. Lined with bookshelves and predominantly occupied by a vast desk on which stood a PC.

She walked in and stopped. Then turned around and looked belligerently at Leo Makarios closing the door behind him.

It was not a small room, but as the solid wood door snapped shut it suddenly seemed claustrophobically confined.

'Well?' she demanded. 'What's all this about?'

Her chin lifted, but behind the belligerent expression on her face she could feel herself paling.

Leo was standing there very still, just looking at her.

Quite expressionless.

The dark padded ski jacket made him look even more formidable than he usually looked.

'I would like you, Ms Delane, to empty your pockets.'

The blood drained from her face completely.

With an effort of will she forced an expression of astonishment to her features.

'What?'

He did not move. 'You heard me. Empty your pockets.'

'No!' she retorted indignantly, trying desperately to stay in character. She took a harsh breath. 'What is this? What the hell is going on?'

'You've gone pale, Ms Delane. Even paler than usual. Why is that, I wonder?'

His eyes were resting on her like weights, but she had to keep staring back at him angrily. Not letting her fear show.

But the fear was there, all right—like pickaxes gouging in her stomach.

'Because I don't want to be anywhere near you. That's why! Isn't it obvious, Mr Makarios?' she thrust defiantly at him.

Did his eyes narrow very, very slightly?

'Obvious—or convenient?'

'What?'

His mouth tightened.

'Just empty your pockets, please.'

'No, I will not. What the hell is this about?'

'Just do it.'

Anna's expression hardened.

'How dare you harass me like this—?'

Leo Makarios's face suffused with instant thunder. His hand slammed down on to the surface of his desk.

'You will not use that word! *Christos*—' He took a harsh, ripping breath. 'Very well—if you do not wish to empty your pockets, you need not do so.' He moved his hand, picking up the phone. 'You can instead let the police search you.'

'The *police*?' With all her nerve she tried to inject as much withering bewilderment into her voice as she could. 'Are you mad?' she challenged derisively. 'I've had enough of this!'

She turned on her heel and headed for the door.

It was locked. Between fear and fury she rattled the handle viciously. She could no longer tell whether she was still in character as someone totally innocent, or succumbing to an overriding instinct to run and run and run.

'Let me out!'

Footsteps sounded behind her across the carpet. Then Leo Makarios was right behind her.

'Of course,' he said smoothly. His arm came around her to unlock the door.

The other hand slid into her trouser pocket and drew out the bracelet.

He stepped back.

For one endless second Anna froze. Then she twisted round, pressed back against the door panels. Like a deer at bay, cornered by a ravening leopard.

Leo Makarios was just standing there, hand palm up, a river of fire draped over his long fingers. He was so close to her his presence pressed on her like a crushing dark weight.

For a moment he said absolutely nothing, just hung her eyes with his as if he were crucifying her.

Then he spoke.

Each word a nail in her flesh.

'Well, well, well,' he said slowly, and the way he spoke was like acid dripping on her bare skin. 'So the virtuous Ms Delane—so virtuous she won't allow her lily-white breasts to be photographed, so innocent she is outraged by a man's touch on her—all along is nothing but a thief.'

She couldn't move, couldn't think. Could only feel the horror spreading through her like freezing water.

Think! Think—say something. Anything…

But every synapse in her brain was freezing.

She watched him walk back to his desk, lay the bracelet on its surface. Then he turned back to look at her.

Fury flashed across his face. Anger so intense she thought it would slay her where she stood. Then, with monumental effort of will, his face stilled.

Behind her back she could feel the hard panels of the door pressing into her. Nowhere to run; nowhere to hide.

Caught red-handed in possession of stolen property. A ruby bracelet worth untold tens of thousands of pounds!

And the only way to clear her name would be to incriminate Jenny.

I can't! I can't do that! Whatever happens, I've got to keep her out of it!

But even as the resolution went through her she felt fear buckle. It was all very well to say something like that, but if she took the can for appropriating the bracelet it would be *her* the police sirens would sound for, *her* the jail would beckon— and her career would be left in tatters.

Oh God—please, no!

Leo was looking at her, just looking. There was nothing in his face. Nothing at all.

Then, softly, he spoke.

'What shall I do with you? My instinct is to hand you over to the police, to hear the prison doors clang shut on you. And yet…'

He paused. His dark, expressionless eyes rested on her.

Into the silence Anna spoke, each word cut from her. 'What's the point of getting the police involved? You've got the bracelet back. No damage done.'

She was speaking for Jenny; she knew she was. Jenny had acted out of desperation, not greed. Pregnancy did things to you—to your head—and, terrified as Jenny was of the man who had done it to her, the balance of her mind had tipped for a few short, fatal moments. It had been an impulse—desperate, insane—to slip the bracelet into her shoe...

She saw his face change.

'You steal—from me—and think no damage done?' His voice was like a thin, deadly blade.

'Well, there isn't, is there?' She made herself give a shrug. Instinctively she knew she had to hide her fear from him. It would show him her vulnerability, and that was something she must never, never show to Leo Makarios.

Another line of defence came to her, and she lifted her chin defiantly. 'Besides, I can't imagine you'd welcome the publicity that would arrive with the police. You're supposed to be getting *good* publicity from this launch bash—not bad! And it would make your security precautions look pretty pathetic— having some of your precious Levantsky jewels walk off from out under your very nose.'

Even as she spoke she wished she had never said a word. Something was changing in his face again, and it was sending icy fingers down her spine.

He fingered the bracelet, looking across at her, leaning his hips back against the edge of his desk.

'How very astute of you, Ms Delane,' he said. His voice was soft, but it raised the hair on the nape of her neck. 'I would indeed prefer not to make this incident—official. Which is why—' his eyes rested on her '—I am prepared to allow you to make your...reparation...for your crime privately, rather than at the expense of the taxpayer.'

Something crawled in her stomach.

'What—what do you mean?'

'Let's just say...' he answered—and his voice still had an edge in it that was drawing along her skin like a blade— '...that I am giving you a choice. I can hand you over to the police—or I can keep you in *personal* custody until such time as I think you have made sufficient...amends.' His eyes held hers. 'Which is it to be?'

She swallowed. Her heart was thumping in hard, heavy slugs.

'What do you mean?' Her voice was faint. She wanted it to sound defiant, but it didn't.

Leo Makarios smiled. It was the smile of a wolf that had its prey in its clutches. Her stomach clenched. His eyelids swept down over his eyes, the lashes long and lustrous.

'Oh, I think you know, Ms Delane. I think you know.' For a long moment he held her gaze, telling her in that exchange just exactly what he had in mind as reparation.

She felt a shiver go through her.

It was revulsion. It had to be.

It had to be.

A sharp breath rasped in her throat.

'No!' It was instinct—pure survival instinct—that made the word break from her.

He raised an eyebrow.

'No? Are you sure about that, Ms Delane? Have you, I wonder...' his voice was conversational, but it screamed along Anna's nerves '...ever been in prison? You're a very beautiful woman, as you know—exceptionally so. And I'm sure that it isn't just men who find you so. In prison, for example, there will be inmates who—'

'No!'

It was fear this time. Naked and bare.

Just for an instant something showed in Leo Makarios's eyes. Something that did not fit what he was taunting her with. Then it was gone. In its place was merely that cold, scarily level regard.

'No? Then, given the choice, which will you make, hmm?'

Her face convulsed. 'Choice? You're not giving me a choice!'

Anger showed like a flash of lightning in his features.

'You think you deserve one? *Thee mou*, you're a thief! A *thief*. You *stole* from me! You had the audacity, the *stupidity*, to think you could do so with impunity?' His eyes scorched her, as if he would incinerate her on the spot.

Suddenly a Greek word spat from him. He turned, seizing up the phone on his desk, and punched in a number.

'*Polizei*—'

Anna jerked forward.

'Please—don't! Don't…don't call the police.'

There was panic in her voice. He mustn't involve the police—he mustn't! They would investigate the theft, Jenny would realise she'd been found out—and she'd confess—Anna knew she would.

And the consequences would be unthinkable. The case would hit the press, Jenny's condition would inevitably be exposed in the time it took to come to trial, and when it did she'd lose her baby for ever.

The man who had threatened to take her child from her would arrive to make good his threat. Jenny would lose her freedom and her baby. She'd be branded a criminal and end up in jail, her life ruined, her child taken from her…

And Anna could not let that happen.

Not if there was some way to avoid it.

Slowly, as if from a long distance, she saw Leo Makarios lower the receiver to the handset and turn back to her.

Faintly, forcing her voice to pass her throat, Anna spoke.

'I need to know…know…exactly what would be involved if I agreed to…to the…the reparation you…you spoke of. I mean—how…how long for…and…when? I mean…'

He was looking at her. Something was in his eyes again, and it made her feel cold.

'How long?' he echoed. His voice was silky suddenly. 'Why, Ms Delane—until I've had all I want of you. Or—' there was a note in his voice that shivered down her spine '—until you please me sufficiently to earn your parole. There—is that exact enough for you? Or would you like me to spell out *exactly*—' his repetition of the word mocked her '—how I envisage you earning your parole?'

He was baiting her, taunting her, wanting her to lash out, scream her defiance, her revulsion at him. She could see it, knew it all the way through her.

And she burned to do it! Burned to tell him to take his disgusting sick 'choice' and—

But she couldn't. Couldn't do anything except just stand there and let him say such things to her.

'And…' She swallowed, forcing herself to go on. 'And if I…if I agree, then…then you won't involve the police, or the press, or…anyone else? No one will know except…you?'

His mouth curved in a contemptuous curl.

'No one will know that you are a thief—is that what you mean?'

'Yes.'

She stared at him. It was essential, *essential* that he agreed that. Because somehow she had to keep this from Jenny. Her mind went racing ahead. If she could tell Jenny that she'd safely returned the bracelet, that no one had found out, that it had all gone quiet, she might just save her friend.

What else am I going to have to tell her?

Oh, God, what on earth was she going to say to Jenny? No, she would think about that later. Not now. Not when Leo Makarios was looking at her with a contemptuous expression on his face that would have made her flush with shame if he'd had the cause for it he thought he had.

But he *didn't* have cause. She knew he didn't!

So was that why she lifted her chin and stared back at him defiantly, *refusing* to let herself be cowed, humiliated, ashamed.

She felt her resolve stiffening as she held his coruscating gaze. What did she care what he thought of her? What did she care if he thought her a thief or not? Because she knew *exactly* what she thought about him—a man who'd walked into her bedroom last night in the sublime assumption that she was just going to sigh with gratitude and lie down for him…

No—don't think about that!

Because if she thought then she might remember, and if she remembered then she might…

She might prefer Leo Makarios to phone the police after all…

But she couldn't let him do that.

Oh, God, it was like being crushed between walls closing in on her, closing in—

With a mental strength she hadn't known she possessed she pushed them apart. She could not collapse now—could not panic, or faint, or burst into tears. She had to keep going—keep going with what she had done. So she went on staring at him defiantly, chin high.

She could see it angered him. See it in the flash of blackness in his eyes, and she was darkly, viscously pleased. She knew it was irrational, and certainly stupid, to anger even more a man who had such cause to be furious with her.

And part of her brain told her it was unjust as well.

He thinks you're a thief. He's got a right to be mad with you!

But reason did not hold sway. Somehow keeping Leo Makarios angry with her made her feel safer—safer than Leo Makarios feeling anything else about her…

Or was it?

As Anna stood there, her back pressed against the door, with those heavy-lidded, hard-as-stone eyes boring into her like diamond-tipped drills, a sense of almost overpowering disbelief shuddered through her.

Oh, God, what have I done…?

The words ricocheted round and round inside her head. Like bullets. Each one a killing shot.

But it was too late to do anything now. Far too late. She'd taken on the burden of Jenny's crime and now she had to see it through.

And the only way to do that, she knew, was not to think about it. Absolutely not think about what she had just agreed to.

A barrier sliced down in her brain. Don't think about anything but *now*! That was all she must deal with.

'Well,' she heard her voice say, and marvelled that it sounded so cool, so unconcerned, 'what happens now, then?' She levered herself away from the door panel, deliberately thrusting her hands inside her pockets, staring, chin lifted, across at the man who had caught her red-handed with a price-less ruby bracelet in her illicit possession.

Again her attitude seemed to send a flash of black anger through his eyes.

'What happens now, Ms Delane,' he intoned heavily, with that killing look still levelled at her, 'is that you get out of my sight. Before I change my mind and get you slung into jail, where a thief like you belongs! Now, get out.'

Leo's eyes were dark, inward-looking, his face closed. He could feel the black deadly rage roiling through him like a heavy sea.

How *dared* she think she could steal from him? And then deny it, defy him as she had? *Christos*, he had heard the word *shameless* used before, but never had he realised just what it meant. His face darkened even more. Now he did.

She stood there in front of me, lying through her teeth. Pretending her innocence even as the bracelet was in her pocket.

And she might even have got away with it.

He saw again in his head the moment when she'd headed towards the front door of the Schloss, walking with her elegant, poised model's saunter, distancing herself completely from the search going on behind her.

And all along…

But she'd given herself away. That tiny but instinctive ges-ture she'd made with one hand, brushing her pocket.

Checking if something was still there…

And he'd known—known with every gut instinct—that the thief was her. He'd already carpeted the cowering Justin, lam-basted the head of security for the shambles that had happened that afternoon. It had been obvious that that was when the theft had taken place, and the only suspects had been those close enough to the spilt jewels to have purloined any.

It had been Anna Delane who'd spilt them in the first place. Anna Delane who'd been the first to scrabble down to the ground. Every finger had already been pointing at her.

But investigating would have been a delicate business. The missing bracelet could have been anywhere in the Schloss— secreted in any of a thousand unlikely places for collection later. Or even off the premises. It could have been miles away, in completely different hands. Searching any of the suspects' rooms would have been fruitless.

And Anna Delane had had the audacity to think she could walk straight past him carrying it on her!

The black rage roiled through him again. That anyone should have stolen from *him*—and for it to be her—her of all people.

His eyes narrowed.

Had he been mad to let her walk out? Mad not simply to pick the phone up again and get the police here?

But the vixen had been right. She'd gone immediately for his one weak spot—his determination to avoid any bad publicity tainting the launch of the Levantsky jewels.

No. Leo let his rage sink down again, congealing into a cold, hard mass inside him. He'd done the right thing. No police— no publicity—no prison.

Anna Delane would make amends to him in a manner he would find far, far more satisfying.

She didn't want him in her bed? Thought herself too virtuous for his desires?

A grim smile twisted at his mouth.

She'd be *begging* for him before he was done with her!

CHAPTER FIVE

ANNA sat in her wide leather seat in the first class cabin and stared unseeingly at the glossy magazine lying across her lap. At her side, separated from her only by a drinks table, sat Leo Makarios.

He was working at his laptop, completely ignoring her.

But then, he'd ignored her almost entirely ever since she'd fled from his office, taking on her shoulders the burden of guilt for a crime she had not committed.

Accepting the blame for having stolen a priceless bracelet.

Accepting the 'choice' Leo Makarios had held out to her.

But she hadn't had any other option. She'd told herself that over and over again, like a litany running in her head. She could not let Jenny be sent to prison and have her baby taken from her, brought up in some faraway desert country, where wives were locked up in harems, kow-towing to every male in sight...

So I'm going to have to go through with what Leo Makarios wants. There's nothing else I can do.

Yet the enormity of it crushed her. Appalled her.

She couldn't think about it; she just couldn't. It was the only way she could keep going. By not thinking about what she had done, what she was going to do...

She willed herself not to think. Because if she thought about it, if for a moment, a single moment, she let her brain accept what she had agreed to, she would, she would...

The grille sliced shut in her brain again. Stopping her thinking. Stopping her doing anything—anything at all except what she had to do.

And it had started straight away—last night, when she'd walked out of Leo Makarios's office, with the word *thief*

73

branded on her, to see the person she had taken the brand-
ing for.

She'd made herself go back to Jenny's room and tell her that
she'd simply slipped the bracelet under the hall table, positioning it such that it was in shadow, obscured by one of the heavy
wooden struts supporting the table's weight.

'They'll just think they missed it, that's all,' she'd told
Jenny.

Her friend had gone white with relief.

'I must have been insane,' she'd whispered, burying her head
in her hands and starting to cry.

Mopping up Jenny had taken all Anna's energies. So had
getting through the evening ahead.

A gala ball, followed by fireworks, opened by a breathtaking
descent down the grand staircase of all four models *en grande
tenue*, glittering, for the last time, with the full panoply of the
Levantsky jewels, to the music of Strauss and the audience's
applause.

It had taken all Anna's professionalism to get through the
evening. Only one thing had been spared her—waltzing with
Leo Makarios.

Or, indeed, being anywhere near him. If the previous evening he'd kept her glued to his side, last evening he'd done the
opposite. He hadn't danced with any of the models, sticking to
high-ranking female guests like the Austrian minister's wife.

Anna had been sickly grateful. And even more grateful to
the kindly German spa-loving industrialist who'd made a bee-
line for her. She'd hung on to him all evening.

When the ball had finally ended, deep in the early hours of
the morning, and the models had been let off duty at last, Anna
had hurried back to her room.

And locked her door.

If Leo Makarios wanted to come in he'd have to break
through it with a sledgehammer.

But he had other plans for her, she'd learnt that morning,
after a nerve-racking, sleepless night.

She'd been packing when the knock on her door had

sounded. It had been Justin, pompously informing her of a new assignment.

'Mr Makarios has very generously extended your booking,' he'd told her. 'It's all arranged with your agency. You'll be leaving in an hour. Please do not be late.'

Leaving for where? Anna had wondered.

Now, four hours later, she knew.

She was flying to the Caribbean, with Leo Makarios at her side.

To have as much sex with him as he warranted would atone for stealing the Levantsky rubies from him.

She felt sick all the way through every cell in her body.

Anna hung on to the strap above the door in the car as it bumped over the potholed island roads. She was dog-tired. In the front passenger seat Leo Makarios was talking to the driver, and she was dully grateful that he was continuing to ignore her.

Anna turned her head away, staring out into the black sub-tropical night. She'd been to the Caribbean before, on fashion shoots, but never to this particular island. At least it had been easy to convince Jenny that that was all this was—an unexpected extra shoot that Leo Makarios wanted done in a sub-tropical setting. Rich men, both she and Jenny knew, were capricious, and they expected others to jump when they said so.

As for Jenny herself, Anna had phoned mutual friends of theirs—a photographer and his wife—who would meet Jenny at Heathrow. The couple owned a holiday cottage in the Highlands, and had promised to keep Jenny there until Anna got back to the UK.

When that would be, Anna did not want to think.

Or about anything that was going to happen. As she had done every waking hour since that hideous exchange in Leo Makarios's office, Anna shut off her mind.

She kept it shut even when the car arrived at its destination, driving through metalwork gates set in a high retaining wall and along a smooth gravelled drive to draw up in front of a large, low villa. As she got out, the chill of the air-conditioned interior evaporated into the hot sub-tropical night. For a moment she simply stood there, taking in the sounds and smells of the Caribbean, the croaking of the tree frogs and the heady fragrance of exotic blooms.

Then she was following Leo Makarios indoors, back into air-conditioned cool and a huge, cathedral-ceilinged reception room. The light dazzled her. She took in an impression of great height, cool marble floors, lazily circling overhead fans, wooden shutters and upholstered cane furniture.

Leo Makarios seemed to have completely disappeared.

Instead, a middle-aged woman was coming towards her.

'This way, please,' she said, with a dignified gesture to follow her.

Anna fell in behind, her eyes automatically registering the unselfconsciously graceful walk of the woman—a walk that managed to be both indolent and purposeful. By contrast, she felt she was dragging her own body along, clumsy and exhausted.

Sleep—that was all she wanted. All she craved in the world right now.

The room she was shown to was vast. Up a short, shallow flight of stairs, off a broad gallery-style landing. Inside the room another high, wooden cathedral ceiling soared. A huge mahogany four-poster bed, swathed in what looked like ornamental muslin but was, Anna assumed, mosquito netting, dominated the room. Again, although the room was chilled by air-conditioning, a ceiling fan rotated lazily.

'May I get you some refreshment?' the woman was saying. Even as she spoke a porter entered, carrying Anna's suitcase.

She shook her head.

'Thank you—I'm just going to sleep.'

The woman nodded, said something to the porter in local patois, quite incomprehensible to Anna, and then they both left. Anna looked around her blearily. Her eyes automatically went to the vast four-poster bed.

Easily big enough for two.

Not tonight, Mr Makarios, she thought sourly—you'll have to wait.

Five minutes later, clothes stripped, *en suite* bathroom perfunctorily utilised, she was fast asleep.

Leo stood out on his balcony. A half-moon glittered over the palm-fringed bay that curved in front of the villa. The location was superb, the scene in front of him idyllic, tranquil and untouched. He'd bought this place five years ago, yet how often had he been here? Not often enough.

Life seemed to be rushing by him at ever faster speeds.

Leo's mouth twisted. *So little done, so much to do*—some politician had said that, and he could identify with the sentiment.

Another line drifted through his head.

Getting and spending, we lay waste our powers.

He frowned. No politician, the poet who had said that. And no businessman either. Getting and spending was what his whole life was about. It always had been.

But then, he'd always known that his destiny was to do that. To continue with the work his grandfather had begun, rebuilding the Makarios fortunes after they had been lost in the debacle of the Greek expulsion from Asia Minor in the 1920s.

He could hear his grandfather's harsh voice even now, in his head, from when he'd been a boy.

'We had nothing! Nothing! They took it all. Those Turkii. But we will get everything again—everything!'

Rebuilding the Makarios fortune had occupied his grandfather's life, and his father's, and now his too. The Makarios Corporation spread itself wide—property, shipping, finance, investment, and even—Leo thought of his latest contribution to the family's coffers—the ultimate in luxury goods: priceless historic jewellery, and the revival of a name that had been synonymous with Tsarist extravagance.

He gazed out over the moonlit sea, feeling the warmth of the Caribbean night, hearing the soughing of the wind in the palms, the call of the cicadas, and, drowning them out, the yet more incessant calls of the tree frogs.

A thought came to him out of the soft wind, the sweet-fragranced air.

Who needed diamonds and emeralds on a night like this? Or sapphires and rubies? What use were they here, on the silvered beach by the warm sea's edge?

What use are they at all?

Into his head jarred a voice—'They're just carbon crystals…lots of other common crystals are just as beautiful.' Anna Delane's lofty sneer at the Levantsky jewels.

His face hardened.

Hypocrite! She hadn't helped herself to the ruby bracelet because it was beautiful, but because it was worth a fortune.

It had been a mistake thinking about her. He'd spent the last twenty-four hours assiduously putting her out of his mind. Even when she'd spent the flight sitting right next to him he'd refused to think about her, let alone look at her, or speak to her, or in any way acknowledge her existence. Now, fatally, she was there—vividly in his mind.

Desire shot through him, hard and insistent. His hands clenched over the wooden balustrade.

No! Now was not the time nor the hour. Sleep was the priority now—and it would be for her, too. When he took her it would not be like this, on the edge of exhaustion, but in the rich, ripe fullness of all his powers.

He would need all night to enjoy her to the full.

And every night.

Starting tomorrow.

How long would it take him to tire of her?

The hard smile twisted at his mouth.

A lot, lot sooner than it would take her to tire of him.

He would see to that.

Anna walked along the edge of the beach. It was one of those crystalline white sand, palm-fringed crescents that were put into travel brochures to make everyone instantly want to go there.

But this beach she had to herself. Completely to herself. It belonged to the beautiful sprawling villa spilling along the shore, and the villa belonged to Leo Makarios.

She could see why he'd bought it.

It was, quite simply, idyllic. Like the beach, a travel agent's dream of what a Caribbean villa should look like. The green tiled roof, the white walls, the wraparound veranda, the palm trees fringing the shore, the crystal beach, the pink and purple bougainvillaea and hibiscus splashing colour, the turquoise glitter of a freshwater pool.

Quite, quite idyllic.

Anna stopped to look out to sea. The sun was lowering, a thin band of cloud just above the surface of the sea starting to pool in the lengthening rays of the sun, like rich dye running into spun silk. Bars of gold were sliding across the azure water. Across the sun's face a large, ungainly pelican flapped lazily. High in the sky a frigate bird soared.

Anna glanced at her watch. Though only just evening, the sub-tropical latitudes meant the sun was going down apace. The night would sweep in from the east like a velvet concealing cloak.

And the night would bring, she knew, Leo Makarios.

There had been no sign of him all day. She'd slept long and when she'd surfaced it had been late morning. She'd eaten breakfast on her balcony, and as she'd gazed out over the beautiful grounds leading down to the sea she'd felt the biting, mocking irony of her situation. Here she was in a Caribbean idyll—and tonight she was going to have sex with a man. Deliberate, cold-blooded sex, with a man she did not want to have sex with—a man who thought her a thief, a man she had already thrown out of her bedroom once but who now she could not throw out.

Deliberate, cold-blooded sex.

She made herself say the words again in her head. And again.

Because that was what it was going to be.

Something flared briefly in the depths of her eyes, but she crushed it instantly.

A sudden panic speared through her. She couldn't go through with this. She just couldn't!

I've got to tell him the truth! Tell him it wasn't me who stole his precious bracelet, that it was Jenny, and that she only did it because she's pregnant and terrified, and has got herself involved with a man so dangerous he makes Leo-Money-Bags-Makarios look like a pussycat…

Cold pooled in her stomach. However much she desperately wanted to, she knew she could not tell Leo Makarios the truth. The risks were far too great. As a woman, she might automatically side with Jenny, but who knew what a rich, powerful man like Leo Makarios would think? His attitude to women was dire—she had personal proof of that already—so why should he think Jenny deserved any favours, any mercy? After what she'd heard him say about Vanessa, and guarding his precious cousin from her, he'd probably think Jenny had got herself pregnant on purpose—picking a rich man to get at his money—and that a man so entrapped was entitled to take a woman's baby from her—especially a woman who'd shown herself so morally lax that she'd stooped to theft… He wouldn't understand.

No—Anna's face closed—there was no way she could take that risk. And that meant—her expression twisted—she just couldn't tell Leo Makarios why she had taken the blame for stealing his rubies.

He had to go on thinking that *she* was the thief. It was the only way she could protect Jenny.

Which meant—the fear pooled in her stomach again, but with a different cause this time—that she was, indeed, going to have to go through with what Leo Makarios intended.

Have sex with him.

She stared unseeingly out over the water. In Austria it had seemed unreal; she'd been in shock, Anna realised, using all her mental energy to tamp down the panic that had been trying to erupt. Here, after being on her own all day, the reality of what she was going to have to do was hitting.

Hitting hard.

For a moment she felt revulsion stiffen through her.

A phrase welled up in her thoughts.

Self-respect. An alien concept to so many people, she knew, moving in the world she did. Men who treated women's bodies as commodities—women who treated them the same way. She could name half a dozen other models she knew who would have thought themselves in paradise to have been offered the choice that Leo Makarios had offered. Queued round the block for it.

I'm not one of them!

Even as she mentally shouted her denial, another voice spoke in her head. With killing, merciless force.

But you will be...

Leo Makarios will reduce you to exactly that. Strip you of every last vestige of your self-respect even as he strips the clothes from your body...

Pincers bit inside her stomach, sharp and painful.

She went on staring out over the darkening sea, her mind even darker.

Facing up to what she was going to do.

What she was going to lose.

Yet, for all that was true, she could not sacrifice her friend's future, her baby, just to protect her own self-respect.

I have to do this.

And after all, she thought, with savage mockery at her own prurience, supposing it was Jenny or jail? What would you do then? Would you still stand by her if it meant losing years of your life?

Instead of just a few days...a few nights...

So why make such a fuss about what Leo Makarios is offering?

Even as Anna let the thought into her mind she tried to suppress it.

Leo Makarios was dangerous. She'd thought him so the very

first time she'd set eyes on him, and every encounter with him had proved it to her. Especially the one in her bedroom…

Memory flooded back like a drowning tide, and suddenly she was there, there again, as Leo Makarios held her, kissed her, caressed her—a sensual onslaught that had simply overwhelmed her, made it impossible for her to resist…

Until, with a strength she'd hardly been able to summon, she had flung him from her…

She shut her eyes in anguish, blocking out memory.

Self-respect? The words stabbed at her. Mocking her. Taunting her.

She wasn't just going to sacrifice her self-respect by having deliberate, cold-blooded sex with Leo Makarios. She was going to lose it for a much, much worse reason…

She turned away abruptly. Grimly, she headed back up the beach in the brief sub-tropical dusk.

Her face had hardened.

She couldn't get out of it now. That wasn't in her power. Not if she wanted to keep Jenny safe, herself out of jail.

But she could, she *must* ensure that it was nothing but deliberate, cold-blooded sex.

Nothing more.

Dear God, let me have the strength I need—please, please!

'More champagne?'

'No, thank you.'

'Smoked salmon?'

'No, thank you.'

'Caviar?'

'No, thank you.'

'As you wish.' There was an amused, baiting quality to Leo's voice. He sat back in his rattan chair on the terrace. From the veranda the gardens were landscaped so that the curve of the beach opened up, framed by palm trees. A light, cooling breeze came off the sea. Moonlight bathed the surface of the water.

It was a beautiful scene—and the woman sitting opposite

him complemented it perfectly. His eyes slid over her as she sat there, ramrod-straight, staring determinedly out to sea.

She was wearing a jade-green loose silk-trousered affair, with long sleeves and a high collar. As she'd stalked across the terrace, her hair caught back in a stark, high knot, not a scrap of make-up on her, he'd read the signals coming from her as if she'd been broadcasting in neon.

She was making not the slightest attempt to look alluring.

It hadn't worked in the least. Anna Delane would have looked alluring in a sack. Her body had a long-limbed grace that could not be disguised, and the bones of her face had been constructed with a natural artistry that meant make-up or hair-style was an irrelevance.

Oh, yes, Anna Delane had an allure that she could not sup-press. Leo gave a mocking, inward smile. Even when she was doing her best to be sullen and monosyllabic, as she was now.

He took a mouthful of champagne and contemplated her. A sliver of irritation wormed its way under his amusement. She really was a piece of work—sitting there as stiff as a board and twice as hostile. He'd caught her red-handed, a proven thief. But was she abashed? Guilty? Contrite?

The words were unknown to her, clearly.

Shameless. That was the only word that fitted her.

He took another mouthful of champagne and washed off the irritation. Well, there was an expression in English that per-fectly captured Ms Anna Delane's forthcoming fate—riding for a fall.

And she would do it, very, very satisfyingly, in his bed.

Anticipation eased through him. He was going to enjoy Anna Delane, every last exquisite drop of her—and the greatest en-joyment would be her enjoyment of him. However galling it was to her.

He reached out a hand and scooped some more beluga with his spoon.

Numbly, Anna took another forkful of grilled fish. Somewhere in her mind she knew it was delicious, but it didn't register.

Nothing registered. She wouldn't let it. Must not. Instead she just sat there, eating grilled fish and salad like an automaton, without will or feeling. Resolutely refusing to look at the man sitting opposite her.

He'd abandoned attempts at talking to her, and she was glad. It allowed her to keep her mind blank—as blank as her expression. She was well trained in that—it was like having to stalk out onto a runway, features immobile, not a person at all, just an ambulatory clothes-horse, walking, posing, stopping, going, all at the direction of other people. No will of their own.

Just as she now had no will of her own.

She set her fork aside, having consumed enough. She reached for her champagne and took a small, measured sip, then set her glass back. She'd contemplated getting drunk, but decided against it. Alcohol lowered your guard. Made you stupid. Weak.

And weakness was something she must not allow.

It was far, far too dangerous.

She'd known it, known it with a hollowing of her insides, as she'd walked out on to the terrace this evening.

And set eyes on Leo Makarios again.

A jolt had gone through her that had been terrifying in its intensity. A jolt that had nothing to do with him thinking her a thief and everything to do with the sudden, instant quickening of the blood in her veins, the surge of emotion dissolving through her, the debilitating weakening of her knees.

She'd taken in the presence of Leo Makarios.

Waiting for her.

And almost, almost, she had turned and run.

But she'd forced herself to go forward. She couldn't run. There was nowhere to run to.

So she'd steeled herself, drained all expression from her face, all feeling from her mind, sat herself down and stared out to sea.

Not looking at Leo Makarios. Not looking where he sat, lounging back with lazy, dangerous grace, the open collar of his shirt revealing the strong column of his throat, the turned-up cuffs showing the lean strength of his wrist and hands, the taut material over his torso emphasising the breadth of his chest.

And not looking, above all, at his face. The wide, sensual mouth, the dark heavy-lidded eyes.

Eyes that pressed on her like weights.

With all her strength she sat there, impassive, indifferent, while her stomach contorted in hard, convoluted knots.

Praying for the strength to get through the ordeal ahead.

But she could not, dared not, put into words what she was praying for.

The meal seemed to go on for ever. She refused dessert, desultorily picking at a slice of mango and sipping mineral water, her champagne abandoned. Leo Makarios, it seemed, was in no hurry. He'd eaten a leisurely first course, a leisurely main course, and had made a considered selection from the cheese board.

Finally he leant back, brandy swirling slowly in his glass, a cup of coffee at his place, eyes resting on her contemplatively.

'Tell me something,' he said suddenly, his tone conversational. 'Why did you steal the bracelet?'

Anna's head turned. Her eyes looked at him, widening slightly as the meaning of what he'd just asked registered. The question seemed extraordinary.

'That's none of your business,' she returned repressively.

For a moment Leo Makarios just stared at her, as if he did not believe what she'd just said. Then a thread of anger flashed in his eyes. Next it was gone.

He leant back in his chair and gave a laugh.

It was an incredulous, disbelieving laugh, with not the slightest trace of humour in it.

'You really are a piece of work,' he said slowly. His eyes narrowed slightly. 'Aren't you going to tell me it was for your sick grandmother, or something? To pay for an operation?' His voice was jibing.

She looked at him levelly. 'No.' Her voice was expressionless, but inside emotion was running. Thank God she had not tried to throw herself and Jenny on his mercy—his taunt just now showed exactly how he'd have received her plea. No. Her face hardened. There was only one way out of this, and that was the way Leo Makarios had given her in his office.

Oh, God, just let it be over and done with!

She just wanted it over and done with. That was all she wanted.

Suddenly, tension spilling out of her in words, she spoke.

'Look, what's with this stupid inquisition? You gave me the choice of the police or you—and here I am. So what are you waiting for? You've had your dinner—why hang around? Just get it over and damn well done with!'

Her voice was terse.

For a moment he just went on looking at her, his face suddenly unreadable. Then, abruptly, he set down his brandy and got to his feet.

'Very well. Time for bed, Ms Delane. Let the reparation begin.'

Was there mockery in his words? She couldn't tell. Didn't know.

Didn't care.

This was it, then. No more tense, fraught waiting. No more prevarication.

She was going to go to bed with Leo Makarios.

Right now. Now.

And have sex with him.

Carefully Anna got to her feet. Her heart, she could tell, seemed to have gone strangely numb as well. Just like the rest of her.

She could only be grateful.

It was the best way to get it over and done with.

She just had to keep her nerve, that was all. Endure. Let him take what he wanted and it would be over.

At least for now. Tomorrow night she'd have to go through it all again, but that was tomorrow. She'd think about that then. Now she just had to focus on getting through tonight.

She walked into the villa ahead of him, every footstep, his

and hers, falling heavily on the marble floor, and let him guide her up the shallow flight of stairs into a room that was not hers.

His, evidently.

She stood for a moment in the middle, not sure what to do. There was a large bed in here, just like in her bedroom, but this one was not a four-poster, and it did not have yards of muslin draped. The air was cool from the air-conditioning, but not as chilly as the setting in her room. On either side of the bed low lamps provided the only illumination, making the room shadowed, intimate.

'Wait there.'

She did as she was told. Leo Makarios disappeared into his *en suite* bathroom. She heard the sound of water running. Anna went on standing there, immobile. Her brain was frozen, her mind empty. She couldn't think, couldn't feel. She was standing in Leo Makarios's bedroom, waiting for him to emerge from his bathroom and take her to his bed. It was impossible, outrageous.

And yet it was happening.

Now.

Tonight.

She should be feeling something, she knew—but she felt nothing. Nothing at all.

Only the hard, heavy thumping of her heart in her breast, the tautness in the line of her jaw told her that, numb though her mind was, her body was registering the anxiety, the tension in her psyche at what was going to happen.

Tonight.

Now.

She went on standing there. Not looking. Not thinking. Not feeling.

Completely numb.

The bathroom door clicked open and Leo Makarios reappeared. He was wearing a white towelling robe. Short. To the knees. Belted tight. The whiteness made his Mediterranean skin tone even darker in the subdued lamplight.

Anna felt some kind of emotion prickle out across her skin.

She watched him as, scarcely glancing at her, he went across to the bed, drew back the covers, and lounged down against the pillows, propping them up behind him. His long tanned legs stretched out bare on the white sheets.

He settled his gaze on her.

Time seemed to stop. Stop completely. As if the world had stopped turning.

His eyes were dark, unreadable. His face immobile.

But something in his eyes made the prickling intensify across her skin.

A pressure started to build.

Inside her—outside her. In the room, in the space between where she was standing, motionless, numb, in the middle of Leo Makarios's bedroom, and where he was lounging back on his bed.

Looking at her.

Waiting for her.

For one endless moment the silence held.

Then he spoke.

'Come here,' he said softly.

For the space of a single heartbeat—which lasted an unbearable agony of time—Anna did not move.

Could not move.

Somewhere deep in her head words were forming. She could hear them, very low. They were telling her to run. To yell. To shout abuse at the man who lounged back against his pillows like some eastern pasha, waiting for his slave woman to come and pleasure him…

But even as she heard the muffled, vehement words they were stifled. Extinguished.

She could not listen to their siren call. Must not.

If she did, Jenny would be doomed.

Slowly, like a puppet, Anna started walking towards him. Feeling nothing, she stood beside the bed.

Docile. Compliant to his will.

Holding down with iron force the voice that was trying to

speak deep inside her head. The pressure that was building, molecule by molecule, inside her veins.

It wanted to get out, she knew. She must not allow it.

Must not.

She went on standing there, motionless beside Leo Makarios's bed, with him lounging back against the headrest.

Looking at her.

There was something in his eyes, dark and hooded, something that made the prickling in her skin intensify again, as if the voltage applied to her flesh had just been increased.

She felt her breath quicken and tried to suppress it.

His eyes washed over her.

Her heart started to slug in her chest; her veins dilated.

Desperately she tamped it down.

Leo's voice was murmuring. Slow, and low, with a creamy, sensual timbre.

'Oh, Anna Delane, you have no idea how much I'm going to enjoy this.'

His voice was soft and heavy. His eyes slumberous with desire.

He reached a hand out to her, taking hers in his. Her hand was limp, inert.

He drew her down on the bed and she sat there, half twisted towards him. Looking at him. Nothing in her eyes. Nothing at all.

She was a doll, a puppet. Capable of no feeling at all…

Slowly, never taking his dark, slumberous eyes from her, he lifted his hands to her hair, pulling out the pins. Her long black hair tumbled down over her shoulders, cascading over the jade-green silk.

Leo spoke again, his Greek accent low and heavy, his lashes sweeping down over those dark golden eyes.

'You come to me like a sacrificial virgin.' His hands sifted through her hair. 'Laying down your virtue for me. Pure, un-sullied, innocent.' Something shifted in the depths of those eyes. Shifted, and hardened.

Like his voice.

'How extraordinarily deceptive appearances can be.'

The words drawled from him.

She did not respond. Did not speak. Did not do anything except go on sitting there as his long, sensual fingers sifted through her hair. Her body was like marble—motionless, insensate. It had to be—it had to be—she must not be anything else! Must not let herself feel his fingers in her hair, feel the myriad pressure points in her skull sending a soft, shivering sensation through her. She must not feel that.

Must remember she was only a puppet. Feeling nothing. Nothing at all.

His fingers stopped, then slid through her hair to stroke the back of her neck. Slowly, sensually...

And suddenly, out of nowhere, sensation started to flow through her. She tried to stop it, tried to remember why she was there, with no feelings, no thoughts, no will, merely a mindless doll that Leo Makarios could touch and stroke, and she would let him, because that was what she had to do...

But it was impossible.

She could not stop herself. Could not stop the sensation rippling through her as his fingers played with the sensitive skin they were touching.

She felt her eyes close. Heavy, slumberous.

Slowly, his fingers tautened around her nape. Leisurely he drew her down towards him. She let him do it. She let him brush her lips with his, slide his tongue within and start to caress her.

She let him slip her top from her, the silky material sliding away, let him pull her over him, let her bared, braless breasts graze against the towelling of his bathrobe, let his hands slide beneath the waistband of her silk trousers, mould over the soft roundness of her bottom. Even as he started to slide off the material, down her thighs she let him do it, wanted him to.

Anna let him go on kissing her, moving his mouth on hers, let the hard shaft of his manhood probe at the juncture of her legs, let his hand palm her breast in slow, rhythmic circles as its peak ripened under his touch.

She let herself lie there, spread across him. His hand was at the nape of her neck, the other at her breast, and his mouth was on hers, his thighs hard beneath hers, his shaft strong and seeking.

She had no will, no emotion, only total, absolute submission to sensation—sensation he was arousing from her, stroking from her, caressing from her. A slow, spreading fire started to lick through her. A long, low pulse started in her veins, and in every cell of her body a warm, dissolving heat began to steal.

She felt herself move, press her body along his, felt the hardness of his hips, the lean strength of his smooth, muscled chest. Felt her mouth move, move over his, felt herself start to kiss him back, to seek his tongue with hers. Felt the hunger start, deep, deep within her. Felt her hands curl over his strong, sculpted shoulders, revelling in the touch of his skin beneath her kneading fingers.

The fire was licking now, like flames at dry grass, spreading through her veins. She could hear low, aching moans, and knew they were coming from her throat, but she could not stop them. She had no will, no power.

Something had taken her over. Consumed her so completely, so absolutely, she was helpless in its thrall, in its overpowering, overwhelming need.

A need to move her body over his, touching, seeking, questing, with her thighs tautening, hips lifting slightly, so slightly, but just enough, just enough…

She wanted…

She wanted…

She wanted to feel his hand on her breast, palming it, scissoring rhythmically, pulling at her inflamed, jutting nipple. Wanted the other breast to feel the same. Wanted more, more—much more.

The fire was coursing through her, hungry for more to feed it with. The low, aching moans were coming again, need and ravening hunger.

Hunger for him. For the lean, hard body beneath her. For the silky moistness of his mouth, the sensuous gliding of his tongue, the rich velvet of his lips. But it wasn't enough. It wasn't enough.

Fire licked again, all through her veins, but with a new focus, a new urgent source of heat.

She wanted...

She wanted...

She twisted her hips, feeling the long hardness of his shaft at her belly.

She wanted...needed...

Again she lifted her hips, straining down on him with her thighs, her hands pressing on his shoulders, her breast ripe in his hand, as she writhed against his body.

She felt the tip of his shaft against her, and the fire flamed within her. She reared up, hands pinioning his shoulders, her thighs over his, hair tumbling over her back. And with a last, low, rasping moan in her throat she caught his tip at the vee of her legs, lifting and positioning it just where it had to—*had* to be.

He let go her mouth, let go her nape, and she threw back her head, rearing up over him. Her eyes were blind, shut, her body one single writhing twist of flame.

His hand glided down her back in a single smooth sweep, splaying over her bottom.

Words came from him. She could not hear them. Could only feel the tip of his probing shaft at the entrance to her inflamed, aching, flooding body.

And she wanted it. Needed it so much that not having it was a torment, a hunger, a desperation.

So she took it.

Took him into her.

His hand splaying across her guided her down on him, slowly, infinitely slowly, and he filled her, stretching and moulding her.

A long, low exhalation breathed from her. He was solid inside her. Solid, and hard and full. For a long, timeless moment she just stayed there, half-reared over him, feeling his fullness inside her, filling her, filling her so completely that she could only stay completely, absolutely still.

Then slowly, very, very slowly, she moved. Indenting her hips, pressing forward.

And the fire inside her sheeted into flame. White hot flame.

A cry came from Anna as her head fell back, helpless, rolling. She cried out again.

'Is that good?' Leo's voice was low. His hand pressed at her, the fingers at her nipple scything her, sending shoots of pleasure through her. 'Because for me it's good. But this—*this* would be better.'

In a single powerful movement he thrust up into her, and the fire sheeted again, burning down through her hands, her feet. She cried out in pleasure again, louder, more helpless.

He thrust again—up, up into her—and there was a place somewhere, somewhere inside her, that was catching fire, and she wanted…

His hand was on her bottom now, kneading and pressing. He thrust again, and the sensation was unbearable. But he thrust again, and her body was melting, and writhing, and burning.

He thrust again. And this time as he thrust she twisted on him with her hips, and again. The rhythm mounted and mounted, and the fire inside her grew hotter and hotter. More cries were coming from her throat, her body one single flame of sensation, and her head was rolling, rolling. She had become a writhing, ravening hunger, and she wanted…needed…

This.

Oh, God, this—this was what she needed!

The place deep within her, which his thrusting fullness had been stoking, stroking, had caught fire. Igniting in a single blazing funnel of sensation, of pleasure so intense, so consuming, that Anna could not breathe, could only gasp.

And then there was another cry, hoarse and urgent, and Leo was thrusting up into her again. Short, rapid thrusts. His hands suddenly on her shoulders, as he jerked powerfully, repeatedly into her, to reap his own unstoppable pleasure.

She collapsed down on him, panting, exhausted, drained. The storm of sensation shaking her even in its dying embers.

She felt a hand smoothing back the hair from her forehead, felt warm breath on her cheek.

'*Thee mou*, I knew you would be good, but—'

His hoarse voice changed to Greek. It seemed to be coming from a long, long way away. Everything was coming from a distance.

Except for one thing. Something black and dark was rolling in, darker than anything she had ever known. Stifling her, annihilating her.

Slaying her.

It was the realisation of what she had just let happen.

The worst thing in the world…

CHAPTER SIX

LEO strolled out onto his balcony. The sun was high already, and he was not surprised. It had been a long, long night—but very little sleep had taken place.

He stretched in a pleasurable flexing of his shoulders.

Thee mou, but it had been good! More than that—it had been mind-blowing.

And not just for him. Anna Delane had responded exactly as he had known she would.

She'd gone up in flames.

White-hot, scorching flames.

Again and again—all through the night. Time after time he had taken her, and every time he had drawn from her a response that had had her body shaking, shuddering, had her crying out helplessly, reducing her time after time to exhausted, breathless satiation. She had threshed in his arms, her spine arching, hair wild like a maenad, eyes blind and unseeing as she'd convulsed in the extremity of pleasure, totally, completely possessed by it.

It had been intoxicating.

And incredibly arousing.

There had been something exquisitely satisfying about her helplessly sensual response to his touch. She had not intended it, that was for sure. She'd tried to hold back from him, to be like a statue, a block of wood—rigid and unresponsive. But he'd ignored her sullenness, her obvious determination to cheat him of what he wanted from her. Of what she owed him.

He'd got what he wanted from her, all right. Had drawn it from her stroke by stroke, touch by touch, kiss by kiss. Caressing her body with his until she was hot in his arms, giving those low little moans in her throat, moving her body on his in helpless, hungry desire…

He felt his body stir. Even though it had been sated time after time on hers. He gave a low laugh. Time enough to indulge—he was going to be here for as long as he wanted Anna Delane, for as long as she still fed his appetite for her—but right now there was another appetite he wanted to feed. It had been a long time since dinner the night before.

He walked inside the bedroom, picked up the house phone by his bed, and gave his order for breakfast. As he replaced the receiver he let his eyes rest on the woman sleeping in his bed.

She really was extraordinarily beautiful—and never more so than now. Her black hair streamed over the pillow, tumbled and tangled. Her skin was white against the white sheets, black lashes splashing on her cheeks. She was breathing softly.

He gazed down at her.

There was something strangely vulnerable about her.

He frowned slightly.

Vulnerable?

That was the last word he should apply to Anna Delane. Even when he hadn't even known her for a thief she'd radiated attitude. Sharp-tongued, difficult—a troublemaker.

And a hypocrite. Oh, yes. His eyes narrowed. A fully paid-up hypocrite! He'd known from the moment he'd laid eyes on her, when she'd met his look, that she was sexually responsive to him. She'd made no secret of it at all as he'd looked her over and signalled to her that he liked what he saw. And she'd signalled back her response to him clearly enough, all the way through that evening when he'd kept her at his side. Hell, what did she think he'd done that for? Obviously it had been to tell her that he was sexually interested in her. And yet when he'd moved in on that response she'd turned on him like a harpy. Even though she'd been halfway to bed with him when she'd done so.

And then, *then* to subject him to a tirade of virtuous outrage as if she'd never melted like warm honey in his arms—when all along…all along, she'd been nothing but a thief. Daring to steal from him—and making the Levantsky jewels her target. A thief without any sense of shame, or guilt, or contrition. A cool, conscienceless, self-seeking, thieving piece!

But she hadn't been cool when he'd been inside her, when she'd been crying out, threshing in orgasm. She hadn't been cool when he'd held her afterwards, her body shaking, convulsing in the aftermath, her hair tangled, her brow sweated, her breathing rapid and shallow, her heart beating like a frantic bird beneath her ribs.

No, she hadn't been cool then…

He turned away and headed for the *en suite* bathroom. Gazing down at Anna Delane and remembering how she'd been in his arms a few short hours ago was not a good idea right now. He wanted breakfast—time enough for more sex later.

A lot more sex.

He hadn't had nearly enough of Anna Delane yet—she had a *whole* lot more to make up for before he'd be done with her.

'Would you like to swim?'

'No, thank you.'

'Take the catamaran out? Or the launch?'

'No, thank you.'

'Do you want to see the rest of the island?'

'No, thank you.'

'As you wish.'

There was no baiting amusement in Leo's curt voice now. Merely mounting irritation. He picked up his coffee cup and drank, then set it down again. His eyes rested on the woman sitting opposite him.

She was reading a book. A thick paperback that was absorbing all her attention. But then everything and anything absorbed her attention except him. Of him she took no notice whatsoever. She was shutting him out of her existence. She never looked at him, or met his eye, or talked in anything other than the briefest, tersest replies.

She'd been like that since he'd sent for her.

The fact that he'd had to do so had been a source of irritation in itself. He'd come out of his shower to find his bed empty. She'd simply disappeared. It hadn't bothered him. He'd assumed she'd merely gone back to her own room to shower and dress.

But she still hadn't appeared even when he'd despatched one of the staff to tell her that breakfast would be on the terrace. He'd eaten on his own, then sent for her again.

That time she'd come down.

And had stalked stiff-backed across to the table just as she had done the night before. As if she'd never spent the night in his bed.

She'd been wearing dark glasses, completely concealing her eyes. Dark glasses, and her hair back in its punishing knot, and wearing tight black leggings and a long-sleeved sweat top. Completely inappropriate for a hot tropical day.

She'd sat down, totally ignoring him, and turned instead to the maid, requesting a pot of hot water and some fruit.

Then she'd twisted her chair slightly towards the sea view, crossed her long legs, opened her book and started reading.

He might not have been there.

For a minute Leo had looked at her, disbelievingly.

Then he'd spoken.

'*Kalimera*, Anna,' he'd said, in a studied tone.

She'd ignored him.

'Are you always unsociable in the mornings?' His tone had been even more studied.

No answer.

'Anna—'

There had been an edge in his voice then.

She'd turned her head towards him.

He'd been unable to see her eyes. The dark glasses were very effective.

Irritatingly so.

'Yes?'

Her tone had been quelling.

'Tell me—' he'd kept his tone light, civil '—what would you like to do today?'

'Nothing, thank you.'

'There must be something you would like to do,' he'd persisted, with punishing politeness.

But she'd said, 'No, thank you.' In the same tone of complete indifference. And she'd gone on doing so to everything he'd suggested.

Now he just sat here, glaring at her, her nose still buried in her book.

Every last vestige of Leo's good mood vanished.

The maid came out again, placing the requested items on the table. Anna lifted her head out of her book briefly and smiled her thanks. A brief smile, but a smile all the same.

Leo was pretty sure it was the first smile he'd ever seen from her.

It did something strange to him.

He pushed the strangeness aside, watching as she took a teabag from where she'd been using it as bookmark, placed it in a teacup and poured fresh hot water over it. A tangy, herbal scent came off it as it infused.

'Do you not drink coffee?' he asked.

'Very seldom.' She picked up a teaspoon and poked the teabag.

Then she forked a slice of fresh pineapple and placed it on her plate. She started cutting it up, lifting small slices to her mouth.

Silently, Leo slid the basket of fresh breads across to her.

'No, thank you,' she said.

'Are you on a diet?' he enquired.

'I'm always on a diet,' she answered, continuing with her pineapple.

'You hardly need to lose weight.' His eyes ran over her slim, elegant body.

She turned her head to him then.

'That's because I'm always on a diet,' she replied caustically.

She went back to eating her pineapple, then took two slices of papaya, ate those, and pushed her plate away.

'What would you like to eat next?' Leo enquired with punishing civility.

'Nothing, thank you.' She picked up her teacup and took a small sip of the hot herbal tea. Then she placed it back on its saucer and resumed reading.

Leo looked at her fulminatingly.

What the hell was she playing at? Pretending last night had never happened? Pretending she'd never cried out, eyes distended with passion, hands clutching at him, shuddering with orgasm in his embrace?

Evidently, yes.

He stared at her balefully. Hell, she should be purring by now! Her body languorous and sensual from its sating last night. She should have undulated towards him wearing something skimpy, like a bikini with a chiffon sarong caressing her hips, wafting up to him, hair cascading down her back, mouth beestung. She should have leant down, draping her arms around his shoulders, murmuring amorously to him, lowering her mouth to his to greet him...

Instead she was sitting ramrod-straight, answering in terse, caustic monosyllables or totally ignoring him.

Christos, who the hell was she to ignore him? Did she really think she'd prefer a police cell to his bed? Obviously not, or she wouldn't have accepted the bargain he'd offered her. She wanted to save her precious skin, all right, and she hadn't been fussy about how she was going to do that. Well—he glared at her—she could damn well earn her parole, just the way he'd told her when he'd caught her red-handed with his rubies.

By working very, very hard to please him.

He took a mouthful of coffee and then pushed the cup away.

'Anna—'

The edge was back in his voice.

She looked up.

'Yes?'

He rested his eyes on her. For a moment he said nothing.

He thought he saw something flicker in her face, then it was gone.

'Lose the attitude,' he said softly. 'If you'd rather go back to a police cell in Austria, you only have to say. But if you don't, then I suggest you remember what you are here to do, hmm?'

Something changed in her face then, all right. It seemed to blanch even whiter than its usual paleness. Then it was gone again. She set her book down.

'You want sex again?'

The question was delivered in such a deadpan voice that Leo just stared. Distaste knifed through him.

'Spare me your crudities,' he said coldly.

The look came in her face again, then disappeared.

'Well, what do you want, then?' she demanded.

There was belligerence in her voice. It set Leo's back up.

'You can start,' he said tersely, 'with some civility.'

A choke sounded from her.

'*Civility?*' She echoed the word as if he'd said *DIY brain surgery*.

Leo's mouth tightened.

'We will be here together for at least three weeks—I have no intention of putting up with your ill-humour for that duration.'

She seemed to have gone pale again.

'Three weeks?' she echoed faintly. 'I can't stay here that long!'

Anger shot through him again.

'You think your time in jail would be less?' he riposted sarcastically.

'I've got assignments booked.'

'I will have them cancelled.'

She leant forward.

'No, you will not. I will not have my professional reputation compromised by you high-handedly cancelling my assignments!'

Once more Leo was reduced to just staring at her.

'Your…professional…reputation…?' he echoed. 'I don't believe I just heard you say that! You, Anna Delane, are a *thief*!
You have committed a criminal act. I could have you slung in
jail. And you dare, *dare* to talk to me of your ''professional
reputation''?'

Leo pushed his chair back and stood up, his hand slashing
through the air.

'Enough! I don't want to hear one more insolent word from
you.' He relapsed into Greek, and vented his feelings in several
choice expletives. Then he stalked away, his mood as black as
thunder.

Behind him, Anna Delane sat very, very still.

She wouldn't crack. She wouldn't. She would not give him
that satisfaction.

Satisfaction.

The word jibed at her with cruel taunting. She could still see
it now, etched on her memory, the triumphant *satisfaction* on
his face as she'd opened her eyes to look down at the man
who had just done what he had to her.

Self-hatred lacerated through her. How *could* she have betrayed herself like that? How could she have responded to him,
been stroked and caressed and kissed into arousal as she had
let herself be?

Until she was helpless, mindless, beyond all control, all sal-
vation.

Beyond anything except the fire that had swept through her
body, flamed it to an ecstasy that she had never known existed.

Nothing had ever been like this—nothing.

It had been incredible, ecstatic, exquisite—a stormfire of sensation that had burnt her flesh to the core in a sensual pleasure
so intense she had not known it was possible to exist.

I never knew—I never knew it could be like this…

And in that same moment of exultant realisation she had
known exactly why she so feared Leo Makarios—just why he
was so dangerous to her. She had opened her eyes and realised,

with a sickening, ravening horror, what she had done, what she had let him do. What she had *wanted* him to do!

And he had known it. Wanted her to want it, and what he could make her feel. She had seen the triumph in his eyes.

Self-hatred lashed through her again.

Oh, God, she'd walked to his bed like an ignorant, arrogant fool! Thinking she could stay detached, controlled. Uninvolved with what was going to happen to her. She had prayed for strength, but she had been weak—devastatingly, sickeningly weak.

So pathetically weak she hadn't been able to resist. Not a single touch or caress; not even a single kiss! Leo had melted her into his arms and she had been able to do nothing, *nothing*, to hold back from him!

A shaft of fear went through her.

Three weeks, he'd said. Oh, God, she couldn't last three *days* here!

Or three nights…

She sat staring out over the beautiful vista of sea and sand as if she were staring at a desert of thorns.

He would do to her again tonight what he had done last night. She knew it. Knew it with a sick, dull certainty. He would take her to bed and stroke, caress and kiss her body until she could fight it no longer. Until her control was stripped from her just as he stripped the clothes from her body, and that mortal, consuming fire would ignite in her again—until she was aching for him…

Anna could feel her body start to respond, feel a prickling in her skin even at the memory of the night that had passed.

Agitatedly she got to her feet, crossing her arms over her chest, crushing down the sensation that was starting to lick at her body. The hunger that was coming to life again, the throb between her aching thighs…

She had to keep busy! Had to do something, anything, to distract her body. She'd already done her morning stretches and skincare routine, using them to blank out her mind as best she could, when she had finally stirred from her exhausted slumber to wake to lacerating consciousness. Sick with horror, she'd bolted from the bedroom, hearing the shower in the *en suite* bathroom, knowing she had to get away before he emerged.

Emerged to enjoy his triumph over her.

She'd stuck in her room, body aching, trembling with over-stimulation, wanting only to sink into permanent oblivion—anything other than face up to what she had done.

But there had been no oblivion—only a maid, insistent, not once but twice, that Mr Makarios was waiting for her on the terrace.

So she had put her armour on. Like one going into battle. Her exercise outfit was hardly the thing to wear in the Caribbean, but it was the only daywear she had brought with her that was not designed for the Alps in winter. She'd tied up her hair, put on the concealing veil of her dark glasses, and gone down to face up to what she had done.

Taking refuge from it the only way she knew how.

And she'd nearly cracked.

So very nearly.

As she'd walked up to him and seen him sitting there, loung-ing back, the strength of his body exposed in a close-hugging polo shirt, in hip-lean shorts, seen the long, strong sinews of his thighs, the smooth, muscled forearms, seen him watching her approach through lazy, heavy-lidded eyes, she had felt her insides start to dissolve.

He had just looked so devastating!

Something had turned over inside her, melting through her.

And then another emotion had taken its place. A familiar one—a safe one. The safest she could ever have in his com-pany.

Anger.

That was what she had to feel in his presence—nothing but anger. It was the only way she could endure what lay ahead.

In the night, she knew, with bitter self-hatred, she would succumb—could do nothing else, was helpless to resist.

But in the day—

In the day the object of her hatred could be someone other than herself. It could be the man who had done to her the thing she could never, ever forgive herself for.

Leo Makarios—the man she both hated and desired.

CHAPTER SEVEN

LEO slewed the Jeep to a halt in front of the villa in the golden light of the westering sun. His muscles ached, but at least his black mood had gone. He'd spent the day on the island's eastern coast, punishing it out of him by wave-sailing the rough Atlantic swell. He'd thought of doing what he'd done yesterday—inspecting his property developments taking shape on the southern shores—but everything was going to schedule and there was nothing more there to occupy him. Besides, he hadn't come here to work. He'd come here to relax.

Unwind.

Enjoy some well-earned R&R with a beautiful woman to warm his bed…

His face darkened momentarily as he tossed the Jeep's keys at one of the outdoor staff and headed indoors. All day he'd deliberately kept Anna Delane out of his head. He didn't want to think about her.

Now he wondered idly how she'd spent the day. Still sulking? A smile twisted at his mouth as he sprinted lithely upstairs. She wouldn't be sulking for long. He'd make sure of it.

There was no way a thieving piece like Anna Delane was going to get the better of him. His smile deepened.

He would start again on her, right now.

He'd just thought of an excellent way to do so.

A massage, personally administered, was exactly what he wanted.

And after the massage…

Anna lay in Leo Makarios's arms. She was facing away from him, drawn back against his body by his heavy, restraining arm. His thigh was heavy across hers.

She stared out across the room.

It had happened again.

The fire had burnt through her, burnt away every last vestige of her self-control, her self-respect.

A massage. She had been summoned to give him a massage.

Like a slave girl!

She'd done it, too. Because what would have been the point of objecting? She'd been brought here for this purpose—the price of keeping her out of jail, keeping Jenny safe. And if a massage was what the man who thought her a thief wanted, then a massage was what he would have.

And what came after.

It had taken very, very little time for her kneading hands to be caught, stilled. For him to turn over with lithe, muscled grace onto his back, for him to draw her down on him again and then, with sudden avid hunger, to tip her over until he was over her. His mouth had been on hers, his hands on her body, peeling the clothes from her as if he were peeling a ripe, luscious fruit for his delectation.

And she had let him. Once more she had let him. Helpless to resist, helpless to do anything except let her body ignite from his, catch the hunger of his kisses, the ardency of his caressing.

Until she had burned with him in the same hot, fierce flame, crying out, her hair whipping, consumed absolutely by the sensation obliterating all sense from her, obliterating everything but its own desperate, urgent need for satiation.

Then afterwards, as the tumult had died, draining away like an inferno that had consumed its own fuel, he had lifted himself from her, rolling to his side, drawing her back against him, smoothing her hair, murmuring to her words she did not understand, his breath warm on her neck, his hands warm on her body.

And now she lay there, her body's conflagration slowly ebbing to its last cooling embers, exhausted, sated, feeling his chest rise and fall heavily behind her spine, knowing her lungs too were replenishing their air, her heart gradually slowing.

She lay staring out into the dusky room, hearing only the susurration of his breathing, only the low hum of the air-conditioning.

Her mind seemed suspended, incapable of operation. She couldn't think, or feel, or make any conscious use of words or thoughts.

She seemed to be somewhere else.

Someone else.

And there was nothing, *nothing* she could do.

Leo lay, Anna enfolded in his arms. His body was warm, inert. So was hers. They were incapable of movement, both of them, he knew. The exhaustion that followed the little death had overtaken them both.

It felt good to hold her like this, spooned back against him.

It was as if she belonged to him.

His mind shifted. Where had that thought come from?

He did not want Anna Delane to belong to him. What would he want that for? She was a thief. A beautiful, desirable thief. But a thief for all that.

He did not want to get involved with her.

But then, he never wanted to get involved with any of the women he slept with. They kept to their own lives and he to his. He felt no desire for more.

Good sex was all he asked for, and a woman who knew not to make a nuisance of herself.

Let alone think she could steal a fortune from him with impunity.

Like the woman in his arms now.

He smoothed the hair back from her face a moment. Her eyes were open, but looking blankly ahead of her. He found himself wondering what she was thinking. What went on in her head?

He frowned. He *never* cared what went on in a woman's head. It was of no interest to him.

Was any other person of any interest to him? he found himself thinking.

His father had died of a heart attack seven years ago, and his mother had moved to Melbourne to be with relatives. But he'd never been close to either of his parents. He'd seen little of his father while he was growing up, because his father, like his grandfather, had devoted his life to making the Makarios fortune. His mother had played her part by being a society hostess, assiduously cultivating anyone and everyone who could be useful to Makarios Corp. Which meant that her son had been handed over to nannies and teachers.

Possibly the closest person to him was Markos, with whom he'd shared some of his schooling, but now, as adults, they met up only sporadically. Both led the highly peripatetic lives of the very rich, each running their own separate portions of the vast Makarios corporation which inevitably took them in different physical directions much of the time.

He had an extensive staff, of course, ranging from key executives to a team of personal assistants. And he had friends. Of course he had friends. Every man in his position had friends. Usually far too damn many.

But were any of them close to him?

Was he interested in any of them other than for what use they were to Makarios Corp? None sprang to mind.

Impatiently, he put the thoughts from him. His life was good—very good. Makarios Corp was riding high, he was riding high. He was in the prime of life, fit and healthy, and he knew without false modesty that he'd been blessed with a physical appearance that would be enviable even in a poor man. Combine that with his riches and he was a man other men envied and women wanted.

Anna Delane didn't...

The words stole into his head before he could stop them.

Anna Delane didn't want you—she threw you from her bedroom. Screeched her head off at you. Rejected you royally!

Deliberately he made himself stroke her arm, slowly, possessively. She wasn't rejecting him now—but the choice had been between him or jail...no wonder she hadn't rejected him! he thought bitterly.

Leo's jaw tightened.

Anna Delane would not have gone on rejecting him. He'd have seen to that. If he hadn't caught her red-handed with the Levantsky bracelet he'd still have pursued her. Whatever hypocritical reason she'd had for rejecting him that evening, he'd have got her in the end. Women didn't hold out on him. His usual problem was quite the opposite—fending them off. No, he'd have got Anna Delane in his bed. Thief or no.

It was a pity she was a thief…

Again, the words stole into his brain before he could stop them. They annoyed him. Obviously he'd have preferred her not to be a thief—after all, she'd come far too damn close to walking off with the Levantsky bracelet!—but that was the only reason for his preference. It would have made no other difference. The end result would have been the same. Her in his bed, a few weeks together, and then he'd tire of her.

His hand moved slowly up her arm again, enjoying her soft, silken skin.

He felt his body begin to stir.

No chance of tiring of her yet.

He shifted his weight onto his elbow, and cupped her chin, turning her head towards him. His mouth lowered to hers.

It felt good. Arousing.

Yes, definitely no chance of tiring of her yet.

Carefully, Anna smoothed total sunblock over her legs. Even though she spent as much time as she could in the shade, and put sunblock on religiously, she still seemed to be browning. She frowned. It was a damned nuisance. Her white skin was one of her selling points, and she guarded it assiduously. OK, so she could have stayed indoors every day, but she couldn't bear to. It was bad enough just getting through the days, without being denied the run of the gardens and the beach. Or the pool.

Thank God for the pool. Swimming up and down occupied hours of her time, and a swimsuit was something she never

travelled without. Although she had enough evening outfits—
brought for her time at the Schloss—daywear suitable for the
Caribbean climate was more of a problem. By dint of washing
her exercise outfit daily, and wearing the jade-green silk trouser
suit during the day, she was just managing to cope. She could
also, during the day, wander round with just a towel wrapped
round her like a sarong. That was because—and she thanked
all the gods there were—Leo Makarios was never around in
the daytime.

Maybe he sleeps in his earth-filled coffin in daytime? she
thought acidly.

The reality, she knew, was more prosaic. He took himself
off on the water. He seemed, thankfully, to have a whole range
of ways of enjoying himself out at sea. Sometimes she saw him
on a windsurf board, racing across the bay in a crosswind;
sometimes—according to her cautious enquires of the house
staff—he went to the Atlantic coast for stronger winds and
wave-sailing and kite-surfing. Often he disappeared off in a
variety of sailing craft. He seemed to have a whole collection
in a boathouse further along the beach. She saw him skimming
along in a one-handed dinghy, or on windier days taking a
catamaran out, spinnaker billowing. He went off diving, too,
some days, and she watched the staff lug oxygen tanks on
board the inflatable dive boat, then him heading out to the reefs.

Whatever took him out to sea, she was just grateful.

It gave her precious respite time—without which, she knew,
she would have cracked.

How many days had passed since she'd been brought here?
She was losing count. It was coming up to two weeks, it must
be. Or was it longer? She had tried not to count, tried not to
think. The moon was changing, at its peak now, sailing serene
and high far above the ocean, mocking her with its romantic
beauty.

But then the whole place mocked her.

It could have been a paradise on earth. Instead it was her
prison. Her place of torment.

A place where Leo Makarios tormented her to the utmost of his malign powers.

Night after night she burnt like a flame in his arms as he wrung from her the response he would not let her rest without.

The response she could not let herself rest without.

He had become a poison for her. A poison that had got into her bloodstream and which she was now utterly, completely dependent on.

And the poison was desire.

Abject, helpless desire.

It mortified her, humiliated her, lacerated her.

But it held her in its thrall.

And she knew she could not free herself from it now—she had succumbed to it abjectly, helplessly. Succumbed to Leo Makarios and what he could make her feel.

Every day when he came back to the villa her heart gave a leap. She tried to crush it, but it would not be crushed. She felt her breath quicken in her lungs, felt a rush of pleasure. Of anticipation.

Sometimes he took her to his bed immediately. Walking up to her, catching her hand, and taking her upstairs. She would feel her body quickening even as she went with him, feel the warm, delicious flood of arousal start in her body. She was as ardent as he; she could not help it. She wanted to feel his mouth on hers, his hands on her body, her hands on his, their bodies seeking, melding, fusing together in a rush of desire so intense it consumed her, time, after time, after time.

It had been a revelation—never had she understood how raw, how powerful, desire could be. Leo Makarios had taken her to a new place, one she had not known existed.

It was a place of passion, of ecstasy, of wanting and needing, of sating and slaking.

She knew no peace. Not during the day, when her restless body waited in forced patience for his return. Not when he was there either, and she went to him and let him take her in that white rush of desire as she took him into her. No peace then, only hunger, a driving, pulsing hunger that was a desperate, ravening need for what he and he alone could give her.

She knew only the brief, strange peace that came after, when their bodies were spent and they lay, exhausted, in each other's arms.

As if they were lovers.

But they weren't lovers. She knew that. Knew it deep in her being. There was nothing between them. Neither knowledge nor intimacy.

They were strangers. Day after day. Night after night.

Nothing but strangers.

A dull, crushing heaviness filled her as she sat, now, putting cream on her legs, before plunging into the warm waters of the pool. She looked around. There was a house full of staff tending the villa and its grounds—other human beings who lived and breathed and had hopes and ambitions and families and friends and loved ones—and yet she was all on her own.

You're always on your own. You always have been.

The thought distilled in her mind. It was true. It had always been true. Her grandmother loved her dearly, had brought her up single-handed after her mother's death, with her father long since disappeared into whatever wasteland involuntary fathers disappeared to. But her grandmother, for all her love, all her protection, was two generations away from her—happy with her little world in the street of terraced houses beside the gasworks, happy to spend the day watching soaps and chat shows, and scared to let Anna go out into the world. Let alone take up modelling.

Her grandmother hated it; she'd always known that. Warning her about the evils of the life she was heading for. But she could not have turned down her one big chance to get away from the gasworks and the beckoning biscuit factory. She'd always visited her grandmother as often as she could, and the years had passed, and she'd become too infirm in body and mind to go on living in her little terraced house. Now she passed her time in an expensive private nursing home, paid for by her granddaughter's modelling fees, sometimes recognising her when she visited, sometimes not.

Who will I have when my grandmother dies? Who will I have then?

The question echoed in her head as she stared out over the azure sea beyond.

She had some friends—good friends like Jenny, with whom she'd bonded in the frenetic, superficial, all too often corrupt and corrupting world of fashion modelling, and a few others that she trusted. But, valuable as her friends were, they each had someone special in their lives. Even Jenny had the child she would bear, in secrecy and safety, in her new life that she would make for herself in Australia.

I could go with her.

The thought came from nowhere.

And even as it formed a terrible heaviness came in its wake.

When Leo Makarios is finished with me—what shall I do?

She had thought she would simply go back to her life. Had thought nothing else.

But now, with punishing clarity, she knew it was impossible, that her life was empty.

She could never go back.

Her life as a model seemed a million miles away from here. On another planet.

She could never go back to it.

And the terrible heaviness crushed at her. She would have to leave here. One day, coming closer day by day, when Leo was bored with her, when he'd decided she'd made reparation enough, when some business crisis cropped up, needing his attention in New York, or Geneva, or London, then he would simply go.

And she would be bundled onto a plane and disposed of.

She would never see him again.

Never.

The word clanged in her head like a stone.

A bitter mockery filled her. Dear God. Once, brief days ago, if someone had said she would never see Leo Makarios again she'd have felt a relief so profound it would have lifted her off the ground.

Now—now it tolled like a funeral bell. Filling her with dread.

And there was an ache in her body that she could not extinguish.

An anguish.

An anguish that filled her being.

She stared out over the silver sand, the azure waters. Paradise on earth.

But, for her, the worst place in the world.

A place of unimaginable, exquisite torment.

Leo limped, bad tempered, out onto the terrace, and looked down across to the pool deck. Anna was swimming up and down with her graceful stroke. He watched her a while. It was strange seeing her during the daytime. Deliberately, he never let himself think about her when he was away from the villa. He just put her out of his mind, focusing instead on things like making a fast tack in the cat, or doing some tricky freestyle move on his board. He glowered. The damn loop he'd been working on yesterday had caught him out—and down he'd gone into the water, foot still caught in the footstrap. The result was a badly wrenched ankle. At least it wasn't a break or a sprain—the doctor had confirmed it just now. But he'd also stipulated resting his foot. No more watersports for a few days.

So what the hell was he going to do all day now? He'd deliberately kept his work to a minimum—an hour morning and evening, communicating remotely with his direct reports and a handful of key people, was all he allowed himself. He didn't want to get sucked back in.

He stood, watching Anna swim up and down. Well, he could swim too—just about. Moodily, he headed down, tossing his dark glasses on a chair. He limped to the deep end and dived in.

He powered down the length, making his turn with one foot only, pushing off, and powering down to the deep end. Over and over—ten, twenty, thirty, forty lengths. Working off something he needed to work off.

As he finally touched the wall at the end of his fortieth length and stood up, shaking the water from his hair, he saw Anna was still in the pool, doggedly breaststroking up and down her side, taking no notice of him as usual.

A familiar stab of irritation went through Leo. The damn girl totally ignored his existence whenever she could. She answered him tersely, her reluctance visible, whenever he tried to talk to her. He'd got to the point where he damned her as much as she was clearly damning him. Hell, he hadn't brought her here for conversation, but for sex—and that she definitely didn't stint him.

Leo stood in the water, leaning back against the stone surround, crooked arms resting on the tiles around the pool. He felt his mood improve. No, Anna Delane certainly didn't stint him on the sex front.

In bed now she definitely, definitely purred.

A slow smile parted his lips. He'd achieved what he'd intended—to have Anna Delane panting for him, hungry for him. No more virtuous outrage when he dared to lay a caressing hand on her. No, now she trembled with her need for him the moment he touched her. He only had to look at her and see the desire flare in her eyes, the hunger...

A sense of satisfaction went through him. Anna Delane purred for him in bed—and now, since he could not go out on the sea, he would amuse himself getting her to purr for him out of bed. It would, he decided, be a personal challenge.

He'd take her shopping. The island had some upmarket designer outlets, and shopping always put women in a good mood. Especially when some man was picking up the tab.

Besides, a woman like Anna Delane was used to the fast life—sophisticated cities and endless parties. Being deprived of them was probably contributing to her sulkiness.

An idea came to him. He'd take her shopping today, and then tomorrow he'd start socialising with her. There was a whole bunch of people on the island—from useful local business and government contacts to wealthy European ex-pats, either living or wintering here—who would always welcome him as a guest. He'd put in a few calls—let people know he was here.

I'll show Anna off to them…

The thought came from nowhere and stopped him in his tracks.

A frown creased his brow. Show Anna Delane off to his friends? Show off a thief? A woman who was earning her freedom from jail in his bed?

No, she wasn't a woman to show off. She was a woman to keep secret, private. Hidden for his own pleasure.

As if he were ashamed of her…

Of himself…

Something stabbed through him. It did not feel comfortable.

Leo shook it away. He did not like to feel uncomfortable about himself.

With a rasp of irritation he levered himself out of the pool. His damaged ankle told him he'd probably swum too vigorously, so a day taking it easy was definitely a good idea. He limped to the other side of the pool and waited until Anna had finished her length.

To his annoyance, even though he was crouched down just where her length ended, clearly intending to speak to her, she still didn't register his presence. She was all set to do a breaststroke turn. His hand shot out, closing around her forearm as she seized the end of the pool with both hands, ready to plunge round.

She stopped abruptly.

'I haven't finished my lengths,' she told him coldly.

'You've done enough,' he told her. 'Up you come.'

His hand closed over her other forearm. Pinioned, Anna glowered at him, then let him pull her out of the pool in a strong, lithe movement. She stood, water dripping off her, hair slicked back in a high ponytail.

'Yes?' she said, just as coldly.

'Get dried and changed,' he told her, limping across to where her towel was draped on another pool chair and helping himself to it. 'We're going out.'

'What?'

He looked at her, dripping and stiff-bodied, as he patted his chest with her towel.

'I said, we're going out.'

'I don't want to go out,' she riposted instantly.

Her attitude annoyed him—as it always did.

'But I do,' he replied. 'And I want you to come with me.'

She just went on staring at him.

'What for? '

'Indulge me,' he returned sardonically.

A slight flush of colour flared over her cheekbones. Then her face tightened.

'I thought I only had to do that in bed!' she snapped.

Something equivalent snapped in Leo. Hell, the girl was hard work. And right now he was in no mood to put up with it.

'*Thee mou*, I simply want to go out for the day. What's the big deal? Lighten up, Anna—you might even enjoy it. After all…' his voice changed, and the sardonic note was back in it, taunting her '…you've come round to enjoying the rest of what I give you, haven't you.'

This time the colour definitely flared out across her cheekbones. For a moment Leo mistook it for embarrassment. Then he realised it must just be temper. Well, Anna Delane could be as cussed as she liked—and, *Christos*, did she like!—but he wanted to go out, and he wanted her to come with him. And what he wanted, he got.

He always did.

He limped off, and Anna watched him go, glowering.

What the hell was going on? she fumed. She didn't want to go anywhere with Leo Makarios. And why was he wanting to take her anywhere anyway? Why wasn't he going off in one of his boats or whatever? She watched him head across the terrace. Was he limping? Yes, he was. Quite badly.

A sudden pang darted through her. For a moment—quite

insanely—she wanted to go after him and express concern. Ask him what he'd done to his foot.

She crushed it down. Leo Makarios could go under a train for all she cared…

Liar…

Emotion twisted in her. She tried to crush that down too, but it would not be banished. Despairingly she shut her eyes.

I can't face a day out with him—I just can't!

It was taking all her strength to cope with the nights, to cope with the terrible, treacherous reaction of her body to his touch. She could cope only because she kept the night to the night, and at all other times either minimised her time in his company or shut him out as much as she could.

But now she was going to have to spend a whole day in his company.

Heaviness pressed on her.

She opened her eyes again. Leo had disappeared inside the house.

With a weariness of spirit she did not want to think about, she followed him.

Anna stared about her. Not only did it make it easier to ignore the man driving the four-by-four careering along the potted road, but it was interesting to see something more of the island than the Makarios villa—exquisite though that was.

From the air-conditioned interior the rolling landscape looked lush, covered in wild greenery. Little villages were dotted about, the West Indian chattel-style board houses surrounded by banana trees and their verandas over-tumbled with crimson bougainvillaea. Roadside stalls every now and then sold fresh fruit, both to islanders and to tourists stopping off in their hire cars to taste fresh pineapple and coconut.

She didn't ask where they were going—what was the point? She would find out when they got there. But when they did, Anna was surprised. It was the capital of the island, and Leo made his way, weaving along a grid of streets, to end up by the harbour. He parked the car and nodded at Anna.

'Time to go shopping,' he announced.

He waited for her expression to brighten at the treat ahead, but she simply kept the same blank expression on her face that she always kept for him. Pressing his mouth tightly, he got out, and waited while she did likewise.

The mid-morning heat hit her, and she instantly felt the inappropriateness of the tight-fitting stretch clothes she was wearing. Had he really said shopping? Well, thank heavens for that, at least. At last she could buy some beachwear.

So it was with more enthusiasm than Leo usually saw in her outside the bedroom that she followed him into the smartest-looking tax-free designer wear shop. Swiftly and methodically she sifted along the rails and took her selection to the cash desk.

Leo was there before her.

'So at last you've seen sense enough to wear something suitable for the beach,' he said pointedly, indicating her armful of brightly coloured clothes.

She stared at him tightly.

'Strangely,' she informed him acidly, 'I wasn't planning a trip to the Caribbean when I packed for Austria. Of course I didn't have any suitable daywear for the beach!'

Leo frowned. 'You mean you've been wearing those idiotic outfits because it was all you had? Good grief, why didn't you just tell me? I could have taken you shopping the day you arrived!' He spoke as if she were stupid.

Anna said nothing, merely smiled at the saleslady and let her start folding her clothes.

'You don't want to try any on?' asked Leo sceptically.

She cast him a look. 'I can tell they'll fit, and I can tell they'll suit me. It's one of the little skills you pick up in my line of work.'

'There is no call for sarcasm,' Leo replied repressively. 'When I take women shopping they usually spend hours trying on everything in sight. It's a dead bore. Your attitude is refreshing, believe me.'

He started reaching inside his back trouser pocket for his wallet. But Anna was already handing her credit card over.

'Anna,' he said, even more repressively, 'allow me, if you please.'

'I don't please,' she said, and nodded at the saleslady to take her card.

Leo sighed heavily. 'Are you trying to prove something, Anna?'

'No. I'm just buying my own clothes.'

With a snap, Leo put his wallet away. Let the damn girl buy her own clothes if she insisted. He watched her sign for her purchases, pick up the bags, and then hesitate suddenly.

'I'd like to change,' she said to the shop assistant, and disappeared with the bags.

She emerged in under two minutes, clad in a brightly coloured blue and orange sundress that floated around her calves.

Leo found his breath stilling. She really was the most stunning female he'd laid eyes on. Effortlessly so. Her hair was still in its high ponytail, and she'd let it dry naturally, without any styling. She wore no make-up except suncream and protective lipgloss. And sunshades. Not a scrap of jewellery either.

And yet in that simple print dress she looked breathtaking.

Something moved inside him. It was an odd sensation. He didn't know what it was.

He only knew it was inappropriate.

'Let's go,' he said shortly, and headed outdoors.

Anna followed him, feeling the relief of finally wearing something that didn't look idiotic in these tropical surroundings.

'There's another designer shop over there.' Leo pointed across the way and started towards it.

'I've got all the clothes I need,' Anna returned.

Leo gave a snort. 'No woman has all the clothes she needs! And this time—' he turned his head '—I am buying. Please do not make another scene.'

Anna's lips tightened.

'I really don't want any more clothes,' she insisted.

'Then what do you want?' He glanced around, eyes lighting

on a jewellery store. For a moment he realised he was on the point of buying her jewels, as if she were an ordinary mistress.

Anna couldn't help but see where he'd been looking.

'No, thank you,' she said sweetly. 'I prefer to steal mine.'

Leo's head whipped round, eyes narrowed.

His eyes fastened on hers.

And for a second—quite inexplicably—he suddenly wanted to laugh. The girl was outrageous, all right! Totally outrageous—and yet...

He broke eye contact deliberately, pointing out a souvenir shop selling island art and mementoes.

Anna shook her head sharply.

'I'll have all the souvenirs of this place I could never want,' she said.

Leo's eyes slashed back to hers. This time he didn't want to laugh at all. He wanted to throttle her.

'Well, your souvenirs from an Austrian jail would be very different, I can assure you!' he shot back tightly. He took her arm. 'I need some coffee,' he announced.

She tried to pull away from him, but he would not let her.

'Let go of me!' she snarled.

He merely tightened his grip, and looked down at her with his long-lashed eyes.

'That's not what you say in bed, Anna *mou*. You want me to touch you then.'

His voice was soft, as soft as silk, his eyes molten, melting her...

Once again he saw colour flare out along her cheekbones, and that look in her eyes. Of all things, it looked as if it was embarrassment. But that was impossible. Anna Delane was a thief, shameless and unapologetic, and the life she lived as a fashion model hardly meant she was embarrassable about sex.

Then he saw her chin go up, her mouth tighten, as if she were suppressing something. Her body was as stiff as a board.

'I thought you said you wanted a coffee,' she bit at him.

CHAPTER EIGHT

ANNA sat at the little harbourside café, watching the boats at their mooring. This was no flash marina—most of the boats were working boats: ferries to other islands, or freighters, or fishing boats.

Opposite her, Leo sat and glowered.

Anna was ignoring him—as usual. Looking at anything and everything except him. Sipping black coffee with a stony face. Exasperation swept through him again. She looked a million dollars in that sundress, and yet she'd insisted on buying it herself—and the others in the bags around her feet. Her insistence infuriated him, and he was annoyed at himself for feeling so unreasonably ill-tempered about it. What the hell was she up to, refusing to let him buy her those paltry clothes?

As if she were making some kind of point to him.

But what kind of point was Anna Delane entitled to make to him? None, that was what. Yet she was as prickly as a hedgehog, trying to make *him* feel bad when it was *she* who was the criminal. Leo's teeth clenched. Why the hell couldn't she just be *nice* for once? Pleasant, attentive, eager to please? Eager, if nothing else, to earn the parole he'd promised her?

But not her. No. No, she was sitting there, ignoring him, chin in the air as if she had a bad smell underneath her fastidious nose.

From the corner of her averted eye, Anna saw Leo glowering at her. She refused to look at him. Every instinct told her not to.

Yet something was pulling at her. Something that made her want to just tilt her head slightly, so very, very slightly. Just a little. Just enough to see more of Leo Makarios than from the corner of her eye. To see him sitting there, lounging back in

123

his chair, long legs extended, lean, taut body displayed for her, dark, molten eyes pouring through her, melting her…

No!

Doggedly she held her head rigid. Refusing to look at him. It seemed suddenly essential that she did not look at him.

She lifted her coffee cup one last time, and set it down empty. And as she did so, of their own volition, pulled by something she could not prevent, her eyes were drawn to him.

To feast on him like a starving man.

Yes! Leo all but punched the air. He'd got her. Her eyes had wandered to him—wandered, and stuck. With absolute self-control he reached for his coffee, holding his gaze impassive. He lifted his cup, relaxing back in his seat, stretching out his legs and flexing his shoulders. He could see her expression register the movement, and his mood improved yet again. He sat back, letting her gaze at him, his own glowering expression quite vanished now.

He luxuriated in her covert observation for a few moments longer, then said, 'Where would you like to go next, Anna?'

Immediately, her gaze cut out. The look of deliberate indifference was back in her face.

'I have no opinion on the subject,' she replied, and pretended to drink more coffee.

'Then I'll choose, shall I?' said Leo, with exaggerated politeness.

'Please do.' She gave her acid-sweet smile again.

And again, for one bizarre moment, as his eyes caught hers, Leo wanted to laugh out loud. The girl was impossible, outrageous, infuriating—yet there was something about Anna Delane that he could not let go of…

Leo got to his feet, tossing some East Caribbean dollars down on the table. Incredulously, he watched Anna open her purse, then pause.

'I don't have any local currency,' she announced. She glanced around and saw a bank on the corner of one of the streets leading back into the town. Without pausing, she darted across and went in. She emerged a few minutes later and came back to their table, putting down some coins next to his notes.

'Take them back, Anna,' Leo said, in a low, dangerous voice.

His good mood had gone—totally. He was right back to wanting to throttle her.

She stared at him. 'I'm paying,' she said, 'for my coffee.'

Greek issued from him in a staccato fire. 'God almighty, is this some kind of joke?' He caught her wrist, halting her. 'You stole a bracelet from me worth at a conservative estimate eighty thousand euros. Don't even *think* of trying to make yourself look virtuous by paying for your own damn coffee and clothes.' He brought his face closer to hers. 'You're a thief—nothing but a thief. Don't ever think I am going to forget that and be impressed by you.'

Anna's face had gone rigid. Her eyes were like pinpricks of green fire.

'Understand this, and understand it well, Leo Makarios,' she hissed at him. 'I wouldn't stoop to trying to impress you if it was my last day on earth. Think what you want of me—I don't give a stuff!'

She twisted out of his grip, and stormed off.

Leo stared after her fulminatingly, then set off after her.

Damn the girl. Damn her to hell! She should be begging him to go easy on her! Should be using all her arts and beauty to try and captivate him, soothe his savage heart and plead for a lighter sentence. She should be making up to him, eager for his approval, his attention.

The way other women did.

Other women always made up to him, sought his attention, his interest. They put themselves out for him, exerting all their charms. They wanted to please him.

And yet Anna Delane, who had stolen *his* rubies and never shown the slightest sign of contrition about it, who had a thousand, million times more cause to want to please him, was as eager to please him as a piranha was to be a vegetarian!

She's different in bed. In bed she wants everything you give her...

His eyes shadowed. Yes, but even there, he realised, eager as she was to take the pleasure he bestowed on her, she never, unless he instructed her, took any initiative sexually. Oh, she did as he bade her, and enjoyed it too, he knew that—taking sensual pleasure in caressing him, arousing him, sating him.

But she never did it spontaneously. Never to please him because she wanted to please him. Because she wanted him to be pleased with her. Indulgent of her.

The way other women did.

He thought of Delia Delatore, his last mistress, and the French countess who had been her predecessor. He thought of the parade of women who had passed through his bed.

Every single one of them had always wanted to please him. Because each and every one of them had known how fortunate they were for having been chosen by him. They had known how lucky they were that his eyes had lighted on them and selected them for his bed.

All except one.

Memory stung in his brain like acid.

Anna Delane—on whom he had looked with desire, with wanting, and to whose bedroom he had come, expecting exactly the same reception as every other woman had given him.

And she'd thrown him out on his ear.

Rejected him and scorned him and berated him.

Anger and chagrin pulsed through him.

Then another thought occurred.

Yes, but she was planning all along to steal the rubies.

But that should have made her even more eager to lull him into a sense of false security with her. He'd have been far less likely to suspect her if she'd been pleasing him in bed—for a start, her motivation would have been a lot less. The bracelet might be worth eighty thousand euros, but that was on the open market. Anna Delane would have had to fence it, and whatever she made out of the sale it wouldn't have been eighty thousand.

Yet as his mistress, pleasing him sufficiently to be kept for several weeks, she must have known she would easily have walked away with gifts of jewellery worth much more than her profit from stealing the Levantsky jewels.

And so much less risky…

So why, *why* had she thrown him out of her bedroom like that?

It simply didn't make sense.

He strode after her, to where she was waiting by the car. She looked like a cat who'd had its fur rubbed up the wrong way. He could almost see her tail lashing furiously.

He unlocked the door and she climbed in, whisking her skirts gracefully inside as she sat. She belted herself up, then stared rigidly ahead out of the window.

He wondered whether her teeth were gritted. He wouldn't be surprised. He could feel his own gritting.

A thought darted into his head.

Why do we keep fighting?

It came from nowhere, and he amended it immediately—*Why does she keep fighting me?* But it didn't work. The original version was the one that bit at him as he headed out of town.

There is no 'we'. There can be no possibility of there being a 'we'.

He put his good foot down, and shot off.

Perhaps a decent lunch would make him feel better.

Anna looked around her. They'd driven for over forty-five minutes across the interior of the island. She'd spent her time as before, gazing around at the landscape and the scenery. Now they were driving along a twisting narrow lane, slowing every now and then as goats wandered, grazing at the roadside. One final twist, and a stone gateway was opening to their left. Leo swung the car through, into a paved area dotted with cars. He pulled into a parking space and cut the engine.

'Where are we?'

Anna stared around, not looking at Leo as she asked her question.

Amazing, thought Leo caustically. She's asked a question. Graciously, he supplied an answer.

'It's an old plantation house that's been converted into a restaurant.' He leant across to open her door, ignoring the way her body automatically stiffened and pulled away, as if to avoid him.

'Shall we?' he enquired, even more graciously.

He drew back his hand and Anna undid her seat belt, breathing out again. She climbed down, feeling the noon-day heat of the Caribbean hit her. She flexed her shoulders and looked around her.

'This way,' said Leo, at her side.

She walked along beside him, doing her best to ignore him, but highly conscious of his presence. But then, she always was conscious of his presence, she thought wearily.

Why can't I be immune to him? Why can't he just be like a block of wood?

She gave a sigh. It didn't help to ask such hopeless questions. Leo Makarios had an effect on her that she could not ignore. Even though she desperately longed to.

How much longer can I endure this? How much more can I take? Wanting him and hating him, and hating myself for wanting him, and...

The questions drummed in her head like a pain in her skull. Numbly she followed the stone-paved pathway that led upwards through tropical gardens. The heat settled on her shoulders, making her feel heavy and tired.

She paused, suppressing another sigh.

'Are you all right?'

Her head twisted in surprise.

'What?'

Leo's eyes flashed briefly.

'Are you feeling all right?' he repeated.

'I'm fine,' she answered shortly, and made to go on walking.

A hand stayed her, cupping around her bare elbow. She wanted to pull away, but there was something about his grip that held her.

'What?' she demanded, this time resisting the impulse to look at him.

'Anna—listen to me.'

There was something different about his voice. She didn't know what it was, but it made her look at him. His face was sombre. The expression quite different from any she had seen. For a moment she just looked at him, a slight puzzle in her eyes.

'Stop—fighting—me.'

The words came heavily, the look he levelled at her even heavier.

A lump seemed to be forming in her throat. It made it difficult for her to speak, but she forced herself. Her chin went up, jaw tightening.

'Tell me something,' she shot back. 'Why do you care less if I fight you or not? Why do you care about anything except getting what you want in bed?' There was a challenge in her voice. A bitter defiance.

Something shadowed his eyes, so briefly she thought she must have imagined it. Then he answered her.

'Because I'm tired, Anna. I'm tired and fed up, and my ankle hurts, and I'm hungry, and you've given me nothing but grief, and I just want—I just want an easy day for once. OK? Is that so big a deal? Can we really not just this once have a civil, civilised meal together, without you giving me the big freeze the whole damn time?'

Anna's eyes narrowed to slits. 'Why *should* I? Tell me that. You get the night times! The rest of the day you can go whistle!'

She saw his jaw clench, then slowly unclench.

'I'll do a deal with you. A one-off special. Just while my ankle is bad. Tonight you can have off, if—*if* you lose the attitude today.'

Anna looked at him. Was he serious? Or was this just another baiting mockery of her?

'Do you mean it?' she demanded.

'Oh, yes. Tonight, providing you behave like a normal woman today, you can sleep in your own bed. If, of course—' and suddenly the baiting, mocking look she'd been expecting was there '—you want to.'

Her green eyes flashed. 'Oh, I want to all right.'

His dark eyes glinted. She thought it was anger, but was not sure. 'Then we have a deal?' he posed.

For one moment longer she went on glaring at him. Then she gave a brief nod. After all, she had no choice, did she? Leo Makarios was blackmailing her into sex—any chance she got to escape a night of 'reparation' had to be grabbed—didn't it?

Of course it does! Grab it with both hands! Because if you don't you'll know—and he'll know—why you don't! And your humiliation at his hands will be complete. Your defeat total.

The thought was unbearable. Only one thing in the world would be worse than Leo Makarios knowing how weak, how vulnerable she was to him.

And that would be him knowing it as well. She would endure anything to prevent that. Even endure having a civil lunch with him.

He let go her elbow.

'Good,' was all he said.

He set off along the path again, leaving her to follow.

Lunch was served at tables set out under a wide awning on a terrace with a breathtaking view down over the bay below. A cooling breeze wafted gently, making the heat comfortable.

Anna took her place, gazing out over the vista. It really was beautiful, she thought, and for a moment a pang struck her so deep that it was like the thrust of a knife.

It's so idyllic, so magical! Why can't I be here with someone else? Why does it have to be Leo Makarios?

But even as the words formed she knew they were not true. The knife twisted painfully.

It's not because it's Leo Makarios—it's because of the reason I'm here with him. That's what's so awful!

Her eyes looked out over the vivid greens of the vegetation, the brilliant azure of the sea, and she felt an ache start inside her—a longing so great that she felt overwhelmed by it.

Oh, God, if only he didn't think me a thief! If he didn't think me a thief I could be—

Another voice cut across her mind. Harsh and punishing.

You could be what? His mistress? His sex toy while he wants you, and then dumped for the next one that takes his eye?

Her eyes hardened. Yes, that was the best she could ever be for Leo Makarios. A man who regarded women as mistresses. To be enjoyed, pampered and then disposed of. Hadn't she heard the way he spoke about Vanessa and his cousin Markos? Why should she assume Leo would think any better of *her*, even if he didn't believe she was a thief?

Heavily, she picked up the menu lying in front of her.

'Anna—' Leo's voice was a warning. She flicked her eyes to him questioningly.

'Yes?' she responded brusquely.

There was a frown in his eyes.

'We have a deal, remember?'

For a moment his eyes held hers, and for a moment she looked back at him with her usual baleful expression.

'Give it a rest, Anna,' he said wearily.

She slapped her menu down. 'How can I?' she breathed vehemently. 'You want me to suck up to you, don't you? Like the rest of your women! Fawn all over you and pander to you and—'

'No.' The negation snapped from him.

Anna's eyes flashed.

'Yes, you do. That's your idea of normality from a woman. You can't cope with a woman treating you without kid gloves.'

A look of annoyance darkened his face.

'You are being ridiculous,' he replied brusquely. 'I require only that my partner is…' he shrugged, clearly searching for a word, then found it '…gracious,' he concluded. 'And why,' he went on swiftly, 'would she wish to be otherwise?'

There was an arrogant question in his expression that exasperated Anna even more, because it showed her exactly what his problem was. Then, with a silent sigh, she subsided. Leo Makarios was rich and gorgeous—no wonder he was spoilt by women. No wonder they sucked up to him, fawning over him, craving him…

Her mind snapped shut. No. She must not think about craving Leo Makarios…desiring him…wanting him so much that night after night she melted her body against his, putting aside, forgetting deliberately, in that burning inferno that consumed her, that the only reason she was in his bed was because the grim alternative was prison…

But I'm in prison anyway—a prison I can never escape from…a prison of passion, of desire, that cages me in night after night…

Except that tonight, if she accepted Leo's temporary bargain, she would have parole from that prison.

If she could bring herself to be 'civil' to the man who was reducing her to such abjectness.

Her chin lifted. She could—she must. For one night at least she might have a reprieve from the prison she went to so helplessly, night after night.

Her eyes went back to the menu, leaving unanswered Leo's arrogant challenge. For a moment longer she felt his gaze resting on her, as if waiting for her to throw yet another pointless dart at his colossal ego, then she felt him relax. So, minutely, did she, and fell to perusing the range of delicious options— none of which, as ever, she had any intention of choosing.

Yet even as she was mentally closing the menu, prepared to

content herself with grilled fish and undressed salad, so, out of nowhere, a spark of rebellion ignited. If she was to get through the day being 'civil' to Leo Makarios, then at least she could have some compensation for her ordeal.

When the waiter came to enquire if they were ready to order, on impulse she lifted her head, closed the menu, and announced that she would have prawns fried in coconut milk, served with rice. And she would drink wine as well.

And calories be hanged! After all, she had something to celebrate—a night off from Leo Makarios.

Without volition, her eyes strayed to him as he finished giving the waiter his own order, and then accepted the wine menu from the hovering sommelier. He was studying the list, brows drawn in faint concentration. She felt emotion pour through her. She waited for it to be anger. That was the safe emotion to feel about Leo Makarios.

The only safe one.

But it wasn't anger. Instead, a different emotion seemed to be taking her over. One she had no business feeling—none at all. None. But she felt it all the same.

She went on gazing at him, drinking him in.

I could look at him all day...

All night....

For ever.

Cold chilled through her as the words formed unbidden in her head. She tried to push them away, undo them, unthink them. She must not let them be said, thought.

Deliberately, she forced herself to keep staring at him.

The dark hair, the planes of his face, those potent heavy-lidded eyes, the wide, sensual mouth, the hard line of his jaw— all were achingly familiar. There wasn't an inch of his face, his body, that she had not kissed, caressed, touched.

But it's the face of a stranger. A complete stranger.

A stranger who can never, never be anything else.

For a moment so brief, and yet so agonising, she sat there, surrounded by other couples, other families, chatting away, eating and drinking in this beautiful place, shaded from the hot sun, yet basking in its balmy warmth, with the deep blue bay and emerald green coastline sweeping before them, and wished, suddenly, deeply, out of nowhere, that she and Leo Makarios were just one of those couples.

Any of them—young or old, good-looking or plain—it didn't matter. But to be here like them, on holiday, together…a real couple…

Not his blackmailed bed partner, not his pampered mistress—but something far, far more to him…

Angrily, she smashed the image to pieces in her mind. She was insane even to think such a thing about Leo Makarios. Her expression tightened and she picked up her glass, sipping sparkling mineral water, making herself look back over the vista beyond. She saw from the corner of her eye Leo give his choice to the sommelier, who then glided away.

She felt a hand tug at her skirt and looked round—then down.

A small moppet of a child was standing beside her, holding up her wrist.

'I've got a new bracelet,' she informed Anna.

Her eyes were blue, her hair curly, her sundress pink. So was the bracelet, of pink polished coral.

'So you have,' agreed Anna with a smile. 'It's very pretty.'

'My mummy bought it for me from a lady on the beach,' the moppet said.

'Lucy!' A woman's voice called from a nearby table. 'Don't bother the lady, darling.'

Anna looked across to where an Englishwoman in her thirties was lunching with her husband and a little boy.

'She's not bothering me at all,' she reassured the woman. 'I'm admiring her beautiful bracelet.'

The woman laughed. 'She's showing it off to everyone she can.'

Anna smiled. 'Why not? It's lovely.' She looked down at

the little girl again. Her smile deepened. 'It's a *very* pretty bracelet,' she told the child again.

The little girl nodded, satisfied with this response, and moved off to the next table to repeat the exercise with the woman there. Her mother got up and gently guided her back to their own table.

'Your ice-cream will be here any moment, Lucy—come along.'

She cast a conspiratorial smile at Anna as her daughter, duly diverted, scurried back to her place.

Anna smiled back, but noticed how the woman's eyes had automatically strayed towards Leo. She was not surprised. Most of the women in the place had cast looks across at him, whatever their age or marital status.

No wonder he's so full of himself, she thought mordantly. She wondered whether they'd still be lusting after him if they knew he'd threatened her with jail to get her into his bed.

Her face shuttered again. She reached for her water glass.

As she did, she saw that Leo was looking at her. He was frowning slightly, as if he'd been confronted with something unexpected.

Leo went on looking at her. That tiny incident just then, with the child, had taken him aback. Anna had smiled—a warm, kindly smile—clearly charmed by the little girl.

He'd never seen her look like that before. It was—out of character. A side of Anna Delane he hadn't seen—that shouldn't be there. Not in a woman like her.

The waiter arrived with their wine and placed the glasses carefully at their places. Anna, he noticed, took a mouthful immediately.

He took a sip from his and leant back, surveying her.

It was strange to see her away from the villa—with other people. Male eyes were drifting across to her repeatedly, but she wasn't taking any notice. Doubtless for a woman as beautiful as her it was a daily occurrence. Yet, unlike all the other beautiful women he knew, she seemed to radiate absolutely no awareness of male observation. Other women showed they could see it coming their way, and sat there almost preening. Anna simply got on with having lunch.

Was that part of her challenge—that she ignored men who looked at her? Did she do it deliberately? Surely she must. He remembered what had struck him most at the gala launch at the Schloss—that she was completely indifferent to her own beauty.

As he watched her, so extraordinarily beautiful, the object of covert and not so covert male looks, he wondered caustically what they would say if they knew she was a criminal who'd help herself to their belongings without the blink of an eye.

His jaw set. She looked so serenely indifferent, sitting there, ignoring him. As if butter wouldn't melt…

It made him feel like needling her, forgetting his deal to have a civil day together.

'So, not tempted by the coral bracelet, then? Tell me, would you steal from a child if it had something you wanted?'

Anna looked at him. 'That's a stupid and offensive question,' she replied coldly.

'Why? I want to know if there are limits to your venality, that is all. You stole from me, why not from a child?' Leo jibed.

She eyed him stonily.

'A crime is not a crime, *per se*,' she said. 'A crime depends upon motive, and on effect on the victim. Is a starving man entitled to steal food from one who has ten times more than he needs? Supposing he stole it for his starving child, to save its life?'

'You're quite a moralist,' Leo observed, eyes narrowing slightly as he lifted his wine glass to his mouth. 'For a thief.' He took a mouthful of wine. 'I asked you once before why you stole from me, Anna—'

'And I told you it was none of your business. That's still the case.'

Leo started to feel the anger running in him again. But, as their food arrived, his attention was diverted.

'Is that what you ordered?' he asked, eyeing the succulent dish sceptically.

'Yes,' Anna said. 'It's by way of celebration.'

'Celebration?'

She gave her acid-sweet smile. 'My night off,' she told him.

For a second his face darkened, then, with visible effort, he made his expression relax. 'It's good to see you eat sensibly for once.'

Anna glanced up at him, midway into spearing a fat, crispy prawn.

'I've told you—I have no choice. Models all have to be underweight for their height. It's part of the stupid fake mystique of high fashion.'

Leo began to eat. 'You sound very hostile to your career.'

Anna gave a shrug. 'I just don't have any illusions about it. I never did,' she added reflectively.

'I thought it was a dream come true for most women—to be a model?'

She ate some more, luxuriating in the rich flavours.

'The fashion industry treats models like garbage—remember the charming Signor Embrutti, wanting Jenny to strip off, not giving a toss that she didn't want to? Think that's unusual? Models have to be incredibly tough to survive.'

'That should suit you ideally,' riposted Leo sardonically. 'I also remember you threatening with your contract terms and conditions at Embrutti.'

Her face darkened. 'That slimeball! I've worked with him before, so I insisted that all four models should have a no strip clause as soon as I knew Justin the Obsequious had hired him for the shoot—'

'*What* did you call him?' Leo set down his knife and fork.

'Should I have called him Justin the Toad?' returned Anna limpidly. 'Oh, for heaven's sake, surely you know the man is a total toerag?'

'He is keen to do his job well,' Leo replied quellingly.

'Keen to lick your boots, more like. *Yes, Mr Makarios. Of course, Mr Makarios. Anything you say with spots on, Mr Makarios.*' She looked at him. 'You don't genuinely want to surround yourself with toadies, do you?'

There was a puzzled, incredulous expression on her face.

Leo's mouth tightened and he started to eat again.

'My staff know that I expect—and get—the highest-calibre performances from them. In exchange they are very well paid indeed. As,' he pointed out acidly, 'you and the other models were for the work you did.'

'And we worked our backsides off, believe me! Do you have any complaints about the quality of our work? You saw us in action, after all.'

'No, you were all perfectly professional,' he allowed. 'Even with you threatening contracts at the photographer. You do that often, do you?'

'When I have to. I learnt the hard way. When I was starting out some ad agency creep insisted on bare boob shots. My agency told me to do it. I walked out. It cost me that job, and a lot of work afterwards. From then on I ensured a no strip clause was in every contract I signed.'

Leo was frowning at her.

'Why is it such a big deal? Nudity is nothing these days.'

Anna put down her fork and stared at him.

'OK, so strip off. Go on. Flash yourself around at these good folk here. Put some flesh shots of yourself in a glossy mag. Make sure your friends and relatives see it. Make sure total strangers on the London Underground see it.'

'Do not be absurd!' Leo retorted stiffly. 'You are a fashion model. You—'

Her eyes flashed green fire.

'Yes—I am a *fashion model*,' she spelt out. 'I model clothes. I do not model *not wearing any clothes*. Can you *possibly* understand the subtle difference?'

Leo glared at her. Her aggression was ludicrous—it was absurd—it was insolent—it was—

It was justified.

He took a sharp, deep breath. He flung his hands up as if in surrender.

'I take your point. But,' he went on, genuine puzzlement showing in his eyes, 'if you dislike modelling so much, why did you become one?'

Leo leant back again, lifting his wine glass to his mouth. Anna's eyes followed the movement, watching the way his long, strong fingers curved around the bowl of the wine glass, the way his sensual, mobile mouth indented as he drank. How the strong column of his throat worked as he swallowed.

Weakness ebbed through her, dissolving and debilitating. Dear God, but he was just so beautiful to look at…

She came back with a start.

'Well, however much I moan about it, it still beats packing biscuits all day long in the local factory,' she returned, taking a mouthful of wine herself, to restore her composure. 'I never did well at school, so higher education was out.'

'You don't strike me as unintelligent,' observed Leo. 'Why did you not do well at school?'

She looked at him, surprised. Leo Makarios didn't look like the kind of man to assess any woman for her intelligence. Let alone *her*. Perhaps, she thought acidly, he assumed that a thief had to have a basic degree of intelligence.

'I'll answer that for you,' he said dryly. 'I can't see you taking kindly to a teacher's authority.'

Anna's face was expressive. 'Some were OK,' she allowed. 'But most of them…' She didn't finish the sentence. Then she shrugged. 'But I was the one who was the fool—I should have been smart enough to make school work for me. Instead…' She shrugged again. 'Anyway, when I was eighteen I got spotted by a talent scout for an agency, trawling the shopping malls of north London. That got me started.' She took another mouthful of wine to wash down the spicy prawns. 'My gran—she'd brought me up—hated it. She thought I'd be dragged into a den of iniquity. She was right, of course. But luckily I wised up pretty fast. And toughened up. I don't put up with garbage any more.'

The wine was coiling slowly through her veins in the warmth of the day and the rare pleasure of eating filling food. The combination made her feel strangely relaxed. Maybe that was why she was able to talk like this to Leo Makarios. She took another forkful of food, her eyes flickering to his face. It was odd, definitely, to be talking to him.

Leo contemplated her.

'Are you as aggressive with your lovers?' he enquired.

Anna's fork stopped halfway to her mouth, and lowered again.

'I don't have lovers,' she said tightly.

Leo stared at her.

Anna Delane didn't have lovers?

He wanted to laugh out loud. Of course a woman as beautiful as she was had lovers. Men must have been swarming around her since she hit puberty!

Did that mean she'd helped herself, though? She certainly threw you out of her bedroom, right enough!

He jabbed angrily at the piece of lamb fillet he'd just cut. It always came back to that, didn't it? Anna Delane throwing him out of her bedroom. Spitting with outraged virtue even while her breasts were still taut and aroused from his caressing...

A hypocrite. That was all she was. Saying one thing with her mouth while her body spoke a quite, quite different language...

'What do you mean, you don't have lovers?'

His own question interrupted his thoughts, which were leading him in a direction he did not want to go on a day he'd told her she could have the night to herself.

Anna resumed eating.

'I mean I don't have lovers,' she repeated. 'What's the big deal?'

'Why not?' There was genuine incomprehension in his voice, as well as underlying disbelief at her extraordinary assertion. 'You are far too beautiful not to take lovers.'

The flash of green fire came again. 'You mean I have some sort of duty to offer myself on a plate to all comers just because they fancy me?' Her voice was shrivelling with contempt.

'Of course not. I merely mean that with your looks you could have the pick of my sex.'

Anna's mouth tightened. 'With you as a prime example? No, thanks.' The green flash came again. 'Look, I thought the deal was we were going to try and be civil to each other. So stop going on at me, all right? Can't you talk about the weather or something?'

He sat back. 'Very well,' he said heavily. There was an expression in his eyes she could not read. 'So, what would you like to do after lunch?'

She shrugged. 'You know the island, not me.'

'Would you like to do more shopping?'

She rolled her eyes. 'Good grief, what is it with you? I don't need or want to buy anything else, thank you. Actually—' a thought struck her '—what I do want is a swim, to cool off. Is there a beach nearby?' Another thought struck her. 'But maybe with your ankle you can't go in the water?'

'That is not a problem,' replied Leo airily, astonished that she'd actually condescended to voice a preference to him. 'And I know just the beach to take you to.' His eyes gleamed. 'Tell me, can you surf?'

Anna stared. 'Surf? In the Caribbean? It's flat as a millpond!'

Leo laughed. 'Not on the Atlantic coast, it isn't.'

Nor was it. To Anna's astonishment the wide, sandy beach that Leo drove to after they'd finished lunch curled with breakers rolling in from the east. He parked the car by a small café-bar just on the sand, and Anna slipped into the restrooms to change into one of the two new swimsuits she'd bought that morning. Leo, it seemed, had his trunks on underneath his trousers anyway. As she emerged, she saw him standing on the sand, stripped to the waist, a pair of colourful boogie boards under his arm, newly purchased from a beach vendor.

'Surf's up!' he told Anna, grinning, and handed her a board. Then, turning on his heel, he ran with a limping gait into the water and plunged over a breaking wave. With a sudden, inexplicable burst of exuberance, Anna ran after him and did likewise.

Foaming water burst over her head—cold for a second, and then warm. She gave a shout, and found herself grinning back at Leo, hair slicked back, torso glittering with diamonds.

'Watch out!' he called, as another wave curled towards them. 'Turn around, board to your midriff—wait, wait… Now!' Leo launched forward, catching the wave and creaming in towards the shore, weaving his route between the other surfers and swimmers.

Anna was less lucky, and missed the wave. But she caught the next one, and the exhilaration of being powered effortlessly into shore was intoxicating. The moment she grounded she was up on her feet, ploughing back out to sea to repeat the process, over and over again. Beside her, Leo set the pace relentlessly, exchanging grins with her as the water's power swept them inshore time after time.

Finally, after what seemed like a million waves, Anna beached herself in the shallows, lying on her board, dragging in the ebbing surf. Leo came and flopped beside her.

'I'm done in!' she gasped.

Leo jack-knifed to his feet lithely and held a hand down to her.

'Time for a cool drink,' he said.

Anna took his hand without thinking, letting his strong fingers curl around hers, and got to her feet. He went on holding her hand as they waded ashore, boogie boards under their arms. The sun was hot on their wet skin, the sea dazzling. Gaining the shade of the wooden café-bar was blissful, and Anna flopped down at a table.

'Enjoy it?' asked Leo, flopping likewise.

Anna grinned. 'It was fantastic!'

For a moment their eyes held, with nothing in them except mutual good humour. Then one of the waiting staff undulated over to them, with the characteristically graceful islander gait, and asked what they would like.

'Long, cool, and a lot of fruit juice, please.' Anna smiled at her.

'Twice.' Leo nodded. The woman smiled, and undulated back to the bar, sandals flapping lazily on the ground.

Anna's eyes went after her.

'They walk so gracefully, the islanders. Even when they are no longer young or slim. It's very striking. I can't work out how they do it.'

Leo leant back.

'It's because they never hurry,' he answered. 'It's too hot to hurry. So everyone relaxes.'

Anna gave a crooked smile. 'Wise people,' she commented. 'They know what's important in life.'

'"Getting and spending, we lay waste our powers",' Leo heard himself murmur, repeating the line of poetry that had come to him when he had been out on the villa's terrace that first night.

Anna's quizzical glance rested on him.

'Somehow that sentiment doesn't go with the hotshot business tycoon,' she said dryly.

Leo's eyelashes swept down. 'Is that how you see me? A hotshot business tycoon?'

'It's how you see yourself,' she riposted.

She expected to see his expression bristle, but instead there was a strange look in his eye.

'It's what was expected of me,' he said slowly. His dark eyes rested on her. 'You escaped your background, Anna. I didn't.'

She frowned, confused. 'Why would you want to—given your background?'

'I grew up with a lot of physical riches—but not much else.'

A snort escaped her. 'Poor little rich boy?'

'How close were you to your grandmother?' he asked, ignoring her sceptical comment.

She looked away a moment. 'Very. She was all I had. My mother died when I was five, and as for my father—well, even the child maintenance people couldn't find him. So it was just Gran and me. Which is a lot more than some kids get in life, so I'm not ungrateful, believe me. But sometimes it was...' She paused.

Something looked different in Leo's face.

'Lonely?' he supplied.

Her expression changed.

'Yes,' she admitted.

'So was I,' he said. He saw her disbelief and went on. 'Oh, there was a houseful of servants—several housefuls!—but my parents didn't bother with me. My father was a workaholic and my mother a society queen. I only became interesting to them when I was old enough to be put to work in an office or tout around socially to catch the interest of young women with commercially and politically influential fathers.'

There was a cynical note in his voice that Anna would have had to be deaf not to hear. But her ear heard something else as well. Something she would never in a million years have associated with someone as sublimely pleased with themselves as Leo Makarios.

It was sadness.

Something moved in her. She did not know what, but it disturbed her.

Made her want to reach across the table.

Take his hand.

Almost, almost, she felt her hand move. Then, with an effort of will, she halted it. Leo Makarios was nothing to her. Nothing except a man tormenting her, night after night, with the hopeless, helpless, shameful desires of her own body.

And yet—

The waitress reappeared, with graceful motion, carrying two tall glasses full of crushed ice and a blend of orange and scarlet juice. Anna was grateful for the diversion—and the quenching drink after so much salty water.

She sipped thirstily through the straw as Leo did likewise.

Then she sat back, lifting her damp, drying hair from her neck.

'It's still so hot!' she exclaimed, arching her throat.

Leo's eyes were riveted to her. He could not help it. The gesture she was making was so unconsciously sensual—her slender arms lifted, her swelling breasts thrust upwards by the movement, her long, loose tousled hair, the languorous tilt of her throat—that his breath caught in his body.

Thee mou, but she is beauty incarnate…

A wave of emotion went through him. It was desire. He knew it must be.

But it was more—what he could not say, could not name. But it was strong, and powerful.

And very, very disturbing.

Abruptly, he pushed his empty glass away from him and got to his feet.

'Time to go,' he said.

'Damn, I've caught the sun!'

Anna examined the skin on her forearm.

Leo glanced away from the road for a moment as they drove away from the beach.

'You haven't burnt, don't worry. A light tan will only flatter you.'

She made a face.

'One of my selling points is my pale skin. I try never to tan—even on a tropical shoot. Oh, well.' She shrugged. 'Too late now.'

It was, too, but somehow she couldn't bring herself to care much about losing her ivory skin tones. After everything else that was happening to her, it seemed very trivial. She brushed off the sheen of salt crystallising on her skin. 'I need a shower,' she said.

Leo kept his eye on the pitted road. Nobly, he forbore to suggest that she take one with him. He even tried extremely hard—and failed—to stop his imagination supplying the details. Imagination, he found, was quite enough to make his body react in hopeful anticipation. Uncomfortably, he shifted in the driving seat. He kept his gaze doggedly ahead. Hell, he must have been insane to make the deal he had at lunchtime— letting Anna have a night on her own.

His eyes narrowed.

And yet—and yet it was extraordinarily pleasant to have their armistice. Have Anna lose her dogged, resentful hostility towards him even for this short interlude.

But why should it just be for an interlude? Why not for as long as we are here?

The thought came unbidden, and took hold.

The afternoon had been good. They had passed it in inconsequential conversation, with him talking about the island, her asking the kind of questions any visitor would ask. And as for that spontaneous surfing session, it had been—

Fun, that was what it had been. The word was the only one that fitted.

A sense of astonishment filled him. Of all the experiences he might have imagined with Anna Delane, having fun—boisterous, seaside fun—was the very last he would ever have thought of.

But fun it had been. Simple, uncomplicated, almost childlike fun...

He eased back in his driving seat. Well-being suffused through him. At his side, Anna's silence no longer seemed aggressive and adversarial—just...peaceful.

He went on driving, heading west into the lowering sun.

Anna was drying her freshly washed hair when Leo knocked on her bedroom door and walked in. For a brief moment his eyes flickered over her in a way she was hotly familiar with. She felt a flush of heat go through her body but crushed it back. This was her night off. She'd earned it. Earned it being 'civil' to Leo Makarios all afternoon. Doing that definitely deserved a reward!

Except—her memory skidded back along the previous hours—it had not exactly proved an ordeal. The afternoon, she could not help but admit with her habitual honesty, had been— OK.

More than OK. In fact, it had been—

She bit her lip, unwilling to let her mind supply the word it wanted to.

Good. It had been good.

Enjoyable. Relaxing. Fun. Nice. Easy.

The words ran on, disturbing her even more than the way Leo's eyes were flickering over her towel-wrapped body.

'Yes?' she prompted.

'We've been invited out to dinner tonight,' Leo said. 'By one of the government ministers responsible for inward investment. Wear something relaxed, but chic. Do you have anything suitable?'

'I dare say I can manage,' said Anna dryly.

That she had succeeded was evident from the expression in Leo's eyes when she went downstairs an hour or so later. The red silk skirt and top were vivid, yet the loose cut on her tall, slender body gave her a languorous elegance that matched the semi-pinned knot of her long, tendrilled hair. Her matching sandals were low-heeled, and her jewellery was a gold torque and matching bracelets. Her make up was subtle.

'You look fantastic,' breathed Leo.

She gave him a polite, social smile, but it flickered uncertainly on her face.

Although she had been apprehensive about the evening, it proved easy enough. While the minister talked tax and finance to Leo, his wife engaged Anna in conversation. With the poise she had acquired in her years since leaving home, Anna chatted pleasantly to her hostess.

By the time his chauffeur-driven car was whisking them homeward, Leo was in a very good mood. The minister had been encouraging about his property development plans, and as for Anna, she had clearly charmed her hosts with her natural, unaffected manner. A memory came back to him, of Anna conversing with Hans Federman at Schloss Edelstein—obviously not in the least bothered that he was dull and middle-aged. His house staff liked her too, he could tell—but then she had an easy air with everyone, he realised.

Even, tonight, with him.

She was asking him now about his villa development in the south.

'It's a complex of villas and low-rise condominiums on one of the undeveloped promontories,' he answered. 'The government are concerned that the site will not be over-exploited. Water, too, is an issue on the island, which has no large rivers, so the villas have to be designed with water conservation in mind.'

Anna let him run on. He was clearly enthusiastic about the project, and knowledgeable too. Every now and then she asked prompting questions.

'I'll take you down tomorrow and show you,' he finished, as the car finally wheeled through the gates of his villa.

'OK,' she answered easily.

She went back into the cool of the villa. Memory slipped back to her—the first night she'd got here, tired and jet-lagged, with a hard, tight knot inside her stomach at the reason she was there.

It seemed, she realised as she walked indoors, a long time ago.

Much longer than the number of days she'd been here.

At her side, Leo caught up, even with his limping gait.

'How's the ankle?' she heard herself ask.

Leo grimaced. 'A damn nuisance—but it has its compensations.' He glanced down at her. 'Like you asking about it,' he murmured.

She gave a half-dismissive, half-embarrassed shrug at having been caught out expressing solicitude.

'Coffee?' he asked.

Anna nodded. 'Thank you, that would be nice.'

They walked out onto the terrace and Anna took her place on the lounger beside the coffee table, looking out over the softly lit pool. In her veins she felt the wine of the evening making her feel relaxed and sleepy. On the other lounger, Leo was resting his bad ankle.

'How did you do it?' Anna heard herself asking as she helped herself to coffee. Without thinking, she poured out a cup for Leo as well, and handed it to him.

'I fell off my windsurf board, like a complete novice,' he answered in self-disgust, taking the cup from her.

She gave a wry smile. 'I don't know how anyone stays on those things anyway,' she commented.

Leo took a mouthful of hot coffee and twisted his head towards her.

'If you can ride a bike you can windsurf. It's not that hard. I'll teach you.'

Anna felt her fingers clench around the cup handle.

'I think I'll pass. My insurance policy doesn't allow me to do dangerous sports.' She kept her voice deliberately light, as though the prospect of being taught windsurfing by the man keeping her in his bed by blackmail was nothing much.

'You are insured?' Leo's voice sounded surprised.

'Against loss of earnings from injury. It seemed a prudent thing to do.'

'Prudent?' echoed Leo. *Prudent?* A woman who thought nothing of stealing a ruby bracelet wasn't someone he'd call prudent. A frown creased his brow. Today had shown him a new side to Anna Delane—as if she were just a normal person, instead of a criminal.

His eyes went to her as she looked out over the beach. The

evening had been so good, the day so good, and he knew exactly how he wanted it to end. Anna looked so fantastic, long-limbed, beautiful, with the grace that took his breath away every time.

Emotion rose in him. It was desire, he knew it was—intense and piercing, making him want to get to his feet, sweep her up into his arms and find the nearest bedroom. It was a familiar feeling, one that came over him every night.

But there was something unfamiliar mingled in with desire. He searched for a moment, then gave up. It wasn't anger, that was for sure, or exasperation, or annoyance, or any of the other frustrations that Anna Delane's cussedness towards him always aroused. But what it was he had no idea. And because he couldn't identify it, he put it aside. Right now he wasn't interested. Right now there was only one thing he was interested in.

He took another mouthful of coffee, then put the cup down.

'Have you finished your coffee?' he asked. His voice had a husk in it.

Anna's head swivelled round to him. Leo reached out his hand and smoothed it along her bare arm. Her skin was warm to the touch, as soft as the silk of her dress. His blood quickened at the touch; his eyelashes swept down over his darkening eyes. In his veins desire creamed, rich with anticipation.

She was just so beautiful, so desirable…

But even as his eyes rested on her, appreciating her delectable body, Anna's expression was changing. Freezing.

He could feel her—see her—pulling away mentally and physically.

'You said,' she enunciated, 'I could have the night off.'

It was like a slap with a wet towel. His hand drew back instantly.

And in the same instant the old, familiar flare of sheer exasperated anger shot through him.

He gave a short, heavy sigh.

'Don't tell me—it's in your contract,' he said grimly.

'It was a verbal contract,' she answered.

Leo's eyes flashed. 'You missed your vocation—you should have been a lawyer. Instead of a thief,' he reminded her nastily.

Her face tightened. 'You said I could have the night off,' she repeated doggedly.

Angrily, Leo reached for his coffee again.

'Do what you want,' he said moodily, and took another mouthful. He wished it were brandy, so he could drink himself into oblivion. His body didn't seem to want to be accepting of Anna's rejection of him. He shifted restlessly.

'Try a cold shower,' he heard her say coolly.

He flashed a killing look at her.

Then went back to staring moodily into the night.

Damn Anna Delane. And damn himself for wanting her so much.

He thrust his cup aside again, and got to his feet. This was hopeless—he couldn't sit there with her beside him, rejecting him.

'I'll see you at breakfast,' he announced bleakly, and limped inside.

Out on the terrace, Anna sat still. It was her turn to stare moodily into the sub-tropical darkness.

Her turn to damn both herself and him. And, worst of all, to damn the desire he had quickened in her, which she was forcing down now with every ounce of her will-power lest it overpower her and send her running hungrily, desperately, after him.

CHAPTER NINE

THE project manager at Leo Makarios's development complex was telling her about the different kinds of hardwood used in construction of the villas, but Anna was hardly paying attention. She was far too conscious of Leo's presence beside her—much too aware of his edgy mood—and of her own.

Instead of luxuriating in an undisturbed night in her own bed she had slept badly, restless and interrupted. Now she felt heavy-eyed and bleary, but running with a tense energy.

Her mood was bleak. A truth was pressing at her that she didn't want to accept—mustn't accept. Her eyes slid past the half-constructed villas out over the endless seas beyond, and a hollow misery filled her. Oh, God, how had it come to this? Tossing and turning all night, staring blindly up at the ceiling, unable to find any peace, any repose—all for the sake of Leo Makarios?

Her eyes hardened beneath the concealing veil of her dark glasses. She had to fight this—she had to. It was nothing but a sick weakness—a stupid, unforgivable, temporary insanity. Nothing else. And she would overcome it! She had to—she just had to...

At her side the project manager had turned his attention to his employer, drawing his notice to something on the sheaf of architectural drawings in his hand. With half an ear Anna heard Leo's deep voice answering brusquely, his voice edged like a serrated knife.

When they left the site she was relieved, and yet it was even worse being incarcerated in the car alone with Leo. He did not speak to her, nor she to him, yet the silent tension between them pulled at her, making her muscles tense in mental resistance. Her hands pressed into each other in her lap. Her throat felt constricted.

He drove for a good half an hour, over twisting coastal roads, until he turned into a private drive that led down to the sea— a low-rise beach hotel his destination.

'Lunch,' he announced tersely, and got out of the car. Silently Anna followed suit, and went into the hotel with him.

She disliked it immediately. It was clearly a boutique hotel, aimed at a clientele bored with mundane tourism and demanding a novelty of design that Anna castigated as pretentious. So was the menu.

'A vegetarian salad, please,' she ordered. 'No dressing.'

'I thought you were starting to eat normally?' said Leo edgily.

Anna shrugged. 'The prices are ludicrous and the menu idiotic.'

Leo's eyes narrowed. 'This is rated as one of the best hotels in the Caribbean.'

Anna stared at him. 'The décor is pretentious, the staff snooty, and the guests are all posers. That place yesterday was a million times better.'

'Well, we're here now,' Leo returned, and moodily studied the wine list.

'Just mineral water for me—sparkling,' said Anna.

'I'm glad something is,' he retorted.

They ate in virtual silence, Leo grim-faced and Anna tense. Had they really been having an almost normal conversation just twenty-four hours ago? she wondered disbelievingly. Now she could hardly say two words to him. Not that he seemed in the mood for conversation. She was grateful. All she wanted now was to get out of here, back to the villa, and lock herself in her bedroom. Or anywhere. She felt jittery, restless. Looking anywhere but at Leo.

And yet somewhere deep inside her it was as if an electric charge were building, dangerously overloading her nerves. Her muscles were tense, her skin prickling. Her body seemed alive, but in an alien, uncontrolled way, as if it wanted something—

something that she must not, would not think about. Her fingers tightened around her fork, she held her neck rigid, so she could not let herself look across at the man sitting opposite her. A man who seemed as restless, as on edge, as she was.

Her teeth clenched. She would not look across at him. She *would* not.

Doggedly she went on eating, though the food tasted like sawdust for all its exorbitant price.

Inside her, coiling tighter and tighter, the electric charge went on building. Silently.

Dangerously.

The meal crawled to its interminable end. Leo seemed determined to drag it out, ordering a dessert and then coffee, when all she wanted to do was jerk to her feet and get out—out of here, away from him.

The tension radiating from him was palpable.

Finally, when she thought she must just scrape her chair back and rush off, he pushed aside his empty coffee cup.

'Anna—'

His voice was edged, serrated. It had been like that all morning. But now it was worse.

Her jaw tightened. She said nothing.

'Look at me.'

What was it in his voice that made her do it? Let her eyes off the leash she had been pinning them down with. Let them lift and meet the dark, heavy-lidded eyes fastening on her.

Electricity cracked through her, the charge arcing across to his eyes.

Telling him exactly, *exactly*, what he wanted to know…

'No.' Her voice was low. *'No!'*

She jerked to her feet—the way every tense, coiled muscle was impelling her to.

Leo followed suit, his hand impatiently, imperiously beckoning for the bill. When the waiter glided over, Leo had his card at the ready. As he handed it over, scrawling his name on the chit, he said something in a low voice to the man, who nodded without a flicker of his eyes. He glided away with the credit card while Anna stood, tension racking through every limb, then returned, handing back the card to Leo—and something else besides. She did not see what it was and did not care. She knew only that she must, *must* get out of here. It was imperative. Essential.

'Let's go,' said Leo, and headed off. His voice sounded harsh, but Anna ignored it. She just wanted to get out of there, the quickest way, and she followed his rapid stride from the dining room without complaint.

But he didn't lead the way back out to the front of the hotel. Instead he went down into the gardens. Shrugging mentally, Anna followed him. She could see palm-fronded beach cottages artfully sited amongst the banana trees and cultivated vegetation, and beyond them the white of the beach backed by the azure of the sea... Without realising it, she saw that she had followed Leo along a paved path and up to the door of one of the cottages. He held the door open for her.

Did he want to change for a swim? she wondered, stepping inside. She could do with one—maybe it would help to drain off this relentless feeling of edgy, restless tension netting her body. She turned to tell him that her swimsuit was in the car.

And froze.

Leo was looking at her.

Looking at her through heavy-lidded eyes focused totally and absolutely upon her. With an expression in them that told her that swimming was the very last thing on his mind.

And instantly, like an electric arc between them, she felt her body flaring. Her heart-rate surged and her breath came raggedly as the hunger she had been fighting all morning suddenly, urgently, took her over. Completely, absolutely.

She couldn't move. Could only stand there, frozen, as he pressed the door shut with the palm of his hand and moved slowly, purposefully, towards her.

He didn't speak, nor she. He only stood for a timeless moment in front of her, and then his hands were spearing into her hair, either side of her head, and his mouth was slanting down over hers.

She opened to him, blood igniting, hunger and desire leaping in her as she twined her mouth with his.

Oh, God, it was bliss! She wanted more, more of him. Now—right now. Her body pressed against his, her breasts swelling and tautening, and she could feel his body respond. The excitement of it ripped through her.

'*Christos*—Anna—'

Leo's voice was harsh, jagged, and then it was cut off as his mouth returned to devour hers. She gave a low moan, wrapping her arms around him, feeling the glory of his hard muscled back beneath her cleaving fingers. She wanted him. Wanted him so much, so intensely, that she felt faint with it. Her body was starving, ravenous for him—deprived of him, of what he could do to her, for a whole agonising long day and night.

Her nipples were hard against his torso, and the sensation aroused yet more and more wanting in her. She pressed her hips against him, feeling his surging masculine response, and she moaned again low in her throat as her mouth mated with his in avid, ravening hunger. Desire and excitement were ripping through her, tearing like a knife, demanding to be sated and slaked on him—*him*—Leo Makarios, whose body she craved, *needed*, now…right now…

Leo's hands had left her hair, had slid down her flanks, curving around the soft mounds of her bottom, lifting her into him so that he could intensify the sensation at the vee of her legs, pressed against his strong, erect manhood. Instinctively she lifted her knee, using her thigh to caress his, winding her foot around his calf, rubbing his leg with hers, her skirts hoisting high.

He was moving her, twisting her around, backing her towards the wide, inviting expanse of the bed, where he could take her, free their bodies of their useless restricting clothes and slake their devouring need for physical satiation.

For a few blinded seconds she surfaced for air, taking a deep, gulping breath to fill her ragged lungs, blood coursing hotly through her veins, her body on fire with desire for him, desperate for him, starving for him…

A shadow of movement stilled her. In the dim light of the shaded interior she suddenly saw a pair of figures outlined in the silvered mirror on the wall.

Writhing, abandoned…out of all control except for the urges of their raw sexuality.

It was like a douche of cold water over her heated body.

She wrenched away, staring, appalled, at the reflection.

Cold, sick horror drenched through her.

What am I doing?

The words seared in her head, and she did not need a translation.

She took a stumbling step backwards.

'Anna—' Leo was reaching for her again, his voice hoarse.

Her eyes flared.

'Don't touch me!'

His expression darkened. 'What the hell—?'

She took another step back.

'I said, don't touch me.'

Mortification was flooding through her, and hot, humid shame. Oh, God, had it come to this? Being bundled into a hotel room for a quick, urgent session of sexual satiation? A room hired by the hour. And afterwards, when he'd slaked himself on her, he'd tell her to get dressed again, and he would do likewise, body sated, and then he'd walk out beside her, his hand under her elbow—the woman he'd just had sex with in a hotel room after lunch—and put down his credit card at the desk to pay for his pleasure, rented by the hour…

She couldn't bear it.

Anguish sheared through her. And shame and anger.

He stepped towards her, his hands reaching out for her.

She stepped further away.

'I don't want this.'

Her voice was high, staccato. Strung on a wire, pulled taut. Unbearably taut.

Something moved in his face.

'Liar—'

His voice was low, eyes intent. Slowly, deliberately, he reached for her.

'Anna Delane—you are a liar to tell me you don't want this. Don't want *me*.'

Leo's hand closed around her wrist, drawing her to him.

She could not resist him. Her breathing quickened again, eyes dilating, heat flushing through her. Oh, God, she wanted this all right! Wanted him...

Leo felt her relax, felt the resistance ebb from her. Felt her go weak, the way he wanted her to be—weak with desire for him. Only for him. Now. Right now.

He started to slide his hands around her waist, to take her back in his arms, feel her soft, slim body pliant against his.

The blow took him entirely by surprise. And in that moment, as Anna drew her arm back with whip-like reaction from where the side of her hand had impacted on his upper arm, she pulled away from him.

Leo stared, disbelieving. She was standing there, in a martial arts fighting pose, balanced on the balls of her feet, one arm drawn back, elbow crooked and her hand fisted loosely at her hip, the other arm extended, warding him off, palm facing him.

'I said no,' she told him.

Her face was set. Only her eyes flared. Showing something in them he would not recognise. Refused to recognise.

'What the hell,' Leo said slowly, 'are you doing?'

She drew her breath in sharply.

'I don't want this. I don't want sex with you now. I don't want sex with you now, here, in a hotel room that you've just tipped a waiter to open up for you. Just because you're in the mood—'

His mouth twisted. 'Anna. Do you think you faked your reaction just now? Like hell you did. You want it, and you've wanted it since last night, when you said no to me and then regretted it and were too damn stubborn to admit it. You've been wanting it all day—that's why you lit up like a volcano just now. The way you always do—always have done with me—every, every time. So don't come the hypocrite with me, Anna Delane, because we both know you want me—you want everything I give you! Everything you give me!'

Leo took a step towards her. Deliberately. Clear intent in his face.

Anger stabbed through her, like a knife slicing through a curtain. Vicious and violent. It had come out of nowhere, like a summer storm boiling out of the sky.

Taking her over.

Taking her over completely.

She felt its power surge through her, coruscating, burning. Released like a tiger, pouring through her.

'I don't *give* you sex at all!' she hissed back at him. 'You *take* it! You take it! And I won't. I *won't* be reduced to having quick, sordid sex like you want now!'

Dark eyes flashed in unleashed fury.

'Sordid?' Leo snarled. His face blackened. 'Do I have to remind you,' he bit out—and there was something in his voice that suddenly made Anna feel sick— 'why you are here at all on this island, with me? You're a thief—a criminal!'

'And so are you.'

'Are you insane?' he demanded.

It was his incredulity that did it for her. Sent the anger searing through her again. She knew she should not let it take over. Knew that, poised like this, her body both her weapon and her defence, she should hold the calm, the dispassion, the control that her sensei would insist on.

But she couldn't. She couldn't control anything.

Let alone her anger. It was coursing through her—destructive, burning.

'You're blackmailing me into sex with you, threatening me with jail, and that makes you a criminal.'

His hand slashed through the air.

'*Thee mou*—I keep you out of jail and you call that *threatening* you?' There were white lines incised around his mouth. His eyes were hard, hard as iron. Black iron. 'I will not have you twist the truth into your own fantasy!' Greek burst from him, staccato and rabid. 'I have taken all I am prepared to take from you. Your stubborn, shameless refusal to show the slightest sign of guilt, or remorse, or contrition for what you did. You spit and snarl at me, *refusing* to acknowledge your crime. And now, *now* you dare to try and accuse me of criminal behaviour?' More Greek broke from him. And a mask came down over his face. She could see it happening. Control. Total self-control of his emotions.

'Put your shoes on. Pick up your bag. We're going.'

He strode to the door, yanking it open. Anna could hear him striding down the path with heavy tread.

Slowly, very slowly, she came out of her blocking stance. Her body was starting to tremble. She felt cold and shaky.

Her breathing shallow, she stooped to gather her bag, her sandals, and then, with a strange, eerie sense of complete emotional dissociation, she left the cottage.

They drove back to the villa in silence. A silence so tangible it could have been cut from a knife.

At the villa, he pulled up at the front entrance.

'Go in,' he instructed.

She got down from the car, but had hardly closed the door when it took off again, pounding back down the drive towards the gate in a swirl of gravel. Slowly she started to move towards the front door.

'Miss Delane?'

The voice that spoke came from one side, and she turned. A man was walking up to her. He had a steady gait that was somehow menacing. A stab of unease went through Anna in her heightened state of excess emotion.

'Who wants to know?' she countered. She looked to the villa. There was no one around—not even a gardener in the gardens. The man approaching her was a stranger.

A car started moving from where it had been parked, in shadow, at the place where the drive swept away round to the garages at the side of the villa. It was black, with tinted windows.

'You will come with me,' the man approaching her said.

Anna backed away. Fear was running in her. What the hell was going on? Why were there no house staff around? She made to turn and run inside, to find someone—anyone.

Her arm was seized. A vice lock.

Automatically she lashed out, striking down at the man's open side. But even as the side of her hand impacted he moved, coming round the back of her and striking her with a blow that all but knocked her out. Before she could recover she was being pushed, head-first, inside the car, thrust face down on the floor, so she could scarcely breathe, hardly think, hardly believe what was happening to her. There were voices—harsh, urgent—the car jerked forward, its engine revving. She tried to surface, fight through the terror buckling through her, but she was thrust back down again, a foot painful on her neck. Darkness rolled over her.

Leo stood, staring out to sea. He was on a rocky headland, where a rough track led to the ruins of an eighteenth-century British fort.

He could still feel anger coursing through him.

Of course it was anger. What else could it be? It was the only thing he was feeling. Burning, biting anger.

Anger at Anna Delane.

Criminal. Thief. Hypocrite.

Who had dared, *dared* to smear her crime on him. Dared to accuse him—*him*—of being a criminal—a blackmailer. Dared to look down her hypocritical nose and accuse him of being sordid.

Just because he'd wanted her so much, needed her right away—

She wanted it as much as I did. Thee mou, *can I not tell exactly when she is aroused, and how much, and—?*

His mobile phone went off. Impatiently he yanked it from his hip pocket and answered it.

'Yes?' he bit out.

He stilled totally as the caller started speaking.

*   *   *

The knife-blade glinted in the light. The man holding it looked at it, and then at Anna.

'You know, Miss Delane, you would be well advised not to withhold the information I wish to have.'

He rotated the blade, so again it caught the light streaming through the windows.

'You are very beautiful,' he said in his accented English. 'It would be a great pity to ruin that beauty. Now, consider your answer carefully. I ask you once again—where is your friend, Jennifer Carson?'

'I don't know.'

Anna's voice was a thread. She had read in a thriller one time that fear was something you had to experience to believe. And now she believed.

The boat she was on rocked slightly over a wave as it continued to head out to sea, and the man holding her arms behind her back shifted his weight to rebalance. The movement caused renewed pressure on her joints, her shoulders. She felt faint again with the pain, her head muzzy, her brain fogged.

And the fear.

It was in every cell of her body. Like a cancer. In every cell.

The man interrogating her had eyes without expression in them.

'I—I told you,' she said again, her voice almost inaudible. 'She went back to London when I left Austria with Leo Makarios. I don't know where she is now. I don't know anything.'

The man twisted the knife in the sunlight again and it flashed. Anna stared at it with a sick terror.

'I am sure, Miss Delane,' said the man with no expression in his eyes, 'that that is an answer you should reconsider.'

He walked up to her, lifting the knife to her cheek and laying the blade flat. She could feel it pressing against her skin.

'All I have to do,' he told her, 'is twist the blade inwards.'

The sickness churned in her stomach. Her eyes were distended, incapable of focus. Her brain was incapable of thought.

Only of terror.

The man holding her said something to the man with the knife. The latter gave a coarse laugh and pulled the blade from her face. He said something to the first man, and they both laughed. Then the first man looked at Anna again.

'Marking you would lower the price we'd get for you—but there are other ways to make you tell us what we want to know. Pain that will not scar…'

The pit of Anna's stomach dissolved.

'I don't know any more than I've told you,' she whispered. Her eyes were blind with fear.

Then, in the mindless terror that possessed her, she heard something. A faint roaring sound in the distance, over and above the noise of the engine of the boat she was on.

Coming closer.

The man with the knife swore, throwing more words at the man holding Anna, and then strode out onto the open rear deck of the motor yacht she'd been taken aboard by her captors.

Then another sound penetrated her stricken brain.

The steady thud-thud-thud of helicopter rotors.

The man on the stern deck jerked his head upwards, staring around to locate the source. Then his eyes went back out to sea.

Anna fought to try and make her eyes focus, but she couldn't make her muscles work. She couldn't make anything work. Terror was eating at her, taking over her body, shutting out everything else.

The man on the stern deck turned and shouted something to the man holding Anna. The noise of a powerboat engine came closer, and so did the thudding of the helicopter rotors. Anna felt the cruiser they were on start to rock more as the approaching helicopter started its descent, whipping up the waves.

The man with the knife spoke to Anna sneeringly.

'Don't get your hopes up, whore. No one can touch us. Not if they want you alive, that is.' His face changed, become a mask of hatred. 'We'll put you to work in a brothel, where you belong!' He strode up to her, and with a sudden violent movement his hand closed over the material of her dress at the bodice and tore it down, exposing her completely. He gave an ugly laugh.

Then suddenly an amplified voice was booming down over the yacht. Anna could not hear the words. Even if she had not been half-dead from fear and pain, she could not have made them out.

The man with the knife strode back to the stern deck and threw his head up, yelled something up at the hovering helicopter.

Out beyond the cruiser's wake, Anna could see another boat approaching. Was that the power boat she had heard? It was closing fast, curving out and round, on an intercepting course to head off her abductors. It was coming closer now. Her eyes twisted to the wide windows lining the side of the cabin. She could see what could only be uniformed police aboard, and then the boat was forcing the yacht to shift to port. She felt their speed slow, jolting her sideways, and the jerking movement on her pinioned arms sent new waves of black pain through her.

Their boat stopped, its churning wake at the rear subsiding to a mere idling. The noise of the rotors increased proportionately, but not enough to drown the amplified voice directed at them—not from the helicopter now, but from the police craft hovering threateningly across the cruiser's starboard bow.

The man on the stern deck shouted something harshly to the man holding her. Anna was jerked forward, forced to go towards the open stern deck.

As she emerged into the brightness she suddenly felt something hard and cold jammed under her ear.

It was the barrel of a gun.

This far out to sea the water was cold as Leo slipped silently into its depths. He ignored it. Blocked out everything except the icy purpose that filled him. Had filled him ever since his blood had run cold when the villa's security head had told him that three gunmen had been holding the house staff at gunpoint, threatening to kill them, and that Anna had been abducted the moment he'd driven off, leaving her at the villa.

The hour that had passed since then had been a living nightmare. The police had been scrambled, but Leo had refused to stay ashore. He and two of his security people had piled into the fastest motor boat he possessed, and headed off in pursuit. A car had been abandoned at the jetty in the next village along the coast, and the villagers there had reported seeing three men drag a young white woman aboard a gleaming cruiser moored, untypically, at the fishermen's jetty. It had left in a roaring wake, heading south.

Cold had drenched through him. This island was one of the safest in the Caribbean—the government extremely protective of its citizens and tourists—especially their very rich ones. So Leo had allowed his personal security at the villa to be minimal.

Too minimal.

Christos—just who the hell had Anna got herself involved with? Who had taken her? And why? The gunmen had been Middle Eastern. That was all his staff had been able to tell him. They had spoken only English. The boat they were using, however, was registered to a South American country.

Drugs? Was that what Anna was involved with? God, he'd known she was a criminal, but stealing priceless jewellery was a world away from drug-running.

Or was it? The criminal underworld was a sick mirror image of the business world—making money out of anything and everything.

Why had his Anna been taken?

He pushed the question from him. It was irrelevant now. Everything was irrelevant except what he was doing. The helicopter-induced swell was running against him, chopping the water and slowing him down, but at least it meant that for the few moments when he had to surface for air he was hidden. The police boat had stopped the cruiser in its tracks, and that and the hovering helicopter were taking all the gunmen's attention.

Getting aboard amidships, well away from the stern deck and the trimmed but still deadly propeller, took all his strength. For a moment he crouched, breathing heavily, just inside the ship's rail, hidden by the bulk of the upper cabin. Then, slowly, he moved.

The man at the wheel was holding the boat as steady as he could in the buffeting from the helicopter, at which he was gazing upwards balefully, as well as keeping his eyes on the police gunmen trained on him from the boat all but grazing his starboard bow. He never even heard Leo in the din.

Cautiously, Leo started to climb up onto the roof of the cabin, sliding along it on his belly. He twisted his head sideways, shaking it warningly at the police on board the boat. Not by a movement or a gesture did they reveal they had seen him. The booming voice from the megaphone was still ordering the gunmen to hand their prisoner over. Somewhere, dimly, he could hear their leader shouting his sneering defiance, telling the police helicopter that if they fired the girl would be dead first. The backs of all three of them were towards Leo, but he could see, with a sick coldness inside him, the gun jammed under Anna's ear. He also saw, with a rage that seared through him like a white heat, that they'd stripped her to the waist.

Silently, like death, he dropped down onto the rear deck.

In a blur, Anna saw the figure drop. For a second terror screamed in her, and then somewhere, in a synapse deep in her brain, she realised who it was.

It was Leo.

Leo—dropping down, pummelling into the man holding the gun to her throat, knocking him to the deck. Anna screamed. And then, from nowhere, she acted. Every muscle in her body went limp and she sagged forward.

Fire shot through her shoulders as they took the full weight of her body, but she didn't care. The change in weight distribution had unbalanced her captor. She hooked her foot around his ankle and, every muscle tensing again, she jerked. He went flying down, almost taking her with him, but at the last moment he released her to try and stop himself hitting the deck. She was on him in a second. Her arms would not work, but her legs would, and she laid in to him, kicking viciously anywhere and everywhere she could to keep him down.

Then, suddenly, she was swept up. Before she could even struggle again she registered that it was Leo—Leo bundling her over the side guardrail of the deck into the waiting arms of one of his security people in the power boat that had come alongside. She heard Leo yell something, and the boat veered off.

'Leo!' She screamed his name, but it could not be heard above the roaring engine.

The police helicopter had shifted, shadowing over the yacht, and she could see two marksmen taking aim from the interior. The swoop of the rotors was ploughing the sea into a frenzy.

The gunman had staggered to his feet, lifting his gun while backing Leo into the cabin, taking aim from the rocking platform. Even through the deafening noise she heard the crack of gunshots, saw Leo launching himself sideways, downwards. Then there were more shots. The police marksmen had shot the gunman and the man was reeling, falling in hideous slow motion, backwards over the churning propellers.

She twisted her head away, hearing yet more shots.

Then no more.

'Leo,' she moaned, 'Oh, God, Leo…'

He was lying motionless, face down on the rocking, jerking deck, and she could see blood staining his shirt. Horror drenched through her.

Leo was dead. He had died saving her.

Grief tore at her like a ravening wolf. Eating her alive.

Then, into the horror, she heard the voice of Leo's security man.

'I think I just saw his hand move!'

CHAPTER TEN

ANNA sat in the waiting room. It was cool. Overhead, a fan rotated slowly. Even with painkillers her wrenched arms and shoulders ached. She didn't care. She didn't care about anything.

Only one thing occupied her entire being.

Leo.

She stared at the clock. How long had he been in Theatre? She didn't know. Knew only that no one was saying reassuring things to her. No one was telling her it was going to be all right.

No one was telling her he was going to live.

My fault. My fault. My fault.

The words tolled through her.

Over and over again.

As she waited, and prayed.

There had been only one other thing she had done since the doctor had discharged her. She had begged the favour of a call to the UK. Across the ocean she had spoken to Jenny, warning her to lie low, that the man who had got her pregnant was prepared to kill for her.

She went on staring at the clock.

My fault. My fault. My fault.

The doors opened. A doctor came out in Theatre garb. He came up to Anna, loosening his mask. His face was grave.

Her throat had a noose around it.

The surgeon looked at her a moment. Then a tired smile formed on his mouth.

'You've got a very tough man there. I've patched him together again, but he needs a reward for all his heroics. Make

168

sure you're there when he surfaces. He deserves a beautiful woman to wake up to.'

Anna burst into tears.

Leo was so pale.

His face like marble.

He hardly seemed to be breathing, and yet the low rise and fall of his bandaged chest told her that he was alive. Blessedly, blessedly alive.

Gratitude flooded through her.

And more, so much more than gratitude.

Shakily, she sat down on a chair and pulled it closer to him. His hands lay on either side of him, inert, pale.

She slid her fingers around the hand nearest her.

Living flesh.

Slowly she lowered her cheek to his hand.

It was wet with tears.

How long she sat there, she did not know. Nurses looked in every now and then—sometimes at her, sometimes to check Leo. The night wore on, and still she sat there, his hand clasped tight in hers, never letting him go.

The dawn came, fingers of pale light stealing into the room. A nurse came to check him again, bringing coffee and sandwiches for Anna.

'His pulse is stronger,' she told her. 'He'll be back with us very soon.' She glanced down at where Anna was holding his hand. 'Don't you let go, now. He knows, you know. You hang on in there.' She gave a last smile. 'Now, drink this coffee while it's hot. And eat.'

She glided out.

Anna went on holding on.

Does he know? Does he know I'm here?

And, if he did, was she helping or harming?

Tears started in her eyes again.

He came for me. He risked his life and came for me. He thinks I stole from him, he thinks me a thief, but he came for me. After everything I said to him...he came for me, to save me.

Her heart swelled with emotion. Emotion so strong it frightened her. Her vision was blurred, so blurred, so it was the infinitesimally slight movement of his hand that she first registered. She caught her breath, her heart squeezing. She wiped her eyes hurriedly with her free hand. The tears just welled again. But this time she saw him move, saw his eyelids lift, saw him gaze without vision for a moment and then, as if his eyes were bearing great weights, they cleared, and moved.

To her.

For a moment there was nothing in his eyes. Nothing at all.

Her heart was crushed. Just crushed.

Slowly, feeling as if a stake were being plunged into her heart, she started to draw her fingers away.

He seized them back with lightning reaction, crushing them, not letting her go.

His eyelids drooped again.

'Anna,' he said. The word was a sigh, faint and low.

His eyes sank shut.

He slid back into sleep.

But at his mouth Anna saw a faint, relaxing curve.

Later still, she was packed off back to the villa, driven by one of Leo's staff. They were all so nice to her, so kind. She wanted to shout at them, tell them it was her fault—all her fault. But the maids bore her off, got her under a shower, fed her and put her to bed.

But not in her own bed. In Leo's.

She slept, hugging his pillow.

It had his scent on it.

And her tears.

When she arrived back at the hospital it was to learn that Leo had already surfaced into full consciousness, then gone back to sleep again. His vital signs were good, his natural physical strength boosting his body's healing powers.

'He'll wake again quite soon,' the nurse told her. 'You make sure you're there when he does. And don't cry, dear. He's going to be fine, you know.'

The admonition was in vain. Anna took one look at Leo's sleeping form, his pale face, his bandaged chest, and started crying again.

Emotion filled her. Filled her and filled her. Welling up and spilling over—just like her tears.

Her heart squeezed.

Oh, Leo, she cried silently. *Leo!*

She sat down, trembling beside him, and gazed at him, her lips murmuring endlessly.

Eyes anguished.

Heart fuller than it had ever been in her life.

Full with love for Leo Makarios.

Leo was dreaming. He knew he was dreaming, because Anna was crying. She was crying, and saying she was sorry—so sorry, so sorry.

So it must be a dream.

Anna never said sorry.

She stole his Levantsky rubies, and she never said sorry.

She got him achingly aroused and then threw him out of her bedroom, and she never said sorry.

She shouted *harassment* at him, and never said sorry.

She accused him of criminal blackmail, and she never said sorry.

She called sex with him sordid, and never said sorry.

Worst of all, she got herself abducted by psychos and he had to go after her and save her and get shot to pieces.

But she was saying sorry now. He could hear her.

His eyes opened.

It wasn't a dream.

Anna Delane was sitting by his bed, her face blotched with crying, and she was saying, 'I'm sorry, Leo. I'm just so sorry.'

Then she saw his eyes open, and fell silent in mid 'sorry'.

For one long, endless moment he saw her mouth quiver, as though she were trying to control something.

Then she burst into renewed noisy tears.

Leo just stared.

Her green eyes were smeared, lashes clogged, cheeks runnelled, colour blotchy, and her nose was red.

She looked awful.

She looked the most precious sight in the world to him.

He reached for her hand. It was twisting with her other hand in her lap. There was a soggy wet tissue in their clutch. He dropped it disgustedly on the floor and took her hand, lifting it back on the bed. It felt ludicrously heavy.

But it felt the most precious thing in the world to him.

He was insane, he knew. She was a thief, a hypocrite, a cussed, unrepentant, shameless, uncooperating, accusatory damn woman, with more attitude than Genghis Khan, and she could make him angrier than he'd ever felt about a woman before. But when he'd seen her standing there, forcibly stripped to the waist, that scum jamming a gun under her ear, he'd felt a rage that he had never known in his life.

No one, *no one* was going to do that to her and live.

Even if it meant he ended up like a damn sieve, full of bullet holes!

With supreme effort he yanked her hand closer to him, possessively.

'*Theos*, but you're trouble, *yineka mou*,' he said, his voice slurring with tiredness.

Her storm of weeping increased. He watched with heavy-lidded eyes he could hardly keep open.

Well, he thought wonderingly, you see something new every day. Anna Delane, crying. His beautiful Anna, crying.

He squeezed her fingers. He wanted to haul her down on him and hold her so tight she'd never storm off again—ever. But he hadn't got the strength right now. So he just squeezed her fingers instead.

It made her cry more.

'Oh, God, Leo, I'm so sorry. I'm so sorry. It's my fault. All my fault.'

He hazed a faint smile. Anna Delane, apologising at last. It was a good feeling.

Irrelevant now, but still good.

'You came after me. You thought me a thief, and I said all those horrible things to you, and you still came after me. You saved my life—and I'm so sorry. I'm so sorry. And I'm so glad, so incredibly grateful, that you're alive.'

Leo went on watching her. He still couldn't get over hard-boiled Anna Delane bawling her eyes out for him.

It was doing the strangest thing to him. The damnedest thing.

He decided to hell with his stitches, and yanked her down to him.

It cut the apologising out instantly.

'Leo! Oh, my God—your wounds.'

She was trying to struggle up from where he'd pulled her to him. He wasn't having that. He definitely wasn't having that. She wasn't getting away from him.

'Hold still. I'm not letting you go.'

'But I'm hurting you!'

'Quiet,' ordered Leo.

He lifted his free hand and brought it round to cup her cheek. His thumb grazed her tear-wet cheek.

'Tears for me?' he said wonderingly. 'Anna Delane, crying over me?'

'Of *course* I'm crying! I owe you my *life*,' she wailed. 'And you nearly got *killed* for my sake. You nearly got killed. And I feel so *bad*. I thought you were just a spoilt, arrogant bastard who believed he could help himself to me because I was a model, that you just wanted a quick lay because you thought I was cheap and easy—and then you got sex from me by threatening me with jail, because I had to let you think I was a thief, and you didn't see *anything* wrong with getting sex that way, and I hated you for that, and I hated you even more because you made me forget that was why you were having sex with me, and that made me even angrier with you—that you could make me so *stupid* over you, wanting a man who was treating me like that—and so I hated you even more, and I was horrible to you—as horrible as I could be—and then you went and came after me when those sicko goons got me, and they would have killed me, and tortured me and you saved me and nearly got killed—you nearly got *killed*—and I thought you were dead. Oh, God, I thought you were dead, Leo, and it was... It just made everything else seem pointless and stupid, and I didn't care if you were spoilt and arrogant, because I just wanted you to be alive. I just desperately, desperately wanted you to be alive...'

Her voice choked off.

'I just wanted you to be alive,' Anna whispered. 'And I'm sorry—so sorry, Leo.'

Leo was staring at her. He'd stopped listening to her saying sorry because the novelty was over—now she was just getting in a state. Besides, it was out of character for Anna. Something else she'd said, however, was not. He forced his gradually unfogging brain to remember what it was.

Then it came to him.

'What do you mean, spoilt and arrogant?' he demanded.

She stopped apologising abruptly.

'Well, you are. You turned up in my room in your Schloss and just thought you could help yourself.'

Leo's eyes darkened. 'You'd been inviting me all evening!'

She pulled back, jerking her hand free.

'I had *not*!'

'Good God, do you think I can't tell when a woman lights up for me?' Leo demanded.

'Well, that can't be hard—considering they all do!' she snapped.

His heavy eyes drooped. 'Not like you, they don't, Anna Delane. No woman has ever lit up for me the way you do. No woman ever will. You made me so angry,' he said contemplatively, looking at her from his weary pose against the pillows. 'Denying what was happening. I thought you a hypocrite. When I caught you with the bracelet I was almost glad, you know. Furious, but glad.' His eyes drooped even more. 'It gave me the leverage I needed.'

'Gave you the chance to blackmail me into bed!' she flashed back.

'Well, I wasn't going to let you go to jail, was I?' he riposted. 'Not when I wanted you so much. And when I knew, *knew* you wanted me too. Whatever you said or did! And you did want me, Anna. You wanted me every night, every time.'

She jumped to her feet. How could he make her so angry, so fast?

'You didn't give me any *choice*!' she exclaimed seethingly.

'No,' he said smugly. 'I didn't, did I? But—' his expression changed '—I could never get you to purr out of bed. You wouldn't, would you, Anna Delane?' He sighed. 'You're a hard case, *yineka mou*, and if I had any sense at all I'd send you packing on the first plane back to London. Coach class,' he said darkly. His voice changed again. 'But I'm damned if I got myself shot full of holes just to lose you now. Not when I've finally got you being nice to me. And, speaking of being shot full of holes…' Yet again his voice changed, hardened, his eyes flashing—the familiar, imperious Leo. 'I need the truth about the bracelet, Anna—the police will want to talk to both of us, and if my security chief doesn't have a full dossier on your abductors by the time I get out of here he'll be looking for a new job!'

There was no baiting tone in his voice now—it was grim and bleak.

Anna opened her mouth, then closed it again.

She owed Leo the truth. He'd risked his life for her.

But she had to protect Jenny. More than ever now, she had to protect her. But she wanted to tell him the truth so much.

He saw her face working and pressed on.

'Anna—I'm not going to press charges about the bracelet. I got it back—and I got you back. But are you involved in other criminal activities? Are you involved with the likes of the scum who took you and damn near killed you? I need to know.'

The harsh edge in his voice showed her he wanted answers. Yet what he had said had made her expression lighten.

'Do you mean that?' There was an eagerness in her voice that took him aback. 'You won't press charges about the bracelet?'

His eyes narrowed again. 'Yes. Why?'

'Do you promise, Leo? Do you?'

'I just told you—'

Anna took a deep breath.

'It wasn't me who took the bracelet!'

Leo looked at her measuringly. If she had not had the truth to protect her a frisson of fear would have gone through her. His voice was harsh when he spoke.

'Anna, I caught you red-handed—'

She shook her head. Surely, after nearly losing his own life, he would see what had driven Jenny to theft? Dear God, even *she* had not thought Khalil that vicious, sending in rabid, murdering gunmen like that to find her.

She swallowed.

'You caught me trying to *return* the bracelet, not stealing it,' she said. 'But the place was swarming, so I had to keep walking. I was trying to think what to do, where I could leave it so it wouldn't point any finger of suspicion at—'

She fell silent again.

'At...?' prompted Leo. His voice was quiet, dangerously quiet.

She took a breath.

'At Jenny.'

Leo looked at her blankly.

'Jenny?'

'The blonde model; the skinny one!' said Anna, with some of her old asperity.

'That one? The neurotic-looking one? Are you telling me *she* stole the bracelet?' Leo demanded.

'Yes. She took it when the jewels spilt on the floor. She must have slipped it inside her shoe to get it into the changing room. I found her with it in her bedroom and made her see sense! I said I'd get it back and no one would know! But—but you caught me. Red-handed.'

She fell silent, biting her lip.

Emotions were working inside Leo. Strange, strong emotions. He was having difficulty controlling them. But he had to. It was essential that he did.

In his head, the world was turning upside down.

'You never stole the bracelet? You were covering for the other model?' His voice was flat.

Anna nodded dumbly.

'And you took the rap for it.' His eyes flashed suddenly. 'My God, you let me go on thinking you a thief,' he said wrathfully.

'I had to!' Anna cried. 'I couldn't let Jenny be blamed. Oh, God, Leo, she's in so much trouble already.'

'She makes a habit of stealing?' jibed Leo harshly. He seemed angry—far angrier than Anna had thought he would be when she told him the truth.

'No! I told you—she was desperate, terrified. It was just an impulse thing—opportunistic. Oh, God, Leo, she needs money to hide—and even I didn't know just how badly she needs to hide. Those gunmen weren't after me—they were after *her*. They thought I knew where she was—I told them I didn't know, but they didn't believe me. They were going to torture me to make me talk. And if they find her they'll—'

Her voice broke off, high with fright.

'Why are they after her?' Leo's voice was grim.

Anna took a sharp, painful inhalation of breath.

'She had an affair with some rich sheikh. I warned her not to. I warned her. But the idiot just went ahead anyway—and now he's trying to find her. So she's got to go into hiding. I know it sounds insane, but it's true, Leo. Look—she's *right* to be terrified. Those gunmen were killers.'

He was just lying there, looking at her. His eyes were still dark with anger.

'Leo.' She bit her lip. 'Please, *please* don't be angry—she isn't really a thief. Not really. She was just so frightened—'

'I'm not angry with Jenny,' he said in a flat voice.

She looked at him anxiously.

'If you're angry with me, I accept it. I lied to you, and covered up the truth. And I'm sorry—I really, really am. But I had to protect Jenny—'

A burst of staccato Greek came from Leo. His dark eyes glittered.

'*Christos*, it's *me* I'm angry with. For being stupid enough to let you get away with fooling me that you were a thief. I was so convinced about you. It tied in with everything I thought about you. Oh, God, Anna, it made me such a brute to you—I can't bear to think of it. And all the time—'

Remorse and guilt shot through his eyes. 'And even when I thought the worst you were getting to me. I kept thinking it was just sex, but it was so much more—so much more. And that day we spent together, when you were nice to me—oh, God, that really started to open my eyes to what was happening to me. And then you turned me down again, as if I were nothing to you—nothing at all. I was so angry with you—angry that you were calling me things I knew were true about me and didn't want to hear! Then, when I heard you'd been abducted...'

He fell silent, and she saw remembered fear stark in his eyes.

Then they flashed again. But something in them seemed lighter. Brighter. 'Damn you, Anna Delane. What I've gone through for you. I had you pegged as a troublemaker—and you are.'

'What do you mean, a troublemaker?' she demanded indignantly.

His eyes were glinting. The harshness had gone, quite gone.

'Oh, you're a troublemaker, all right, Anna Delane. I knew that from the first moment I saw you, lashing out at that jerk Embrutti. Quoting your contract at him. And it went on, didn't it? Thinking you knew better than me about not wearing all the damn Levantsky diamonds at once. Let alone not even *caring* that they were the Levantsky diamonds. And as for your *pièce de résistance*—turning virtuous on me at the last possible moment and slinging me out of your room as if I were some kind of animal in rut. *Thee mou*, what do you call that except a troublemaker?'

She bridled. 'Just because I stand up for myself you call me a troublemaker? That is just so bloody typical! I said you were spoilt and arrogant, but I let you off lightly. You're the most—'

But what he was the most Leo never heard. Because he simply grabbed her hand, hauled her down against him, and kissed her.

It silenced her completely.

For a considerable length of time.

And when, at length, Leo released her, he cupped her cheek.

'Once a month,' he said to her, gazing into her eyes, which were not flashing or glinting now, but simply glowing with a light that had never been in them in her life before, 'on a Friday evening, for one hour, *yineka mou*, you can yell insults at me. For the rest of the time...' he brushed her mouth caressingly with his '...you purr. You purr for me, Anna Delane, because I am the only man who can make you purr, and you are so very, very good at it. You'll purr for me in bed and out, and you will be very, very happy. And so will I,' he added.

She tried to pull away, but he wouldn't let her. She didn't try again. It might hurt his wounds. Wounds he had taken for her sake—to save her life.

So she just lay there in the crook of his arm.

It felt a good place to be.

A very good place.

'You see,' he said, smoothing her hair, 'you're doing it already—aren't you, *yineka mou*. Purring away in my arms.'

She eyeballed him suspiciously. 'What's *yineka mou* mean? Troublemaker in Greek?' she demanded.

He gave a wry smile, his eyes softening.

'Truer than you know, Anna Delane. It means *my woman*—and you *are* my woman. For the rest of our lives you are going to look after me, and cosset me, and do everything you can to please me and— Ouch!' He looked at her, outrage in his face. 'I took bullets for you, woman. And, besides, I hadn't finished.'

He laid a hand against her cheek, gazing into her green, green eyes. 'For the rest of our lives I am going to look after you and keep you safe—from psycho gunmen, from anything and everything—and I'm going to cosset you and cherish you and take care of you and buy you everything I want to buy you—including cups of coffee, and all the jewellery you don't want—and I'm going to do everything I can to please you and—'

He broke off, eyeing her again sternly.

'Why does the prospect of that reduce you to tears?'

It was hard to explain to a man who asked stupid questions, so Anna didn't. She just went on crying.

Leo's arm tightened around her.

'You're getting my bandages wet,' he complained.

She went on sobbing.

There was a low knock on the door, and then it opened. The doctor standing on the threshold stopped. Anna jerked upright, face swollen, eyes bleary, nose running.

'*Tsk, tsk,* I told her you needed to see a beautiful face when you surfaced,' the doctor told Leo, shaking his head.

'I know,' agreed Leo. 'She looks awful, doesn't she? Fortunately, I love her, and she loves me, so it's all right.' He looked back at Anna. 'You do love me, don't you, *yineka mou*?' he asked conversationally.

'Yes!' wailed Anna, and burst into tears again.

EPILOGUE

'WHAT would you say to having our wedding right here on the island?' Leo asked Anna as they walked along the beach towards the villa, barefoot in the silvery sand.

He'd been out of hospital for a week now, and though his gait was slower than normal he was well on the way to a full recovery. And every day, and every night, Anna gave thanks to all the powers that be for his safety. She loved him so much she thought her heart would overflow and burst. She cherished him and fussed over him and cosseted him.

It was a daily miracle to her that he had forgiven her for nearly getting him killed, for lying to him about having stolen the rubies, for having so stupidly, idiotically, kept on denying that he had only to touch her to melt every bone in her body. And he kept feeling so bad about the way he had treated her when he'd thought her a thief—so completely different from the way he was treating her now. Cosseting her as if she were made of porcelain. Cherishing her and fussing over her, day and night, all the time. Desperate to undo the way he'd treated her.

But now, as he spoke about a wedding, she halted, staring at him.

'Wedding?' she echoed.

'It's the usual way to get married,' he said.

'Married?' she echoed again. She swallowed. 'I—I didn't know you were thinking of marrying me.'

It was his turn to stare. 'You have some objection?' he posed. She could hear the slightest, just the slightest, edge in his voice.

Her expression was troubled. 'Leo, I know what you think

181

about women wanting to marry rich men—you think they're gold-diggers, trying to trap them.'

This time it was her voice that had an edge in it.

'*Thee mou*, of course I don't think that of you! No gold-digger gives a man as hard a time as you gave me!' He shook his head in sorry memory. 'So, any more objections, *matias mou*?'

But her expression stayed troubled, despite the lightness of his tone.

'Leo—we come from very different worlds. I was brought up in a two-up, two-down next to the gasworks. Whereas you—'

He placed his hands on her shoulders. 'So now you think me a snob, do you?' He sighed. 'Anna, my family fled Turkey in the 1920s with nothing. They lived in the slums of Athens for years. It was my late grandfather and my father who made the Makarios fortune—it's all new money.'

'But there's so *much* of it!' she wailed. 'And you keep making more!'

He gave a laugh and dropped his hands.

'Anna Delane, you're the only woman I know who'd worry about that.' He replaced his hands on her shoulders and looked at her, the expression in his eyes serious now. 'If you're worried I'm going to be the kind of husband who spends all his time in the office, obsessed with making money, you couldn't be more wrong.' His dark eyes searched hers. 'I've got enough, more than enough, for the rest of my life—and for our children and their children. I want to be there for my children—our children—as my parents were not for me. So I'm not wasting any more of my life getting and spending—I've got two holes in my chest to remind me that life isn't for ever.'

Anna clutched at his arms, her eyes stricken.

'Oh, God, Leo. I'm so sorry for—'

He placed a hand over her mouth.

'I cannot believe,' he told her, 'that I used to have fantasies about you saying sorry to me. It's the biggest bore in the world!'

She flushed and pushed his hand away.

'But it's all my fault that you—'

He lowered his mouth and kissed her.

'There's just no stopping you, is there?' he asked rhetorically.

'No,' she said.

And kissed him back.

Then, reluctantly, she drew away.

'Leo, I still don't think you should marry me. We could just—well, you know.'

'Live in sin?' His voice was wryly caustic.

'Yes. You see…' She gazed up at him earnestly, her eyes troubled. 'None of this was meant to happen, was it? You only really wanted a night with me—maybe one or two, whatever else any other woman you went after got. It was only because you wanted your pound of flesh after the stupid rubies, and then all that nightmare with the gunmen, and you nearly dying, and—well, all that stuff. Otherwise it would have been over ages ago. I think we're really still in post-traumatic shock—well, you mainly, I guess—and it's making you a bit doolalley. Thinking about weddings and stuff like that. If you waited a few weeks you'd be back to normal again, I'm sure.'

Leo had taken a step backwards. An expression of outrage was gathering strength on his features.

'I have taken,' he said grimly, 'everything I am going to take from you, Anna Delane. You have been absolutely nothing but trouble since I laid eyes on you. But this—this is too much. You actually dare to stand there and look me in the eyes and tell me I must be insane to want to marry you. Good God, woman,' he roared, 'I love you! Do you understand? Yes, I was a fool, a total idiot, thinking it was just sex I wanted. But I've wised up now. It took a couple of bullets to wise me up, but I have. And so have you. Now we both know it's love, not just sex. So from now on that's what we both do. *Love each other.* For ever. All our lives. You see that sun out there, Anna Delane? It shines out of me. Understand? You'd better because I can tell you it damn well shines out of you. Now—' he heaved a big breath '—I don't want to hear any more of this. Understand?'

'Yes, but I—'

He silenced her with a kiss.

'Stop arguing,' he told her.

'But I—'

'Stop—' he kissed her '—arguing.'

When she surfaced, after a long, long time, she gazed up at him. He was right, damn it, she thought.

The sun really did shine out of him. It was infuriating. But it was true.

He read her expression, eyes twining with hers.

'It's the same for me, Anna,' he told her softly. 'It really, really is.'

She went on gazing up at him adoringly.

Leo let her do it, and did it back, because he was helpless, quite helpless to do otherwise—all his life. For ever.

A stray memory flickered in his brain. The redhead at the Schloss, gazing adoringly up at his cousin. Markos ought to marry her, he thought. He must remember to tell him so. He would lend the girl the Levantsky emeralds for her wedding day.

And speaking of the Levantsky jewels...

'Don't move.'

'I can't anyway!'

'Good.'

Leo stood back, surveying his handiwork.

'Two last pieces.'

He dipped his hand into the almost empty crystal bowl. He picked up a pair of sapphire earrings and carefully arranged them symmetrically.

Then he surveyed his handiwork once more.

'Perfect,' he said.

He reached for the camera.

'Are you sure? I don't want anything showing that shouldn't!'

'You have my word.'

'OK—well, go on, then. Get it over and done with!'

Leo looked disapprovingly down at her.

'You really have no soul, have you?'

'I've got a stiff back, an itch behind my knee, a clasp is sticking into me somewhere sensitive, and if I sneeze, Leo Makarios, you are going to have a roomful of flying jewellery!'

'Don't even think of it, Kyria Makarios,' he said, and started snapping.

'I must be mad,' muttered Leo's brand-new wife.

'Just besotted,' said Anna's brand-new husband.

He clicked away again.

'OK, darling—give me sexy!' he instructed.

'Stuff off,' growled Anna.

'Pouting and sulky—just as good,' returned Leo.

'You're a pervert, you know that? Taking photos like this!'

'It's a one-off private art show, my beloved. Indulge me. You'll never let me do this again, will you?'

'Too damn right,' she growled.

He lowered his camera.

'Anna—if you could see yourself now you would understand. You simply look—unbelievable.'

His eyes swept over her lying in his bed, her naked body covered in jewels.

He lifted his hand helplessly.

'You outshine every one of them,' he said softly. 'And all of them together.'

'They're just crystals, Leo.'

He looked down at her, at her glittering rainbow body.

'And you are just a woman—but you are *my* woman, the most precious in the world to me. And if I lost you my life would end.'

Slowly, he raised the camera, and took one last picture.

Then he put the camera aside and came towards her.

'And do you know the best, the very best, part of this, my adored bride on her wedding night? This,' he told her.

Carefully he lifted up a diamond ring from her navel and slipped it inside the crystal bowl.

'This,' he said, and removed a sapphire collar from where it lay around her arm.

'This,' he said, lifting a ruby tiara from where it circled her left breast.

It took him a long, long time to remove them all.

Until at last only the necklace of diamonds was left, cascading from her throat.

'That stays,' said Leo.

He bent over to kiss her, long and languorously.

Anna's eyes gleamed. 'Don't you want me to wear the whole *parure*?' she asked.

Leo frowned disapprovingly. 'That would be vulgar,' he told her loftily.

Her mouth pressed together. 'Leo Makarios, you are the most—'

'I know.' He smiled with insufferable self-satisfaction, and grazed one bare, beautiful breast with his velvet lips. 'The most irresistible man you've ever met.'

Anna locked her arms around his neck and dragged him down to her. 'Yes! Damn it!' she said.

A MISTRESS FOR
THE TAKING

BY
ANNIE WEST

Annie West spent her childhood with her nose between the covers of a book – a habit she retains. After years preparing government reports and official correspondence she decided to write something she *really* enjoys. And there's nothing she loves more than a great romance. Despite her office-bound past she has managed a few interesting moments – including a marriage offer with the promise of a herd of camels to sweeten the contract. She is happily married to her ever-patient husband (who has never owned a dromedary). They live with their two children amongst the tall eucalypts at beautiful Lake Macquarie, on Australia's east coast. You can e-mail Annie at www.annie-west. com or write to her at PO Box 1041, Warners Bay, NSW 2282, Australia.

Look for a new Modern™ romance from Annie West in the New Year.

To Claire, Andrew and Geoff —
for your inexhaustible patience and support.
To Joanie for the encouragement. To VGs for believing
(and re-reading). And to the superlative Karen — where
would I be without you? Thank you all.

CHAPTER ONE

RONAN CARLISLE scanned the glamorous crowd filling the hotel reception room. A snake like Wakefield couldn't have this many friends.

Yet there were always people wanting to get close to the rich and powerful. Ronan had no time for sycophants himself, but then he didn't have Wakefield's need for fawning admiration.

He glanced past the Sydney Harbour view to where Wakefield preened amongst his cronies. The sight made him want to plant his fist in the man's smarmy face. But that would only bring temporary satisfaction.

Soon, very soon now, Wakefield would get his just desserts. Ronan would make sure of it.

He felt a swell of savage anticipation. Tonight he'd let slip a hint as to his next major commercial move. No doubt by morning Wakefield would be eager to follow suit. And that was when Ronan would bring him down. It was simple. It was ruthless. And it was long overdue.

Ronan shrugged his shoulders free of their stiffening tension and turned to leave. But something in the colourful, noisy room caught his attention. *Someone.*

Over the artistically coiffed heads he saw her move away from the entrance to plunge into the crowd. She was alone, starkly dressed among the throng of decorative trophy wives and well-fed executives. A woman with a purpose, he decided, as she carved a path through the party. It was there in her glittering dark eyes, in the jut of her chin, in her palpable aura of determination.

She paused to ask a question, then changed direction. Towards Wakefield.

In that moment Ronan decided he'd stay a little longer.

Instinct told him the party was about to get a whole lot more interesting.

Marina took a deep breath and forged on. Triumph warred with fear as she neared her goal, and her heart thumped a telltale double beat. Her palms were damp, but she resisted the impulse to wipe them down her skirt, just as she ignored her trembling knees and the nervous roiling in her stomach.

You can do this, Marina. You have to do it.

It's your last chance.

She almost wished she'd grabbed a glass of Dutch courage from the waiter. But she needed all her wits, not to mention luck, for this confrontation. Failure was a luxury she couldn't afford. Not when her whole future and her family's depended on it.

So she pushed her way through the crowd, as out of place as a household tabby cat among a coven of pampered Persian thoroughbreds. She felt curious eyes on her and lifted her chin a notch. She had important business with Charles Wakefield and nothing, not his evasion tactics nor her own trepidation, would stop her this time. Previously, his minders had stonewalled, pretending he was too busy to see her. But tonight he'd have no choice!

She was almost at the windows when her skin prickled.

She raised her eyes and stumbled to a halt, ensnared by an intense indigo gaze that seemed to blaze straight past her protective barriers and delve into her inner fears. Her throat dried as she stared up into the face of the man who stood head and shoulders above the crowd.

A stranger. She'd never seen him before. And she knew from the press cuttings that he wasn't Wakefield. But his unblinking scrutiny held her motionless, confused.

The party hubbub faded, replaced by the heavy beat of her pulse, loud in her ears. And still she couldn't look away from that compelling stare.

His was a stark face, hard and intriguing. Beyond handsome. His height and the breadth of his shoulders signalled pure masculinity. But, more than that, she was mesmerised by the barely leashed tension in him, as if he were poised for action.

Potent. Vital. Commanding. The words tumbled through her brain as she swallowed hard and fought against the swirl of heat, heavy and low, that rippled through her.

Then there was a shout of laughter, someone jostled her, and a movement ahead revealed her quarry.

Wakefield stood by the windows, smiling confidently. He looked exactly what he was: one of Australia's wealthiest men, scion of a famous business dynasty.

This was her chance. She had to concentrate on her mission, on Wakefield. Yet she didn't move. She stared at him, but it was the presence of the dark-haired man looming nearby that filled her mind. She felt his eyes on her still, and her skin heated with sizzling awareness.

She resisted the temptation to turn her head and meet his look again. She couldn't let herself be sidetracked. Not now.

Taking a deep breath, she marched over to Wakefield, the man who'd ripped her world apart.

He was shorter than she'd imagined, barely her height. But he had a smile like a crocodile. A shudder of apprehension slithered down her spine at the sight of it.

'Mr Wakefield.'

Her voice was too strident, loud enough to make all eyes fix on her. Heat flared in her cheeks as conversation around them stalled. At the same time the stranger moved forward into her line of sight. A group of women gathered close, welcoming him.

Annoyed that she'd even noticed, Marina dragged her attention back to Wakefield.

His eyes flicked over her, cataloguing the plain suit, flat shoes and neat hair. His brows rose, and she stiffened at the dismissal she read in his face. She'd had a lifetime to get used to the fact that looks weren't everything, and she'd be damned if she'd let him judge her like that.

'I'm Marina Lucchesi, Mr Wakefield.' She plastered on a

smile and held out her hand. If her face felt stiff and the smile forced, it was the best she could do.

Recognition flared in his eyes. Then it was gone, lost in the give-nothing-away blandness of polite enquiry.

'Ms...Lucchesi.' His grin made her long to snatch her hand away. 'Welcome to my little celebration.' His handshake was brief. 'Do you work for me?'

Before she could answer he continued. 'If it's a message from the office, sweetheart, you'd better talk to my assistant.' He half turned. 'Damien! Take the message.'

'No, Mr Wakefield, I'm not an employee.' Her voice betrayed her anger, but she didn't care. He knew exactly who she was. 'But I am here on business. I was hoping to arrange a private meeting with you.'

'Ah. Damien.' He turned to the sleek young man who'd appeared beside him. 'Ms Lucchero wants an appointment. Organise something for her. Perhaps with recruitment.'

'It's *Lucchesi*, Mr Wakefield. Marina Lucchesi.' She stepped forward, deliberately crowding his personal space, and felt a jab of satisfaction as she got his full attention. 'I'm sure you remember the name. After all, you know my brother, Sebastian.'

Know him well enough to strip him of everything he owns. And a few things he doesn't own as well.

She didn't say it out loud, but the knowledge pulsed between them, raw and undeniable. His eyes widened and Marina waited, poised for his inevitable acknowledgement.

But it didn't come.

'I'm sorry, Ms...*Lucchesi,* but I don't recall. I meet so many people.' He spread his hands and looked around his entourage. 'Very few of them make an impact on me.'

Marina ignored the stifled titters and kept her gaze fixed on her nemesis. A wash of embarrassment scalded her cheeks and throat. It was the final straw.

Fury such as she'd never experienced surged through her, stiffening every sinew in her body. She'd expected stonewalling, murmurs of regret or, if she were lucky, a reluctant agreement to meet and discuss the situation. Naïve as she was, she'd actually believed she'd be able to reason with the man. Bargain for more time.

She hadn't expected scorn. Not from someone who had nothing to gain from humiliating her.

'You surprise me, Mr Wakefield.' Her voice was harsh and unsteady, but no way would she back down now. He might have her brother's measure, but he was about to find out she was a completely different proposition.

She pitched her voice to carry. 'Surely you should remember the name of the man whose company you stole.'

The whispering voices ceased abruptly and a tense hush fell. Marina felt her heartbeat thrum heavily once, twice, three times, before she continued.

'Or is that such a common occurrence you don't recall those details either?' She stared straight into his wrathful eyes.

The frozen silence lengthened as Wakefield's companions leaned closer. A decisive movement to Marina's left caught her attention and she looked up.

And up. Into the deepest, most amazing eyes she'd ever seen. Ink-blue and fringed with long black lashes, those same eyes had held her in thrall only minutes before. Now they sizzled with a dangerous heat.

Up close, the man was stunning. It wasn't just the aura of power he wore like a mantle, or the innate authority of a height well over six feet. It was the combination of strongly angled cheekbones, sharply defined jaw, authoritarian nose and slashing dark eyebrows. No wonder the women clustered so close around him.

Abruptly the stranger moved. He broke eye contact, inserting himself between her and the avid onlookers, murmuring something that made them reluctantly step away. He made the manoeuvre seem deceptively easy.

A minder of Wakefield's, she decided, still dazed by the inexplicable fizz of reaction that bubbled through her veins. She'd never felt anything like it before. And then to discover he worked for her enemy, was a yes-man to Charles Wakefield… The moment shattered in ridiculous disappointment.

Wakefield found his voice again, his smooth tone laced with

a venom that demanded all her attention. She turned back to face the ire of the man she'd just accused.

'I'm afraid, Ms Lucchesi, you're completely in error.' His eyes iced over and she shivered. 'You shouldn't make such accusations when you don't know the facts.' He lowered his voice. 'That's slander, sweetheart. And it can be a costly mistake.'

A cold, hard knot of fear plummeted through her stomach and she sucked in a gasping breath. What more did this man want? Blood? Hadn't he taken enough?

Dimly she realised that the tall bodyguard and Wakefield's assistant had moved the onlookers aside. Nearby people laughed and gossiped. But here, in this small circle of quiet, she stood alone. Face to face with the man who'd destroyed her brother's future and her own.

'I see you're having second thoughts about your accusation.' Those wintry eyes regarded her steadily, and she read satisfaction in the slight curve of his mouth.

It was the look of a man who knew he'd won.

What the hell! He couldn't take anything else from her. There was nothing left to steal.

'No,' she responded. 'No second thoughts. You and I both know it's true. What else would you call duping an innocent out of his inheritance?'

To Marina's surprise, Wakefield cast a frowning glance at the imposing man beside them. Did he have qualms about airing his dirty linen in front of his staff? Surely his underlings were used to cleaning up the mess left behind by his dubious business practices?

'Ms Lucchesi.' Wakefield spread his hands and offered the semblance of a smile. If it weren't for his eyes, as cold as a reptile's, she might have been taken in by it. 'There's obviously been a misunderstanding,' he continued. 'Your brother hasn't told you everything.'

'So you admit to knowing Sebastian?'

He shrugged. 'I remember him now. A very…impetuous young man. But hardly an innocent.'

Not by the time you got your claws into him, she thought.

'And you call it legitimate business practice to steal a prosperous company the way you did?'

She saw his sidelong look at the man to his right.

'Come, come, Ms Lucchesi. Marina. It was hardly theft.'

He was denying it, damn him. Brazening it out. Marina clenched her fists at her sides so no one would see how they shook. She'd never hit anyone in her life. But now, face to face with this slick playboy, she was so close.

'You say it's normal commercial practice,' she asked in a voice no longer her own, 'to get a twenty-one-year-old so drunk he doesn't know what he's doing? Then get him to sign your legal documents?'

For a single shocked moment no one spoke or moved. Even the two men flanking Wakefield seemed to stiffen. Then he spoke, as smoothly and patiently as if reasoning with a child. 'Your brother obviously knew you'd be upset and didn't give you the full picture.'

'That's a lie! I know exactly what happened and—'

A deep voice interrupted before she could get into her stride. 'Surely this isn't the time or the place, Charles? Why not take this somewhere more discreet?' It was the bodyguard who spoke and, despite her anger, Marina couldn't ignore the responsive shimmer of deep-seated excitement as his words seemed to roll across her skin.

Wakefield scowled. 'And give this lunatic accusation any more credibility? Thanks for the suggestion, but I can take care of my own business.'

'Like you've taken care of Ms Lucchesi's?' came the dry response.

Marina stared at the man who dared to interrupt the tycoon. One of his dark eyebrows rose in a slashing line of enquiry as he stared down at his boss. His square jaw was tensed but his tone had been mild. He didn't seem at all fazed by the fact that he'd just taken issue with his furious employer.

Whoever the guy was, he didn't scare easily. Charles Wakefield had looked at her with dislike. But it was nothing compared to the naked hatred in his eyes as he glared at the man beside them.

'I'll thank you to keep out of this, Carlisle. The woman's misguided, but I can handle it.' He looked over Marina's shoulder, not even sparing her a glance. 'Ah, here's the chief of security now.'

'No need for that,' said the man, Carlisle. 'I'll escort Ms Lucchesi.'

Like hell he would! She still had plenty more to say to Charles Wonderboy Wakefield.

'No way! I'm not finished yet.' Incensed, she glared up at the man beside her. 'If you think you can keep me quiet about what he's done you're dead wrong.'

Slowly he shook his head, and she thought she saw understanding in his eyes. Maybe he didn't always like doing his job, but that wouldn't stop him performing his duty. That much was obvious from his determined face and the implacable set of his broad shoulders.

'It's not a matter of keeping you quiet,' he said, dropping his voice and moving close so that the heat of his body radiated against hers. 'You can't win this now. Not here, like this.'

There was a bustle of movement and Marina tore her gaze away to take in the group of thickset men in dark suits that closed in to circle them. Charles Wakefield was already talking in an undertone to their leader.

'Official security,' said the man beside her, nodding at the newcomers, who seemed all brawn and muscle. 'You've got a choice now. You can let them frogmarch you out of here as an intruder. They'll probably hold you till the police come to investigate Wakefield's complaint that you're trespassing or disturbing the peace.'

He paused, his gaze holding hers.

'Or you can leave with me.'

As if she could trust him. He was Wakefield's man. And, more than that, her sixth sense warned her not to take him at face value. He was up to something.

Outraged, Marina spun round, but another dark suit blocked her view. Piggy little eyes stared back blankly at her from a face that gave nothing away.

of her accusations. Then, as the throng pressed close and she saw
the rampant speculation on so many female faces, she realised
the crowd's interest centred on the man beside her.

Several people spoke to him, faces eager. And each time she
heard the deep tones of his reply. But he didn't stop till his way
was blocked by a man, vaguely familiar, with an air of authority. Her companion introduced her, so she stretched her lips in a
smile and held out her hand. But their short conversation was a
blur, muted by the throb of pain passing through her aching
body. Then they were on their way again, step by slow step
towards the exit.

Through the doors and into the foyer, where the relative
silence was like a comforting blanket. Almost as welcome as
finding it deserted. No bodyguards. No police. Relief was a
buzzing hum in her ears.

She stumbled to a halt and took a long, slow breath, combat-
ing her physical pain and the sudden renewal of that dreadful
roiling in her stomach. Reaction, that was what it was, after that
horrible scene.

'Here.' Carlisle's voice was peremptory as he ushered her to
a low divan tucked against the wall.

'Thanks. I'm fine now.' She tried to disengage herself from
his hold.

'You don't look it,' he responded, watching her carefully.
'You look like you're about to fall down.'

She gave up trying to push his arm away and stared back at
him. 'Well, I'm a lot tougher than I look,' she said, with a spark
of her old self.

Deep blue eyes stared straight back, and she had the unnerving sensation he could see everything she tried so hard to hide.
She swallowed convulsively and looked away.

'Please let me go.' To her surprise his arm dropped away immediately, making her shiver again, this time at the loss of his
body heat. 'Thanks for your help. I appreciate it. But I can look
after myself from here.'

Still he didn't leave, but stood watching her, head tilted
slightly, as if considering her words.

And then there was no time for dissembling. With more haste than grace she collapsed abruptly onto the cushioned sofa as her knees gave way.

'Don't move,' he ordered, as he spun on his foot and strode back into the reception room.

As if she could.

She grimaced, wondering how on earth she was going to get out of here under her own steam. She let her head fall back on the upholstery and felt her exhausted muscles relax.

'Here, drink this.' A hand, enveloping and warm, took hers and curled it round a cold glass.

'Thanks, but I can manage *that* all by myself.' There was nothing wrong with her hands, just her legs. She took the glass and sipped iced water, ignoring his harsh expression as he hunkered beside her.

Immediately she regretted her spurt of temper. It wasn't his fault she'd wrecked her chance to make Wakefield see reason. Or that she was as weak as a kitten. And he *had* stuck up for her back there with his boss.

'I'm sorry,' she said. 'You've been great, really.' She sighed, 'It's just—'

'Don't worry about it,' he cut in, his tone impatient.

His gaze held hers, and she wondered what a man like him was doing working as hired muscle for Charles Wakefield. His take-charge attitude and the intelligence she read in those stunning eyes seemed to fit him for so much more.

'You'll be all right if I leave you?' He cut across her thoughts as he stood up to loom over her, making her even more aware of her own physical weakness.

'Of course. I'll just catch my breath.'

He nodded brusquely and turned away, pulling a mobile phone from his pocket as he headed across the lobby.

Idiotically, she was disappointed he'd taken her so readily at her word. She'd insisted on being left alone, but now she felt bereft.

Rather than watch him return to his post, she shut her eyes, trying to work out how she'd get home. She'd come by bus, several of them. Did she have enough cash for the luxury of a cab? If not, she was in trouble. She didn't have the strength to walk four blocks to the bus stop.

She sighed and leaned back against the cushions, weary beyond belief. Now her head was thumping too. Tension, she decided. And the way she'd scraped her hair back from her face didn't help. She reached up, pulling out the pins that kept up her unruly hair. No matter now if she looked like a wild woman. She'd blown her chances with Wakefield—the one she'd wanted to impress.

She groaned at the memory of that disaster, and knew she had to get away. Now. She slid closer to the edge of the sofa, ignoring the way her skirt rode up in her haste.

Psyching herself for the effort to stand, Marina opened her eyes. And caught her breath at the sight of the man standing in front of her.

It was him, Carlisle, frozen as if in mid-stride on his return. For the first time she saw him whole, not as a shoulder to lean against or a pair of probing eyes. And what she saw made her stare, transfixed.

He had *it*. Sex appeal, animal magnetism—whatever you wanted to call it. Something more vital and compelling than mere good looks. And infinitely more dangerous. Especially when he looked at her like that.

Heat prickled as her skin seemed to contract across her. The sensation made her intimately aware of all those completely feminine places that responded immediately to the promise of such a man.

And right now his look *was* a promise. All masculine intent and blazing energy that made the air between them crackle with electricity.

Her shallow breath stalled in her throat even as her heartbeat accelerated into overdrive.

Then, as suddenly as if it had never been, his expression changed, morphing into hard, unreadable lines. She blinked. Was she seeing things, or had that scorching look been real?

He returned her gaze steadily, hiding nothing, and she felt the guilty heat creep up her neck, as if he'd been able to read her crazy thoughts.

Yeah, sure. As if a man like him would look at her that way. Marina Lucchesi, the least glamorous woman she knew. Too tall, too buxom, too outspoken Marina. She dropped her gaze to the empty glass cradled in her hands.

'Marina.' Reluctantly she looked up. He stood over her, brows together and legs planted apart. Again she felt the flood of physical awareness that made her tremble. 'It's time to go. I'll take you home.'

'And why would you want to do that?' she asked, still breathless.

His lips tilted up in a smile that disturbed rather than reassured. 'Because I'm the man who can get you what you want—Charles Wakefield's head on a platter.'

CHAPTER TWO

A KNIGHT in shining armour, come to slay the dragon and rescue the damsel in distress?

Yeah, right.

Marina stared back at him, wondering whether she'd developed a hearing problem. Or maybe it had been a double vodka and not mineral water in the glass he'd given her.

One thing was for sure—no man, other than her father, had ever offered to solve her problems. And she was old enough to know it was never going to happen again.

'I don't believe you,' she said flatly. 'No one's got that much power.'

Something shifted in his expression. Nothing she could put her finger on. But the effect was clear—creating a look of pure arrogance. One that would have done Charles Wakefield justice. It was enough to make her shiver again.

'You think not?' he murmured eventually. 'Perhaps you're right. Decapitation might be too drastic. Maybe we could settle for him getting his just desserts.' And still there wasn't so much as a flicker of humour on his face.

'And pigs might fly,' Marina muttered.

She ignored his outstretched arm and reached over to place the empty glass on a low table. Then she planted both hands on the edge of the sofa and levered herself up.

Immediately he put a hand to her elbow, steadying her. But it wasn't enough, not with the way her knees shook. In one decisive movement he scooped her off her feet and gathered her close.

It happened so fast, shock held her speechless for several seconds. His eyes locked with hers. Dimly she registered the hard heat of his body against hers, the seductive aura of safety, the temptation just to let go.

'What do you think you're doing?' she breathed, all too aware of the reception in the next room. 'Put me down!'

'Why? So you can fall at my feet? I'm not that desperate for female adulation, thanks.'

All the fear and hate and anger she'd felt towards Charles Wakefield coalesced instantly and unreasonably into a blaze of fury directed at this new tormentor. Her palm tingled with the barely repressed impulse to smack him on the cheek.

'I said, put me down. Now!'

He didn't move a muscle, simply stood, watching her, as if her weight was no strain at all. While she felt as helpless as a newborn. And ridiculously conspicuous. Any second now someone would come out and see her, slung like a sack of potatoes in his arms. It would be one more humiliating detail in the saga of her defeat.

'I'll yell,' she threatened.

This close, there was no missing the spark of interest in his eyes. 'I thought you wanted to leave with a minimum of fuss,' he countered. 'Or was I wrong? Do you get some sort of turn-on from being the centre of attention?'

She gritted her teeth at the injustice of that remark, fearing if she responded she'd do something stupid like shout.

Meanwhile he looked her over slowly, cataloguing her reaction to his question. Her hands clenched into tight fists, her chin lifted and her chest rose and fell rapidly in her agitation. His gaze paused as she took a deep breath, and instantly heat blossomed and spread through her. She tried to slow her breathing, calm the riot of confused emotions that had tipped her out of control.

Her eyes dropped, following the direction of his, and she saw that her jacket had come undone, revealing her plain white shirt and, through the fine material, the equally plain white bra that covered her ample breasts.

She opened her mouth to say something, anything, but he turned his attention back to her face and the babble of outrage died in her throat.

His eyes looked *hot*. There was no other way to describe them. They seemed to sear her with their intensity, and she blinked, trying to read his expression. But he gave nothing away. Nothing but that odd, compelling flare that made her want to wriggle out of his grasp.

Or curl in closer to his solid strength.

No one had ever held her like this, and she was aware of a myriad of disturbing new sensations. His arms curved round her body and stockinged legs, generating an intimate warmth that both teased and comforted. Her head rested against his shoulder, cheek pressed to the hard plane that sloped down to his massive chest. His own scent, clean and masculine, teased her senses. No heavy manufactured aftershave for this man. Why bother when you had the real thing?

'Well, what's it to be?' he asked, in a deep, soft voice that stirred a swirl of response low inside her. 'Do we go quietly or do you make a scene?'

'Of course I don't want a scene.' She glared at him, furious that he had the upper hand. Furious that she'd just discovered another fatal weakness to add to her list: chocolate, black and white romance movies, speaking her mind, and deep blue eyes that sizzled with promise.

Damn it. She didn't need this now. She just wanted to go home, where she could lick her wounds and regroup.

As if he'd read her mind, he swung round and strode across to the lift. Automatically she reached out and pressed the button.

'Shouldn't you be getting back to the reception?' she asked, trying for a tone of polite interest. As if being cradled in the arms of the sexiest man she'd ever met was no big deal.

'No, I was ready to leave,' he said, watching the numbers above the lift light up as it ascended.

'But don't you need to get back to your work? To Charles Wakefield?'

He looked at her then, one dark eyebrow raised. 'Work for Wakefield? Just who do you think I am?'

The bell pinged above her head and the steel doors slid open with a refined hiss. The mirrored walls of the lift reflected images of the pair of them as he carried her in.

Those images were enough to banish any last shred of Marina's self-confidence. She hung like a broken doll in his arms—skirt hiked up, long legs dangling, jacket askew and, worst of all, her wild tangle of dark hair frothing in all directions.

'You can put me down now,' she urged as the doors slid to, shutting them into the confined space.

'Push the button, would you?' He ignored her request, and when she didn't move to help hefted her closer, so that her face was half buried in the silk of his shirt while he hit the button for the ground floor.

His heart beat strongly somewhere beneath her face, and the scent of him intensified, musky and compelling. Despite her better judgement she breathed deeply, and felt stupidly disappointed when he relaxed his hold a little so she lay back against his arm again.

'Honestly, you can let me go now. I'm perfectly capable of standing.'

'You still haven't answered me.' His eyes locked with hers. 'Who is it you think I am?'

She shrugged with the shoulder that wasn't tucked in against him. 'Aren't you some sort of minder? The way you moved those people away so they couldn't hear...'

Her words petered out as he laughed. It started as a grin, then grew to a rumble in his chest and eventually to a deep, infectious sound that almost made her smile.

'You think I'm one of Charlie's lapdogs?' For the first time since they'd met his expression was uncomplicated and un-guarded. Sheer amusement lit his features and dazzled her. He had the sort of smile that was guaranteed to melt the most level-headed woman in ten seconds flat.

'I wouldn't say lapdog,' she answered, remembering the way he'd put Wakefield on the spot. 'But you sure had his interests in mind. The way you manoeuvred that crowd away was obviously to protect him.'

His smile faded. 'It didn't occur to you that perhaps *you* might have been safer accusing him somewhere private? Didn't you stop to think how he'd react if you confronted him in front of his adoring fans?'

Anger resurfaced at his accusations. Especially since she knew he was right. She should have kept her cool, not lashed out at Wakefield's provocation.

'If I spoke the truth, you mean?'

'Exactly.' His tone held no apology. 'When you deal with a man like Wakefield you need to understand there's a time and a place for open honesty.'

'It sounds like his dubious morality has rubbed off on you,' she accused. 'Is that how you operate? By choosing to be dishonest? I don't know how you stomach working with the man.'

His hooded eyes met her gaze as he let the silence grow between them. And, though he didn't react visibly, something about the increasingly tense atmosphere in the enclosed space made her uneasy, convinced she could sense a barely leashed anger thrumming through his big body.

The doors slid open, but still he didn't respond to her jibe.

Marina didn't know whether to be relieved or dismayed as he stepped out and, without pause, carried her straight across the glossy mosaic floor of the huge foyer. They were in Sydney's most expensive hotel. And as they made their way past a smiling concierge and a couple of curious guests she wished she could simply disappear.

'If you plan on fighting Wakefield, Marina, you'd do well to remember that things aren't always what they seem.' His words were low, for her ears only.

Then they were outside. She felt the warm air brush across her hot cheeks as they left the air-conditioning, and she concentrated on avoiding eye contact with yet another uniformed employee. She needn't have bothered—all his attention was focused on Carlisle.

'Your car's right here, sir.'

'Thanks…Paul.' He read the young man's discreet name tag.

'Here you are, sir, madam.' The employee stepped out under the enormous *porte cochère* and opened the passenger door of a car.

It was a long car, silver and streamlined. Marina didn't know much about the latest models. But you'd have to live on the moon not to realise that this fine beauty had cost more than several times the average annual wage, and was probably one of a kind in Australia.

For some reason the sight of it scared her almost as much as the confrontation with Wakefield.

'I *said* you can put me down, and I mean it,' she whispered fiercely. 'I'm not going anywhere with you. I don't know who you are. And even if I did, I'm okay now. I can make my own way home.'

His answering smile probably looked intimate to any onlooker, but this close Marina could see the anger in Carlisle's eyes. It radiated from him in waves, so sudden and so unmistakable that her own eyes widened.

'By all means don't trust me,' he said as his gaze pinned hers. 'That's probably the most sensible thing you've done all evening.'

And now once more his expression was unreadable, but something there, something unsettling, sent a tickle of apprehension down her spine. She knew without being told that this was a man she didn't want to mess with.

'But,' he continued, 'don't for one minute expect me to let you wander off at this time of night, alone and barely capable of standing, let alone driving.'

'I wasn't going to drive,' she burst out. 'I'm not that stupid.'

'My car can get you home just as safely as any taxi,' he said implacably.

No way was she going to tell him she'd planned to use the buses. It was absolutely none of his business. But at the moment she didn't have the strength to fight it out. She felt as forceful as a rag doll.

'Mr Carlisle? Is everything all right?' asked the youth waiting at the car door.

'*Mr* Carlisle?' Marina repeated. She'd assumed that was his first name.

'That's right,' he said as he strode over to the sports car and carefully lowered her into the embrace of butter-soft moulded leather. 'Ronan Carlisle.'

His smile flashed, devastating despite the dimness of the car's interior. He took her right hand in his. 'A pleasure to meet you, Ms Lucchesi.'

Marina's hand was limp in the hard warmth of his. The brief pressure of his fingers curling around hers sent a tide of sensation tingling across every nerve-ending. But she barely noticed. She was too busy absorbing the truth of his identity.

If the sheer power of his personality and his arrogance in the face of her protests hadn't been sufficient to convince her, this car would have been proof enough. Or the look of hero-worship from the guy who'd opened it for them. And then there'd been the cluster of women crowding around them as they left the reception. She remembered the avid excitement on their faces, the hungry looks.

Marina sagged back into the luxurious leather and tried to make sense of it all.

'Don't faint on me now, Marina.' His voice was a low purr near her ear as he leaned across to snick her seatbelt shut.

'I'm not about to faint!' How dared the man? He must have an ego as big as Charles Wakefield's. 'I'm just tired.' She lifted her chin a fraction and glared into the knowing eyes mere inches from hers. 'And I never said you could take me home.'

His silent laugh was a puff of fresh, warm breath across her cheeks. More intimate than the embrace of his arms about her. She felt again that insidious, melting sensation begin deep inside her.

'Come on, Marina,' he urged, voice grave despite the twinkle of amusement in his eyes. 'Let me take you home. I'd worry all night if I left you to make your own way.'

Staring back at his handsome, determined face, Marina wondered why she'd even bothered to argue. Suddenly exhausted, she gave in to the force of the inevitable.

'Thank you. I'd appreciate it.'

And that was how, still reeling from the debacle with Charles Wakefield, Marina found herself chauffeur-driven home by the most disturbing man she'd ever met.

Ronan Carlisle.

Who also happened to be one of the richest, most powerful businessmen in the country.

CHAPTER THREE

RONAN let the silence lengthen as he buckled his seatbelt and started the car.

He didn't need to look at his passenger to know she'd used her last reserves of strength. Despite her fighting spirit, Marina Lucchesi had almost reached breaking point. The shadows of fatigue under her expressive dark eyes, the uncontrollable tremor that racked her body. The exhaustion etched in the pallor of her face. They all told their story as eloquently as any words could have done.

She wasn't up to dealing with a piranha like Wakefield.

Hell! She was so physically weak she shouldn't be out of bed. The woman had more spirit than sense. And how she'd managed to get past security in the first place to confront Charlie-boy was a mystery.

Easing the car into the street, he stopped at a set of traffic lights and flicked a curious glance at her.

She stared straight ahead, either not seeing or not acknowledging his look. Her shoulders slumped and she bit down hard on her full bottom lip. His gaze lingered a moment on her mouth before he turned his attention back to the street.

Who was she? A virago with a grudge against an ex-lover? Wakefield was a womaniser who played the field. Or was she what she claimed, the sister of an innocent victim of his dirty business tactics? Ronan's gaze narrowed. And why was she in camouflage, wearing that shapeless suit? He'd felt the seductive curves beneath that prim navy outfit and there was no doubt in his mind Marina Lucchesi would be worth much closer investigation.

He'd lay odds no one had spoken to Charles Wakefield like that in a very long time. If ever. Ronan silently applauded her nerve. If the confrontation hadn't been so dangerous for her he would have laughed outright at the look of shock on Wakefield's face.

She'd managed to stun Wakefield into rare silence. And even on the verge of collapse she'd used her sharp mind, and tongue, to keep Ronan at a distance as well, when he'd tried to help her.

She had guts.

And that mouth. She used it like a weapon.

He'd like to see her use it for other things. Those luscious ripe lips, with their natural pout, had to be the most erotic he'd ever seen.

His lower body tightened as his mind lingered on the possibilities.

The lights changed and he slid the car forward. Over the noise of the engine revving he caught another sound. A groan or a sob?

'What is it?' he demanded, shooting her another look.

'Only the usual,' she answered, with obvious sarcasm. 'Wondering how I came to have public arguments with two multimillionaires in one night. It must be some sort of record.'

He smiled. Down, but not out. Marina Lucchesi was some woman.

She sighed. 'Not my usual Friday night.'

'And what *is* your usual Friday night?' He was genuinely interested. She was the most intriguing woman he'd met in a long time.

'Not business launches with the jet-set.'

'Hardly the jet-set,' he countered. 'There were a lot of hardworking people there.'

'And a lot of glamorous ones who'd never worked a day in their lives.'

He let that slide. There'd been the usual hangers-on. The sort who loved a free party.

'You should have told me,' she said after a minute's silence.

'Told you what?'

'Who you are,' she said flatly. 'I feel a complete idiot.'

'I don't see why.' He worked hard at keeping his face, if not his name, out of the press. Unlike Wakefield, he shunned the media hype, enjoying his relative anonymity. He didn't look for or want instant recognition.

But her silence was accusing, not understanding.

'Maybe you're right,' he admitted. 'I could have told you earlier. But it didn't occur to me at first—I was too busy wondering if you were going to slip into a dead faint.'

'And later?' she persisted.

Good question. Why hadn't he told her? Because he'd got such a kick out of their verbal duel? Because he'd been too intrigued by his immediate reaction to her to bring the interlude to a close? The combination of her no-holds-barred attitude and obvious fragility had aroused his protective instinct. And his hormones.

'It was refreshing talking to someone who didn't watch every word they said. Who wasn't worried about making an impression.'

That was an occupational hazard these days.

'You shouldn't beat yourself up about tonight,' he continued, knowing how mentally bruised she must be after the confrontation. 'Why do you think Wakefield was so worried? He couldn't keep you quiet. He knew you had the mettle to make trouble for him.'

She shifted in her seat. 'But it didn't help, did it? He's got away with it and there's nothing I can do. Absolutely nothing.'

Did he imagine a quiver in her voice? He swung the car over to the kerb.

'Why are you stopping?' she asked, turning swiftly as if to get her bearings. Her long hair flared round her and he caught her elusive scent again—warm and fresh as spring sunshine.

'I'm waiting for directions,' he answered. 'I don't know where you live.'

'Oh.' Her lips formed a perfect inviting circle, and it was an effort to force his gaze up to her eyes.

'Head north,' she said. 'Either the bridge or tunnel will be fine. But if you're going in the other direction you could drop me at a taxi rank.'

'I'm on the north shore myself.' He watched her steadily. 'Tell me where you live, then sit back and shut your eyes. You look dead tired.'

She frowned, and he knew it wasn't what she'd wanted to hear. What woman would?

True to form, she straightened her shoulders. Then she pushed her hair back behind her ears, twisted it round and up high in a style that seemed too heavy for her slender neck.

'Damn,' she whispered.

'What is it?'

'No pins,' she mumbled, and let the long tresses fall in a rippling curtain that hid her profile and the over-bright glitter of her eyes.

He felt a surge of protectiveness and almost reached out to touch her. But he guessed it was only pride that held her together right now. She wouldn't thank him for his sympathy.

And he knew instinctively it wasn't only sympathy he wanted to give.

'Give me your address,' he repeated. 'I'll take you home.'

She didn't know what woke her, but suspected it wasn't the car stopping. She sensed they'd been stationary for some time when she opened her eyes and found them parked in her driveway. Then she realised that the movement-activated sensor light at the corner of the house was off, confirming they'd been sitting there for a few minutes at least.

There was no light in the car, and very little from the street at the end of the drive. She could barely make out the man beside her in the gloom. Yet she knew instantly that he was watching her. The intensity of his scrutiny raised goosebumps of awareness across her flesh, bringing it to tingling life.

'You should have woken me,' she said, her voice grating with accusation. For there was something unsettling about his very stillness. And the sensation that he'd been focussed on her so totally, watching her as she slept.

Despite the sultry summer air she shivered, conscious of an unfamiliar expectancy in her shortened breathing and rapid heartbeat.

'We've only just arrived,' he countered, his voice giving nothing away. 'And I didn't think another minute or two's rest would hurt.' He opened his door and she blinked at the blaze from the interior lights.

Then he was out of the car and opening the passenger door, while she fumbled to get her seatbelt undone. She looked up to see him lit by the exterior house lights that had switched on as he moved.

Big, broad across the shoulders and powerful, he loomed over the car. Even his exclusive tailored clothes couldn't conceal the aura of dominance that he projected, his sheer potency. His sleek silk shirt, stylish jacket and dark trousers should have branded him as one of the socialite A-list crowd they'd left behind at the reception. But instead they revealed him for what he was: a man used to command, utterly formidable.

And, to any woman, a danger. Attractive was too bland a descriptor for him. With those strong, sharply defined features he was compelling. And the passion that seemed to lurk in the indentations at the side of his mouth was enough to warn her that she was way out of her league.

Just looking up at him made her heart race.

'Marina?' His brows drew together, then in a single fluid movement he bent to lift her out of the car and tuck her close against his chest.

The heat of his body, the faint male aroma, the strength of his arms were familiar now. Almost welcoming.

She must be out of her mind.

Last time he'd carried her she'd been in shock—almost able to pretend she didn't react to his blatant maleness. But now she couldn't think of anything else. He filled her senses, deluging her awed brain into overload with a new awareness. The firm texture of his jaw when she accidentally brushed it. The way her body fitted so perfectly in his arms. The odd incendiary flare of excitement in the pit of her stomach.

'I can stand, thanks.' But her voice sounded breathless instead of sure. She cursed this stupid feminine response to sheer masculine appeal.

Typically he ignored her, and strode instead to the patio and up the steps towards the door just as easily as if he carried a child. Not a woman a mere couple of inches under six feet.

Hastily she dug out her key and slipped it into the lock. 'Thanks very much.' She looked up at his face, deliberately not meeting those eyes that seemed to see far too much. 'I'm really grateful for the lift. So much better than waiting for a cab,' she babbled.

'My pleasure,' he responded, in a low voice that brushed, like the sensuous silk of his shirt, right across her nerves. But instead of lowering her to her feet, he nudged the door open and stepped inside. Automatically Marina reached out and hit the light switch by the door, illuminating the wide hallway.

'Which way?' he asked as he followed the hall.

'I'm fine now that I'm home,' she countered, wriggling in his arms, as if she could make him release her. 'I can stand by myself.'

'Marina.' He stopped and looked down at her, eyes unfathomable, but with an infinitesimal smile that deepened those tiny grooves beside his mouth. 'You've got nothing to worry about, I promise you. Tonight, all I want is to see you safely tucked up for the night.'

Of course that was all. A man like him would never be interested in someone like her. Even if he were a playboy like Wakefield, who apparently couldn't resist the lure of the chase, she'd have nothing to fear. She wasn't beautiful, or glamorous, or sexy. She didn't even have experience on her side.

He simply felt sorry for her because she'd made a fool of herself in front of Sydney's business elite. And because she couldn't get her damned legs to work properly. That was all.

She didn't want his pity.

Her eyes burned with the glaze of unshed tears. Tears of anger at her failure tonight. At her inability to make Wakefield atone for what he'd done. At the sheer physical exhaustion that had hit again so suddenly. And at the knowledge that this man, this unsettling stranger, had seen her at her most vulnerable.

She tilted her chin and pointed down the hall. 'The third door on the left is mine,' she said, refusing to look at him. His intentions might be charitable, but, selfish as she was in her pain and frustration, she wasn't in the mood right now for anyone's charity.

He paused at the open door and once again she reached round to flick on the switch. Soft lights illuminated the familiar room, with its soothing blues and creams. She almost sighed aloud at the sight of the bed, with its coverlet turned down ready for her.

Every bone in her body ached with tiredness, and she couldn't even summon the energy to be annoyed any more that Ronan Carlisle had ignored her protests and invited himself into her home.

And then he was lowering her onto the bed, as gently as if she was some fragile piece of glass.

She sank back gratefully against the pillows propped at the headboard.

'I'm sorry I snapped at you,' she offered as his gaze took a swift inventory of the room. She saw the way his eyes lingered on the crutches in the corner and the medication on her bedside table. Then he turned to look at her and she hurried on.

'It was churlish of me. And I do appreciate your help. I don't think I could have made it back here by myself.'

He ignored her thanks and asked brusquely, 'There's no one else home? No one to help you?'

Marina bit her lip against the sudden shaft of pain his words evoked. She was tired. She was having trouble holding her emotions in check.

'I live alone,' she said. 'And I'm quite able to take care of myself.'

His frown told her he wasn't convinced, so she added, 'My brother lives ten minutes' drive away,' and gestured to the phone on her beside table. 'If I need anything I can always call him.'

Male that he was, Ronan Carlisle would be satisfied with the idea of a man to look after her. He wouldn't have any idea that it had always been she who'd looked after Seb.

For long moments he stared down at her, and then he nodded. 'Okay. Do you need any medication?'

She glanced at the box of pills. Surely not tonight. She'd been trying to do without them because they left her feeling so woolly-headed. And after what she'd been through she was so exhausted she'd sleep as soon as her head touched the pillow. But you could never be sure.

'If you could get me a glass of water that would be great. The kitchen's down the hall and the glasses—'

'I'll find them,' he said as he turned on his heel.

As soon as he was gone she felt better, not tense with the need to appear self-sufficient. The tightness in her chest eased and she carefully swung her legs over the side of the bed. The *en suite* bathroom was only a few feet away, and the unsteadiness in her legs had abated. It must have been brought on by the stress of confronting Wakefield.

She'd washed her face and finished brushing her teeth when she heard him in her room.

'The water's on the bedside table,' he said in a low voice from just the other side of the door. 'Do you need any help in there?'

'No, I'm okay now.' Wimp that she was, it was easier to stay there in the bathroom than open the door and face those penetrating eyes.

'Thanks very much for your help,' she said, in what she hoped was a bright voice. 'If you wouldn't mind pulling the front door closed firmly behind you, it's self-locking.'

Silence for a moment, then he said, 'I'll remember.'

'Thanks again…' What should she call him? Mr Carlisle was too formal after all that had happened, but she couldn't use his first name. 'Goodnight, then,' she murmured eventually. But there was no response.

She stood by the basin listening, but there was nothing. He'd already left.

See? He just felt sorry for you. He knew you were safe now at home and he couldn't get out of here fast enough.

When she opened the door the bedroom was deserted and dark. Only the bedside lamp spilled its warm glow. He must have been trying to save her a trip across the room to switch off the overhead lights.

Ronan Carlisle was thoughtful, all right, as well as stubborn and self-opinionated and way too good-looking. Marina yawned again and reached under the pillows for her nightie.

She undressed and slipped the cool midnight-blue silk over her head. It cascaded in lovely concealing folds down her body and she smiled at the thought of this one private indulgence. You didn't have to be a size eight beauty queen to enjoy the feel of sexy lingerie against your skin.

She put her folded clothes on the blanket box at the foot of her bed and straightened to reach for the crutches. She'd better find the energy to go and check the front door or she wouldn't be able to sleep.

'Here, let me.' That familiar dark voice came from the doorway and she swung round, stunned, to meet Ronan Carlisle's shuttered gaze. Her pulse beat a crazy tattoo that might have been shock—or excitement.

In one hand he held a large steaming mug, and as she watched he strode across the room and snagged her crutches in his other. He put the mug on her bedside table and reached for her, his big hand hard and hot against the tender bare skin at her elbow.

A shimmer of exquisite excitement emanated from his touch.

'Where do you want to go?' He held the crutches out to her, but she couldn't tear her gaze from his face. It was there again, the blaze of heat in his deep blue eyes that liquefied her bones.

And then, seemingly in an instant, it was gone. His faced showed only polite enquiry. Mild concern. No more.

'Marina?'

'I thought you'd left. I was going to check the front door,' she said, wishing she had a robe at hand to cover herself. Though, she reasoned, the nightgown covered a whole lot more than some of the dresses she'd seen tonight.

Still, she couldn't shake the awareness that she was almost naked in her silk and lace. And he was so close his body heat radiated against her. It seemed to stoke a fire down low in her abdomen. She felt the flames curl and flare as his indigo gaze meshed with hers.

'Come on, you shouldn't be on your feet.' He sounded gruff, and his expression was stern. As if he feared he'd have to scrape her up off the floor when her legs gave way.

But it wasn't her injuries that turned her knees to jelly. Not this time. It was something else. Something new.

Desire.

An unfamiliar tension gripped her body and slowed her brain as he guided her to the bed. Automatically she leaned against his arm as he supported her to sit down.

Without a word he swept the sheet further aside, then bent to swing her legs up. His hands closed round her heels, lifting them onto the bed. She sucked in a breath at the tingling shivers that spread in ripples up her legs.

Immediately he stilled.

He must feel it too—her uncontrollable trembling. Fervently she hoped he'd put it down to her weakened physical condition and not realise it was reaction to his touch.

She stared at the dark head so close to her own, at the way his ebony hair flopped down over his brow. The fan of his dark lashes against his skin. What was he thinking?

Her heart thudded against her ribs as she waited, willing him to let her go.

That was what she wanted. Wasn't it?

He moved infinitesimally and the tremors grew. His long fingers slid from her heels to her ankles, encompassing them in the lightest of caresses.

Marina bit down hard on her bottom lip to stop the sigh of pleasure welling in her throat. The slide of his hands against her skin felt so unbelievably good. Warm and gentle and…erotic.

Her fingers curled, twisting into the sheet beside her. She held herself rigid as his hands skimmed higher, inching up her calves.

And all the while the swirling heat in the pit of her stomach intensified. The tremors became shudders as he reached her knees and discovered the sensitive flesh behind them.

She couldn't contain her automatic jolt of response to his touch. It was as if shards of white light splintered through her, numbing her brain and momentarily blinding her.

What was happening?

This had to stop. Now!

'Please…' To Marina's horror her voice was a hoarse plea, revealing exactly how little control she had over her body.

'Please, I—' Abruptly the words were lost as he raised his head.

Was this the same man? His face seemed pared down to the arrogant bone, his mouth a taut line, nostrils flared wide. And his eyes… She shrank back against the pillows. Those eyes were voracious, glittering in a way that unnerved her.

'Since you ask so nicely, Marina.'

She heard his low murmur through a haze of disbelief as he

settled beside her, hip to hip, on the bed. His body heat burned her through their clothes.

Her throat closed on her instinctive protest, so she raised her hands to ward him off.

She was stunned, but she wasn't stupid. She didn't want him to—

He leaned forward and her hands pressed into the silk of his shirt, felt the solid muscle beneath and the rapid thump of his heart.

She tried to concentrate on pushing him away. But somehow her fingers slid instead across the sleek fabric, moulding the hard, living heat of him. A heady surge of scorching sensation coursed through her fingertips, her palm, right through her body, fusing all thought.

Transfixed by a wanton tide of longing, Marina felt his hands settle on her bare shoulders. The slight roughness of his skin against hers, masculine against feminine, made her shiver.

Dangerous. Far too dangerous.

She had to protest, find the words that would stop this madness.

But he leaned close and her vocabulary disintegrated.

He lowered his head to hers and she forgot to breathe.

CHAPTER FOUR

RONAN'S lips were hot, hard and demanding. At their touch, Marina gave up all effort of resistance.

Suddenly she knew with absolute certainty: this was exactly what she wanted.

His tongue thrust into her open mouth and dark heat consumed her, blotting out everything but him. He pressed her back into the pillows, his body conquering hers, his arms pinning her against him.

There was no hesitation in his kiss. No doubt. Just a driving urgency that should have frightened her. She felt consumed by his power, his remorseless, compelling energy.

But Marina wasn't afraid. She exulted in the hard strength of his body against hers. In the insistent thrust of his tongue caressing her and the hot, musky, drugging taste of him in her mouth. The erotic flavour of him was surely addictive. Like the spicy scent of his skin that filled her nostrils and short-circuited her brain.

She was on sensory overload, absorbing and responding to layer upon layer of new experience. There was nothing about this man she didn't want. Didn't *need*.

She loved the sensation of his torso pressing her down against the bed, the weight of him both comforting and tantalising.

Desire, like hot honey, flowed through her, loosening her muscles, making her pliant in his arms.

His hands splayed across her cheeks, fingers speared into her hair, holding her so he could deepen the kiss, delve further into her mouth. She welcomed him, eagerly answering his demands with her own.

She gave him back kiss for kiss as the fire inside her grew into a molten flow deep in her belly and right down to the junction of her thighs. She arched into him, revelling in the amazing sensation of his chest crushing her breasts.

Yet she wanted more.

His hand slid across her shoulder and she shuddered as every nerve-ending exploded at his touch. It was like fire, delicious flame, stroking down her body. She trembled as his hand closed on the silk at her side, exploring the curve of her waist. She couldn't prevent the sinuous twist of her lower body in response.

And lower went his palm, circling over her hip and dipping down.

Sanity crashed upon her like a breaker on soft sand.

His hand slid across her thigh. She stiffened, rigid under his touch, as the magic shattered. From the sensual fog of desire reason slowly emerged. Then caution. And fear.

Instead of clawing into his shirt her hands pressed, frantic to lever some distance between them.

For an instant he didn't budge. But his hand stilled.

Then with one final, heartbreakingly seductive caress of his tongue against hers, he released her mouth and pulled back.

Marina sobbed in a gulp of air, distraught at the mix of relief and longing that swamped her. She could still taste him on her lips.

She told herself she was relieved he'd stopped. She'd done the right thing in pushing him away.

She just wished she'd never let it start.

Her body was on fire from their shared passion. But it was embarrassment that flamed in her cheeks.

She couldn't meet his eyes.

'I don't want—' But his finger on her lips stopped her.

'Of course you don't.' His deep voice cut across her whirling thoughts with the precision of a stiletto.

Startled, she raised her eyes, but he'd already got to his feet, was turning away. All she saw of his face was the taut angle of his jaw and the furrow of his down turned brow. And then he was walking away across the room.

Marina let her hand slide to the crumpled sheet beside her, still warm from his body.

She wasn't regretting her last-minute qualms. Of course she wasn't. Nor was she upset at how readily he'd agreed to end their kiss.

Their sensuous, mind-blowing, once-in-a-lifetime kiss.

She drew another slow, calming breath.

He turned in the doorway to face her, but in the dim lamp-light his face was shadowed. She couldn't read his expression, could only see the enigmatic gleam of his eyes.

Even that was enough to send another spiral of fierce need twisting through her. What had this man done to her? How had he breached a lifetime's defences so easily?

And how had she been reckless enough to let him do it?

'Goodnight, Marina,' he said, in a voice blank of all emotion. 'I'll make sure the front door is locked on my way out.'

Marina slumped back against the pillows, her heart pounding.

She strained her ears, listening to the faint echo of Ronan Carlisle's footsteps on the polished wood floor. The sound of the front door closing behind him.

Silence.

Except for the roaring of blood in her ears.

She lifted unsteady hands to her cheeks. Her face burned. Her chest heaved as if she'd been running for her life and her nipples were sensitive peaks. Even the delicate touch of her silk night-gown created an exquisite tension there.

She could taste him on her tongue. Feel his powerful hands on her face, in her hair. And deeper, lower, where the sensation of need still agitated, she registered the searing liquid heat of desire.

So this was lust.

She covered her swollen lips with her fingers, stifling the rising bubble of hysterical laughter.

Marina Lucchesi in lust!

It had taken her long enough. After spending a lifetime attending to her family, her home and honest hard work, she'd finally discovered temptation in the form of an attractive man.

And what a man!

If the situation weren't so awful she'd have to laugh. Either that or cry.

How could she have given in to the rush of insane desire that welled at his touch? She'd been pathetic.

Nothing had prepared her for this torrent of emotion, this longing.

Her only hope was that he'd attribute her reaction to the strain she'd been under, to her physical weakness.

And, of course, to his own stunning attractiveness. He probably had women melting at his feet all the time. He'd have the pick of them. Wouldn't have to settle for second best.

She guessed he'd only kissed her out of curiosity.

Or worse: pity.

She squeezed her eyes shut against the scalding tears of embarrassment that filmed them.

Stupid. Stupid. Stupid.

At least he'd had the decency to stop when she had changed her mind. He'd pulled back when she'd stiffened in his arms. If he'd kept up his sensual onslaught, she knew the interlude would have ended very differently.

She hiccoughed on a laugh. Or was it a sob?

Even her strict upbringing and her own inclination not to be noticed by the opposite sex hadn't saved her. She'd made an utter fool of herself.

If only she'd used her brain rather than simply let herself drown in sensation. If only she hadn't willingly colluded with his sensual demands.

Her pride wouldn't be so bruised if she'd repulsed him because she never slept with strangers.

But she didn't even have that salve to her pride.

It hadn't been morality or caution that had made her pull back. It had been the realisation that at any moment his big callused hand might slide up under her nightgown to discover the disfiguring network of scar tissue that deformed her thigh.

Maimed, and anything but beautiful. That was her.

Even if pity had motivated Ronan Carlisle to kiss her, he couldn't feel *that* sorry for her. The sight of her injured leg would make any man recoil. Especially a man used to the sultry charms of glamorous women.

At least there was an upside, she realised with a bitter twist to her lips. Her injuries would undoubtedly have repulsed Ronan, so she'd escaped the final humiliation.

She'd never have to reveal to a man of his experience and expectations that, at twenty-four, she was still a virgin.

The next day dawned hot and bright, but it was late by the time Marina showered and breakfasted. A night of broken sleep and the unsettling memory of Ronan Carlisle guaranteed she was slower even than usual. Desperately, she thrust the image of him from her mind.

She was impatient for the day she'd be fully healed. The physiotherapist said she was almost there, but to Marina it sounded like hollow reassurance, designed to keep her trying.

She shouldn't complain. Others weren't so lucky. Blinking away a tear, she busied herself, packing her towel and purse into a tote bag ready for her aqua therapy.

The phone rang as she headed out the door.

It would be Seb. She didn't want to break the news that Wakefield wouldn't give them more time. Or admit that she'd blown it and got the man so incensed he'd called Security to throw her out. The memory of Wakefield's cold, uncaring eyes made her shiver.

With a sigh she dropped her bag and trudged into the kitchen. Might as well get it over and done with. Delay wouldn't make the task easier.

She reached for the phone, but stopped dead as the answering machine clicked on and the deep voice that had echoed through her confused dreams filled the room.

'Marina, it's Ronan Carlisle. We need to talk. I know how you can get your company back.'

He paused for a long moment and her stomach muscles

spasmed tight. She swayed and reached over to lean on a straight-backed chair. Dismayed, she registered the sense of deep fore-boding that held her rigid.

And, worse still, a flare of unwelcome excitement.

Then his voice continued smoothly. 'Call me. I have a proposition for you.'

CHAPTER FIVE

RONAN leaned back in his chair and watched the restaurant entrance.

He was early, deliberately so, staking his claim on the territory. It was second nature to take the advantage when beginning an important negotiation.

He smiled, savouring the thought of it.

Marina Lucchesi. She'd be obstinate, he had no doubt. And critical, accepting nothing at face value. She had a quick mind and enough guts to make her a formidable negotiator, even though he was the one in the position of power. He held all the cards.

A flicker of heat flared in his belly. He recognised it instantly. Anticipation. It had been there last night, and again this morning, when he'd woken to the dawn light and lain in the semi-darkness thinking about Marina.

She'd been so passionate, so responsive, that he was eager for more. Eager for the intimacy his frustrated body had craved through the long hours of darkness.

It had taken every shred of his resolve to pull back from her as she lay in his arms. Even now the tension in his lower body was almost painful at the memory of her generous sensuality. But he hadn't mistaken her change of mind. That sudden recoil from his touch had been obvious. It had been the wrong time. He shouldn't have let things go so far and so fast.

He'd bide his time. Marina would be worth the wait.

There'd been reluctance in her voice earlier today when he proposed this lunch meeting. Perhaps she was embarrassed at how completely she'd responded to him. Women had some strange ideas, he knew.

Or was there another reason? He propped his elbows on the table and tapped his fingers together. Despite all he'd learned about her, Marina Lucchesi was an enigma.

She was confident, capable, supremely passionate. But there was an unusual reserve about her.

When they'd kissed, for an instant she'd been startled, unco-operative. She'd seemed…unsure, even clumsy, as if untutored.

He shook his head at the absurd notion. After a few moments she'd kissed him back with a fervour that had sent his temperature soaring and his blood pressure rocketing off the scale. She was one seriously sexy woman.

So why had she seemed uncertain at first?

Innocence? He discarded that possibility. There was too much innate sensuality in Marina for it to have remained untapped until now.

Was she playing some sort of game? Trying to pretend to a hesitancy she didn't feel? What could she hope to gain by that? He sat back, sure he'd find out soon.

He knew she had misgivings about meeting him, but she was desperate too. And desperation would win out over caution. He counted on it.

Marina wanted her family company back, for herself and her brother. And to protect their employees. His digging had un-earthed some interesting facts. Including her absolute loyalty to the firm's workers. No way would she leave them to Wakefield's tender mercies without a fight.

And then there was her other weakness. He savoured the memory of last night's promising interlude. She might be wary, but she couldn't hide the way she reacted to him. He could use that knowledge to ensure she didn't walk away.

A movement outside caught his eye, and he sat up straighter as he saw her approach from an avenue of trees in the park opposite. No crutches today. She walked slowly but steadily. He was relieved she hadn't done any permanent damage after the way she'd almost collapsed at the party.

She'd pulled her hair back again, this time in a long plait, and she wore…what was it? Some sort of loose tunic dress, a couple of sizes too big for her and styled for a middle-aged matron.

He frowned, wondering what message that outfit was supposed to convey. Hands off?

He grinned. *Too late for that, Marina.*

Then she stepped out from under the trees. The flicker of heat inside him transformed into a rush of scorching physical response that stiffened his whole body.

Whatever her intentions in wearing that sack, she couldn't have realised it was transparent when backlit by the glaring midday sun. Now he had tantalising glimpses of her long, shapely legs and sultry curves. The flare of her hips and the voluptuous dip to her waist. It was like watching a seductress dancing behind a veil, all that hidden, enticing treasure barely concealed.

His pulse quickened. The camouflage only heightened her body's natural eroticism. So much more effective than the blatant allure of most women he met. Especially as he knew first-hand what treasure she attempted to hide.

Ronan enjoyed every single step of Marina's approach, until she walked into the shadow of the restaurant awning.

Then he settled back in his seat and schooled his features into an expressionless mask.

Marina paused in the shade to draw a steadying breath.

Ronan Carlisle had sounded so certain he had the answer to her problems. Yet surely there *was* no solution. Not after the way she'd stuffed up with Wakefield.

And how could she face Ronan again after last night's debacle? Heat filled her at the memory. Her pride insisted she ignore his summons.

But family duty dictated she attend.

The temptation to turn tail and run was strong. Her inner voice warned Ronan Carlisle was trouble. But she had no choice. She'd meet with the Devil himself if there was any chance to drag her brother out of this mess.

She'd have to brazen it out. Pretend the scene in her bedroom hadn't happened. It was only a kiss, after all. A sensuous, cata-clysmic experience for her. But to Ronan Carlisle it probably meant nothing.

She pushed open the restaurant door then stood, eyes adjust-ing after the brilliant January sunlight. A man at a secluded table instantly captured her attention. He was framed by a pair of French doors that opened onto a picturesque courtyard. The sunlight em-phasised the arrogant tilt of his head, the breadth of his shoulders.

Her eyes met his. A jolt of heat held her still. As he looked straight back at her, eyes unreadable, a thrill of something like excitement rippled down her spine.

Or was it apprehension?

Her immediate response to him was too strong, too over-whelming. It scared her.

Drawing herself up straight, she ignored the frantic inner voice urging her to get away, fast. There was too much at stake to turn coward now.

A waitress ushered her across the room. And then Ronan Carlisle was standing. He held out his hand as if this were any other business meeting and he hadn't gathered her close in his arms last night, kissing her till her mind shut down and sensual oblivion beckoned.

A flush spread up her throat and across her cheeks as his hand enveloped hers. Somehow the hard warmth of his hand enclos-ing hers was appallingly intimate. Deep inside, a quiver of unwanted anticipation trembled into life.

He was just as stunning as she remembered. In tailored linen trousers and a casual blue shirt a few shades lighter than his eyes, he could have graced the cover of an opulent fashion magazine. Editors would pay top dollar for a model like him. That aura of command, with his starkly attractive face and powerful body, made a seductive combination.

'Marina, I'm glad you could make it,' he murmured, his low voice sparking a thrill of reaction through her straining nerves. His expression was bland, but was that a hint of mischief in the curve of his lips?

'Mr Carlisle,' she said, reminding herself that this was business and she had no right to wonder about his smiles. If she kept this formal and pretended nothing had happened between them he'd have to follow suit. 'It's good of you to make time for me.'

Then he did smile, a wide, white, brilliant slash of amusement in his tanned face. 'No need to be so formal.' He squeezed her hand and a corresponding clenching sensation in her chest snagged her breath. 'Call me Ronan.'

'Thanks,' she said, nodding briskly as she withdrew her hand. But she wouldn't take him up on the offer.

His expression reminded her all too vividly of his unnerving stare when he'd walked in to find her ready for bed. And look where that had led!

She sat in the chair he held, and placed her bag beside her. When she swung her head round to face him he was leaning back in his chair, lazily watching her.

His indolence set her teeth on edge and she stiffened. However diverting this might be to him, however foolish she'd been, swooning in his arms, this meeting was important. For her and Seb it meant their whole future.

'How are you feeling today, Marina?'

'Much better, thanks.' The quicker they got off the subject of her health the better. 'You said you had a proposition for me?'

'No need of the crutches today?'

'No.' She stared back at him, but his expression revealed nothing other than polite enquiry. She drew a slow breath, reminding herself that this man might be able to help. No need to go out of her way to antagonise him because she was embarrassed and didn't want to talk about herself. Or because her instincts screamed that he was dangerous.

'I rarely need the crutches now,' she offered. He opened his mouth and she hurried on. Her injuries weren't something she wanted to discuss. 'I was surprised to get your call. I don't understand what you can do to help us.'

One of his sleek dark eyebrows rose, reminding her of the immense power he wielded. If he deigned to help them then maybe there was a chance things would work out.

'Have a little faith, Marina. And in the meantime—' he glanced at the waitress, who'd reappeared beside them '—let's order lunch.'

There was no budging him. As he sat, relaxed and amiable, discussing the menu, and as he made small talk while waiting for their meal, Marina realised this was a man all too used to getting his own way.

He'd invited her to lunch, and lunch they would have. Obviously food was a higher priority than her predicament. Or even last night's explosive embrace.

It took all her patience to sit back and pretend this was a social occasion.

He, on the other hand, was totally at ease. The perfect host, he was solicitous of her comfort, drew her into conversation on general topics and added some amusing anecdotes that made her smile despite her tension.

It wasn't what she'd expected. For an unsettling moment she toyed with the idea that he had another reason for inviting her. That Seb's problem was merely an excuse.

But that was preposterous. Not by look or word had he referred to *that* incident. By mutual consent they'd put it behind them. This was a business meeting.

By the time their seafood meal was served, Marina realised she was ravenous. Last night she'd been too nervous to eat, and this morning it had been tea and toast.

'*Bon appetit*,' he murmured, and lifted his wine glass towards her. Automatically she responded.

His eyes held hers, and this time she couldn't look away. An invisible thread seemed to link them across the small table, drawing them together in a cocoon of intimacy that shut out the muted activity beyond them.

His expression changed, as if some force drew his skin tight over the strong planes and angles of his face. He looked harder, stronger, even more compelling.

Oh, how she remembered that look.

Heat ignited inside her and her palms itched at the temptation he presented. Breathless, she realised she only had to reach out to feel the fine-textured bronze of his flesh, mould the hard line of his jaw.

Even as the insane idea surfaced his eyes widened, almost as if he could read her thoughts. Her pulse skittered. She would *not* be stupid enough to respond that way to him again. She clenched her free hand in her lap and bit down hard on her lip.

'To the success of our plans,' he murmured.

'To a second chance,' she amended, not trusting his expression. It looked like possessiveness. But that was impossible. Her imagination was working overtime.

The white wine was cool and soothing as it slid down her dry throat. She took another sip and nearly sighed with relief as Ronan Carlisle put his glass on the table and dropped his gaze to his plate.

Abruptly the tension that had held her spellbound dissipated. She slumped back in her chair, heart racing as if she'd just swum twenty laps of the pool at top speed.

She needed to get a grip. She'd never had problems concentrating on business. But she'd never had to deal with a man like Ronan Carlisle before. She couldn't let a pair of blue eyes and a handsome face unsettle her.

Fighting the urge to watch him, she turned her attention to the meal. Sooner or later he'd explain this brilliant idea of his.

'I've done some digging since I left you,' he said eventually, 'and I know something of your situation.'

He had her attention now. All of it.

'But I need to know more.'

'You said you knew how we can get the firm back.'

He nodded. 'All in good time. First I want to make sure I understand the circumstances completely. My contacts could only provide so much information for me last night.'

'You rang them last *night?*' It must have been nearly midnight by the time he'd left her.

'Not all work is conducted between nine and five,' he said, as if the middle of the night was a perfectly reasonable time to call business contacts.

She shook her head, wondering about the urgency of his actions. But that didn't matter. All that mattered was the fact that he was willing to help.

'What do you know?'

'That our friend Wakefield is in the process of acquiring another company to add to his portfolio. A medium-sized and quite profitable freight company.' His eyes bored into hers. 'Marina Enterprises. It's owned by a family called Lucchesi.'

She laid her cutlery on the plate carefully, as if it was important it shouldn't fall and clatter.

'That's right,' she said flatly. 'My father started the firm. Built it up from nothing.' She twisted the stem of her wine goblet between her fingers. 'But it's jointly owned by my brother Sebastian and me.' She drew a deep breath. 'Or it was.'

'Until Charles Wakefield came on the scene.' She thought she heard the echo of sympathy in his deep voice.

She pushed back her shoulders and took a sip of the crisp wine he'd ordered. She didn't need sympathy. She needed action.

'Seb owes Wakefield a lot of money,' she said brusquely. 'The company was security for a debt, and Wakefield's demanding payment in full. Immediately. Legally, he's within his rights.' She swallowed down the bitter taste of nausea at the injustice of it and forced the words out. 'Seb's tried everything to raise the money, but he can't get his hands on that sort of cash.'

'So Wakefield gets the company.'

'I don't see what you can do about it,' she burst out. 'I thought if I met Wakefield I might be able to persuade him to give us more time. We could look at a loan, sell some of the firm's assets.'

Never mind that it would gut the company and they'd never recover financially.

'But he'll never agree to it now. Not after what I said to him.' She shuddered. Her stomach churned at the memory of last night's disaster. She couldn't have done a better job of sabotaging any last chance to reason with Wakefield if she'd tried.

She couldn't believe how easily that slimeball had got to her. All because she'd been tired and stressed. That was no excuse. She should have done better. Should have found a way past his arrogance and her own stupid pride.

Just as well her parents weren't around to see how badly she and Seb had mismanaged their legacy. It would have broken their hearts. She blinked furiously as her eyes blurred and pain radiated from that inner well of grief.

'Slow down, Marina.' He reached out and covered her hand, where it fisted on the pristine linen cloth. His touch was warmth and reassurance. And something else. Something that made her flesh tingle beneath his palm. But she knew the contact meant nothing to him.

'Tell me what happened.'

Her lips pursed at the thought of laying bare Seb's naïve stupidity to this man who dealt in billion-dollar deals. She tried to pull her hand out from under his.

He wouldn't release her. No fuss, no pain, but his hold was unbreakable. Just like the intensity of his stare.

'Tell me,' he urged.

She looked at his square hand engulfing hers. It made her own look almost dainty, her wrist slender and feminine. And it warmed her in a way that made her hot all over.

Damn, but she didn't like this. It felt all wrong.

'Dad was grooming Seb to take his role as head of the company,' she said at last.

'And you?'

She lifted her face to find him leaning close, so close she could see tiny flecks of azure in his dark eyes and inhale his clean, spicy scent. Something clogged in her brain, and for long moments she stared at him, unable to concentrate on anything else. Dimly she was aware of her clamouring senses, of her racing heartbeat.

Her eyes dropped to his sculpted lips. A surge of longing engulfed her.

For God's sake, concentrate!

She straightened in her seat. 'I'm a qualified accountant. I work in the firm's financial team and I'm a company director.' No need to tell him she'd been co-running the company for the last year or so with her dad.

'My father died several months ago in a car accident.' Her tone was matter-of-fact, giving nothing away. But his hand tightened round hers, squeezing warmth into her suddenly chilled flesh.

'And you were injured in the same accident.' It wasn't a

question. His gaze was sharp. 'Tell me, just how long ago did you get out of hospital?'

'That's hardly relevant.'

'Humour me,' he said softly, as his thumb stroked tantalisingly over her knuckles.

The tiny movement created a lush wave of seductive warmth that spread across her hand, over her wrist and up her arm. Some of her brittle defences shattered.

'I moved out of physical rehabilitation two weeks ago.'

She watched anger add brilliance to his glittering eyes. 'And I can take care of myself.' As if it was any of his business. 'I've looked after Dad and Seb since I was thirteen.'

'And now who's looking after you?'

Furious, she yanked her hand away. This time he released it, and she tucked it safely in her lap, steadfastly ignoring the way it tingled from his caress.

'I'm perfectly fine on my own. And Seb can't be at my beck and call. He has a new bride.'

'Married at twenty-one?'

He must have a phenomenal memory to recall that from last night's barrage of accusations.

She shrugged. 'They were in love.' And, her father had assured her, marriage to Emma was just what Seb needed to help him settle down.

Absently she rubbed a finger over her right hand, as if she could erase the lingering sensation of his touch.

'I don't see why you need to know all this.'

'Because I like to know what I'm getting into,' he countered, and the look he gave her was all business. Only an unwise woman would argue now. The angle of his jaw and the steely glint in his eye belonged to the wealthy corporate powerbroker, not the charming lunch partner. Nor the passionate lover who'd almost seduced her twelve hours ago.

'So,' he recapped, 'you and your younger brother jointly own Marina Enterprises. And…?'

'Dad was gone, and I was stuck in hospital.' She leaned back in her chair, suddenly exhausted. She stared out into the courtyard. A soothing trickle of water splashed from a wall fountain into a pool surrounded by ferns.

'My brother was eager to make his mark. He wanted to prove himself.' Their dad was a hard act to follow. But she'd never realised how much Seb felt he had to show himself his father's equal.

'Even before the accident he'd been working on plans to expand the firm. He'd made some new contacts and talked about borrowing to diversify while the market was right. It would be a good scheme, so long as he did it properly.'

'But he didn't.' It wasn't a question but a grim pronouncement.

She shook her head, feeling once more that swooping feeling in the pit of her stomach, the nauseous horror at the enormity of Seb's stupidity.

'Some of his new business contacts were extremely successful and had plenty of disposable income. There were weekend-long parties and gambling for high stakes. Seb got invited to a few.' She still wondered about that. Couldn't understand why Seb, handsome and ambitious as he was, had been welcomed so readily into that *milieu*.

'Charles Wakefield hosted a racing party,' she said, eager now to get this over. 'Emma was away, so Seb went alone. He gambled till he'd lost all he could afford, but Wakefield persuaded him to stay on. Later, after Seb had been drinking far too much, Wakefield mentioned how easy it would be to raise the money for the expansion if he had one good win, rather than bother with a bank loan.'

She took a ragged breath and plunged on. 'Seb knew he had no more money to bet, but Wakefield assured him it was all right. Said something about a gentlemen's agreement.' And in his sozzled state Seb had actually believed him!

'My brother lost. And the next day Wakefield told him he'd signed over the company as security.'

'It was definitely his signature?' Ronan Carlisle leaned close across the table, his only sign of animation.

Marina nodded, reliving the sickening moment of revelation. 'Oh, yes, it was his.' Her voice was bitter. 'Wakefield didn't leave anything to chance. One of his lawyers just happened to be on hand to witness it. The document is legally binding—we've checked. And Wakefield had witnesses there to testify that Seb knew what he was doing when he signed it.'

'Greedy bastard.' Ronan Carlisle sat back and rubbed a hand over his jaw.

'Precisely.'

Looking down, she saw the scraps of her meal, cold on her plate. She shuddered and pushed it away. If only this had all been a bad dream.

'But you own the company jointly. Your brother couldn't sign away what wasn't his.'

'And what would you have me do?' she demanded on a surge of fury. 'Watch him struggle with a debt he'll never be able to pay? Have him blacklisted by every potential future employer and finance company because of bankruptcy?'

She sank back in her chair and regarded him wearily. Every bone in her body ached with tiredness. She was so close to giving up the fight that it scared her.

'He bet the company and more besides. Wakefield won't accept any alternative.'

'So you're selling your family home to help?'

'How did you—?'

'I drove you home last night, remember? There was a real estate agent's sign on the footpath.' He paused. 'Where will you live?'

Marina stared. What did it matter where she lived? She'd just returned home after the shock of her father's death and months in hospital. She hadn't even been able to attend her dad's funeral, and for a while there she'd thought she'd never overcome her grief. But then she'd discovered her family company was as good as in a stranger's hands. Everything her parents had worked towards all their lives.

Right now nothing else mattered. Not even her frighteningly intense feelings for this man.

'I'll worry about that when the time comes. You said you knew what we could do to keep the company,' she challenged, waiting for him to prevaricate.

Instead he returned her gaze, unblinking and confident.

Whatever he had in mind, he was sure he could bring it off. Certainty was there in his relaxed posture, and in the tiny smile that curved his sculpted lips.

'You *do* have a plan, don't you?' Excitement stirred.

He inclined his head. 'It's unorthodox.'

She sat back in her chair, wondering exactly what that meant. 'Illegal? Is that it?' she asked suspiciously.

His lips twitched and she watched, mesmerised. Did he have any idea just how sexy that made him look?

'No. I may be creative in my approach to business, but I always stay on the right side of the law.'

Absently she nodded, aware of his reputation not only for success, but for fair dealing. The corporate regulators never had problems with Ronan Carlisle's companies.

So what was his plan? And why was he bothering? Marina Enterprises was a solidly successful company and worth saving. But what was in it for him?

Her earlier unease returned. She knew where she stood with Wakefield. He was a womaniser, a louse and a cheat.

But Ronan Carlisle? She knew his public reputation as rich, innovative and successful. She'd learned last night that he was determined, confident and surprisingly considerate for a mega-wealthy tycoon. And that his shuttered expression hid a passionate, incredibly sensual nature. That he kissed with the expertise and ruthless eroticism of a fallen angel.

And now he knew so much about her. He'd delved into her personal life and stripped her bare of all defences. She felt totally vulnerable.

'Why are you getting involved?' she asked breathlessly.

Again that half-smile that made her heart somersault. He leaned towards her. The scent of him assailed her, clean and male and provocative.

'You and your brother aren't the only ones to suffer at Wakefield's hands.'

He was silent for a moment, as if choosing his words. 'He can be dangerous when he wants something, and the results can be disastrous.'

The grooves bracketing his mouth deepened as his lips compressed. A flash of raw emotion burned in his eyes.

Pain? Marina was an expert at recognising it. After all, she'd seen it for so long now, reflected back if ever she looked in the mirror.

'So you want revenge?' she said.

There was no discernible change in his expression, but he looked so uncompromising, so far removed from her urbane lunch companion, it sent a chill through her. She had no difficulty believing he could be totally ruthless in getting whatever he set his heart on. No matter what the opposition. Or the cost.

'Perhaps,' he answered. 'But, more important, I want Wakefield so busy working to keep his head above water that he won't have time to destroy anyone else.'

Destroy. It was a strong word. But that was what Wakefield was doing. Destroying Seb's future and her own. Stealing her father's hard-won legacy.

She nodded, steadfastly ignoring the aura of danger emanating from Ronan Carlisle. Hadn't she decided she'd do a deal even with the Devil if she had to?

'What do you have in mind?'

He sat back and watched her through narrowed eyes. 'It will only work with your co-operation,' he warned.

'All right. You need me and my brother.'

'No.' He didn't raise his voice, but the single syllable cut across her jumble of thoughts. 'Not your brother. Just you.'

Marina's pulse thudded, slow and heavy, compounding the dull roar in her ears. All her senses were on alert, as if she was an animal stalked by a predator, on the lookout for certain attack.

This smelt like danger. It felt like impending catastrophe. But she couldn't pull back.

'What do I have to do?'

The grooves beside his mouth folded deeper, not with humour this time, but with satisfaction.

'I want you to become my mistress.'

CHAPTER SIX

MARINA jerked back as if she'd been slapped. What sort of game was he playing?

He met her stunned look with arrogant assurance.

For a moment she even wondered if she'd heard him right. Then her chair scraped across the polished wood floor as she shoved it back.

But the way he sat there, calm and unruffled, goaded her. Instead of thrusting up out of her seat she leaned across the table, the full blaze of her fury and hurt consuming her. She might have made a fool of herself when he kissed her, but she didn't deserve this.

'If that's your attempt at humour, I don't think it's funny.'

No response. Only the steady regard of hooded eyes scrutinising her like a beetle under a microscope.

'And if it's a reference to what happened last night…' She slammed a lid on the memory of his body against hers, his lips so utterly persuasive. 'You can be sure there'll never be a repeat performance.'

Not even to herself would she admit how much she'd wanted to trust Ronan Carlisle. The realisation of her mistake was a raw, scalding ache deep inside, making it hard to breathe.

'This isn't about last night, Marina, delightful as that was.' His voice was as smooth and seductive as rich chocolate, and a responsive thrill of pleasure skated through her body, stoking her anger.

She glared into his indigo eyes, trying to discern his expression, but it was shuttered. All she had were his words.

'My proposal is unorthodox, but it *will* work. I'll get you back your company…if you co-operate with me.'

'Yeah, sure. Me as your mistress. I can see that!'

'Why not?' He leaned towards her across the small table so their faces were only a breath apart.

Furious, she registered her body's response to him: tingling awareness, a telltale flush of heat. And she despised herself for it.

'Your boyfriend would object? Is that the problem?'

She swung away, but his hand closed over hers, clamping it uncompromisingly to the table.

She tugged, but her strength was no match for his. He didn't even seem to exert any pressure—to an onlooker his touch would seem intimate, not imprisoning.

'Let me go,' she snarled.

'In a moment. After you tell me why it wouldn't work.' He paused, his gaze raking her face. 'Is it because there's some man in your life? A lover?'

She shook her head.

'So what's the problem?'

'First,' she spat out, 'your sex-life has nothing to do with Charles Wakefield, and it's not going to get back Marina Enterprises. And second, it's just ridiculous.'

His eyebrows slanted up. 'Why is it ridiculous?'

'I've had enough now. Let me go.'

'After you explain.'

She tried to prise her hand from under his, but he refused to release her and she couldn't break his hold. His ability to keep her there was the final straw. She had enough arrogant men in her life. She'd be damned if she'd put up with another one.

'I'm not mistress material. Anyone can see that.' If she had been, maybe he wouldn't have found it so easy to walk away from her last night. A shaft of burning pain pierced her. She knew her limitations.

'On the contrary,' he said, his voice so low and sensuous that she shivered. 'I can see you in the role.'

Marina sucked in a breath at the image he evoked in her wayward imagination. Her and this man. Together. Intimate.

Something inside her melted into swirling sensation at the thought of it. Her nipples peaked and moist heat welled low in her body as she remembered how close they'd come to being lovers.

'I'm sorry I didn't make it clear, Marina,' he said softly. 'I should have said *pretend* to be my mistress.'

Pretend?

She stared, trying to make sense of his words.

'If we can convince Wakefield that we're involved,' he murmured, 'it will create the opportunity I need. With you as bait I can entice him so far out on a limb that releasing Marina Enterprises to your family will be the least of his worries.'

His words fell like a pledge into the silence. He was serious now, both face and voice grim.

He really meant it!

Her mind boggled. His suggestion that she pose as anyone's mistress was in the worst possible taste.

Marina shook her head. 'I wouldn't be convincing.' Not if she had to play the role of *femme fatale*. The whole idea was ludicrous, cruelly so. 'Whatever you have in mind, it won't work.'

'Of course it will work. Can't you find it in yourself to trust me, even a little?' His lips quirked in a half-smile that she was sure he'd practised on countless gullible females.

She took a slow breath and marshalled her thoughts, tried to calm her pounding heart. Saving her family company. That was what counted. She should hear him out.

'Not trust,' she said, surprised at how steady her voice sounded. 'But I'll listen.'

'Good.' His hand slid back, releasing hers. To her dismay she missed the lingering warmth of his touch.

'We'll go somewhere more private to discuss it.' He stood and tucked a hand under her elbow.

In anyone else she would have thought the gesture merely solicitous, especially after her physical weakness last night. But to her dazed mind his touch against her bare skin felt like a brand of ownership. She shivered.

* * *

'You were going to explain,' she prompted as they sat in her living room. He turned his gaze from the family photos covering one wall and watched her with those unreadable eyes. Uncomfortable under his scrutiny, she steeled herself to remain motionless, apparently at ease.

'I decided to act against Wakefield some time ago.' Ronan's voice was dispassionate. 'He's extended his personal resources recklessly in the last year, grabbing at opportunities but not consolidating. Despite his wealth, that leaves him vulnerable. A single major loss at the wrong time would leave him desperate.'

His lips curved, easing the stark lines of his face. But it was a predatory smile with a ruthless edge. When he looked like that Ronan Carlisle scared her. Something Wakefield, for all his money, had never managed.

'I need a diversion to preoccupy him while I spring the trap.' His gaze held hers. 'That's where you come in.'

Marina tried to ignore the flare of heated awareness his obvious approval evoked and concentrate on the facts. 'I still don't understand.'

He stretched his long legs towards her. She felt the brush of his shoe against her sandalled foot and shifted uneasily.

'You're perfect,' he said, his voice a low purr of satisfaction that made the hairs on her arms rise. His eyes were warm as they rested on her. 'You have reason to hate Wakefield, so you won't fall victim to his charm.'

'Charm?' Her voice rose in amazement. 'That snake has as much charm as a tax auditor.'

'You're judging him with the benefit of inside knowledge. He's handsome and rich, and, believe me, he can convince most women he's the man of their dreams.'

'Not this woman!'

'That's exactly why I need you.'

Ronan held her bewildered gaze. She sat forward in her chair, luminous eyes fixed on him and lips slightly parted. A surge of exultant heat filled him.

She was like some seductive earth goddess, hiding herself

beneath a prim hairstyle and shapeless, sexless clothes. But she couldn't conceal the passion, the voluptuous femininity he'd discovered in her. The memory of her mouth alone had been enough to keep him awake into the early hours. And that body…

Why was she so adamant she couldn't pretend to be his mistress? He could imagine it so clearly he was burning up. But she acted as if she didn't have beauty on her side, or intelligence. Or the innate sensuality that drew him irresistibly to her.

Yet she was born for the role.

All he had to do was get her to admit it.

He was sorely tempted to throw common sense to the winds. To lean over right now and skim his fingers over the tender flesh of her cheek. To release the vibrant luxury of her long hair so it caressed him as he claimed the softness of her flagrantly erotic mouth with his own, fast and hard.

Heat pooled in his belly.

It would be a mistake. Reason was an ice-cold douche to his fervid imaginings. Instead he contented himself with the promise that one day soon the time would be right.

One day very soon.

He had plans for Marina. Plans he had no intention of revealing yet.

In the meantime there was still much to do. First he had to assuage her doubts. He didn't share his feelings easily, and dredging up the past held no appeal. But it was necessary if he was to convince her.

'Wakefield is dangerous,' he said. 'He's hurt too many people and he needs to be stopped before he ruins any more lives.' He paused, deciding how much he needed to reveal.

'We met at boarding school,' he continued eventually, his voice clipped. 'Wakefield's father and grandfather were old boys there. But I was the son of an entrepreneur; Dad started from nothing. Wakefield thought that made us second rate, but I was proud of my father. Still am.'

He saw a glimmer of understanding in Marina's face, a nod of approval. So that explained her fierce determination to wrest her birthright back from Wakefield. If her father had been her hero, then guilt at the loss of his company drove her on as much as a desire for justice.

'Wakefield never took to me. He lorded it over his cronies but I wouldn't kowtow to him. He tried to make school hell, but I refused to leave. He even tried to thrash me once, but he didn't manage it.' Ronan looked into Marina's wide-eyed gaze, reading surprise there, and something he couldn't identify. Distaste?

'After that we were rivals in everything: studies, sport, you name it.' He paused, remembering Wakefield's brutal methods— anything to win. Wakefield had been a vicious young thug, and the years hadn't improved him.

'And then, in our final year, there was a girl.'

'Your girl?' she interrupted, her dark eyes probing.

'No, his. He broke up with her. She was upset, not him. He was too busy bragging about—' Ronan shot Marina a piercing look. Her expression told him she got the picture.

'Her brother was a mate of mine. But Charlie-boy decided there was something between me and her. He didn't want her, but he didn't want me to have her. He warned me off.' He shrugged. 'When I ignored him he turned nasty. He couldn't hurt her, or me. But there was her kid brother. They found him one night, beaten and bleeding.'

Marina's hiss of indrawn breath was loud, and he nodded. He remembered vividly his own horror the night they'd carted Simon off to hospital. And his rage.

'He claimed not to have recognised his attacker. But Wakefield made sure I knew he'd done it. When there weren't any witnesses around, of course.'

'You're joking!' she gasped. 'He'd have to be mad.'

He inclined his head. 'Definitely unhinged when he's crossed.' A pity the bastard hadn't been forced to get professional help years ago. That might have prevented him inflicting so much damage on innocents.

Silence filled the room as she absorbed his story. She hunched in her chair, arms wrapped protectively round herself.

Good. It was time she realised how dangerous Wakefield could be. The way she'd stood up to him last night had filled

Ronan with admiration, but it was clear she hadn't realised the man was an unprincipled lout.

'We've had little direct contact until recently.' He wrested his attention back to the present. 'But lately, for a number of reasons, I've kept a close eye on him. Even attended one or two of his functions. Our commercial interests are in different spheres. Or they were. In the last twelve months he's been sniffing at my heels, trying to expand into the transport industry.'

Ronan's business empire had been built from a base in international air freight. And he had no doubt that was precisely where Charlie would like to diversify.

Her eyes narrowed as she realised the significance of his words. He'd been right. Marina was no one's fool.

'You've made the connection.' He nodded. 'It's not coincidence that he wants Marina Enterprises. He'd like to become a serious competitor.'

'And that bothers you?' she asked, brows arching.

He shook his head, relishing the idea of an up-front battle. 'Let him bring it on. I'd be fascinated to see how well he manages in a field other than commercial property.'

Marina frowned, and he saw the inevitable question in her gaze. 'There's more, isn't there?' she asked.

As he'd thought: definitely an intelligent woman.

Yet he hesitated. Could he risk revealing the truth to this woman who, essentially, was a stranger? Would she keep it to herself or try to use it for gain?

He stared at her through narrowed eyes, wondering if she was as innocent as she seemed. Whether this morning's lightning-fast security assessment was reliable. Was she indeed principled and talented, as well as hard-working and supremely unlucky? His gut instinct urged him to trust her.

But if he was wrong… No, he couldn't take that chance. This was Cleo's life. Not ancient history from his school days. And she'd worked so hard to claw her way back towards regaining what she'd lost. He couldn't risk it. If the truth leaked out it would destroy her.

He surged to his feet, striding to the window and swinging

round to face Marina. Tension throbbed across his shoulders and up his neck, holding him rigid.

'Wakefield hurt someone I care for. Hurt them badly.' He paused. 'I don't want them hurt again.'

'I don't gossip.' Her voice was matter-of-fact. 'But if there's more to know about Charles Wakefield I'd like to hear it. Fore-warned is forearmed.'

The acrid taste of guilt seared his mouth. If only he'd warned Cleo… If only he'd suspected the lengths that twisted bastard would go to with his sick games.

And here was another of his victims. He looked into Marina's lustrous eyes, read concern in her furrowed brow, and knew a surge of protectiveness so strong it rocked him.

'I can't tell you the specifics. It's not my story. But I can tell you to watch out, because Wakefield will use *any* tactic to get what he wants. And what happened to my…friend was done de-liberately. The only reason he targeted her was because of her link to me.'

He shoved his hands deep in his pockets. 'It sounds melo-dramatic, but what started as a schoolboy rivalry has become a dangerous obsession. Wakefield is fixated on besting me any way he can.'

'I…see. But where do I come in?'

He doubted if she did see. But she was listening.

'Wakefield's reputation as a ladies' man is well deserved,' he said brusquely. 'And that's his weakness. One of the few things that can distract him from making money.'

She nodded. Wakefield's playboy reputation was public knowledge.

'In the last few years he's taken a particular interest in the women I've dated. Occasionally dated some of them himself later on. It's happened often enough for it to be no coincidence. A few have even complained that he was too persistent, virtually stalking them.'

Marina's confusion was obvious from her knitted brow.

'His marked interest in them, like his new interest in freight, tells me that the old rivalry is still alive in his mind. He's so predictable it's almost laughable.' Except for the fact that people were getting hurt again.

He watched Marina, hands clasped as if in prayer, her face like a luminous Madonna's. That sack of a dress only hinted at her sensuous curves, making her look like a temptress hiding in a nun's habit.

He needed her. Badly. But he had to tread warily.

He swung away from her dark questioning eyes.

Marina stared at those wide shoulders, hunched as if against the cold. Or with the strain of painful memories.

This tale of a jealous rival was so far-fetched. She could hardly credit it. In any other circumstances she wouldn't believe it. But she had the evidence of Ronan Carlisle's voice, his body, his torment, to convince her.

No one was that good an actor.

His pain was so intense, so raw, it vibrated from him in waves. And the flare of hatred in his eyes when he'd blamed Wakefield had been truly terrible. She wondered if Wakefield understood the force he'd unleashed when he'd hurt Ronan Carlisle's girlfriend.

For she had to be his lover, not a mere friend. The anguish in his eyes had been so absolute.

'He's destroying people,' Ronan said at last. 'But I'm his real target, so I'm the one who has to end it.'

He paused, turning to meet her gaze in a way that made heat rise in her throat. 'Wakefield will sit up and take notice if he thinks you're mine.' The heat spread to her cheeks, and down much, much lower.

'His competitive instinct won't let him rest. He'll try to win you for himself. And while he's chasing you he won't be concentrating on business.'

'But he looked at me as if I'd crawled out from under a stone!' Her voice rose to a protesting squeak and she cleared her throat. 'No way would he chase after *me*.'

'You underestimate yourself,' he assured her, his eyes holding hers. 'And you underestimate his egomania. He believes he can get any woman he wants. The harder the chase, the more important it is for him to win.'

'You didn't see the way he looked at me. I embarrassed him at his party. He's not going to see me as a trophy!'

'I know Wakefield,' he said, and the confidence in his voice had the ring of truth. 'If he thinks you're mine he'll try to seduce you away. Your confrontation with him won't matter if he thinks there's a chance to best me.'

She shook her head. Why couldn't Ronan Carlisle see what was in front of his nose? He was so set on revenge that he was blind to the obvious.

'You need someone glamorous,' she said eventually, ignoring her outraged pride. 'You need someone who *looks* like they might be your mistress.' *Someone with the experience to carry it off.* It was only sheer determination that allowed her to meet his eyes.

'And you don't?'

She kept her lips firmly closed, refusing to answer.

He stared back at her. 'What if I said you were wrong? That I like women with fire and passion, who stand up for what they believe in no matter what the odds?'

For a moment her heart stopped. She so wanted to believe him. But she wasn't into fantasy. This wouldn't work.

'I don't look like anyone's mistress,' she repeated.

'Clothes,' he said dismissively. 'That's soon fixed. You need something sensational. Not that suit you wore last night.'

'There's nothing wrong with my suit.' It was comfortable, and perfectly respectable.

'Except it's a couple of sizes too large. It conceals too much.'

'And maybe I want to be concealed.'

He shook his head and paced across the room to her. She had to tilt her head up to meet his gaze, the strain in her neck making her feel even more vulnerable.

'Most women with a body like the one I saw last night would happily flaunt it. I'm sure you could manage it for a few weeks. To save your brother.'

Her jaw sagged as she heard his words. A body worth flaunting? She blinked and stared. Had she heard him right?

'But I'm too…' Her voice trailed off under his scrutiny. 'Too tall,' she finished lamely. No way could she bring herself to use any of the other labels: big, buxom, oversized.

'Too tall.' He sat down opposite her and leaned back. His rigid control drained away as his mouth curved into a smile that creased his face, stunning her with its vibrancy. He laughed, and the sound, rich and mellow, melted the hard knot of unhappiness deep within her.

'I'm hardly in miniature myself,' he said at last. 'I'd look ridiculous with a tiny woman on my arm. My women are always tall.'

Marina swallowed hard at the thought of being included in the list of his women.

If things had been different last night…

'But Wakefield's only my height,' she said, as if it really mattered. As if it were even possible that a handsome multimillionaire would give her a second look.

Ronan Carlisle's eyes gleamed. 'Don't you know lots of men fantasise about tall women? Buy the highest stilettos you can find. You'll have him drooling in no time.'

She shook her head, denying the ridiculous ideas that filled it. Her dressed to kill. Her as a sexy vamp, playing off one wealthy tycoon against the other.

If it weren't so pathetic she'd laugh. Ronan had had no difficulty keeping his distance from her, even though she'd all but offered herself to him on a platter. She cringed. Oh, no, her *charms* definitely weren't up to the role.

Her eyes strayed across the room to the photos on the wall. Her mother looked out of the central one, her smile brilliant and alluring. She was dressed for a party, her pocket-Venus curves emphasised by the gorgeous cocktail dress she wore. Now, *there* was a beautiful woman.

'It's all academic anyway,' she said harshly. 'Even if I could lure Wakefield's attention away from business for a short time, that won't get the company back for us.'

Ronan Carlisle watched her silently for so long she shifted in her seat, wondering how much of her inner turmoil he sensed.

'You're wrong. I've worked towards this. I know how precarious Wakefield's cash flow is. He's overstretched. Which is probably why he used such desperate measures to grab your company.' Ronan leaned back and crossed one ankle over the other, the picture of male confidence.

'I've got a deal coming up that will put him just where I want him. He'll think it's the opportunity of a lifetime to catch me unprepared. And when he reacts, tries to get the better of me by grabbing first for another company, he'll overreach the mark. That's when I'll reel him in, and call in a few of his debts.'

His face glowed with savage satisfaction. His grin looked carnivorous, and Marina experienced a fleeting pang of sympathy for his enemy. Ronan Carlisle wouldn't show any mercy to the man who'd hurt his woman.

'The timing's perfect,' he continued. 'With your help we can get Wakefield where it will hurt most: his ego and his hip pocket. I can engineer it so he surrenders Marina Enterprises. You and your brother will be shot of Wakefield *and* the debt if you help me.'

He made it sound easy. Too easy. She knew nothing in life was that simple. Such multi-company dealings were far more complex and risky than he'd described.

She stared across at the man who had taken over her life in one short day. Who did she think she was kidding, even pretending she could play in his league? She was a minnow who'd unwittingly ventured among barracudas.

And even though he understood Wakefield, and could no doubt manage a hostile takeover bid as easily as she did a bowl of steaming pasta, Ronan Carlisle had miscalculated.

She wasn't the sort of woman men burned for. She'd never even had a serious boyfriend. What did she know about tempting a man?

'I'm sorry,' she said at last, squashing a pang of regret. 'This isn't going to work.'

Hours later, and still Ronan Carlisle's words played in her ears. His presence haunted her. She paced the bedroom, too wide awake to sleep, her thoughts tumbling over each other as she racked her brain for a way out of this mess.

She halted at the mirror tucked behind the door, her attention caught by her outrageous mop of curls. She should cut her hair.

With her father gone no one would complain if she did. She pulled the locks away from her face.

She looked different since the accident. Her cheekbones were more defined, the curve of her lips more pronounced. She frowned. Or maybe she was just getting older and she'd never bothered to look properly before.

Mirrors had never been her favourite thing. Not since she'd turned thirteen and developed womanly curves before all the other girls. It took confidence to carry off a figure like that so young, and she hadn't had it. Not then. And especially not after her mother's death in the same year.

Marina had taken refuge in the kitchen, comfort-eating and trying to take her mum's place there, organising the family. And after that it had been easy to slip into the habit: focus on study and work and family. Ignore the jibes of slim, sexy, confident girls who had no idea there was anything more important in life than their next boyfriend. Not worry about frivolous things like parties and fashion.

Marina's gaze strayed down over her silk nightgown, wondering how Ronan Carlisle had seen her the night before. Her hands smoothed the sensuous fabric over her stomach and hips, down across her thighs, remembering his touch.

He was right. She stepped closer to the glass, peering at her outline. The curves of her bust and hips were still there, nothing could take those away, but they were sleek, streamlined, with none of the excess she'd so dreaded in the past.

One of the benefits of a stint in physical rehabilitation. Sensible eating and exercise to get her legs working again.

The phone rang and she scowled. Who'd ring so late?

Fifteen minutes later she hung up, feeling dazed. Could life throw any more curve balls?

The looming loss of the company had brought Seb to his senses. He'd worked night and day, trying to find a way to stop Wakefield's takeover. He'd matured, realising his responsibility to his family, and to his employees. But clearly today's news had unnerved him.

She sat motionless, wondering what to do. Her glance fell on the plain business card resting on her bedside table. Ronan Carlisle had insisted she take his private number in case she changed her mind.

One slow breath. Then another.

Had she changed her mind?

It didn't matter whether she had or not. Not with Seb's news that they weren't the only ones losing their inheritance. Not with the news that Emma was pregnant.

She knew what her father would have done: whatever it took to secure the firm for the next generation. She faced the truth now, with a sense of leaden detachment. They had one chance only to retrieve their birthright.

She reached out a hand and grabbed the phone, refusing to stop and think about what she was doing.

He answered almost immediately. 'Carlisle.' Just that, in a voice that even at this distance created a dangerous whirlpool of need and longing deep inside her.

She was going to regret this, she knew. But she didn't have the luxury of choice.

'It's me,' she whispered. 'Marina Lucchesi. I've changed my mind.'

CHAPTER SEVEN

'AREN'T they a bit much? Too extreme?' Marina asked, as she turned to peer down at the four-inch stiletto heels.

The dressy sandals had the narrowest of diamanté-studded black straps across her toes, and pairs of shoestring ribbons that curled up around her ankles to tie on her legs.

'You've got to be kidding,' Bella Montrose said in her smoky drawl. She leaned forward in one of the boutique's exclusive designer armchairs for a better view. 'Dynamite is what you want, honey, and that's exactly what you've got there.'

Marina looked at the elegant personal stylist who'd been her companion for the past three days. Ever since Ronan Carlisle had rung and announced she'd be arriving at nine a.m. sharp to oversee Marina's transformation.

The arrogance of his announcement still rankled. Almost as much as his calm acceptance when Marina had changed her mind and agreed to this charade. As if there'd never been any doubt that she'd agree to do what he wanted.

'Well?' Bella raised one artfully sleek eyebrow, returning Marina's look with what might, in a less refined woman, be a grin of self-satisfaction. 'You know you love them. You're just being obstinate again.'

'If I might say,' chimed in the saleswoman, 'for a special evening they *are* the most stunning shoe we have. The straps draw attention to the lovely curve of your leg.'

Marina twisted her foot and stared at the full-length mirror.

It was true they were unlike any shoes she'd worn before. In height, price and sexiness. She'd been afraid she'd look like a tart, or, worse, a clown, in sandals so outrageously provocative. But her feet were well-shaped, something she'd never appreciated before. Her ankles were trim and her calves did look…feminine.

Even wearing her favourite loose summer dress, the one Bella had threatened to burn, she looked different in these shoes. As if she might be a seductress in disguise.

She almost laughed out loud at the absurdity. But then, as so often today, her eyes lifted again to the reflection of her newly trimmed and treated hair.

What a transformation. The hours at the expensive salon had been worth every minute. She still didn't understand the intricacies of what the team of stylists had done. But the result bore no resemblance to the untameable mop she'd started with. Her curls had been persuaded into lush waves that flowed invitingly over her shoulders and framed her face perfectly.

Even her hands looked different, more feminine, with their elegantly shaped and painted nails.

She blinked.

Was that really her in the mirror?

'I'll take them,' she said on impulse. Maybe the sandals went with her new image after all. Or maybe she'd just given up a lifetime's habit of choosing sensible over glamorous.

With Bella, she was almost learning to enjoy shopping.

'And she'll take the red ones as well,' Bella said.

Marina opened her mouth to protest, then caught the older woman's eye. Bella was right; the red would be perfect with the outfit they'd bought earlier. Even Marina, with her inexperienced eye, could see that.

Though after three whole days with Bella, Marina couldn't claim any longer to be untutored in the secrets of fashion. They'd discussed colour, body shape, face shape, dress design, jewellery, posture—though apparently she had no problems there—and make-up.

She'd been bullied into hundreds—or was it thousands?—of outfits, until eventually she'd understood why Bella so emphatically approved of some clothes and shuddered at others.

Forced to look in the mirror again and again, she could see now that the cover-up dresses she wore did her no favours, while some of the styles she'd avoided were almost flattering.

She'd even let herself be talked into new underwear that was silky, seductive and utterly decadent. She'd insisted it was unnecessary, had almost blurted out that no one else would see it. But Bella had been adamant that she needed a makeover from the skin out.

And Bella knew what she was talking about. The delicate caress of silk against Marina's body did make her feel…different. Not like her old self at all.

By the time they'd made it to the discreet salon this morning, Marina had been eager to have her hair cut short, ready to embrace a whole new image. Even the chief hairstylist's disapproval hadn't dimmed her enthusiasm. It had taken Bella's throaty murmur, stating that Ronan had specifically ordered her hair be kept long, to stop her. After all, he was financing this masquerade.

But it had stuck in her craw—him dictating something as intimate as the way she wore her hair. She'd been tempted to ignore his wishes and suit herself. Yet she'd known as soon as she saw the results that he'd been right.

Blast the man! How had he known? And, more to the point, why had he even bothered to think of it? Surely the length of her hair was a trivial detail.

She sat down and took off the delicate sandals. They were so fragile, so extravagant. So not like her.

A pang of misgiving speared her. Would this plan of Ronan's work? Could she really snare Charles Wakefield's interest and hold it long enough to distract him even a little from his business?

She shook her head at the ridiculous notion. A change of clothes couldn't make that much difference. She was still essentially the same: too lacking in feminine wiles, too scarred to attract a man. She had about as much sex appeal as double-entry bookkeeping.

Then she looked up and caught sight of the stranger in the mirror. She didn't look like herself any more.

A discreet chirrup interrupted her reverie, and she watched Bella flip open her silver cellphone.

'Ronan!' There was genuine delight in the other woman's voice.

Immediately Marina tensed. It was nonsensical, but just a call from Ronan Carlisle was enough to disrupt her equilibrium. He'd burst into her life like a hurricane, turning everything topsy-turvy. Nothing was like it had been before. And she had a sinking premonition that *she* would never be the same again.

She bent over and concentrated on slipping on her flat sandals.

'Sure, I'll put her on.' Bella held out the slimline phone. There was no way Marina could avoid it.

'Hello?' She half turned away, to stare out of the door.

'Marina.' His voice was deep and smooth. Inevitably, stupidly, a thrill of excitement skittered across her skin and she shivered. 'How's the shopping? Has Bella finally convinced you to spend my money?'

Marina darted a look at her companion, but Bella had moved away, talking to the sales assistant as she boxed the shoes. Just how much had she told him about Marina's reluctance to use his platinum credit card?

'It's going fine, thanks. It's impossible to shop with Bella and *not* spend a small fortune.'

'I'm sure it will be worth every penny.' His voice lowered to a soft burr that made her pulse gallop. 'I'm looking forward to seeing the results.'

'Why are you calling?' She sounded brusque, but that was better than letting him hear the unevenness in her breathing.

'To invite you out. Are you up to it?'

Fleetingly she wondered if she'd ever be up to coping with Ronan Carlisle. Just the sound of his voice, low and intimate in her ear, was enough to turn her inside out.

'Of course. I'm not sick.' She paused. 'When did you have in mind?'

'Tonight.'

All the breath in Marina's lungs disappeared in a sudden whoosh of fear. Tonight! That was way too early. They'd only agreed to this crazy plan a few days ago. She still wasn't sure she could manage her part in it.

More to the point, she didn't yet know how to control her

responses to Ronan Carlisle. No man had ever affected her like this. He was even disrupting her sleep. And if she played the part of his lover she'd have to stand close to him, maybe touch him, let him touch her…

'Marina?'

'I'm still here,' she said quickly.

'I'll pick you up at seven.'

Seven. That was only a few short hours away.

'I…' she gulped. 'Sure. I'll be ready.' As ready as she'd ever be. 'Where are we going? What should I wear?' This was the beginning of their masquerade, and she was determined to do the best she could.

'A cocktail party first. Then a quiet dinner. We'll go somewhere we'll be seen, but where we can talk privately. Discuss it with Bella; she'll help you choose something suitable.'

There was the sound of voices in the background, then he said, 'I've got to go. I'll see you at seven.'

And then there was silence.

Marina closed the phone carefully. Her palms were damp as she rubbed them over the cotton of her sundress. Her pulse still raced, and there was an edgy, swirling sensation in the pit of her stomach.

Three hours to transform herself. Just three hours until she had to play the part of Ronan Carlisle's mistress. She'd have to persuade a bunch of critical strangers that she was the sort of sexy female who'd catch Ronan Carlisle's interest. *And* she had to ensure Ronan had no inkling of the devastating effect he had on her.

She had to convince both herself and him that her reaction to his kiss had been an aberration, a one-off event. That he could look at her with that intense flare in his eyes, share a whispered conversation, even perhaps hold her close, and she would feel nothing.

She shivered.

Would she have the nerve to go through with it?

In the end Marina had more time than she wanted to prepare. Too much time to think and worry. She showered and carefully put on her make-up, following the instructions they'd given her at the salon. And all the time she tried to ignore the deep-seated fear that she was about to make a complete spectacle of herself.

But then how much worse could things get? No business and probably no job soon, if Charles Wakefield brought in his own staff. And Seb and Emma with a baby on the way.

Which meant she *had* to co-operate with Ronan Carlisle. If there was any chance, no matter how small, that he could get back for them what they'd lost, then she had to take it. Her personal discomfort didn't matter.

For a moment another fear edged into her thoughts. The idea that Ronan might want her to do more than put on a public show as his mistress. Was it possible he'd expect her to be so grateful for his help that she'd play the part of his lover in private too?

Her breath clogged as she froze, transfixed by the possibility.

Then common sense reasserted itself. She was letting her imagination run away with her. He'd kissed her, but only after she'd made it shamingly clear how much she craved his touch. He'd been curious. But he didn't want her. He just saw her as a tool in his scheme.

She had nothing to worry about on that score.

Marina zipped up the new dress and walked over to the mirror. There she stopped and stared, eyes wide with disbelief. The outfit looked even better now than it had in the changing room.

It had been over a year since she'd bought new clothes, and since then she'd dropped a dress size. She was slimmer. But it wasn't only that.

Her hands spread over the silky fabric that skimmed her curves so lovingly. It was unbelievable. She turned, trying to discover just what made the dress so different. So intriguing, so sinful.

It wasn't too tight, but it clung in all the right places. Places that now seemed just right. Curvaceous, not bulging. The neckline wasn't especially low—only a shadow of cleavage showed at the deeply cut square neck. She frowned, unable to put her finger on what made the dress so special.

And turned her into a different woman.

Then, suddenly, there was no time left to wonder. The doorbell pealed and she grabbed her purse. She wouldn't allow herself time for doubts now. It was too late.

But her hand shook as she reached for the front door.

Ronan stood back as the door swung open. Anticipation fizzed through his bloodstream. He hadn't seen her in days. He'd forced himself to keep away, working with renewed vigour on his commercial plans. But it had been harder than he'd expected to maintain his distance. Far too hard. For it wasn't business that had been paramount on his mind. Marina had eclipsed all else since the moment he'd seen her, vibrant and determined, at Wakefield's party.

And suddenly there she was. Marina Lucchesi, ready to play the part of his lover. She stared up at him with liquid-dark questioning eyes.

He should say something to break the thick tension in the air. But he couldn't. He stood, absorbing the body-blow to his solar plexus that had robbed him of oxygen.

By God, she was gorgeous. Arresting, with her sculpted face and hourglass figure. Why she'd hidden herself under those frumpish clothes was a mystery.

He'd imagined her like this during each restless, frustrated night. Her hair was seduction itself, a silken invitation to touch that made him clench his fists so he wouldn't reach out and grab. Her lips were a glossy dark pout that promised all the passion a man could want. Her body was a siren's: the sort a man would dream about for the rest of his life.

The telltale tightening across his belly and thighs was testament to the power of her.

'You look lovely, Marina.' He watched confusion and delight flare in her eyes, and wondered at her reaction to the simple compliment. She obviously wasn't used to praise.

'Is it okay for the party?' She gestured to the dress, as if unsure.

'Perfect,' he assured her. 'You'll be the sexiest woman there.'

Her eyes widened at his words, and her full lips parted just a fraction.

It was pure invitation. Impossible to ignore.

He stepped close, bending his head before she could protest or move away. But he dredged up a sliver of restraint at the last moment and pressed his lips to her brow, not her luscious mouth. He'd discovered how dangerous her kisses were, and he was determined not to be sidetracked again. For the moment at least.

He inhaled her delicate scent, trailing his mouth for one exquisite moment over her whisper-soft hair, feeling her intimate warmth against him.

He couldn't repress the tremor of raw desire that racked his rigid muscles. She was pure, feminine invitation. He breathed deep and forced himself to move away.

She wore black, a shimmering dress sprinkled with silvery starbursts, that clung to her like a lover's hands. On her feet were the sexiest shoes he'd ever seen. And those legs…

Hell! Tonight would be the ultimate test of his control. He'd much rather lead her to her bedroom, strip the clothes from her and lose himself in her body.

But he knew how stubborn she was. Had seen the obstinate tilt of her chin when she'd argued against his plans. He remembered her sudden reserve, how she'd pushed him away. Despite her body's undeniable weakness for his caresses, her mind was set against any further intimacies.

This wasn't the time. Not yet. Somehow he'd have to find a way to ignore the primitive instinct to reach out and simply take her.

Tonight was the night he introduced Marina to the world as his lover. A ploy to lure Wakefield, yes. But, more importantly, a means of keeping Marina exactly where he wanted her.

And he was a man used to getting exactly what he wanted. Every time.

CHAPTER EIGHT

MARINA sank back into the embrace of the leather seat and tried to slow her beating heart as the sports car cruised the city streets.

From the moment she'd opened the door to Ronan Carlisle it was as if she'd stepped out of her mundane world and into a fairytale.

No fantasy prince had ever looked more handsome or more potently male. The sight of him had set off a deep-seated fire of need and a ridiculous longing that had robbed her of words. She hadn't been able to read his expression. But there'd been a tension about him, as if he was poised on the brink of decisive action, that had held her in thrall with its intensity. Then he'd stepped close, and the world had tilted on its axis.

Marina's eyes fluttered shut as scorching desire rose at the memory.

She'd almost expected him to sweep her into his arms and kiss her like he had before, till reason disintegrated in an explosion of new sensations. She'd *wanted* him to.

But of course he hadn't. The other night had been a mistake. He probably regretted it as much as she should—*did.*

Instead it had been a chaste kiss, a gentle salutation that a brother might give. A little much-needed encouragement. That's all.

Yet, no matter how firmly she told herself that, her reaction was the same. An urgent craving—not only for his approval, but his passion. Her whole body had come alive, awareness had ignited as he'd stepped close. Her senses had clamoured for more, more, more.

How stupid was that? She was on fire for a man who viewed her simply as an asset in a business manoeuvre.

She had to cling to that knowledge and keep her feet firmly on the ground. She was no match for his sophistication, could never compete with the type of woman he *really* wanted. She had to remember what this was all about.

She opened her eyes and slid a sideways glance at him. Even with his jaw clamped hard and his brow furrowed, he was the handsomest man she'd ever seen. He looked almost grim, and Marina wondered if he too was having second thoughts about his scheme.

'Tell me if you tire,' he said abruptly. 'We'll only stay at the party long enough to make an impression.'

'I'll be fine,' she murmured, wondering just how big a lie that was. She wasn't worried she'd collapse—her difficulty the night she'd confronted Wakefield had been due as much to stress as physical weakness. And now, after just a few days, she was feeling much stronger.

But would she be able to carry off this masquerade? Despite the new clothes, she couldn't imagine anyone believing she'd captured Ronan Carlisle's attention. He could have any sultry, gorgeous beauty he wanted.

And would she be able to hold her own tonight among Sydney's elite? She was a homebody. An ordinary office worker. She had no practice at rubbing shoulders with the rich and famous.

She turned her head to stare out of the side window. For one unguarded moment she allowed herself to admit the devastating truth. Parading herself as a *femme fatale* was preposterous. She was sure to be found out.

But that was the risk she had to take. If there was a slim chance of setting things right for Seb and Emma and the baby, then she'd do it gladly.

But her secret fear was much worse. That by playing this charade of intimacy with Ronan Carlisle, he might discover how she felt about him. Learn how devastating he was to her peace of mind and her willpower.

That secretly, in some hidden inner chamber of her heart, she wished it was true: that she and Ronan really were lovers.

An hour later, Marina was stunned at how easily she'd slipped into this role of Ronan's devising. No one had shown by word or look that they thought it odd, her being with the most powerful, most drop-dead gorgeous man at the crowded party. Maybe they were all too polite to hint at what they really thought—that she didn't belong.

All she'd had to do was stand close and look as if she had eyes for no one but him.

No acting required!

Awareness vibrated through her every time Ronan moved or gestured at her side. It was frightening how attuned to him she was, even now, when his attention was on the man who'd come up to discuss business trends. She remembered him from Wakefield's reception of course, where he'd waylaid them on their way out. But it was only now she recognised him. After all, it wasn't every day you bumped into a senior government minister in the flesh.

Ronan turned and caught her gaze. A shaft of heat seared her. Shaken, she dropped her eyes and bent her head to sip champagne.

The men finished their discussion. The politician excused himself for interrupting them. She smiled and shook his hand, then watched him turn away.

But her smile died as, through the shifting colours of the crowded room, she saw a face she knew. A pair of eyes fixed on her, absorbed. She swallowed hard and froze.

Charles Wakefield.

Her illusion of confidence shattered in an instant.

How would he react to her presence? Would he embarrass her in front of everyone? Or would he ignore her?

'Marina, look at me.' Ronan's voice was low and compelling. She turned. 'Did you see him? Wakefield—'

'I know.' He moved in front of her to eclipse the room so she could see no one else. She tilted her head and looked up into his mesmerising eyes. 'There's no need to be nervous,' he said. 'Wakefield's not going to make a scene. Not with me here to stop him.'

Marina wished she could absorb the confidence that radiated from the big man in front of her. Dread carved a hollow sensation in the pit of her stomach. A few days ago she'd wanted nothing more than a meeting with Wakefield. Now the very idea of it made her feel sick.

Ronan took the glass from her trembling hold and placed it on a nearby table.

'Touch me.' His lips moved bare inches from her face.

She couldn't have heard him right. 'Sorry?'

'Touch me, Marina. Now, while he's looking at us.' His eyes blazed with an inner fire and the curve of his lips as he smiled down at her was a sensual promise.

She swallowed, stunned at how realistic that lover's smile of his looked. Scared by the inevitable reaction it stirred low in her body.

Tentatively she raised her hand, closed her fingers round the soft weave of linen on his arm. The muscle beneath shifted and bunched. She felt the gentle exhalation of his breath on her upturned face. Without thinking she leaned in to him, drawn to his heat and to the subtle male scent that had teased her senses all evening.

'That's it,' he encouraged. 'Perfect.'

For a heartbeat they stared at each other. Then he wrapped an arm round her, drawing her close so his heat seared her right through the thin fabric of her dress. Her breath stopped in her throat at the forbidden images that simple contact evoked.

Ronan turned her towards the full-length windows that opened onto the roof garden. They stepped into the warm, scented evening, not pausing till they reached the shelter of a secluded loggia. His fingers splayed across her hip in what must look like a mark of ownership. To her it felt like a brand, pure fire that sizzled across her skin and deep into her soul, marking her very being.

Nonsense! She was letting her imagination run away with her. This was all make-believe.

Here in the shadow of overhanging jasmine they were virtually invisible from inside. But Wakefield must have seen them leave. Was he curious enough to follow them outside?

Ronan obviously thought so. He stayed close enough to look like a lover.

And that was what she had to remember. It was an act. She had to concentrate on playing her part.

She drew a deep breath, heady with the perfume of flowers, and stared out over the spectacular cityscape, fighting to block out all sensation and concentrate on the view. The harbour below them glowed like shot silk with the last reflection of the dying sun. Around it a multitude of lights from the surrounding city had sprung to life like sparkling gems.

'Beautiful.' Ronan's deep voice was like the brush of rich silk across her skin. She looked up and found him watching her, intent. Her stomach plunged in a bottomless dive as excitement sped up her pulse another notch. The shadows of an overhead vine cast his features in shade, but she could make out the strong lines of his throat and jaw, the glitter of his eyes as he looked down at her.

Whatever she'd been about to say died. The passion in his voice, the tension vibrating from his body, seemed so real.

A game, Marina. Remember it's a game.

But despite that knowledge, despite the last vestiges of common sense, she responded, swaying closer, forgetting her vow to be strong.

In the distance a melody sounded, a shout of laughter. But here there was only the sound of her heartbeat, drumming like a hammer. Her breath, raw and shallow in her throat.

What would it be like if Ronan Carlisle, so virile, so tempting, were to look at her with real desire? Not as a ploy to convince Wakefield. Not because he felt sorry for her, as he had the other night.

Her mind skittered away from the dangerous idea.

'Is he watching?' she asked, hoping Ronan would mistake her breathlessness for a whisper.

He didn't respond, just wrapped his other arm around her and pulled her close, so that the heat of him enveloped her. His elusive male scent invaded her senses, potent and musky, like a taste of velvet against her lips.

Something inside her flared into life, shimmering and exciting. Expectation.

Staring into his eyes, she wondered frantically how she'd got herself into this. She was playing a part, but she was way out of her depth. This man who was supposed to be her ally had suddenly become a threat.

Ronan Carlisle was far more dangerous, she now realised, than Wakefield, the man who'd stolen her birthright. More dangerous than any mere business competitor or swindling cheat could ever be.

Ronan was out of her league, a master player in a complex game where she was just a pawn.

He made her feel like she'd never felt before. Like a woman, vibrant and passionate. Wanting.

Wanting what she couldn't have. What she shouldn't want from him.

She opened her mouth to speak. To break the spell of the seductive setting and her own fantasies. Of the passion Ronan projected for the benefit of the man she guessed watched them from the shadows.

But it was too late.

Arms as unyielding as steel drew her up to a body that was all hard muscle and bone and flaring heat. His head lowered, lips warm and sure against hers.

And Marina melted into his embrace, promising herself that she would give herself up to these glorious sensations once. Just one last time, to convince Wakefield. And then she'd step away.

Ronan's mouth was surprisingly soft, coaxing her to kiss him back. There was none of the ravaging energy she'd experienced before. Yet this kiss was just as stunning, destroying all thought, inviting complete capitulation.

He lifted a hand to her hair, cupping her head as he sought better access to her lips.

He tasted like sparkling wine and pure, intoxicating man. Like all the sins of temptation put together. And she couldn't get enough of him. She wanted to burrow closer to his warmth, to the easy caress of his mouth, to the exciting hardness of his big frame.

The sensations exploding through her were like firebursts. They flared and spread, searing every nerve with a need she fought desperately to resist.

But the desires he awakened were too compelling to deny.

She lifted her hands, sliding them up against his shirt to rest against the heat of his chest. His heartbeat thudded beneath her palm, strong and steady, and her head swam at the intimacy.

It wasn't enough. Involuntarily she squirmed against him, fighting her own weakness. But common sense had deserted her. Instead she gave in to the primitive need that pounded in her blood, slipping her hands down so she could wrap her arms round him, beneath his jacket. Holding him tight, as if he were hers.

He stepped closer, his thighs settling on either side of hers so she was cradled in his intimate heat. His other arm lashed tight round her waist, making breathing difficult.

But she barely noticed. For his tongue slid along her lips, inviting her to open for him. And of course she did, responding mindlessly to the sensuous promise of his expertise.

Heat. Velvety darkness. Mingled breaths. The delicious rasp of tongue against tongue. A shared erotic awareness that scorched all rational thought from her brain. And, above all, the rising need for more.

She clutched at him, dimly aware of being bowed back over Ronan's arm by the power of his embrace. He was closer than ever, pushing against her breasts, her hips, her thighs. Comprehensively claiming her mouth.

His arm moved from her waist, slipping down over her hip, and then lower still. His long fingers splayed over her bottom, pulling her higher and tighter against his hard body. It was a movement so explicit that she gasped.

Not with surprise or outrage.

With the realisation that she wanted still more.

She wanted everything she'd dreamed of from a lover. All the heat and passion. All the love. Everything she'd never had.

And she wanted it from Ronan.

For an instant the illusion held. Then his mouth relinquished hers and she gulped in a shuddering breath. He straightened, pulling her up with him, but he stepped back a tiny pace too. Enough to keep the illusion of intimacy, but, she realised achingly as her body throbbed with unfulfilled desire, not close enough.

Flame scorched her cheeks. It was only the strength of his hands that kept her upright. Her legs trembled with a weakness that had nothing to do with her injuries.

He didn't speak, but she saw the way his chest heaved. Lack of oxygen. She'd clung to him like a limpet. It was a wonder he'd been able to breathe at all.

It was a miracle she hadn't climbed up his big body in her desperate passion.

And all he'd done was kiss her.

Hell!

She squeezed her eyes shut, knowing she couldn't have been more embarrassingly transparent if she'd tried.

So much for being wary. For doubting his plan. For being a self-sufficient, independent woman. For telling herself she could control her reaction to him.

Nothing had mattered except the craving his touch had evoked. Not her self-respect, nor their situation, nor the knowledge that to him she was no more than a temporary business partner.

'Marina.' His husky whisper set need spiralling anew in her abdomen. She opened her eyes and looked at his shirt, not ready to lift her chin and meet his probing gaze.

One of his buttons had slipped undone. Had she done that? Horrified, she kept her gaze fixed on it, wishing she had the nerve to reach casually across and do it up.

But that would mean touching him again.

Yes! screamed the savage woman he'd awakened.

Absolutely not, dictated the grim voice of self-preservation.

How had she succumbed yet again to this man? He'd only had to touch her and her defences had melted to nothing.

'Marina,' Ronan said again. 'We've got company.'

Even as he spoke she heard the voices coming nearer. Just as well they'd stopped when they had.

She darted a look up at him and, sure enough, he watched her intently. His face was expressionless, but the throb of his pulse at the base of his neck testified to the urgency of their embrace.

Marina pushed back her shoulders and tilted her chin. But she wouldn't look him in the eye again. Instead she swung round towards the approaching couple. They paused beside a huge potted tree strung with lights. No mistaking that profile, she realised as she recognised one of the pair. Charles Wakefield.

She waited for the dread to engulf her. The trepidation. But this time it didn't come. Instead all her senses were alert, trying to read the body language of the man beside her.

Ronan Carlisle must have been born a natural poker player. Not by so much as a movement did he betray his thoughts or feelings.

'So, it looks like the mountain is coming to Mohammed. I knew his curiosity would get the better of him.' Ronan leaned close to whisper the words against her ear, and it took all her control not to shiver at the delicious sensation of his hot breath against her skin.

'Are you ready, Marina?'

'Of course.'

'Marina?' His hand lifted her chin, forcing her to look at him. The touch of his hard fingers against her flesh sent another riot of sensation through her and she set her jaw, desperately searching for her shattered defences.

His expression was quizzical. 'Just remember, you're besotted with me. Don't worry about Wakefield or anything else. Okay?'

'Okay.'

Nothing could be easier, she decided glumly, as he draped his arm round her shoulders and pulled her in close against his side, so they looked like lovers. Even that casual embrace made her heart thud out of control.

She wouldn't even have to act. She had a sinking feeling that *besotted* described her feelings all too accurately.

A cynical voice in her brain told her it was simply to be expected. Ronan was gorgeous, powerful, sexy, rich, and he had a take-charge attitude that appealed to her despite her own need to assert herself. The fact that he kissed like every woman's erotic fantasy had nothing whatever to do with this appalling weakness.

'Chin up, Princess,' he said. 'Just remember what we agreed and it'll be fine.'

What they'd agreed. Right. Marina ticked off the points in her mind.

One: she was to focus on Ronan. She could check that one off.

Two: as far as Wakefield was concerned, Ronan was looking after her now. She'd be angry with Wakefield, but she'd appear to have other things on her mind. Double check.

'Oops, sorry. I didn't see you guys.' A giggling voice interrupted her thoughts, and she turned to see a blonde who looked all of seventeen on Wakefield's arm.

Righteous anger surged through her. Not only a thief and a cheat. A cradle-snatcher as well.

The kid was unsteady on her feet, and Marina wondered if it was due to the teetering heels she wore or the oversized cocktail glass she waved in one hand.

Marina frowned, and immediately Ronan's arm slipped down to tighten round her waist, snatching her breath away as she experienced again that incredible melting sensation deep in her body.

'Charles.' It was Ronan who spoke.

'Carlisle. Loitering in the dark?' Wakefield's smug tone set Marina's teeth on edge. Despite Ronan's embrace, she had to fight the urge to spit venom at the man who'd cheated her brother.

Wakefield turned to face her, the curiosity obvious in his expression. He eyed her up and down so thoroughly she felt queasy. Her dress was designed to catch a man's attention, but this was one man whose regard made her feel as if she needed a wash.

'And Ms Lucchesi. I must say I didn't expect to see you here.'

Marina stared back at him, wondering what sort of guy could threaten her with a lawsuit for slander, plan to throw her out of his reception, and now act as if she were an interesting specimen for study.

An arrogant son of a bitch who believed he had to answer to no one, she decided.

'I could say the same,' she retorted. 'If I'd known you'd be here I wouldn't have come.'

'Now, Ms Lucchesi. Marina.' He spread his hands in a show of openness. 'No need for that, surely? Our conversation the other day wasn't helpful, but it was hardly the most appropriate time or place.'

His patronising tone made the hairs on her neck prickle, and

Marina was grateful for the reassuring sweep of Ronan's hand against her waist as he held her against him. She looked up to see him watching her, his gaze giving nothing away. It was good to have an ally. Even one who made her feel far too much.

'I see you have someone else to speak for you now. How very convenient.' No mistaking the sarcasm in Wakefield's tone.

Ronan's baritone cut across him. 'My relationship with Marina is private, Charles, but I can tell you this: *convenient* isn't how I'd describe it.'

'Hardly,' added Marina, fixing Wakefield with a glare that should have burnt the smarmy grin right off his face. 'Nor is it any of your business. But I speak for myself and always will,' she added in freezing accents.

The girl with Wakefield looked uncertainly from one to the other, clearly wondering what she'd walked into. But Wakefield's expression was intent. Marina could almost hear the wheels turning over as he sifted their words, read their body language.

Could he really be putting two and two together and coming up with five?

'My mistake,' he said smoothly. He looked at Ronan, then back to her again, and Marina held her breath, wondering what was coming next. Had he already decided this was a far-fetched plot? She'd known no one would believe they were an item.

'We still have unfinished business, Marina,' Wakefield continued in a suave tone. 'Our last discussion didn't resolve anything, and, on reflection, I feel I owe you an explanation of what took place between your brother and me.'

Marina bit her tongue rather than blurt out that she knew exactly what had occurred. Seb had told her.

Wakefield took her silence for agreement. 'We should meet.' He paused, bestowing his toothy smile. 'And we can discuss the situation.'

Stunned, she nodded. Surely it couldn't be so easy? Could it? Was he really promising her a chance to negotiate?

'That's exactly what I'd like.' She had to remind herself that it was easy to arrange a meeting. That didn't mean Wakefield had any intention of making redress.

'Good,' he said, and his smile widened disconcertingly, re-minding her again of a hungry carnivore. 'Give me your number, and I'll get my PA to organise it.'

She'd opened her mouth to respond when Ronan spoke. 'Good idea, Charles. Just have him call my home to arrange a time.'

She gaped as he continued blithely, 'Marina's moving in with me.'

CHAPTER NINE

A FEW minutes later Ronan watched Marina steer the younger woman across the roof garden and into the penthouse. The girl looked green around the gills, and Marina had decided they both needed to freshen their make-up.

He suppressed a smile, wondering if she'd use the privacy to give vent to feelings she'd been unable to acknowledge in front of Wakefield.

When he'd dropped the news that they'd be living together she'd stiffened in shock, her whole body taut as a bowstring. He knew what it had cost her not to ask what the hell he was up to. He'd felt the anger well inside her, a palpable force. But she'd restricted herself to a burning stare which might have been mistaken in the shadows for passionate.

Wakefield had been ogling her like a kid staring in a candy shop window. But that bombshell had made him jerk back in disbelief, then shoot an assessing glance between the two of them. Obviously he'd made it his business to know Ronan never invited lovers to share his home.

But instead of it warning Wakefield off, he was still sniffing around Marina. The 'private property' signs Ronan had posted didn't deter him.

Just as he'd expected. Wakefield found her attractive in her ultra-feminine clothes and make-up. Any man would.

The news that she belonged to Ronan, and apparently meant significantly more to him than any previous lover, had sent the man into a frenzy of curiosity.

But Wakefield felt much more than curiosity. There was no mistaking the leer on his face as he watched Marina support the other girl through the door of the apartment.

That look told Ronan all he needed to know. Wakefield would take the bait and chase her, as much for her own sake as for the opportunity of besting his rival. All he had to do was play Wakefield a little longer, choose his moment, and then reel him in.

Ronan waited for the surge of elation. Of satisfaction.

And waited.

Why wasn't he pleased at how easy this would be? He took a moment to assess the emotion gripping him so rigidly round the shoulders.

It was sheer bloody anger. Fury that a low-life like Wakefield thought he stood a chance with someone as intelligent and classy as Marina.

Marina was *his*! His alone.

His pulse quickened at the thought of how much he'd enjoy wiping that leer off Wakefield's face.

'I have to hand it to you, Carlisle, you're a quick worker.' Wakefield took a swig of what smelt like pure Scotch and grinned at him. 'It's less than a week since she gatecrashed my reception, and I'd bet you hadn't even met her before that.' His eyes narrowed. 'Or was it you who put her up to that little stunt?'

Ronan settled his shoulder against a pillar and crossed one leg over the other, projecting nonchalance. It was a child's ploy, but he knew how much Wakefield would hate it.

'Sorry to disappoint you, Charles, but I had no idea Marina was going to be there. You know I've always left the Machiavellian stuff to you.'

But things have just changed.

And he was going to get a hell of a lot of satisfaction from making Wakefield pay for the damage he'd inflicted. And for daring to leer at Marina.

'I'd never seen or heard of Marina before that night,' Ronan added.

Wakefield flicked a glance in the direction of the penthouse.

'And obviously you took her home afterwards.' Ronan caught an undercurrent of pique.

He nodded. 'That's right.'

'Well, well.' Wakefield spread his lips in a lascivious smirk. 'She must really be something in the sack if she's hooked you in less than a week. What's her secret? Does she play the innocent or the tart?'

The impulse to grab the slimy bastard by the neck and crush the air from his windpipe was almost overpowering. Ronan's hands flexed convulsively and he straightened to loom over him. There was a savage satisfaction in seeing the immediate flare of terror in Wakefield's eyes. Ronan had to fight the temptation to deck the little weasel, since he couldn't throttle him.

Years of ignoring his petty games had taught Ronan control in the face of provocation. He'd even reined in his thirst for blood when he'd learned what Wakefield had done to Cleo. It had been almost impossible, but that was the only way to protect her. If Wakefield learned the truth about her recent 'illness' he'd make it public knowledge in the blink of an eye.

But now Wakefield had gone too far. The surge of primitive emotions was too strong for Ronan to contain. And that was a warning sign in itself.

'Don't go there,' Ronan growled, in a voice that was pure intimidation. He took a single pace forward and saw Wakefield shrink back.

He got the message all right. It was clear in the whites of his eyes and his defensive posture. But Ronan wasn't taking chances.

'Just one word like that to Marina, or about her, and you'll wish you'd never been born. Have you got that?'

'Sure, sure.' Wakefield took another step away. 'No need for threats. Obviously I got the wrong idea. I didn't realise you were serious about the girl.' His gaze, intent and assessing, swept Ronan.

'Your mistake. Just don't make it again.'

And so the trap closed, with an echoing clang.

This time Ronan recognised the sizzle of anticipation as he saw his plan swing into action. Wakefield wanted what Ronan had: Marina. His ego was so colossal he actually thought he could entice her away with his brittle charm and empty promises.

Wakefield waved his drink in the direction of the party. 'Here she comes now.'

Ronan turned to see the two girls heading towards them. His mouth dried at the silhouette of Marina's figure, backlit by the lights of the apartment. The enticing sway of her hips as she walked towards him matched the urgent tattoo of his pulse. Blood drummed through his body as he remembered the feel of her luscious curves pulled up hard against him. Of her hands, tentative but seductive, stoking his need wherever they touched.

'I have to admit, Carlisle, you can pick them. She really is something.'

Wakefield was trying to lighten the atmosphere. But the sense of primal ownership Ronan felt as he watched her made him want to whisk her away somewhere private. Somewhere secluded from every other man. He didn't want Wakefield looking at her. Not when he knew what was going on in that gutter that passed for his mind.

'If she'd dressed like that when she came to see me I might have taken her more seriously,' Wakefield muttered.

Which just confirmed what Ronan had always known— Wakefield was as shallow as they came. It was surface glitter that caught his eye. Hadn't the guy seen beyond Marina's god-awful suit and scraped-back hair that first night?

Ronan shook his head in disbelief, remembering her spirit and intelligence, her determination, her sheer bravery that night as she'd fought a losing battle and ignored the odds. The way passion had lit her from within, the fire in her eyes and the classic sculpted lines of her face. All had accentuated her vibrant beauty.

Wakefield was worse than a conniving bastard.

He was a fool.

* * *

Ronan must take her for a fool, Marina decided half an hour later. Avoiding his probing gaze, she looked around the exclusive restaurant. After the dizzying flash of lights from the paparazzi as they entered, the dining room was quiet, elegantly opulent and very discreet.

She didn't understand what Ronan was up to. That lie about moving in with him had been totally unnecessary. Yet it seemed he expected her to accept it without argument. Why should she move into his home? Surely they didn't need to go so far to convince Wakefield they were lovers?

And after tonight she was even less certain she had the stamina to play the part of Ronan's mistress.

When she'd returned to the roof garden to see both men watching her, she'd wanted to turn tail and run. Wakefield's sly looks had made her want to hide. And Ronan's steady, impenetrable gaze had heated her body to tingling, sensuous excitement.

He scared her witless.

A single touch of his hand sent her nervous system into overload. If she had to pretend to intimacy with him for an extended period he was sure to discover she wasn't acting. That her desire for him was shamingly real.

She was in lust with Ronan Carlisle.

He'd only have to crook his finger and she'd have the fight of her life trying to keep her sanity long enough to resist him. Even worse, the way he made her feel—as if she were precious, protected and cared for—appealed far too much. If she weren't careful her emotions would override her common sense.

And that would be disastrous. He would never want a woman like her.

'All right.' Ronan's low murmur sent a shiver of delicious awareness through her. 'The waiter's gone, so you can say it. No one will hear but me.'

She lifted her gaze. He leaned back in his chair on the other side of the small table, the epitome of arrogant assurance. His eyes glittered in the subtle candlelight and his smile would melt the hardest female heart.

Pure sex on legs. That was what he was.

Too much man for you, Marina.

'I've changed my mind,' she said flatly. 'I want out of this charade.'

She read a flicker of emotion in his face but couldn't pin it down.

'I didn't have you pegged as a quitter, Marina. Or are you just frightened?'

'What would I be frightened of?'

He shrugged. 'You tell me. I don't pretend to know what goes on in your mind.'

'I'm not scared,' she said, lifting her chin and looking him in the eye so he wouldn't guess how big a lie that was. She felt colour wash across her throat and cheeks as he surveyed her but she refused to look away.

'If it's not fear, why give up so easily?'

She shrugged. 'This isn't going to work. I never really believed it would, but I was desperate enough to think we might make Wakefield change his mind.'

'And you're not desperate now?'

Her breath caught. Trust him to remind her of her obligations. Of course she was desperate.

'That's not the point,' she answered. 'I can't make Wakefield give back what he's stolen just because he thinks I'm your...'

'*Lover* is the word you're looking for.'

Marina watched his mouth shape the word, and something short-circuited in her brain. All she could think of was the feel of those lips against hers, the intimate caress of his tongue, the way his hands had splayed so possessively, so knowingly, over her body.

And of how she'd all but begged him for more. Not once, but twice. And the second time, on the roof terrace, not even the fact that they were being watched had stopped her.

She reached for her water and drank half of it.

'You may not be able to make Wakefield surrender it, but I can.' From anyone else the words would have sounded glib. But not from him.

She read the grim implacability in his face and knew a fleeting twinge of sympathy for Charles Wakefield. He should never have messed with Ronan. Marina couldn't conceive of anyone besting Ronan in this mood. His angular jaw looked dangerous and his eyes shone bright with purpose. A man who played for keeps.

'I know what I'm doing, Marina. I have every intention of succeeding.'

She believed him. As far as his pursuit of Wakefield went.

But further than that she couldn't trust him. Not when he held all the cards and used her to suit his own ends. He might need her now, but she was part of a bigger scheme that he alone understood. That made her vulnerable.

And something about his plan didn't sit right. Instinct told her it wasn't what it seemed. That there was more to it than Ronan had told her.

Worse still, she knew that against Ronan Carlisle she didn't have enough defences. Her sixth sense screamed at her to get away while she still could.

'You'd be unwise to back out now.'

'Why? What do you know that I don't?' She leaned forward and caught of glint of satisfaction in Ronan's eyes as he crossed his arms. The action drew her attention to his shoulders, wide and powerful beneath his jacket.

'You didn't see the way he looked at you?'

'He made my skin crawl, if that's what you mean. But that doesn't prove anything.' If the situation weren't so ridiculous it would be pathetic. The night she finally looked half convincing as a desirable woman and it had to be for a toad like Wakefield!

'He's definitely interested. He swallowed the bait.'

'How can you be sure?'

'Let's just say he made himself obvious when you weren't around.'

Marina registered Ronan's disapproving tone and decided she didn't want to know what Wakefield had said.

'So he's interested. So what? There are lots of women in Sydney, and I'm sure he spreads himself pretty wide.'

'The difference is your connection with me. I made it clear you were someone special. I posted "no trespassing" signs even he couldn't miss.'

Despite her resolve, Marina was intrigued. More than intrigued. Delighted. Some idiotic, credulous part of her wanted to pretend Ronan had done that for real, because he cared for her. How pathetic was that?

'You did?'

'I did.' His expression held her spellbound, sucked the air from her lungs. 'Why do you think I told him you were moving in with me?'

'That's what I've been wondering.'

His lips twisted in wry amusement. 'Wakefield knows I've never invited a woman to share my home.'

Marina reached for her glass again and drained it. Anything to counter the fatuous smile that threatened to spread across her face.

He was playing a part. He didn't really want her living with him. But illogically she was pleased none of his previous lovers had shared his house.

Even though she was a lover in name only.

'The guy's hooked.' He interrupted her train of thought. 'One good look at you and he wasn't thinking with his brain. And when I threatened him—'

'You did *what?*'

'I warned him off my territory.' He shrugged those massive shoulders. As if Wakefield was merely a nuisance, not a danger.

For a bedazzled instant, for more, Marina wondered what it would be like to let this dominant, powerful man share her burdens. Solve her problems. Protect her. Let her relinquish the weight of responsibilities she'd accepted at thirteen.

As if.

Anyway, it would probably drive her crazy.

'When Wakefield learned I was serious about you he could barely contain his excitement. He's decided you're my weak spot, and he can't wait to try luring you away. Especially now he holds a trump card.'

'Sorry?'

'Your business, Marina. He'll use it as a bargaining chip.'

As if she could be bought for the price of the company. Or, she realised, a bitter taste in her mouth, just for the promise to discuss it. Wakefield would never relinquish it.

Which meant she had no choice but to go along with Ronan's scheme.

She felt trapped, as if the walls had closed in on her. All avenues were barred except the one he held open. She couldn't turn away.

There was Seb and Emma. And the baby. Seb could find another job, start from scratch. But he'd struggle for years because of a single stupid mistake.

And it was her family business. She couldn't let it go so easily. Not to a shark like Wakefield. He'd strip its assets and move on, leaving their employees out of work. People who'd been with them for years: loyal, hardworking, many of them too old to find another job easily, despite their experience.

They were all links in the heavy, inescapable chain that bound her to Ronan Carlisle.

Marina stared at him. The subdued lighting couldn't conceal the hard decisiveness of his angular jaw, the powerful set of his shoulders as he leaned back at ease in his chair. His face was un-revealing, but even in repose it spoke of strength and determina-tion. He was a man who played to win. A man who could get her what she needed.

As long as she survived the experience.

'But if he thinks I've moved in with you he won't make a move.'

Ronan shook his head. 'He'll see you as a greater challenge. He has an ego the size of Antarctica. He won't consider the pos-sibility that he can't get you.'

His lips turned up in a taut smile that made her shiver. 'He won't be able to resist, now he believes you're my woman.'

The shiver turned into a thrill of forbidden excitement at his words.

She was being ridiculous, but she couldn't help it. Not when the touch of his eyes was a hot caress across her bare skin. His elusive scent, dark and masculine and provocative, drew her heightened senses to fever-pitch.

Ronan's deep blue gaze pinned her. 'Whenever he sees us together he'll be convinced I'm serious about you.'

Marina gulped. The fire in his eyes made her skin sizzle. How would she cope playing up close and personal with him for Wakefield's benefit?

'But I don't have to move in,' she countered.

He raised one eyebrow in disbelief. 'Of course you do. Everything has to be as it seems. Wakefield may be an egotistical bastard but he's cunning. That's what makes him so dangerous.'

Marina sagged back in her chair, suddenly exhausted as the inexorable net closed round her again. She'd committed herself to this dangerous game. She had no choice, other than defeat. And she refused to give in.

But a dark fear welled deep inside her. She was way out of her depth. No longer in control.

She stared at the man who'd taken over her life. Could she really trust him to succeed, to deliver what he promised? Could she trust herself to play this role and no more? No stupid dreams, no pathetic hopes and longing?

'And your house is for sale,' he added. 'You'll be moving soon anyway.'

'It's been sold,' she blurted out. Seb had been waiting with the news when she arrived home today. He'd been a picture of guilt, knowing it was his folly that had driven her out of the house their father had built.

Ronan raised one dark eyebrow. 'So soon?'

She nodded, not trusting herself to elaborate. Of course it was just what they'd needed—the news of a buyer, and one willing to pay full price at that. And in the circumstances she'd felt unable to object to the request for an immediate settlement. She'd planned to spend tomorrow searching for a flat. No way could she take up Seb's offer of a room with him and Emma.

The sooner she moved out the better. The place was too full of memories. A lifetime of them.

She shouldn't pine for an empty house. Yet she had to swallow down the lump of grief in her throat. This loss was the final straw.

After all she'd been through she'd used up her reserves of strength, just forcing herself not to give up. Now she was too tired, too physically weak, to fight any more.

The warmth of Ronan's large hand enfolded hers, and she blinked back the film that blurred her eyes.

'In that case you can move in straight away.'

'I suppose I can.' She slumped in her seat, conscious again that she didn't have a choice.

It had been a hectic couple of days, an emotional few months. Right now she felt every minute of them weighing her down.

His thumb brushed across her wrist and her pulse jumped. 'It will be all right.' His voice was low and husky, as if he understood her despair.

She nodded. But she didn't look up at him till he lifted her hand. Her eyes widened as he lowered his head, the expression in his eyes concealed. She felt his warm breath on the back of her hand and shivered.

Then her own breath caught in her throat as he turned her hand and pressed a kiss to the centre of her palm. A tender, slow, utterly seductive kiss that ignited a roaring burst of sensations and made her arm jerk. But he held her firmly, cupping her fingers so that she in turn caressed him: his jaw, his lips.

'I promise, Marina,' he murmured, his mouth brushing her sensitive flesh with each syllable.

Shafts of fire ran along her arm and through her body, arrowing to the secret centre of her femininity. She trembled at the intensity, the sheer blatant potency of her reaction.

He curled her fingers around his and lifted his head. Then he signalled to a waiter, and moments later the sommelier appeared with a bottle of vintage champagne.

Through it all Ronan held her hand. And for the life of her Marina couldn't summon the willpower to pull away. Not when it felt so good.

The wine was poured and they were alone again. Ronan handed her a glass. His eyes were bright with an emotion she couldn't read and his body seemed to pulse with leashed energy, as if he couldn't wait to put his plan into action. Just being near that intense power was exciting.

'I'll take care of everything, Marina. Don't worry.'

He paused and raised his glass in salute. 'To success.'

Fervently Marina added her own silent toast. *To survival.*

CHAPTER TEN

'WELCOME to my home.' Ronan held out his hand to help Marina from the car. She hesitated, but he deliberately stood close, blocking her exit, so she had to accept his assistance.

'Thank you.'

He repressed a smile as she placed her hand in his. Did she experience it too, that frisson of superb sensation when they touched?

She turned her head away as she stood up, looking at the house rather than meeting his eyes.

Of course she felt it. She'd been avoiding his touch ever since they'd met. Almost jumped out of her skin whenever he allowed himself the luxury of brushing into contact with her.

The realisation tightened the coil of ever-present need deep inside him.

But once again she was shying away from him, nervous as an unbroken filly. For an otherwise confident woman, her anxiety when he got near was intriguing. And he was sure it wasn't an act.

Now he cursed himself for insisting on her new wardrobe. He'd promised himself he wouldn't rush her. Would give her time to adjust to the incandescent physical attraction between them since it so obviously unnerved her.

But hell! It was *killing* him.

He wasn't used to shy women. Usually he was kept busy fending them off. And nor was he used to waiting for something he wanted as much as he wanted Marina.

What he needed right now was to have her camouflaged

in one of her old sack dresses. Not the new Marina, with her rippling hair loose, her voluptuous curves and slim waist discreetly accentuated in trousers and a sleeveless waistcoat top.

Ronan dropped his eyes. Five buttons. He swallowed. Only five buttons between him and—

'Your house is lovely,' she said, snapping him out of his distraction.

He stepped back, allowing her space. Then he turned, put a proprietorial hand to the small of her back and drew her towards his home, the perfect host. As long as he could ignore the warmth of her body, the scent of her hair just a touch away.

It was an old house, heritage-listed. Gravel crunched underfoot as they approached the wide front doors.

'I'm glad you approve. I want you to be comfortable here, Marina.'

She darted a glance at him, filled with such a mix of emotions it was impossible to read. He knew she didn't want to be here. She'd made that abundantly clear, right up to this morning, when the removalists had stripped her home bare.

But she had no choice other than to accept his hospitality. He'd made sure of that.

'Come and meet Mrs Sinclair, my housekeeper. She's looking forward to having another woman in the house.'

The tour of the property took some time. And Marina's reactions were fascinating.

He'd been asked more than once if his home could be featured in one lifestyle magazine or another. But it wasn't the multi-million-dollar waterfront location that made Marina catch her breath, or the sleek yacht moored at the private pier. Instead it was the simpler things—the things that didn't shout out money. Like the small jewel-coloured leadlight window at the end of the hall, the collection of antique pewter in the kitchen, and the rose arbour, filled with the fragrance of summer.

By the time they went upstairs she'd finally lost her stiff formality. Her fingers slid up the curved cedar banister, caressed the marble sculpture positioned in the angle of the corridor, stroked the vibrant petals of a vase of liliums.

Watching avidly, Ronan felt his control fray further. Heat rose to combustible levels. She was so tactile, so sensuous. It was there in her sigh as she breathed in the scent of flowers, her instinctive need to touch.

He wanted those hands on him, knowing his body. Just as he wanted to learn every secret of hers.

He'd realised when they kissed how responsive she was. How dangerous to his control. But nothing had forewarned him about this. He was aroused just watching her sensory pleasure in her surroundings.

'This is your room,' he said, his voice almost brusque at the effort of restraint. He pushed the door open and stood aside, jamming his hands into his pockets as she stepped past him.

'Oh.' Her soft sigh of pleasure enticed him, dragged him into the room behind her.

'It's beautiful. Thank you.' For the briefest of moments her eyes, bright with pleasure, met his. Then she walked forward to investigate, obviously intrigued by the antique furniture.

'My pleasure.' His voice was wooden as he watched her skim the silk coverlet on the bed with her palm. He would *not* think about pushing her down onto its wide expanse, imprinting his naked body on hers.

'There's an *en suite* bathroom.' He gestured to the door in one corner, trying not to envisage her in the enormous spa bath that took up half that room. Or standing nude in front of the massive mirror.

Not yet.

He strode across to the French doors and flung them open. Fresh air, that was what he needed.

'And there's a view from here.' He stared out at the harbour, dark and choppy now as the wind picked up. That must be why the air seemed heavy and close, making breathing difficult. They were in for a summer storm.

'I can't thank you enough.' Her voice came from close beside him. 'You're doing so much for us, for me and Seb.'

He turned. Was that a quiver of emotion in her voice?

She stood watching him, chin up in that characteristically courageous pose. But her eyes gave her away. He didn't miss their bright, over-moist sheen.

And here he'd been, imagining how easy it would be if, in tonight's thunderstorm, Marina needed company. He was only a couple of rooms away, down the corridor or the balcony that so conveniently stretched between their rooms.

Deliberately he drew a steadying breath. Passion had burned white-hot between them whenever he'd taken her in his arms. But clearly this wasn't the time to accelerate their relationship to a more intimate level.

It was support she needed right now. Not sex.

He set his jaw. She was hurting. She'd just lost her father. Had been almost disabled in a horrendous smash. And then she'd had to face the loss of her family enterprise, her livelihood, her home, the future as she knew it.

He curved his lips into a smile that he hoped was reassuring. 'You're helping me achieve something that's long overdue. We're in this together.'

That's it. The scheme against Wakefield. His promise to retrieve her company, make things right for her. If only he'd been able to make things right for Cleo. The knowledge of his failure was like acid, eating away at him.

'Just the same…' she walked past him and onto the balcony '…you've been an enormous help.' She smiled briefly and turned to lean on the balustrade. 'I could never have organised removalists so fast, for a start.'

An unfamiliar pang of conscience shafted through him. It wasn't sympathy that had produced the removalists in record time. It had been sheer selfishness and a hefty wad of cash. He'd wanted Marina here, close by him, so it had happened immediately.

'I have to admit the idea of arranging it all was daunting,' she added.

Ronan watched her swallow, saw the way her mouth turned down at the corners. She'd left the only home she'd known, forced out by her brother's stupidity at a time when she needed care and cosseting. And she'd been thrust into a perilous battle of wills with Charles Wakefield.

It astonished him how angry he felt about that. The tidal surge of protectiveness he felt was totally unexpected. Unprecedented. Except for his response to Cleo's situation. But that was different.

He frowned, perplexed.

Marina was different.

His desire for her, his concern, his total absorption in her, were unlike anything he'd experienced. It wasn't her vulnerability—he'd never been attracted by lame ducks. Or simply her looks—there'd been some stunning beauties in his life. But something about her, something he couldn't put his finger on, drew him like a needle to a magnet.

He had to have her.

And he needed to keep her safe from sharks like Wakefield.

He'd been ready to tell Seb Lucchesi just what he thought of him. The kid needed to grow up, fast. He should be caring for his sister, not relying on her to clean up his fiascos.

But it hadn't been necessary. Reality had hit Seb hard. He'd looked sick with guilt this morning, as he'd helped Marina pack her personal possessions. And it sounded as if he'd been working himself into the ground trying to find some alternative to Wakefield's takeover.

It would do him good to work and worry a little more. But Ronan had been compelled to take him aside and give a sanitised version of his own plans to stop him fussing around Marina, upsetting her. When Seb and his wife had finally left on their trip to visit his in-laws, Marina's relief had been palpable.

Ronan uncurled his white-knuckled fists, fighting the urge to stalk over and wrap her in his arms, pull her close and—

The buzz of his phone sounded and he fished it out of his pocket. The dialler's number was highlighted. It was just the distraction he needed.

'Make yourself at home, Marina. I have to take this call.'

She didn't turn, just nodded and stared out across the garden to the water.

He lifted the phone to his ear as he walked away. 'Hi, babe. How are you?'

Marina watched Ronan cleave through the crowd and out onto the Sydney Opera House terrace, where he could carry on his phone conversation.

It was his sister again. Marina had known the instant he elected to answer the phone. Very few people had that private number, and he answered her calls no matter where he was. He was a caring man, a loving brother, who took his family responsibilities seriously.

The contrast to the indefatigable, implacable businessman still fascinated her.

The first time she'd heard him talk to his sister—the day Marina had moved into his house—she'd thought it was a girl-friend calling. His voice had softened, like rich chocolate, melting right through her defences.

And it had made her jealous as hell!

She'd craved his tender endearments for herself, even then, when she'd hardly known the man. And the sound of his intimate tone, calling some woman 'babe', had made her want to rip the phone out of his hand.

'Your Ronan is a devoted brother.'

Marina turned and looked up at the man to whom she'd just been introduced. Tall, silver-haired and beak-nosed, Sir John Biddulph had a daunting presence. He was obviously one of Ronan's friends, but she wished Ronan hadn't left her alone with him. He looked sharp enough to see through their deception. And without Ronan by her side she felt vulnerable.

'They talk every day,' she said, trying to look relaxed.

'She's away somewhere, isn't she?'

'In Perth.' Marina nodded. 'Having an extended holiday with her mother, I believe.'

'Then it's high time she found a young man of her own to talk to. Ronan should be reserving his attention for you, m'dear, before some other fellow cuts him out.' There was mischief in his smile and a distinct twinkle in his eye, and Marina felt some of her reserve dissolve.

'Ronan tells me you're in freight?'

'Oh?' Ronan had been discussing her? 'Well, yes, but in a very small way.'

'Marina Enterprises, isn't it?'

She nodded, amazed that he knew so much about her. Astounded that Ronan had even mentioned her to him.

'A good sound company. Now, tell me, what do you think of the current fuel excise? How is it affecting your business?'

Discussing the transport industry with Sir John was like a guppy comparing notes with a whale. He was the head of a multinational company and she was—what? Ex-director of an ex-family company?

But his interest seemed genuine and his comments were instructive. Soon Marina forgot the disparity, intrigued by their discussion.

It wasn't until an arm slid round her waist, pulling her close to a solid male body, that she looked round. And lost her breath, as she always did when Ronan came close. The sizzling intensity of his gaze, the tantalising male aroma and that smile. Her train of thought disappeared.

'Don't let me interrupt you.'

'You shouldn't leave this girl on her own, Ronan,' said Sir John. 'Someone unscrupulous, like me, might try to steal her away.'

The sally was gallant and very sweet, considering Sir John had to be pushing seventy.

'You're right, of course. I should have switched off my phone.' Ronan curled his arm further round her, so that his heat scorched through the silk of her gown and she forgot to breathe. 'Intellect and beauty together are a powerful combination. Marina's a very special person.'

Marina felt her eyes boggle. Beauty? Even for a man apparently besotted, wasn't he laying it on too thick? But Sir John merely nodded approvingly.

And then, instead of changing the topic, Ronan steered the

discussion straight back to Marina's last point about duties and charges.

For a moment she was flummoxed. She was used to guys who wanted to hold the floor themselves, cap someone's comment with an even more incisive one of their own.

The conversation lasted another fifteen minutes, till the bell went for them to take their seats. And in that time Ronan didn't try to direct the discussion. He seemed as interested in her opinions as Sir John's. But he didn't humour her.

He made her as if they were equals. That was it.

Marina walked inside, conscious of Ronan's large hand, deliciously warm on her back. And all the while she scoured her memory of their previous conversations.

That was how Ronan always made her feel, she realised.

As if she mattered.

'Marina, are you all right?'

She nodded, keeping her face turned away. 'I'm okay. The carpet's just a little uneven.'

He moved, drawing her arm through his and keeping her close against him. Inevitably she felt it again, that unique, exciting sensation, as if something deep inside her dissolved into a swirl of warm emotion.

But while her body responded her mind was busy, sifting and assessing. Whenever they disagreed he didn't bully her or condescend. He didn't use his wealth and power, or his size, to intimidate her. He always treated her as his equal. Her eyes widened. More than that, he treated her as if she were special.

'After you.' His low voice at her ear made her shiver, and she hurried forward to their allocated seats. When they were settled he linked his fingers with hers, drawing the inevitable response as excitement budded and heat skittered up her arm. As he chatted about the performance they were about to see, Marina's responses were mechanical.

Ronan's attentiveness and charm made her heart race, even though he was simply playing at the role of lover. His strong personality, his integrity and his stunning physical presence were what she'd secretly dreamed of in a partner.

He was the most dangerous man she'd ever met.

With a sinking feeling she turned and looked at him, automatically bracing herself for the impact of his dazzling smile and his intent gaze.

He was gorgeous.

He was out of her league.

Their relationship was pure make-believe.

And she'd just realised she was in serious danger of falling in love with him.

CHAPTER ELEVEN

'COME and have a nightcap?' Ronan asked as he ushered Marina into the house.

'I don't think I—'

'I promise not to bite.'

He watched her eyes widen. Her lips round in a prim circle.

The trouble was, Marina's mouth wasn't at all prim. It was luscious, inviting, seductive. It was enough to give the lie to his statement. For if she stood there much longer, close enough for her delicate scent to waft around him, he'd be tempted to lean over and nibble at her lips until she responded like she had that first night.

A surge of volcanic heat shot through him at the memory of her—so passionate, so responsive in his arms.

Just one taste—

'It's late,' she said, taking a step back.

Immediately frustration clawed at him. She'd been like this almost from the first—blowing hot, then cold. Stoking his libido with her seductive body and smouldering glances. Then pulling back like an ice maiden. But Marina wasn't devious. He was convinced she wasn't playing hard to get.

So what was going on here?

'But you're not tired, are you?' He kept his tone light and cajoling.

Of course she wasn't. Tonight's performance had exhila-rated her. That had been obvious from her enthusiastic conversation as they drove home and the unguarded smiles that had slipped past her usual reserve. Her eyes still shone with delight, and she glowed. So, despite his plans to do some late work via e-mail, he found it impossible now to say goodnight and turn away.

'Come on, Marina. You're wide awake. You need time to unwind before you turn in.'

He knew he wouldn't sleep for hours. But that had nothing to do with tonight's world premiere performance and everything to do with the woman before him. She haunted his nights, so tantalisingly close that his body ached at the inhuman restraint he placed on it. He mustn't allow himself to touch. Not yet.

But for how much longer? He couldn't keep this up. And, after all, did he really need to hold back? He could overcome her reserve, obliterate her caution. Seduce her.

Did it really matter that she wasn't yet ready to admit she wanted him? Did it matter that she was still traumatised by recent events?

'Well, I suppose just half an hour. It's been a long day.'

Ronan hoped his answering smile was enigmatic, devoid of the hungry heat that ripped through him, tearing at his resolve. He turned and shepherded her into the sitting room, conscious of her slow steps.

Was she in pain? She never referred to the weakness in her legs but he knew she was still recuperating. From what he'd been able to discover, she was lucky to be walking again.

The thought of her narrow escape still brought him out in a cold sweat.

'What would you like? Liqueur, wine, a soft drink? Or would you prefer coffee?'

'Something light would be good, thanks.'

When he turned from the drinks cabinet she was sitting in a wing chair, looking away from him. Her hand splayed over her skirt, smoothing the soft material.

His attention snapped immediately to the slow movement of her hand. But she didn't look to be in pain. It was a nervous gesture. Instant heat flared, and his temperature soared as he pictured his hand on her leg, sliding up its enticing length. Up the sheer silk of her pantyhose and under her skirt. Or maybe she wasn't wearing pantyhose. Perhaps they were stockings.

He shuddered at the potent eroticism of the image. He could almost feel her warm thighs under his trembling fingers.

He stopped mid-stride and slammed back his drink. Heat scorched down his throat. It was no way to treat an aged single malt.

Marina had no idea how her gesture revealed the long, elegant lines of her legs. How it drew his attention to her innate sensuality.

She was utterly without guile when it came to her body. He'd realised it that first night. She had the body of a seductress, every sensational curve, every long line innately sexy. But she acted as if it was something to hide.

Even now, after days dressed in a wardrobe designed with the sole aim of driving men insane with need, she acted as if she wore a sack. Like the suit he remembered from Wakefield's reception.

How amused Bella Montrose must have been as she'd helped Marina spend his money. He wondered if Bella had any idea what torture he went through now.

'Thank you,' Marina said as she took her drink from his hand. She didn't meet his eyes and, as usual, she was careful not to touch him. He made her uncomfortable.

Uncomfortable!

He'd been in pain since she'd moved in. His whole body was brittle with the strain of self-control. With the agony of repressing lust so incendiary he thought he might self-combust if he couldn't have her soon.

She was driving him crazy.

He dropped in a seat well away from her and put his empty glass on a side table.

'It's a lovely room,' she offered, looking around.

Ah, a nice, polite, pointless conversation. He gritted his teeth, wondering now much longer she could avoid looking at him. 'Thank you.'

'I suppose you got a decorator in to do it?'

'Not a qualified one. At least she isn't yet. My sister did it for me.' At the mention of his sister, some of the fire in his belly faded, replaced with another inevitable tension.

'She's very talented.' And Marina meant it. He could tell by the way her gaze lingered approvingly on the antique Celadon ware in its display alcove, and on the eclectic furniture positioned in comfortable groups. He'd always liked this room, with its elegant proportions and its unparalleled view. But Cleo had transformed it. She really was a genius with interior design.

'Thanks. I'll tell her you like it.'

'You mentioned the other day that she's in Perth. Is she studying there?'

'No.' His voice was too brusque. He saw Marina flinch. 'She's not studying at the moment.'

'Oh. Well, I'm sure there are lots of things to keep her busy there. I've heard it's a lovely city.'

She sipped at her soft drink. She'd given up smoothing her skirt, and fidgeted instead with her tiny beaded purse.

Damn! That was his fault. He hadn't been prepared for her interest in Cleo.

And Cleo had been so interested in Marina, demanding all sorts of details over the phone. She'd even given him permission to tell Marina exactly what Wakefield had done. She'd said Marina needed to hear it, to know what she was up against.

He frowned. He could protect Marina.

Like you protected your sister?

His hands fisted at the recollection of his failure. Guilt pierced him, hollowing his gut.

Was this how he'd feel if Wakefield hurt Marina? He shuddered at the idea. Wakefield couldn't get to Marina now. He'd see to it.

Then he remembered the insistent calls his staff had fielded. The bastard was trying to contact her. And one day he might just succeed.

Tell her, Cleo had urged.

'Ronan, what's wrong?'

He turned his gaze to Marina. She sat up straight in her chair, her eyes huge as she watched him. He felt the tension in his face and knew he'd been scowling.

'Nothing's wrong—' Then he realised the futility of the lie.

If he trusted Marina, if he wanted to protect her, he should tell her the truth. That was what Cleo had said, and he knew she was right.

Yet it went against the grain. The words clogged in his mouth, tasting like betrayal of his sister.

But as he looked into Marina's dark, worried eyes he knew he'd prevaricated long enough. She deserved to know. And he trusted her to keep Cleo's secret. Marina was as honest as anyone he'd ever met.

'It's my sister. Cleo,' he said finally.

'Is she ill?' Marina's smooth brow furrowed.

'She's fine. Now.' He dragged in a deep breath and forced the words out. 'I told you before that Wakefield had hurt a friend of mine.'

Marina nodded, comprehension dawning in her face.

'It wasn't a friend. It was Cleo he hurt.'

'Oh, Ronan!' Her voice was a horrified whisper. 'I'm so sorry.'

He shook his head. It was over. Or almost over. Cleo was so much stronger now. Almost ready to pick up the threads of her life again. It just remained for him to ensure Wakefield got his just desserts. Which meant concentrating on business and not the delicious dilemma now watching him with wide eyes and the most sinful pouting lips imaginable.

'Cleo thought I should tell you what happened.'

'You talked to your sister about me?'

'She wants to meet you. She's got a lot of time for anyone who can see Wakefield for what he is and stand up to him.' A pity Cleo hadn't seen through him earlier.

'You don't have to tell me.' Marina put her glass down on a nearby table, her gaze skating away from his. 'It's private, I know. And it's late. I really should—'

'Stay!' She stiffened and he began again. 'I mean, I'd like you to stay. You need to hear this.'

She slipped back into her chair. A nearby lamp spilled its warm glow over her, picking up the highlights in her glorious hair, revealing the delicate flush of colour high on her cheeks. In that moment Ronan realised that lust was only a fraction of what he felt for this woman. There was a protectiveness and a warmth too, that made him feel—complete.

He held her eyes with his as he spoke, drawing strength from her.

'Last year I spent a few months overseas. I had some negotiations to complete and I was long overdue for a holiday. When I returned…' His hands clenched tight on the arm of his chair. 'When I returned I found Wakefield had given up sniffing around my girlfriends. He'd turned his attentions to my sister instead.'

He should have attacked the bastard then. Taken his fists to him and made him sorry he'd even dared approach her. But life was rarely that simple.

'Cleo is much younger than me. She had no idea of my history with Wakefield, or of what he's really like.' He'd never carried that back to his family. 'She's bright and clever, and full of life, but in some ways naïve.'

Or she had been.

'She was duped by him, completely bowled over. She was in love, and she believed he was too. Nothing anyone said made a difference. She was waiting for his marriage proposal.'

He watched the dawning horror on Marina's face. It echoed his own feelings when he remembered Cleo's face, vivid with excited expectation. The bitter taste of bile rose in his throat at the thought of how much she'd changed since then. Of how much Wakefield had damaged her.

'Ronan?' Marina's voice was low. She perched on the edge of her chair, concern in her expressive eyes.

'The proposal never came,' he said abruptly. 'She discovered she was pregnant instead. She went to him, eager to tell him the news in person. But she never got the words out. That was the day he dumped her, in the cruellest possible way.' His fists grew white-knuckled as scorching fury swept through him.

'He let her find him in bed with another woman. Then he told her their relationship had all been a joke. Just a bit of light relief to see what it was like, screwing Ronan Carlisle's sister.'

He barely registered Marina's outraged exclamation.

Instead it was Cleo's ashen face that riveted his attention. The memory of her, distraught with pain and fear, clutching his hand in a death grip as the doctor confirmed she'd miscarried.

She hadn't cried, not then. She'd been silent and dry-eyed with shock. The tears hadn't come till later. Not till depression had taken her in its grim hold. The downward spiral had been appallingly rapid. The separation from her friends, the insomnia, the burden of self-doubt and, eventually, the desperate bid for release.

His heart pounded against his ribs as he remembered the frantic trip to the hospital, the wait while they pumped her stomach of the sleeping tablets. The crumpled face of his mother as they told her Cleo was lucky to survive.

Marina's skin crawled. Could Wakefield really be that callous?

It would be so much easier to believe Ronan had exaggerated. Except it was no exaggeration. She remembered Wakefield's cold eyes. There had been something inhuman about their icy intensity.

Instinct told her this was the truth, or as much of the truth as Ronan chose to reveal. For it was clear there was more to the story. The expression on his face was so bleak, the pain so real, that she almost reached out to comfort him. His anguish ripped at her. She lifted her hand towards him and then faltered, remembering.

She didn't have the right to comfort him. Their recent intimacy was a charade, and she wasn't really his friend. Her heart plummeted as reality intruded like a blast of white-hot blinding light, forcing her back in her seat.

He wouldn't want her sympathy. She was just another of Wakefield's victims. Ronan had taken her on as a charity case. He'd told her the truth only so she understood the gravity of the situation.

Distress left her wounded and empty.

Even his ferocious scowl and the grooves of pain indenting the corners of his mouth couldn't detract from his charisma. He fascinated her, attracted her, made her feel things she'd never felt before. She wanted to cradle his dark head in her arms and soothe him, ease his hurt. Offer him solace.

Offer herself.

She drew a shuddering, horrified breath.

Even if she found the courage to give herself to him, even if he accepted, she knew he'd be disappointed. He might even be revolted by the sight of her injuries. No, she couldn't bear to see that in his eyes.

'Cleo's been...unwell ever since,' he said, cutting across her thoughts.

'And the baby?' She dreaded the answer.

'A miscarriage.'

Marina sank back against the cushioned upholstery, feeling sick to her stomach. She stared out of the window towards the harbour lights. But all she saw was the fierce pain and hot fury in Ronan's eyes.

'Doesn't Wakefield *expect* you to act against him?' He'd be the world's biggest fool if he didn't. 'After what he did to your sister—'

Ronan shook his head. 'Wakefield's not sure I know about that. Cleo may not have confided in me. And he certainly doesn't know about the pregnancy.' He looked across at her with glittering, unreadable eyes.

'But it's my responsibility to stop him before anyone else gets hurt.' His mouth was a severe line, his jaw set implacably. It was obvious nothing could sway him from his purpose.

Now it all made sense. His obsessive need to obliterate Wakefield. His willingness to champion her cause against a common enemy. Ronan's protectiveness. Even the scorchingly intense looks.

It wasn't attraction he felt for her. She'd always known that with her head. But in her heart had lurked a secret, stupid hope. She felt it wither at last, shrivel to nothing inside her.

Ronan saw her as another vulnerable woman.

She probably reminded him of his sister.

He'd decided she was weak and helpless. A poor, homeless, injured victim. Someone who couldn't take care of herself and needed protecting from a rapacious wolf like Charles Wakefield.

She bit back a sob of despair at the futility of those secret longings she'd clutched to her heart. How foolish she'd been, even to dream there might be something more between them.

Ronan pitied her.

CHAPTER TWELVE

MARINA turned in the water and pushed off from the end of the pool. A couple more laps and she'd quit. Ronan wouldn't be home for hours, even though the shadows were lengthening. But she always played it safe and finished her swim well before he arrived home.

Whenever he was near she needed her wits about her, ready to repress her traitorous reactions.

To her dismay, she'd discovered her weakness for him grew stronger each day. He only had to walk into a room, or look at her in a certain way, to make her pulse gallop and her breath shorten.

Mercifully, they hadn't played their charade often. There'd been the opening night at the Opera House, another cocktail party, and a few dinners at expensive restaurants. Each time he'd been the perfect attentive lover. His arm around her had been like a brand, a searingly exquisite mark of possession that she enjoyed far too much. His show of solicitous interest came so easily she almost believed it was real.

Even here in his home, where they didn't pretend, he made her long for what she couldn't have. He didn't encroach on her space. It wasn't his fault she yearned for a reprise of their passionate kisses. Or that the knowledge that he slept just two doors away kept her awake through the long, hot summer nights. Awake and wanting.

She knew he felt not one iota of desire for her. Yet that knowledge didn't have the power to blunt her craving.

The idea of playing his lover filled her with excitement and apprehension.

She couldn't imagine deceiving his close friends. Someone was sure to spot her as a fake. She had the glamorous clothes, and she didn't wobble any more in high heels. But the woman beneath the gloss was just the same as before. Ordinary. Scarred.

So it was strange how, when Ronan was at her side, smiling down at her, she felt anything but average. Felt almost pretty.

Who did she think she was kidding?

Her palm slapped against the tiles at the end of the pool and she lifted her head, heaving in a deep breath. She needed oxygen. Too much thinking about Ronan and not her pacing. She let herself slide under the water. But closing her eyes didn't obliterate the image of his sexy smile.

She bobbed to the surface. A hand, well-shaped and large, appeared before her. She looked up into Ronan's face and caught her breath at the intensity of his gaze.

'Come on.' His deep voice had a rough edge. 'It's time you got out of there.'

Ignoring his outstretched hand, she propelled herself back from the wall, automatically seeking safety in distance. No man had the right to look so good in business clothes, with his sleeves rolled up over tanned, sinewy forearms and the top buttons of his shirt undone.

'I'm not finished,' she panted. Anything to get him to leave.

His brows drew together. 'Yes, you are. Mrs Sinclair said you've been out here for forty minutes.'

'You set your housekeeper to spy on me?' Marina had liked the woman, with her easy manner and no-nonsense attitude, and felt disappointed.

'Don't be absurd. She happened to notice when you went out, and she's concerned you don't have a relapse. She knows you're recuperating.'

Feeling stupid, Marina concentrated on treading water, ignoring his hand still imperiously outstretched.

'I'll be out in a minute,' she said. 'I'll see you inside.'

'You'll get out now.' This time it was an order. 'Look at your breathing, woman. You need to stop.'

Her chest was heaving, it was true. But it was as much to do with the effect he had on her as the exercise.

'I said I'd get out soon.' After he'd gone safely indoors and she had some privacy. It was bad enough when strangers at the local public pool stared at her. She didn't need that from Ronan.

'Marina.' His voice was a low growl that sent a message of primal power. 'Take my hand now, and let me help you out, or I'll come in and get you.'

She opened her mouth to protest that he wouldn't be so stupid, not when he was fully clothed. But one look at the grim set of his mouth convinced her it was no idle threat.

Still she hesitated, and in that moment his hands went to his shirt, rapidly unbuttoning, his eyes holding hers.

'Okay,' she all but shouted, feeling ridiculous now. 'I'm coming out.'

Instead of gripping his hand, she swam to the side of the pool, keeping her left side away from him. Then she grabbed the ladder and hauled herself up. He was right, she realised with annoyance. She'd swum too long and her legs were trembling. But she'd make it to the sun-lounge and her towel.

He was there before her, walking towards her with a towel held out in both arms.

She stiffened as his gaze swept over her, briefly but comprehensively. Heat rose in her cheeks as she pictured what he saw. She barely resisted the temptation to cover the ugly scars that marred her left thigh. But it was too late, and they were too massive to conceal.

She lifted her chin to stare squarely into his face. His closed expression gave nothing away, neither distaste nor pity. But his eyes seemed darker than usual, almost stormy with emotion. She supposed he wasn't used to anyone crossing him.

He made no comment on the disfiguring legacy of her car crash, and she was too proud to refer to it. Right now it was only stiff pride that kept her upright. The swim and the stupid confrontation had sapped all her energy.

She took a step towards him, her hand reaching for the towel, and one leg buckled. She recovered quickly, shifting her weight to her other foot so she could balance again.

But not fast enough. In a single stride Ronan closed the

distance between them and swept her up into his arms, towel and all. His swearing, low-voiced and pithy, sounded just above her head.

'There's no need for that. I can stand.' Her protest was an indignant hiss.

'There's every need,' he countered, as he pulled her dripping body closer and swung round towards the house.

She stared at the set line of his jaw, at the tension in his strong neck, and knew she should be wishing herself anywhere but here in his arms. Even though excitement fizzed through her bloodstream and the inevitable tendrils of forbidden desire unfurled low in her abdomen.

He strode across the wide paved courtyard and through an open door, kicking it shut behind them with a savagery that made it crash. The sound reverberated through the house.

Her stomach clenched in a mixture of fear and exhilaration, and she shivered. Surely she wasn't enjoying the sight of Ronan, the most controlled, unreadable man she'd ever met, losing his cool.

She had to get a grip.

'Ronan,' she said as calmly as she could, trying to ignore the rapid thump of his heartbeat near her ear and the spicy male scent of him teasing her senses. 'You're right. I should have got out earlier. But you don't need to do this. I can walk.'

'Perhaps I enjoy carrying you.' His voice was sharp, impatient. 'Did you ever consider that?'

Marina hadn't. Couldn't conceive of it. And her mind boggled at the possibility.

She darted a look at his face, reading only annoyance in his furrowed brow and the tight line of his mouth.

Surely he didn't mean it. Even to a man of his size she'd be a burden. He felt sorry for her, that was all. Was worried she'd fall flat on her face.

The trouble was that, cradled in his arms, she felt cherished and ridiculously feminine in a way that was far removed from her usual assertive style.

Even that first night when he'd held her, she'd been ready to drop from exhaustion and bitter defeat, but there'd been magic in his embrace.

He hitched her closer, his arms like warm steel and his hands splayed wide against her wet body. His touch generated a heat that seared and spread through every vein.

With a sigh of surrender she gave in to the inevitable. She let her head relax against him, her hands curve into his hard muscles as he carried her up the stairs.

She shut her eyes and, despite her better judgement, concentrated on collecting a memory of the moment. One she could savour when she was alone again. There was the steady rhythm of his steps ascending the long sweep of staircase. The reverberating thud of his heart beating in the wide wall of his chest. The aroma of him, stronger than the tang of salty pool water, curling around her. The tension of his bunched muscles beneath her fingers.

Face it, Marina, you've got it bad.

He shouldered his way through a door and her eyes flew open at the sound of it slamming shut behind them.

She looked up to see the delicate plaster tracery of the ceiling in her room. And then he strode across to the four-poster bed and lowered her, half dropping her, onto it.

'The bedspread,' she protested, scrabbling to find purchase to lever herself up and off the exquisite silk bedcovering.

'Damn the bedspread.' With one large hand he pushed against her shoulder so she flopped back onto the mattress.

'What the hell did you think you were doing, Marina? Or didn't you think?' He loomed over her, eyes sparking. 'Don't you care that you might do yourself an injury? Cause a relapse that could undo all the work the surgeons have done?'

Her mouth opened, but no words came out. She was transfixed by the sight of Ronan Carlisle, his face stripped of its usual veneer of urbane sophistication. She'd wondered time and again what he was hiding behind his mask of control. Now she had her wish.

Pure, unadulterated fury blazed at her. It was there in the glitter of his darkened eyes and the flare of his nostrils. His feet were planted wide apart in a stance that radiated machismo. Tension corded his neck, and his hands alternately fisted and unclenched at his sides, as if seeking an outlet in action.

And she wanted him.

Big, angry, utterly masculine in his thwarted fury, but he didn't scare her. She knew he'd never hurt her. He wasn't that sort of man.

Instead, the sight of him physically battling such strong emotion stoked the spiral of excitement and need in her own traitorous body. It was all she could do not to squirm beneath his hot stare, revel in the sensations he evoked.

She had to be depraved. Turned on by his anger? Where had that come from?

Marina shook her head, trying to dredge up some sanity from the fog of emotions that deprived her of common sense.

She struggled to keep her breathing even. 'I'm okay. I just took the laps too quickly and—'

'And nothing! It's a good thing I came home when I did, or I could have found you floating face-down in the water.'

'Oh, don't be ridiculous,' she snapped, forgetting her resolution to be calm in the face of his overreaction.

'Ridiculous, is it?' He bent close to glare at her. 'And I suppose you weren't being ridiculous when you refused to get out of the pool?'

'I can make my own decisions.' She propped herself up on one arm, refusing to take this lying down. 'I'm a grown woman, in case you'd forgotten.'

His bitter laugh sent a puff of warm air across her face. 'I haven't forgotten, Marina. Believe me.' He paused to drag his gaze from her face, down her body, to her legs.

Immediately warmth, the telltale pooling of desire, welled low in her belly. Her nipples hardened and puckered, so that it took every ounce of willpower not to draw attention to them further by covering her breasts with her hands.

'And I suppose you thought it made sense to stay in the water rather than let me see this?'

He lowered his hand to her left thigh. It wasn't the tentative touch of a fingertip tracing the unsightly scar tissue. It was the solid warmth of his whole palm, flat across her wet skin, long fingers splayed to cover the mess of her injuries.

She flinched and caught her breath.

His hand slid round her thigh, caressing the worst of the scars she'd tried so obstinately to keep from his view.

'Don't!' The word choked her.

'Why not?' His eyes were on hers, reading the emotion she couldn't hide. 'You've got to face it some time, Marina. It's part of you now, and you have to learn to live with it.'

Tears of sheer fury blurred the lines of his face and she blinked rapidly to clear her vision.

'You arrogant bastard! Don't you think I know that? I lived with the pain of it for months. How am I supposed to forget when I see it every time I shower? Every time I dress? I feel the weakness and I remember…'

Her throat closed as memories came rushing back. Being in the car with her father—the last time she'd seen him alive. The banshee screech of the truck's brakes as it slewed straight into them on the wet road, tossing their car end for end.

And now this man, who knew nothing about the pain of losing someone so tragically, or how it felt to be disfigured, had the hide to preach to her because she wanted to preserve what little dignity she could muster.

She glared at him, not knowing at that moment which was stronger—her need for him, or the wish never to see him again.

'You don't understand.' Her voice was hoarse.

'Oh, sweetheart, I understand all right.' His words were a whisper of breath against her forehead as he leaned close and stroked his hand gently from her cheekbone to her chin.

There was tenderness in the rough timbre of his voice and in his feather-light touch. And she knew it would be her undoing. She could cope with anything but that.

Spurred by the need to wrest some control again, by the anger that hadn't abated, she shoved his caressing hand away. Grabbing his shoulders, she pulled herself up and kissed him— right on the mouth.

Not with tenderness or subtlety. But with all the roiling mass of conflicting emotions that surged through her: anger, grief, despair and longing. Her mouth was urgent, hard with desperation against the pliant warmth of his lips. She barely felt the strain in her neck and arms at holding herself inches above the bed, clinging to the solid, real strength of him.

And he let her kiss him, tilted his head to accommodate her. But he didn't kiss her back, not properly.

He was letting her use him. He felt sorry for her, and was letting her work off her pain and frustration on him.

Damn him! She was *not* an object of pity. She wouldn't let herself be.

She slid her hands from his shoulders to the back of his head, allowing herself to fall back against the bed as she did so.

For a minute she felt resistance in his strong frame, his wide shoulders unyielding despite the tug of her weight against him. And then, at last, her urgency won out. He allowed her to pull him down. His body covered hers.

Marina barely noticed the way he braced himself on his arms so as not to crush her. She only knew that he was here with her, the taste of him enticing, the feel of his hard strength inciting her kiss to transform from furious to passionate.

Her fingers thrust through his silky hair, splayed over his skull. She tugged at his bottom lip, nipped it with her teeth, and then tasted him with her tongue. His lips parted and at last she delved into the haven of his mouth.

Her hands gentled, cupped his head, and she sighed, realising how completely she wanted him. The clean musky scent of him excited her. The feel of his long body blanketing hers was comforting and unsettling. She twisted beneath him, revelling in the sensations.

And then in a heartbeat it all changed.

He came alive in her arms.

Like an unstoppable force he drove her down against the mattress. The kiss she'd thought she controlled turned into a lush, achingly sensuous, fiery mating of their mouths. She hung on to him desperately, afraid to lose her one point of reference in their dizzying passion.

He surged against her, no longer passive but arrogantly masterful. He thrust her legs apart with one knee, pushing them wider so he could plant himself intimately in the cradle of her hips. The soft friction of expensive pure wool suiting against the sensitive flesh of her inner thighs, the weighted hardness of him pressing down against her, brought a gasp of awareness to her lips.

And a rough growl to his. It rumbled in his throat and vibrated against her bruised mouth.

And still she couldn't get enough.

She moved beneath him, urgent in her need to get closer. As close as it was possible to get to this man who filled her every sense. He eclipsed her mind so that nothing mattered but the passion that bound them.

One large marauding hand palmed her hair, spanned her throat, skimmed her bare shoulder, then slid unerringly to cup her breast. He squeezed gently and every muscle in her body stiffened as darts of sizzling heat shot through her. His thumb brushed her nipple once, twice, and a jolt of pure desire shook her. She ached for more.

And he gave it. He released her mouth, lowering his head in a trickle of kisses down her jaw, across the ultra-sensitive flesh of her neck, then, as if impatient himself, directly to her other nipple, laving it through the slick Lycra.

She sucked in a gasp of air for her oxygen-starved brain. But thought was impossible as she watched his dark head bent over her, his mouth and hand on her breasts. The feel of his teeth nipping at her was exquisite torment.

And through it all the lava-hot flow of desire swirled and centred deep in her body, throbbed between her legs.

She pushed up against him and was rewarded with the solid weight of his own need thrusting hard against her. It soothed the ache of emptiness, but only for a moment. Even that wasn't enough now.

Disjointed thoughts swirled through her mind, but she couldn't make them connect. Not when Ronan, the man she'd dreamed about since their first meeting, was doing such outrageously wonderful things to her. With her.

When his hand slipped from her breast along the taut line of her body to her thigh, she struggled to breathe. And when his hand moved, firm and deliberate, from her bare thigh to the thin fabric between her legs, she thought her heart might stop.

His fingers spread and swirled and rubbed till she strained up to meet his touch.

'Ronan,' she murmured. Her voice was unrecognisable, husky with longing. She wanted so much from him. More than she'd ever let herself admit. More than he'd ever know.

'Mmm?' He kissed up her throat, along to the base of her ear.

And then, as if he knew exactly what she wanted, his long fingers slipped beneath the edge of the Lycra, insinuating themselves across the tender skin of her belly and dipping down to the core of her heat.

'Ronan!'

Helpless, in the grip of sensations stronger than she'd ever encountered, she felt her body lift to his touch, begging for more.

And again he met her need. His hand slid down until his fingers probed, circled, and entered.

'Don't!' she panted. Frantic thoughts whirled in her head. It was what she wanted. But it wasn't. She wanted more. She wanted him. All of him.

But his caress was deliberate, rhythmic, and she moved restlessly against his stroking hand.

'Don't what?' His words were hot in her mouth. His lips demanding against hers.

And suddenly she felt the world tilt and slide. There was a roaring in her ears, a dazzle of bursting light. Her body stiffened, pulled taut by a surge of unbelievable sensation.

'Don't…stop,' she gasped as he took her mouth with his and brought her to glorious, mind-numbing ecstasy.

She shuddered uncontrollably, held close in his embrace.

It was long minutes before she surfaced from the spiral of physical and emotional intensity. A lifetime before she came back to herself, aware of her body, sated and pliant beneath his. Of his mouth, gentle against her neck. His heartbeat, throbbing fast within his chest. The unmistakable rigidity of an aroused male, tense and unfulfilled, above her.

Tentatively she raised a weighted hand to stroke the firm line of his jaw and he froze. She felt his sudden inhalation against her skin.

He shifted his weight, moved his leg over hers, and her breath caught. Despite the wonderful climax he'd given her, she was wanton enough to want more. She yearned for the physical completion that no one but he could give. She needed him. And it was obvious that he wanted her.

Make love to me, Ronan.

That was what she wanted to say.

But she knew he wouldn't want to hear that from her.

'I want you,' was what she whispered.

He froze above her, and even his breathing seemed to stop.

Tentatively she slid her hand down his body, past the finely woven shirt, the sleek leather belt, the soft wool of his trousers, till her hand closed round him, long and hard and inviting.

Oh, Lord.

'No!' He reared back, pushing her hand away and bracing himself at arm's length above her. His wide shoulders blotted out the room and she felt almost small, and very vulnerable beneath him.

She frowned, unable to decipher anything beyond the feverish glitter in his eyes. Wasn't she supposed to touch him?

'But you haven't…' Her words petered out as his expression settled into grim lines.

'That doesn't matter.' He looked as if he was gritting his teeth.

'But…' She bit her lip, wondering what she'd done wrong. She lifted her hands to cup his jaw, feeling the infinitesimal abrasion of his burgeoning stubble.

'Please, Ronan.'

She was beyond pride now. He must know how she felt. How infatuated she was with him. She had nothing more to lose.

'Please,' she whispered. 'I want you inside me.'

This close, she could see the way his pupils dilated, feel the way his jaw clenched in violent spasm. And then he was pushing himself up on his arms, away from her.

Bereft of his heat, she shivered. Or maybe it was because of the shuttered expression in his eyes. It wasn't the look of a lover. Or even a friend.

They were a stranger's eyes.

'No,' he said, thrusting himself to his feet. His eyes swept her body once, comprehensively, then he jerked his head round to look out of the window. 'You don't know what you're asking.'

But suddenly, shatteringly, she knew exactly what she'd been asking. She bit her lip hard, hoping the pain would help her concentrate on keeping the tears at bay.

She'd fallen in love with him. Had been hiding from the truth for days. Pretending that love at first sight wasn't a family weakness despite the way it had struck both her parents and Seb.

Despite all her efforts, all her stern self-admonition, she'd succumbed to the fantasy. Had fallen under the spell of the role she played and Ronan's irresistible attraction. She'd drifted into a pleasant daydream where Ronan cared for her. Had even deluded herself that the flare of heat she sometimes discerned in his eyes was desire. She'd succumbed to the pathetic fairytale: her as the beautiful maiden and Ronan as the handsome prince who rescued her.

But it was pity he felt for her. Pity and, judging by his expression when he'd just looked at her, distaste for the way she looked. For the grotesque scars she couldn't hide.

You don't know what you're asking.

She rolled over on her side, so he couldn't see her face crumple.

He'd been angry that she might have put herself in danger. He'd been sorry for her because of the damage to her body on top of everything else. He felt responsible in some way for her.

He hadn't caressed her out of desire. Or anything remotely like love. She supposed the aroused state of his body was a simple male reaction to watching a woman climax in his arms.

She blinked furiously and burrowed her face into the bedspread. He'd taken pity on her, but he didn't want her.

And who could blame him?

Despite the new look and the expensive clothes she was still the same old Marina. She'd been kidding herself.

Nothing had really changed.

The truth was so devastating she didn't even hear him stride out of the room and leave her alone.

CHAPTER THIRTEEN

HE WAS on fire.

His chest heaved, about to burst. His skin stretched too tight. His breathing was a harsh rattle in his throat.

He gripped the basin of the *en suite* bathroom with both hands, striving for control. Then he wrenched on the tap, bent low and soused his head. He rubbed the cold water down his neck, scrubbed his face with it, let it beat down on him.

It did no good. His need was still a physical pain, throbbing through his body. So strong it made his teeth ache.

He shut off the tap and straightened, flicking water from his hair, feeling it trickle down from his neck and shoulders.

His reflection met him as he stood up. Shirt half unbuttoned and soaked. Hands unsteady. Eyes almost black with lust. Facial features taut, pared down to stark lines of raw desire.

I want you inside me.

He groaned. Marina hadn't known what she was asking.

A decent man would walk away. As he'd done.

A decent man would put those words from his mind.

But he couldn't.

I want you.

The words echoed in his brain, growing louder, not softer.

A decent man would remember that she was hurting. Grieving. That she needed protection, even from herself, as she struggled to re-establish her equilibrium and salvage her damaged pride in the face of others' pity.

A truly decent man would know that it was her bruised ego talking and wouldn't take advantage.

But his reflection wasn't that of a decent man. Though he'd tried, heaven help him. He'd worked long hours on his scheme to bring Wakefield undone and it was succeeding. The moment of triumph drew closer each day. But it was a hollow victory when he knew the real reason for his compulsive drive was to avoid the temptation that had taken up residence in his home. Marina.

Having her in the house had been his own brilliant idea, but now she was here he'd discovered, too late, how dangerous she was. Like a glass of wine set before an alcoholic, she was pure temptation.

He thought of her passionate mouth and groaned. Her fiery eyes and soft-as-seduction hair. Her quick mind and determination. Her independence, that wouldn't let her be cowed by a rich bastard like Wakefield. Or by him. Her body, ripe and lush with its hourglass figure no man could resist.

He turned away, knowing he was no longer a decent man.

She was still on the bed when he returned. Her eyes were bleak as she stared out of the window. Her legs were tucked up and her wet hair spilled like a protective shield around her hunched shoulders. She looked so vulnerable.

He should do the right thing—turn his back and leave her alone.

Her head jerked round when he stalked across to the bed, eyes widening as he threw the packet of condoms onto the bedside table.

'No!' She pushed herself up from the bedspread. 'I didn't mean it. I don't want you to…'

The rest of her words were lost in the heavy rush of blood in his ears that half-deafened him. And the sound of his shirt ripping.

His hands were on his belt when she found her voice again. 'Ronan, no. I don't want this.'

He kicked off his shoes as he undid his trousers and let them fall.

'Are you sure?' His voice was a husky growl. Definitely not the sound of a decent man. Or even a reasonable one.

Stepping away from his discarded clothes, he bent to peel off his socks and heard the hiss of her indrawn breath.

When he straightened she was reaching towards him, her hand half raised. His breath jammed in his chest as she leaned forward. Her lips were sultry invitation, her breasts superb, her body meant for his.

'What's that?' Her words were almost inaudible over the hammering beat of his heart.

He twisted round and saw realisation freeze her features, as he had known it would.

'It's scar tissue, Marina.' He stared at her, challenging her. 'Is it so ugly you can't bear to make love to me?'

'Of course not!'

She hadn't thought that one through. But he didn't mind as she scooted forward on the bed and he felt the tentative brush of her fingers at his side. He shuddered and prayed for control.

'What happened?'

'Like you,' he said harshly. 'An accident. But mine was a plane crash. Our Cessna went down in the bush.' He felt her warm palm slide around to his back, spreading hesitantly over the burn mark that marred his skin. 'I was twenty and my best mate was twenty-one. He was the pilot and he died in the smash.'

'Oh, Ronan.'

'Save your pity.' Right now he wasn't interested in reliving the loss of his friend, or his three-day fight for survival in the wilderness.

Right now his mind was fixed on one thing. Marina. And how good this was going to be.

'So you *do* know.'

'What?' He frowned, trying to follow her words.

'You do know what it's like,' she repeated, her hand a soft caress across his skin. 'Loss,' she explained. 'And injury.'

He grabbed her wrist and pulled her hand away from him. He couldn't take much more. Not if he was going to retain any shred of control. Already the tension in his strained muscles had ratcheted almost to breaking point.

He planted his hand against her shoulder and pushed her back against the pillows. She looked like a stranded, sexy mermaid. All that long glossy hair spreading across the bed. Her eyes so wide he could drown in their velvet depths. Her lips parted in a naturally seductive pout that made his muscles spasm.

Pure sexual bliss beckoned. Already he knew the taste of her and the petal-soft feel of her bare skin. The sweet scent of her arousal. The erotic little cries of her ecstasy. And her raw, unfettered responsiveness to his touch, the biggest turn-on of them all.

'Now's not the time for that discussion,' he managed to say over the tightness in his chest. He shoved down his boxers and reached for the box on the bedside table.

'The only thing that matters right now, Marina, is how badly I want you. And from the look on your face I know you feel the same.'

He paused long enough for her to protest. But she didn't. Instead she watched him with a mixture of longing and awe that would have been a treat for his ego if he hadn't been in such pain.

He sheathed himself and knelt on the bed before her, slowly closing the distance between them. She gulped, then licked her lips as if her mouth was dry, but she didn't retreat.

'Take it off,' he whispered.

She fumbled at the straps of her one-piece swimsuit, dragging it jerkily from her shoulders. She struggled with it, hunching a shoulder to manoeuvre the slick material down. Then her arms were free.

'All the way,' he ordered, holding her gaze. Her eyes were wide with shock and excitement.

Slowly she bared one creamy breast, and then the other. They were just as he'd imagined. Perfect. Proud and full and utterly seductive.

She shimmied, pushing the wet cloth lower. The suspense became too much. He reached out, ripped the black fabric away in one surge of violent energy and tossed the swimsuit across the room.

He heard her gasp. His own breath stopped somewhere in his aching chest.

She was beautiful. Sultry, sexy curves. The enticing dip to her waist. The feminine flare of hips just meant to cradle him against her body. Glossy dark curls below a tiny belly. Long, long, shapely legs. His hand hovered over her, close but not touching. If he touched he'd be lost before he even started.

He darted a look at her face, wondering if she knew what she'd just unleashed. But her eyes weren't on his face. She was looking lower, and he throbbed in response.

Was that anxiety he read in her face?

'Lie down.' His voice was strangled, a rough whisper, but she understood and settled herself back on the bed.

He moved up to straddle her, knees on either side of her hips, and lifted a hand to her face. She was trembling and his heart squeezed.

'It'll be all right, Marina,' he promised, wondering how the hell he'd salvage the willpower to make it right for her.

She raised a hand to his heaving chest and he shuddered. Heat seared his skin, radiating from her touch and sparking a potent erotic response. Right now he couldn't withstand her caresses.

He captured both her wrists and lifted them above her head, gripping them lightly in one hand, watching the way the movement tilted her body slightly, raising her breasts towards him invitingly. His tension notched up unbearably as he reminded himself he had to share, not ravage.

Unsteadily he settled himself beside her, shivering at the sensation of her soft skin against him. He let one thigh splay over hers, pushing them wide.

Her breasts rose and fell with her rapid breathing, but he didn't dare suckle them, not now. Instead he cupped her intimately with his palm, grinding the heel of his hand against the sensitive spot between her legs so that her hips bucked and she pushed against him. His fingers slid against her, feeling the slickness of her arousal. He could smell her musky, feminine scent. Soon, he promised himself.

She shifted, trying to break his grasp. 'Ronan, please,' she gasped. 'Ronan…'

'Shh. I know, honey. You want more. So do I.'

He rolled over, positioning himself above her, revelling in the embrace of her satiny thighs encompassing him. Molten heat flared deep inside as he nudged at the very core of her and looked into her eyes. What he saw there made him feel like a king. And her pliant, welcoming woman's body beneath his was all the enticement he needed.

Releasing her hands, he braced himself above her as he slowly, inexorably, thrust forward.

Oh, God. It was heaven and hell combined. Ecstasy and torture. She was so tight, so—

His brow furrowed. She couldn't be…

He stopped, quivering from the effort of holding back, and tried to force his mind to work.

Her face was drawn in stark lines. Whether of delight or pain he couldn't tell. But she was tensed, her whole body taut as if in shock. Her breath came shallowly, pushing her breasts up against him in an agitated rhythm.

Taking his weight on one arm, he brushed a shaking hand across her collarbone, down the fine porcelain skin of her breast, to skim her dusky nipple. She shuddered and her breath caught. But still she kept her beautiful eyes shut, as if trying to block him out.

He stroked her breast with his whole hand, cupping its feminine weight, then slid lower to kiss her there. Immediately her heady, unique fragrance filled his nostrils. She tasted so sweet. He loved the way she trembled at the deliberately slow lap of his tongue against her nipple.

'Ronan.' It was a throaty whisper of need. He smiled against her breast, sure of himself now. He let himself concentrate on enjoying her breast under his tongue, licking, kissing, sucking.

'Ronan!' More desperate this time. He felt her hands slide down him, restless and seeking. She smoothed over his back, trying to draw him up again. He hooked an arm under her knee, tilting her hips up to him and slid forward, deep into the waiting warmth of her.

Her eyes opened then: wide, bright and dazed. But their expression was welcoming, wanting, and he knew it was all right now.

'Marina.' He'd never felt it before: savage wanting paired with such tenderness, such a need to give her everything. She was so much more than he'd ever imagined.

He lowered his head to kiss the frenetic pulse in her neck and she shuddered. Her hands went to his shoulders, fingers splayed, gripping possessively. He moved infinitesimally and her hips rose to him in an invitation he couldn't refuse. He rocked against her and she met him. Again. And again.

Her breathing was a raw rasp in his ear. She lifted her knees higher, wrapping her long, gorgeous legs around him, holding on tight as his movements quickened. He almost lost it then, aware of her silken body everywhere against his.

He struggled to control the pace, not race to completion as his body urged. But soon he heard his name on her lips, felt her contract around him, pulsing and drawing him further and faster. That was when he let himself go in the sheer, mindless ecstasy of making love to Marina.

And through the mind-numbing barrage of sensations and turbulent emotions—triumph, fulfilment, and finally exhaustion—he realised he'd been right all the time. Nothing could rival making love to Marina Lucchesi.

Afterwards, limbs weighted and drowsy, he just managed to roll off her. His arms bound her fast to him, pulling her close as he settled on his back. Her hair, still damp, spread over him like a mermaid's tresses. Her warm body, hazed with sweat like his, sprawled in utter abandon.

No, he hadn't been a decent man.

Lord help them both. He hadn't cared about what was right. Just about satisfying that blood-hot craving.

She'd been a virgin. Against all odds he'd been her first. The very idea of it still dazed him.

And the realisation filled him with a wholly masculine thrill of ownership. He felt his lips curve in a self-satisfied smile he couldn't prevent. His hand skimmed possessively over her body, down her smooth back to the seductive curve of her hip. No one but he had touched her like this. The realisation was such a turn-on that he had to force his thoughts away.

She'd been trusting and, despite her sassy front, hurting badly. Needing his care, relying on his honour to help and protect her.

But he'd failed her. He hadn't been honourable. Hadn't protected her. Instead he'd been completely, inexcusably selfish, taking advantage of her weakness when she was most vulnerable. He should be ashamed of himself. He waited for the arrow-sharp pang of conscience to hit him.

But it didn't come. Instead he felt a smug satisfaction that he had exactly what he needed.

She didn't know he'd wanted her from the first. Had wanted to help her almost as much as he'd wanted her in his bed.

He let his fingers trail possessively over her fine skin, already planning their next sensual encounter. After he'd given her time to recover.

He'd guessed at the start she was different, special. And how right he'd been!

One thing was clear—he couldn't make love to her once and walk away.

For as long as this incandescent passion burned bright between them Marina would be his lover.

CHAPTER FOURTEEN

MARINA woke to the slide of soft silk being drawn over her. She sighed and burrowed her head into the pillow, emerging slowly from sleep.

Her body was alive in ways it had never been before. She revelled in the weighted sensation of fulfilment and in the tingling hint of expectation in her blood.

She felt wonderful, completed. And all because of Ronan. The man who'd made her feel beautiful, desirable, special. As if she really *was* the woman of his dreams. As he was the embodiment of all her longings.

Tentatively she reached out to caress him, slip her hand across the solid warmth of his chest. She needed the reassurance of his embrace to remind her that this was no dream. But her fingers found only the empty bed, still warm from his body.

It couldn't be.

Frantically she swiped her arm out as far as she could reach.

A dart of something like panic jabbed her. But when she opened her eyes she found it was true. She was alone in the darkening room.

He'd even closed the door when he left.

Her chest squeezed and she swallowed against the hard lump of distress that lodged in her throat. For the second time that day unaccustomed tears filmed her eyes.

What had she expected? A declaration of love? A promise of for ever?

Her lips compressed bitterly at her own stupidity.

At least he'd shown the common decency to cover her naked body when he went.

Hell! She screwed up her eyes against the flood of despair. What had she done?

On a surge of bitter energy she slid off the bed to stand, swaying with shock and the effort of holding back her pain. Life had taught her not to believe in miracles. So why was she surprised that he'd taken what she'd offered—what she'd pleaded for—and then walked away?

Marina pulled the silken cover up and around her with trembling fingers, needing its warmth against her chilled body. It trailed heavily behind her as she stumbled towards her private bathroom.

She averted her eyes from the sight of her swimsuit, torn asunder and crumpled in two pathetic heaps by the window.

She knew exactly what she'd done.

She tugged the voluminous coverlet through the door, then snicked shut the lock. Sighing, she dropped the bedspread and yanked on the shower tap. Instantly steam rose and she stepped under the spray, gasping at the heat and reaching to adjust it.

She'd given herself to Ronan Carlisle. Begged him, offered herself so shamelessly that he'd overcome his distaste and his scruples to take her. They'd had sex.

But she'd made love.

She'd been a fool. A ridiculous, pathetic fool. She prayed that he hadn't guessed the truth about her feelings.

Feelings. Hah! Such an insipid word. She had feelings of affection for friends and neighbours. Feelings of tenderness and regard. But her emotions for Ronan were like a whirlpool, a surging, tugging vortex of pressure that overwhelmed her in spite of every last shred of common sense and self-preservation.

She bent her head and let the drumming water wash down over her entire body as if it could wash away this fatal weakness in her.

For even now, faced with the brutal truth, she couldn't honestly say she regretted what had happened. It had been wonderful. Ardent and exciting and downright earth-shattering. His power. His almost unwilling tenderness. His passion. The strength and beauty of him. She'd revelled in it all.

Despite his lack of true feeling for her he'd made her feel like a queen.

She'd loved it. And she wanted more.

That made her sick in anyone's book.

He hadn't lured her with soft words or false promises. He couldn't have made it clearer that he didn't want a relationship. He'd walked away rather than face her.

But there was no denying what they'd shared was wonderful.

Imagine what making love with Ronan would be like if he felt for her as she did for him.

No! She wasn't masochist enough to go there. She couldn't afford to let herself dream the impossible. Unrequited love was bad enough. She couldn't afford to live in a fantasy world any longer, deluding herself that wishes might come true.

She turned off the water and stepped out of the shower, drying herself quickly with a huge towel and wrapping her hair in another.

She had to work out what she was going to do. How she could drag herself out of this impossible situation. Or whether she even wanted to.

Five minutes later the bed was made, pristine, as if it had never been the scene of such a disaster.

A pity her hands were shaking so badly she had to clasp them tight together to stop them shaking. All she wanted to do was curl up and sob herself hoarse.

She straightened her shoulders and walked to the wardrobe. Deliberately she dressed in one of the new outfits Bella had convinced her to buy.

Now, if ever, she needed confidence, and this outfit would give her the boost she needed so desperately. The red fitted dress complemented her curves in a way that made her feel feminine and not, for a change, oversized. The high-standing collar gave way at the front to a neckline that plunged low. She'd seen the way Ronan had looked at her breasts, hot and hungry. The memory sent a thrill of exhilaration through her. She wasn't about to deny herself the chance to make him hunger for them again.

She was sitting on the bed, untangling her wet hair and wishing she could untangle the mess her life had become, when the phone rang.

'Hello?'

'I want to speak to Marina Lucchesi.' Charles Wakefield's unmistakably impatient tone shocked her into silence. 'Can you put her on?'

'It's Marina speaking,' she said, carefully lowering the hair-brush to the bed. What on earth could he want?

She didn't think she could deal with him now. Not when it felt as if her heart was bleeding.

'At last. Charles Wakefield here,' he said, and paused as if waiting for her to respond. 'You've been hiding yourself away, Marina.' His voice was smooth now, playfully chiding, but she picked up a current of anger. 'You haven't returned my PA's calls.'

'Sorry,' she said, frowning. 'What calls?'

Silence.

'My assistant has been ringing you every day. You say you didn't get the messages?'

She shook her head, wondering if she should believe him. 'I haven't had any messages from you.' What was going on? 'Who did he speak to?'

'Does it matter? Whoever it is your lover employs over there.'

Marina sank back against the headboard of the bed, rubbing her temple where a headache had begun. Why would Mrs Sinclair—or Ronan, for that matter—not pass on the messages?

'It sounds like Carlisle doesn't want you to see me,' said the voice on the other end of the line, and Marina had to agree. That was exactly how it sounded.

Mrs Sinclair was too organised to forget messages. She must have been told not to pass them on. But why, when the whole point of Marina being here was supposed to be as a lure to Wakefield?

Her head whirled with a jumble of questions. Nothing made sense. And she couldn't get her mind into gear to work it out.

'I'm sure there's been some mistake,' she offered finally, won-dering how she was supposed to play this. She didn't want to deal with Wakefield, but he was the man who held Marina Enterprises, the key to her future and Seb's. And she was supposed to be inviting his interest, not hiding from him.

'Why are you calling?'

'Ah. Now there's a question.' He paused, and she could picture his crocodile smile. She shivered.

'We agreed to meet—don't you recall? Just the two of us. You wanted to discuss Marina Enterprises.'

'That's right.' Her pulse quickened despite her reservations.

'Good. Let's arrange a time to get together. The sooner the better.'

Marina looked up at the sound of her door opening and her breath stalled.

There was Ronan, in faded jeans, open shirt and bare feet, staring back at her across the room. She felt the shock of it deep in her solar plexus. How had she managed to forget how sexy he was? Or that her body thrummed into needy awareness just at the sight of him?

Ashamed, she gripped the phone harder, anchoring herself against the need to forget sanity and plead for more of his lovemaking.

She was a self-destructive idiot. Surely she had more self-respect than that.

'Marina?' Wakefield's voice was sharp. 'I said let's make it soon.'

At last she found her voice. 'I agree...Charles.' She almost grimaced at the sound of his name on her lips. 'As soon as you like.'

Her eyes widened as Ronan strode across the room, tension manifest in every rigid line of his body, his brow folding into a black frown.

'How about tonight?' Wakefield prompted.

Ronan loomed over her now, disapproval clear in his eyes. He stood aggressively close, feet apart and arms akimbo.

She trembled at his aura of barely leashed power. It was too much, too soon. Suddenly she'd have given almost anything for a reprieve before she had to deal with him again. Even if it meant meeting Wakefield.

Tonight? Why not?

'That sounds perfect.' Her voice was husky and she cleared her throat. 'I'll meet you for a drink.' No way was she signing up for a whole evening in Wakefield's company, no matter how desperate she was. 'Where and when?'

She glanced at the bedside clock as he named an expensive bar in the city, realising she'd have to leave soon to make it in time.

'Fine. I'll see you there.' She put down the phone abruptly before she could change her mind. Then she grabbed her brush, began tugging it through her tangled locks.

'You're meeting Wakefield?' Ronan's voice was tight.

'Yes.' She avoided his gaze. 'I just have time to put my make-up on and dry my hair.'

'You're not going to see him now!' He sounded outraged.

'Why not?' She couldn't think when he stood so close—pure invitation to such a needy female. Swallowing down the sour taste of self-knowledge, she pushed to her feet and stepped past him.

Tension pulsed through him, charging the surrounding air and she shivered. 'That was the whole point of this preposterous charade, wasn't it?'

His hand snapped out and clamped around her wrist, pulling her up short. Her senses sang, remembering the magic he'd wrought a mere hour ago. She yearned for his passion and his tenderness.

And that made her furious. How could she be so weak? So self-destructive? To want a man who saw her as no more than a convenient lay and a pawn in a commercial manoeuvre?

She spun round to face him. 'Why didn't anyone tell me his PA has been calling? That he wanted to talk to me?' Her voice rose unsteadily. 'What sort of game are you playing?'

Through the fizz of tension in the air, Ronan felt the inevitable pulse of his driving need thrum into being. Marina's eyes flashed and her body vibrated with indignation. She was totally alluring.

'You needed rest. You've been through a lot recently, and you needed time to recuperate. Letting Wakefield think you were un-attainable hasn't done any harm. It's just whetted his interest.'

That was something he didn't want to dwell on. Wakefield had been all but drooling last time he'd clapped eyes on Marina, triggering a violent proprietorial response in Ronan. Wakefield had been lucky to escape that night in one piece.

Ronan watched her eyes narrow as she assessed his logic. Eventually she spoke. 'Well, in future I'd appreciate it if you'd consult me before you interfere.'

He shrugged. 'I've had Wakefield in my sights for so long, I'm used to calling the shots.'

'Not with me, you don't.' Her face was closed, unreadable, except for the angry passion that lit her eyes.

How badly he wanted that passion for himself. Now. Again. Right through the night.

Marina was like a drug in his bloodstream, heating his body to combustible levels.

The only reason he'd forced himself from her bed and into some clothes was the knowledge that it had been her first time. She'd be tender, possibly even sore. And if he'd stayed there, naked against her, nothing would have stopped him taking her again.

'I'll deal with him.' His voice was rough.

'No!' She tugged her hand free and turned away to the open bathroom door. To the wide mirror and the array of cosmetics spread before it. 'I'll meet him. It's my business, after all.'

He scowled.

She was right. It was time she met him. Keeping her incommunicado had served its purpose. Wakefield's interest had reached fever-pitch, judging from the number of calls he'd made. He was the sort who couldn't bear delay—was used to instant gratification.

And while Wakefield had been absorbed in his futile efforts to approach her Ronan had been busy dealing with a few of Wakefield's creditors, as well as acquiring some useful shares.

So why did he revolt at the idea of Marina and Wakefield together? Why did his whole body tense, ready to prevent her leaving?

He heaved in a deep breath and forced his mind to claw back control from his instinct. His eyes skimmed her figure in that clinging red dress, the swathe of her long, inviting hair.

And he felt again the jab of fierce possessiveness.

You can't go tonight because we've just made love and I want you again. Because you were a virgin an hour ago and you need me to cosset you. Because it revolts me to think of you going to meet Wakefield when you're mine. Because he'll take one look at you in that dress and spend the rest of the time imagining you without it.

Because I'm jealous.

He was *jealous*? Of Wakefield?

Impossible.

Wakefield was nothing to Marina but an enemy.

It was *he*, Ronan, who had her in his home, his bed. He'd just initiated her into the secrets of lovemaking and he had the prospect of long, hot nights ahead, expanding on her education.

He was Marina's lover.

Yet there was no denying the unreasoning surge of fury at the idea of Marina spending time with Wakefield. Or with any other man.

What the hell was happening to him? He'd never been a jealous lover. Protective, yes. But this raw possessiveness?

He wiped a hand over his face, as if to scrub away the strange miasma.

'Yes.' He forced himself to nod, to be sensible. 'You'd better see him. But it will have to be a short meeting. I'll get the car out and meet you downstairs.'

Her eyes met his in the bathroom mirror and he almost changed his mind about letting her go. Her glossy lips parted invitingly, and she'd done something to her eyes that accentuated their brilliance. He didn't want her looking like that for anyone except him.

'I'll catch a taxi.'

He shook his head. 'You'll go with me.'

She swung round to face him, skirt flaring around those long, lovely legs. 'Wakefield will think it's odd if you take me to meet him. What lover would do that?'

'Let Wakefield think what he likes. I'm taking you.'

Or you're not going.

She stared at him for the space of two heartbeats, then turned back to the mirror.

He swung round and left the room before he gave in to one of his more primitive urges: to scoop her into his arms, pin her to the bed and keep her there. The way a caveman would react. The way he'd already behaved tonight.

No. Logic dictated that he let Marina and Wakefield meet. And so they would.

All he had to do was find a way to deal with the storm of jealousy that bombarded him at the idea of her going out to meet another man.

CHAPTER FIFTEEN

MARINA pushed her way towards the exit of the trendy bar, ignoring the bustle of activity near the window where Charles Wakefield now sat alone. Except for the waitress mopping up the spill.

A pity he'd ordered a bottle of champagne. Red wine would have left a much more satisfying stain on his silver-grey suit. One that would last.

As she emerged onto the pavement a shadow detached itself from the darkness and fell into step beside her. It was Jackson Bourne, Ronan's chief of security. He'd been detailed to wait, then drive her back. When Ronan had snapped out the order she'd been affronted that he thought she needed a minder. Now she was grateful.

Bourne's large presence reminded her of Ronan. She longed for him. She wanted to throw herself into Ronan's strong arms and rail at the unfairness of it all. Ronan would put his arms around her and tell her it would be all right. That together they'd defeat Wakefield. And that the most important thing to know right now was that he loved her.

Yeah. Right.

Abruptly the righteous indignation that had buoyed her through the scene with Wakefield dissipated. Its loss left her feeling hollow and weak. Her legs trembled and she pulled up abruptly, locking her knees to steady herself.

'Ms Lucchesi? Are you okay?' Bourne's gravelly voice was concerned.

'I'm fine, thanks. Where's the car?' The last thing she needed now was a sympathetic ear. Not if she wanted to get back with her composure still in place.

'Here it is.' He gestured to a gleaming dark sedan.

She got in, watched him pause for a quick conversation on his cellphone before taking the driver's seat. Probably reporting to the boss that he was delivering her back, she thought sourly.

In their different ways Ronan and Wakefield had made her feel like a commodity tonight. Something to be bought and traded and possessed. But she wasn't a chattel, or a prize. She was a woman with her own needs and dreams.

She bit her lip, wishing she could go back now to her own home. She needed the comfort of its safe familiarity. But it had been sold—she had no home.

Marina shivered, recognising the symptoms of exhaustion. She was emotionally vulnerable and her body was tender in places that didn't bear thinking about. Why had she thought she could handle Wakefield tonight of all nights?

Self-pity was tempting. But she couldn't give in to it or she mightn't stop. She bit down hard on her trembling lip and stared out of the window, blinking back tears of defeat and disillusionment.

The car pulled up on the gravel drive before Ronan's home. She opened her door before Bourne switched off the engine.

'Thanks for the lift,' she said over her shoulder as she got out. Her legs were steady now, just leaden with tiredness.

The entrance door opened and Ronan stood there, his broad shoulders and the confident tilt of his head silhouetted against the glowing lights of the vestibule. She checked as a flood of hot, intimate memories surfaced, stealing her breath.

'Marina.'

'Hello, Ronan.' She didn't meet his eyes, and he stepped aside to let her sidle past him into the house.

As she crossed to the stairs, her heels click-clacking on the tiled floor, she heard the murmur of male voices. It crossed her mind to wonder if Bourne had witnessed the scene with Wakefield.

But what did it matter? Half of Sydney could have been there for all she cared.

She'd reached the top of the stairs when Ronan caught up with her.

'Marina.'

'I'm tired, Ronan. I want to go to sleep.'

'We need to talk.' He followed her down the hall.

'Not tonight.' She was too keyed-up to sleep, but she craved solitude. She didn't have the strength to maintain this crumbling façade of independence much longer. She just wanted to lock herself in her room and sob her eyes out in the welcoming darkness.

'Have you eaten?'

'I'm not hungry,' she said, her attention on her bedroom door a few rooms away. Sanctuary.

'Good,' he said, and she felt his hand, large and uncompromising, shackle her wrist. 'Then you won't mind if we talk rather than eat.' He drew her towards his own bedroom, shoving the door open with his other hand.

'No!' She jerked back, desperate to break his grasp.

'Yes,' he said, pulling her inexorably into his private space. 'Don't worry, I'm not going to bite you.'

But Marina had had enough of managing, manipulative men tonight. She squirmed, pulling with all her might, trying to inch her way back into the hall. 'Let me go!'

'Damn it, Marina, I need to talk to you.'

She was past caring. Past hearing. She'd finally reached breaking point. Her struggles grew wilder, her breathing shallow as she fought to break his hold.

And suddenly it was over. With one powerful movement he swung them both round and she was trapped, her back flush with the wall. Ronan pressed his hard body against her from breast to knee. His hands splayed flat on the wall at either side of her head.

She couldn't get enough purchase to move. Could barely gasp for the air she needed with his chest weighting hers. She was surrounded, helpless.

But despite her impotent fury an insidious curl of desire unfurled and spread through her body. It drew her skin tight and made her mind race.

Being jammed up against his hard body was intoxicating. Suffocating. Tension pulsed between them, a palpable force.

She sagged, her body surrendering to the overwhelming power of her emotions.

How had she ever found the strength to walk out on him this evening? To turn her back and meet Wakefield? It wasn't simply that Ronan dominated her with his physical superiority. It was her heart, her own longings, that held her in thrall to Ronan Carlisle. She didn't have the strength left to fight that any more.

He didn't love her, didn't need her. But she loved and needed enough for the two of them. Her pride was dust.

'Marina.' His voice was a husky whisper across her temple and she raised her face, deluding herself that she heard longing in that single word.

She licked her parched lips, knowing she should say something, anything, to shatter the intimacy that threatened to destroy the shreds of her self-control.

And then, so abruptly she almost slid on useless legs down the wall, he stepped back, allowing her freedom. Her soul cried out in torment, bereft without him.

For a silent moment he stood, watching her. She felt the touch of his gaze but she wouldn't meet his eyes.

She blinked as his hand enfolded hers and he led her across the room. She didn't even protest when he pulled her down to sit beside him on the huge bed. Her brain had atrophied, overloaded by a tide of emotional turmoil. She felt numb.

He cradled her hand in his palm and she watched, fascinated, as he covered it with his other hand. His thumb rubbed slowly, rhythmically, over her wrist, sending quivers through her body.

'Marina.' She could read nothing in his voice except soothing reassurance. 'What happened when you saw Wakefield?'

She felt a flicker of emotion burn, then fade. Disappointment. He really did want to talk.

Surely she hadn't thought he'd want to make love with her again? Once had clearly been enough for him. Where were her wits? Her self-respect?

She stared at his hands: large, capable and well-shaped. Against his sinewed strength her own hand looked delicate.

'Marina,' he urged softly. 'What happened?'

She frowned, swallowing down the bile that rose in her throat. She could see Wakefield now, suave and elegant with his custom-made suit and solarium tan. And his sly innuendo.

Ronan raised a hand to her jaw and tilted her head so he could see her face. His own was unreadable but for the tension he couldn't hide.

'Well? Are you going to tell me?'

And that was when she recognised it. Impatience. And more than that. Concern. He was worried for her.

She watched the muscles in his jaw shift and clench. The pulse in his neck grew more pronounced. And she knew beyond a shadow of doubt that Ronan would inflict savage retribution on Wakefield. There was suppressed violence in his rigid stillness. All it would take was a word from her to unleash it. Wakefield was his sworn enemy.

She pictured herself giving him the excuse he wanted. Telling him Wakefield had been interested, but he hadn't bothered to exert his fabled charm on her. Oh, no. He'd taken particular delight in being crudely forthright about what she had to do to make him rethink his ownership of Marina Enterprises. Dump Ronan and become his own 'special friend'.

She'd known Wakefield was scum. Tonight had merely confirmed it. His filthy suggestion was only what she should have expected from the man who'd cheated her brother so ruthlessly.

She felt unclean at the memory of Wakefield's insult, of his leer and his hungry smile. And she knew Ronan's response to her revelation would be swift and violent. He'd probably end up on an assault charge.

Wakefield wasn't worth that.

'If he's hurt you I'll destroy him.' His fingers stiffened against her chin. 'Right now.' Ronan's voice was a savage rumble. She knew instinctively he meant what he said.

'No!' She lifted her hand to clasp his strong wrist, and felt the pulse thud roughly under his hot skin.

'No. There's nothing to get worked up about.' She stared straight back into his electric gaze, willing him to believe her. 'He was interested, but non-committal,' she lied. 'I just don't like being alone with him.' That much at least was true. 'He gives me the creeps.'

Ronan's scrutiny was so intense she felt it slide across her heated skin. She managed to hold his gaze until he lifted his hand and rubbed his thumb over the frown creasing her brow. Such a gentle caress, so intimate.

'He didn't try to touch you?'

'No.' He'd expected her to make all the moves instead.

'You won't be alone with him again.'

She swallowed hard at the sound of his low-voiced pledge and acknowledged the seductive desire to let Ronan shoulder her burden. She'd never let anyone fight her battles in the past. No one had offered. But now he was assuming that right. And, Lord help her, she couldn't find it in her to argue any longer.

He didn't love her, but he'd protect her from Wakefield.

'I should never have let you see him alone.' Fury vibrated in his voice. 'In future I'll deal with him. No matter what he promises, you keep away from him.'

She nodded, glad to be on safe ground. 'I will.'

'You trust me to take care of everything?' he murmured. His hand stroked from her brow to her cheek, sending thrills of delight through her, making a mockery of her attempt to control her responses. She lifted her eyes to his.

She had no qualms now about leaving everything in Ronan's hands. If anyone could retrieve Marina Enterprises, he could. He had the power and the business savvy. And his protectiveness showed he had her interests at heart, if only because he felt sorry for her. He'd do what he could for her and Seb.

'I— Yes. Yes, I do.' It was a relief to admit it.

Heat flared in his eyes. Her breath snagged at the intensity of his gaze. His hand cupped her cheek and he brushed his thumb across her lips once, twice, parting them with gentle pressure. Her mouth tingled and she fought the desperate urge to sway closer to him. To press her aching, sensitive nipples against the wall of his chest and invite him to take her again.

She needed to leave. Before she was lost. She shut her eyes, trying to summon the strength to move away. But the darkness only intensified the intimacy of his touch, the overwhelming surge of longing that weakened her body and her resolve.

When she opened her eyes his face was closer, and a shiver of urgent expectancy raced up her spine.

'I should go now,' she whispered. Even to her own ears she didn't sound convincing. Where was her willpower? Hadn't she decided he was too dangerous for her peace of mind?

He lifted his other hand to smooth up her bare arm, sending shivers of awareness over her flesh as he caressed her shoulder, then brushed the nape of her neck. Her breath hissed out as he tunnelled his fingers through her hair, massaging her scalp in slow, sensuous circles that liquefied her bones.

'Ronan. I really think…' Her words petered out as he leaned close and touched his lips to the corner of her mouth. It was a tiny, barely-there kiss. And it ignited an explosion of desperate need in her. Her recently awakened body responded with voracious hunger to the memory of ecstasy. Ecstasy wrought so easily and so devastatingly by this man.

He drew away just enough to look into her eyes and his hands stilled. He held her, but a single movement would break his hold. She could leave him now if she wanted to.

She should be relieved. Instead she was confused, appalled by her own lack of resolve.

He was giving her a choice. She read the question in his expression, the controlled energy in his bunched muscles.

She *should* leave him. Now. While she could still think. She'd invite heartbreak if she let him make love to her again. Such intimacy could only bind her closer.

After just one time the sensations were scorched into her brain. His erotic caresses, the slide of his body against hers, his ragged hot breath in her ear, his shuddering climax, the raw power of him thrusting inside her: every memory was addictive.

Her chest heaved with her rapid, uneven breathing as the now-familiar need pulsed through her, shattering the last of her control.

This man excited her. More than that, he held her heart.

How could she deny herself when he was everything she wanted?

Tentatively she reached out and touched him, her trembling palm flat against the cotton of his shirt. Beneath her fingers thudded a heartbeat as rapid as her own. It throbbed, vibrating against his powerful chest, testimony to his desire for her.

That shouldn't make a difference. If she knew what was good for her she'd get out of here now.

But inevitably it made all the difference in the world. He cared for her. Unlike his rival, who merely saw her as a tool to be used in a crude power contest. Ronan felt something for her, even if it wasn't love. And in this moment he desired her.

Her, Marina Lucchesi. Big, buxom, scarred Marina. The woman who'd fallen headlong into love with him.

She didn't have a hope of letting her head rule her heart. Especially when he chose that moment to spell out his intentions.

'I want to make love with you, Marina. Properly this time. I want to show you just how good it can be between us.' His low voice was a husky burr that alone was enough to seduce. 'You deserve more than I gave you before. Much more.'

Heat washed her cheeks and she shivered helplessly, knowing she was lost. She barely registered the rest of his words. It was the raw desire in his fever-bright eyes, the urgency of his hungry growl, that she understood.

Gaze still locked with hers, he took her hand, raised it to his mouth and centred a slow, erotic kiss on her palm. She felt his tongue flick across that sensitive point and a riot of sensation burst through her body. It heated the very core of her. Need was a potent, writhing force consuming her. She had no defence against it.

His eyes told her he was waiting for her response. Her shuddering delight at his caress wasn't enough.

She slid her palm up his chest to the radiant heat of his bare neck. His muscles strained with tension, but he sat rigidly still as her fingers spread up through his hair. It was marvellously soft and sexy on such a hard, masculine man.

She watched him swallow convulsively and registered the finest of tremors in his long fingers.

He leaned close, till his face was bare centimetres from hers, till his hot breath seared her skin. Deliberately, unhurriedly, he kissed her full on the mouth, and she thrilled to the way his strong arms gathered her close. They lashed around her needily, protectively. And she responded, melting against him like wax before a flame.

He was all strength and power and tenderness. A fantasy come to life.

Slowly, with intense deliberation, he laid her on the bed and stripped her clothes away. She lay pliant beneath his sure touch, her breath arrested at the promise of ecstasy to come. His burning gaze held her still, dazed by the enormity of her emotions.

And then it was impossible to lie passive any more. He'd dispensed with her clothes, and now his fingers skimmed, stroked, teased and excited. He caressed her so sensuously, making her quiver with delight and longing.

Finally he lowered his head and kissed her again.

Desire. Love. They welled up inside her. She thought she'd explode then and there at the perfection of the moment as she felt his lips slide against hers, his tongue delve into her mouth, his hot breath mingle with hers. His weight upon her, as she pulled him close, stimulated a wild yearning.

But there was more.

When he took her nipple in his mouth, first delicately laving and then suckling hard, she sobbed with relief. She was wound up too tight, the tension building in her till she thought something would break if he didn't love her soon. She was desperate for him, her hands skimming restlessly, urging him close.

Yet he refused to rush. He moved on, exploring, nuzzling and kissing and smoothing his hands in the lightest of caresses, all over her. Over her shoulders, down her hips and calves, to the arches of her feet, and back up along her inner thighs to the place between her legs where the fire blazed brightest. Liquid heat seared her veins and pooled low in anticipation.

She throbbed with unfulfilled need as she twisted beneath his ministrations, eager for so much more. But he used his strength to overpower her frantic attempts to undress him. His hands clamped her wrists. His heavy thigh restrained her legs. His solid weight pushed her down against the mattress.

He heaped sensation after amazing sensation on her, denying her the fulfilment of his own body. Hoarse gasps filled her ears and whimpering mews of need. The sound of her falling apart, mindless with wanting him.

He slid low, licked from her waist to her ribcage. She shuddered and slipped her hands from his hold. Blindly she scrabbled at his shirt, popping buttons in her haste.

One large hand captured both of hers, pressing them to his chest, curbing her frenzied movements. And then he met her eyes. She sucked in her breath in shock. His eyes scorched so hot that they should have burnt her to cinders. His face was a tight mask, almost of pain, that told its own story of the immense self-control he was exerting.

'Ronan.' She swallowed hard, her throat parched, raw with desperation. 'Let me!'

He shook his head and lowered his mouth to her breast.

'Ronan, please!'

He stopped, his mouth a breath away from her nipple. Then he lifted his head and held himself above her. His storm-dark gaze probed, as if testing the truth of her words. He looked grim, utterly unyielding.

'I *need* you.'

Something flickered in his expression, and suddenly she was free. Ronan rolled away, ripped his clothes off in savage haste. Her breath caught at the sight of his body. Beautiful. Rampant. Hers.

He reached for protection and then he returned. But now his movements were careful. His deliberation belied his haste a moment before. But the way he trembled told her just how much it cost him to move slowly.

He lowered himself to lie over her, trapping her in a world that began and ended with his strong, gorgeous body. She loved the feel of him. The scratch of his hairy legs against hers. The erotic sensation of his torso, solid and lightly covered in hair, heaving against her breasts. The weight of him pressed hard against her abdomen, inciting a fever of shuddering desire.

She wanted all of him, every glorious inch of his magnificent body. And she wanted him now.

She almost cried with relief when he spread her thighs and braced himself, poised above her. His sex nudged her, tested, and then slowly, with the inexorable power of a swelling tide, he entered, stretching her taut muscles. Her eyes widened. He filled her further and further, till surely any more was impossible.

'Lift your knees,' he whispered.

Tentatively she obeyed, felt a momentary relief of the pressure, and then gasped as he slid right to her core, coming to rest deep within her.

Had it been this impossibly magnificent before? She was anchored to him, part of him, whole.

She tilted her hips up a fraction, amazed at the feel of them together.

'No!' His voice was hoarse. 'Don't move,' he gasped.

He propped himself above her on arms taut with strain. His mouth was a line of pain, and every clenched muscle in his hard body spoke of iron-willed control. Sweat budded on his brow and at the base of his throat.

But Marina was greedy for more. He smelt musky and sensual, inviting. She lifted her head and licked his neck, taking the salt tang, the pure essence of Ronan, into her mouth.

He groaned and shuddered.

She wrapped her arms around him, hugging him to her, knowing that she never wanted to let him go.

'Yes,' she said, tilting her hips provocatively, revelling in the surge of sensation where their bodies joined.

For a moment his control held, and then, with a whoosh of hot air, he expelled the breath he'd been holding and metamorphosed from human statue into pure energy. He took control, moving swiftly, expertly, in a primitive rhythm she instinctively matched. Faster and harder and stronger.

Marina clutched at him, holding tight, as if she could contain the erotic energy that pulsed through him. It frightened as much as it exhilarated. But then it erupted into her body—a storm unleashed. Sparking heat like lightning flashed through her, blinding her, electrifying her senses. She juddered, the shocking intensity of power too strong for her. The world spun and she cried out in pleasure so fierce she thought she'd die.

Fulfilment crashed upon them both: long, bone-jarringly intense and utterly wonderful.

Through a haze of sensation she felt him pulse hard within her, heard his rough groan of release against her hair just as she started floating back to earth, his name still on her lips and ringing in her ears.

CHAPTER SIXTEEN

SHE was trapped, unable to move on with her life. But not because of Wakefield's takeover, or Ronan's plans to wrest her company back.

Her priorities had changed.

Marina stared across the flagstones to the brilliant azure of the pool. Yet it was Ronan she saw in her mind's eye.

With his relentless energy, his passion and tenderness, he had taken up residence in her heart. He was the strongest, most fascinating man she'd ever met. He made her feel like a new woman and she loved it.

She told herself he didn't need her, didn't really need her. But the knowledge made no difference to her feelings. She craved him. As a lover, a partner, the other half of herself.

For now it was almost enough to be desired. Even with her rounded body and her smart mouth and her scars—all the things she'd believed would keep any man away. But not Ronan. A spasm of excitement lanced through her when she remembered his hot wanting looks, as if he couldn't get enough of her. He desired her so blatantly that she felt powerful—confident and sexy as never before.

Even now, away on urgent business, Ronan made her feel special. He rang daily, and the sound of his voice, husky with intimate shared memories, made her blood race and her body come alive. The calls came from Tokyo, Beijing and Perth. They made her realise how pathetically she loved him, when the high point of her day was the sound of his voice from thousands of kilometres away.

To make it worse, she felt guilty about lying. She hadn't admitted she was there under false pretences. Her value to Ronan's plan had vanished as soon as she'd reacted to Wakefield's suggestion that she prostitute herself for Marina Enterprises. Wakefield wouldn't chase a virago. Yet she hadn't told Ronan about that incident. If she did she'd have no reason to stay. Her part in his scheme would be over.

She had no illusions. Ronan cared for her, desired her, and pursued their affair with a voracious appetite. But he'd never mentioned permanency. This was a fling. Sooner or later his passion would burn out.

Despite the afternoon sun she felt a bone-deep chill.

Marina stared past the glittering pool, dreading the decision she had to make. The specialist had told her this morning that her recovery had been excellent. She could return to work soon, part-time. She should be pleased.

That was what she needed: to focus on her future. She'd strived hard to get her accounting qualifications, had worked just as hard for the company, and had thrived on the knowledge that she was darned good at what she did. She still had a job, even though the transfer was complete and Wakefield now owned Marina Enterprises. He hadn't sacked her—yet. She could work there while she found another position.

Then she'd need somewhere to live.

She swallowed the sour taste of reality and forced her mind to the future. A future that didn't include Ronan. She ached at the idea of leaving him. But eventually he'd want her to go. Better she went with dignity and had her departure planned. She couldn't risk him finding out how badly she wanted to stay.

She'd had enough of being an object of pity.

Reluctantly she reached for the newspaper on the patio table before her. She'd already circled some flats to let. She should ring about them, but the action seemed so final, like the end of a dream, that she couldn't do it.

Abruptly she pushed her chair back, strode to the pool-edge

and dived in. The silken water closed round her, cool against her tense muscles. Maybe if she pushed herself hard enough the pain would go away.

When she stopped, gulping air and blinking water from her eyes, her breath jammed in her throat as she saw Ronan. It was as if she'd conjured him from her troubled thoughts.

Lovingly she scanned his powerful body. He wore only swimmers, a towel slung over his shoulder. Her pulse quickened, excitement filling her. What was he doing back two days early?

She watched the play of muscles across his back as he threw his towel down beside hers. He was like a sun god, bathed in the golden light of late afternoon. His perfect physique utterly masculine.

Trembling awareness weakened her limbs; the heavy coil of desire began to spiral within her. Would she ever break this spell he had over her?

He turned and she saw his frown, unmistakable strain evident in his fisted hands. Her own brows creased and she wondered what was wrong as she swam towards him.

She'd only done a couple of strokes when she felt his powerful slipstream as he turned in the water beneath her. A pair of strong hands fastened on her ribs, pulling her up. She surfaced in his arms and couldn't prevent a smile as she tilted her head up towards his.

'Hello, Ronan.'

'Marina.' His voice was deep and mesmerising, just as she'd remembered it in her dreams each night. And then he was kissing her, pulling her hard against him in a display of power that was as unnecessary as it was wonderful.

She felt her heart tumble over in her chest. How she loved him. How would she cope when she had to leave him?

When he broke the kiss he kept his arms around her. She clung to him, loving the sensation of his body pressed against hers. All that refined power, that tensile strength so close and so tempting.

'What's wrong?' she asked, seeing the grim line of his mouth.

'You're looking at flats to let?' His voice was harsh, accusing.

It was the last thing she'd expected him to say, and she hesitated, uneasy, as if she'd been caught out at something. 'I was just checking what's available.'

His arms tightened round her, but he didn't say anything. She could feel the tension in his rigid muscles and in the rapid thud of his heart against her chest.

Was he angry that she was showing some of her old independence? That must mean he wasn't yet ready to end their liaison. That he still wanted her. A thrill of excitement curled through her at the knowledge. It was quashed seconds later by the chill voice of common sense, warning her she'd be an emotional wreck if she waited for him to end the affair, as he inevitably would.

'I need to think about the future.' She watched him intently, foolishly wishing he'd interrupt and declare her future was with him. Of course he didn't.

'I went to the doctor today.'

A flash of potent emotion appeared in his eyes, lighting the indigo depths with blazing heat. But it was gone before she could put a name to it.

'What did he say?' Ronan's voice was clipped, almost as if he'd braced himself for news.

Marina wondered if she'd grown fanciful, reading significance into a simple question. His face was enigmatic, no emotion at all.

'He said I've made a terrific recovery.' She forced her lips into a smile, knowing she should be ecstatic at the news instead of feeling that her heart would break. 'He says I can go back to work soon. Just a few hours a day to start with. Isn't that wonderful?'

'Wonderful.' His tone was expressionless, as was his shuttered face. She frowned. She didn't know what she'd expected from him, but this grim watchfulness wasn't it.

'You want to return to work?'

She nodded slowly.

'And you want to find a place to live?'

'Well, I... Yes. Yes, I do,' she lied, over the sound of her giddy dreams of love crashing around her. This was so much easier than she'd expected. Much easier than she wanted it to be. She schooled her features to match her calm tone. He'd never guess how hard this was for her.

'Your plans will just have to wait.' His face was all harsh lines, and his eyes flashed fire as his arms stiffened around her.

'I don't understand. Why should they wait?'

For a long moment he stared at her, almost as if stumped by her question.

'We haven't finished with Wakefield—or had you forgotten? I need you here with me till that's finished.' He paused. 'You don't want to jeopardise our chance of making him pay for what he's done.'

'I'd be happy just to get Marina Enterprises back,' she said. 'But me being here won't make any difference.'

'You think not?' His eyes glinted. 'Then you have no idea how valuable a diversion you've already been. He hasn't been alert enough to the warning signs in his own companies.'

Now was the time to tell him the truth—that Wakefield was no longer interested in her. 'It won't make any difference—'

'And there's another reason you need to stay.' He lowered his head till his mouth was a breath away from hers. She swallowed hard, trying to ignore the burgeoning need as his voice turned low and harsh. Forbidden excitement swirled deep inside her.

'There is?'

'Yes.' He nodded, his eyes never leaving hers. 'This.'

Water rippled around them as he pushed her against the tiled wall of the pool. She was out of her depth and grabbed his shoulders for support, though she wouldn't have sunk. His body was jammed against hers, trapping her.

Then she stopped thinking as he kissed her. It was unlike anything they'd shared before, even their urgent, almost angry passion the first time he'd loved her.

It was compelling, fired by a frantic hunger and fuelled by his recent absence. He plundered her mouth with a marauder's kiss, hot and urgent and breathtaking. She wanted all that and more, revelling in his fierce need, meeting his desire with her own. He surged against her as if he couldn't get close enough, his hands heavy and hot on her slick skin.

He felt so good. So right. Even better than she remembered. How could anything so wonderful be so destructive?

'I missed you,' he murmured against her lips, and even that

was enough to make her heart sing. 'And you missed me,' he said, as he stroked the tender flesh behind her ear with his tongue.

'Didn't you?' he demanded.

'Yes,' she whispered as she clung to him. 'I missed you, Ronan.'

He nipped at her earlobe and she shivered, knowing that she didn't have the strength to leave him. Not yet. Not when he kissed her like this, wanted her like this.

It was only the roughness of his hands on her swimsuit that brought her back to realisation of their surroundings. He pushed her arms off his shoulders and tugged at her shoulder straps, sliding them down.

'Ronan! We can't. Not here.' She peered over his shoulder towards the house.

'Of course we can.' He palmed her now bare breasts and squeezed. Darts of hot sensation speared her, arrowing down to the place where he pushed, hard and ready, between her legs. She gasped and tried to control the shudder that rippled through her. The desire burning within, the loosening of all her muscles ready for lovemaking.

And he could see it all, damn him. The knowing gleam of satisfaction was there in his eyes.

'Mrs Sinclair…' she began, fighting for control.

He shook his head and rubbed her nipples between his fingers, making her gasp. 'I gave her the rest of the day off.' His look was pure predator. 'We're all alone. No one can see us. The gates are locked. There'll be no intruders.'

Marina felt him pulse against her and gave up the fight. She didn't know how much longer she had left with him. But she wasn't masochistic enough to deny his passion while she had it. It made her feel dizzy, reckless with desire and love.

'Good.' She shoved at his broad chest.

He backed a scant few centimetres and she thrust his hands away. She was beyond thought when he touched her like that. Then, with a single sinuous movement, she slid her swimsuit down past her waist, over her hips and thighs, submerging to bend and kick the Lycra off her legs.

She had a perfect view of Ronan's legs, planted wide apart,

of his erection straining against the fabric of his swimmers. She reached out to snag her fingers over his waistband.

There was a flurry of movement as he grabbed her wrist and hauled her to the surface. Before she could protest he pushed her up against the tiles again. Her breath expelled in a single whoosh of surprise and thrilled expectation. One large hand pulled her thigh up and round his waist as the other disposed of his swimmers.

She closed her eyes in relief at the feel of him against her. This was what she wanted so badly. It was like fire in the blood, blazing stronger all the time. He lifted her other leg, wrapping it round him, and she pulled herself up so that her nipples brushed the firm contours of his chest. She shuddered at the erotic friction.

'Yes,' he urged, his voice thick. 'Higher.' Then, with one abrupt, decisive movement, he pushed up into her.

Her eyes snapped open to meet his as the tremors started.

'Yes,' he said again, and the tenderness she read in his eyes filled her heart with answering emotion.

'Hold on.' His face clenched into a mask of concentration as passion took over. She clung to him as he thrust harder and faster, and the world began to spiral out of control in the most wonderful way.

Still his eyes held hers, till she could hold back no longer and she shouted his name in her ecstasy, needing him, loving him.

As if it was the signal he'd been waiting for, Ronan thrust one last time, gathering her up against him, and buried his face in her neck as shudder after shudder thundered through him.

Marina wrapped her arms around him, feeling the most ridiculous urge to protect him. This big, strong man who held her life and her happiness in his hands.

She shut her eyes, wondering how she could find a way to fight against love.

Ronan straightened his tie as he looked down at Marina, sleeping in his bed. She was curled up right in the middle. Exactly where she'd lain with her head on his shoulder till he'd forced himself to move. She hadn't even stirred when he slid out from the bed.

Hell, he was exhausted too. After breaking all records to get two weeks' work completed in barely five days, and after the long flight back from Perth, he'd spent the whole night making love to Marina.

And he wanted to rip the suit off right now and resume what they'd been doing as the first dawn light had crept into the room.

But he couldn't do it. Not today. He had one last item to finalise in the office before he took a well-deserved break.

He had everything organised.

He scowled, remembering the surprise that had greeted him yesterday. The news that Marina was planning to leave had stopped him in his tracks. How ironic that she planned to go now, just when all his efforts had come together and his hostile takeover of several Wakefield enterprises was complete.

And the fact that she'd been to visit a doctor had stunned him.

Instantly his mind had filled with an image of Marina turning to him with her sultry smile and saying she was pregnant. That she was going to have their child.

Even now the idea tripped his pulse, caught his breath in his throat.

Marina, swollen with *his* child.

He'd never thought about having kids before. It had always been part of some nebulous future. He'd never been envious of his mates who'd settled down to marriage and family life.

But now… The intensity of his excitement shocked him.

His hands fisted as that hot, possessive hunger took hold of him again. With Marina he was a man driven by his most primitive instincts. They overrode logic, even his careful plans.

The situation was out of control.

But he knew exactly what he was going to do about it.

CHAPTER SEVENTEEN

'Ms LUCCHESI? There's a call for you.'

Marina looked up from her breakfast.

Mrs Sinclair frowned as she held out the cellphone. 'It's Mr Wakefield.' Her carefully controlled voice told Marina the older woman's opinion of him matched her own.

She shivered. It was like being told the serpent had arrived in the Garden of Eden. Which was stupid. Wakefield couldn't hurt her now. Ronan had promised he'd see to it, and she knew he would.

'Thanks.' She nodded to the housekeeper and made herself reach for the phone.

'Marina Lucchesi,' she said at last, pushing away her plate and sitting back in her chair.

'About time,' Wakefield said in her ear. 'I've got some papers for you. We need to meet.'

And hello to you too. He had to be the rudest man she'd ever met. But if he thought he could make her jump at his bidding he was mistaken. She wasn't meeting him again. Once had been enough.

'I'm sorry, Mr Wakefield, we no longer have any business to discuss.'

'That's just where you're wrong, sweetheart.' His honeyed tone barely concealed some strong emotion that made the skin at the back of her neck prickle. 'This is your business. Yours and your brother's. I've got the transfer documents for Marina Enterprises with me.'

Marina froze in her chair. It couldn't be. Could it?

She knew Ronan's plans were progressing. But surely he'd have told her if they were this close to victory?

'Did you hear me?' Wakefield barked in her ear. He certainly didn't sound like a man on a winning streak.

'I heard.'

'Good. Get them to open the security gates. I'm a couple of blocks away. I'll be there in a few minutes.'

Let him in here? The idea appalled her. And she'd told Ronan she wouldn't meet Wakefield alone again.

But how could she refuse? If he was here, ready to sign back the company, could she risk turning him away? Who knew what devious scheme he might find to keep control of it after all?

'Or aren't you interested any more?' the detestable, silky voice taunted, as if confirming her fears.

Marina straightened her shoulders. 'I'll have the gates opened for you,' she said, and took a savage delight in ending the call before he could.

She didn't want to see him again. Her skin crawled at the thought. How she wished Ronan were here, instead of closeted in some high-priority meeting. Mrs Sinclair had said he'd be tied up all morning. And she had no chance of getting her lawyer here so quickly.

She'd have to deal with him herself.

Charles Wakefield still looked brashly successful, she decided ten minutes later, as they faced each other over a coffee table in the sitting room. He was the picture of sophisticated prosperity, with his Italian suit, glossy shoes and whiter than white teeth. Yet he'd changed since she'd last seen him.

This close, she saw how the frown lines were carved deeper on his forehead. The pouches under his eyes bulged more prominently. His deep bronze tan couldn't conceal those signs of strain, or the pinched tightness of his thin lips.

He wasn't the same smug powerbroker he'd been only weeks before.

His eyes flicked over her, assessing, like a bidder in a sale yard, and she stiffened. She stared straight back and watched with satisfaction as his eyes narrowed and he shifted in his seat.

'Your friend Ronan has been busy. I congratulate him.' His sarcasm gave the lie to his words. 'It's obvious he's had quite an incentive.' Again his gaze skimmed her, in a leer that undressed her as she sat.

'What do you want?' she demanded, ignoring the heat flooding her cheeks.

He smiled at her obvious discomfort. 'I told you. I've got those papers you wanted.' He leaned forward. 'You do still want them, don't you, Marina?'

She nodded.

Slowly, eyes still on her, he opened his attaché case and drew out a wad of documents. He glanced down, his smirk transforming into a frown as he scanned the cover sheet.

'The papers transferring my ownership of Marina Enterprises,' he said slowly. 'Just how much are they worth to you?' Abruptly he lifted his head, spearing her with his hungry gaze. 'Enough to give me what I want? To give me what you've been giving Carlisle these past weeks?'

Nausea welled in her throat. So that was why he'd come to see her rather than let the lawyers finalise everything. He just didn't give up.

'You've already had my answer on that.' She surged to her feet. 'This is about my business, not my body!'

'I thought so.' Wakefield grinned at her, leaning back in his seat. 'You really do believe it, don't you?'

'Believe what?' she snapped.

'Such innocence,' he mocked, shaking his head. 'And such a waste. You've obviously fallen in love with Carlisle. Which means you won't get to find out how superior I am to him in so many ways. Especially in bed.'

Bile rose in her throat, almost choking her. 'Get out of here. Now!'

But he merely smiled back at her. 'Such a waste,' he murmured again.

That was it. Marina marched across the room. She'd have no

hope of ejecting Wakefield if he refused to shift, but Ronan's security staff would see to it.

'If you leave now you won't get the papers I've brought you,' he taunted. 'They're already signed.'

Signed? She paused. If they were already signed then it was all over. Warily Marina turned to face him. He shuffled the documents on his knee, then slapped them down on the coffee table.

'There,' he said, in that smooth voice she didn't trust. 'Signed and delivered.' Then he sat back in his chair, arms stretched out over the upholstery.

Marina frowned. It had to be a trick. But she was already heading back, compelled to find out what was going on. He made no move to stop her picking them up. She walked round the coffee table and sank onto the sofa.

'This isn't for Marina Enterprises,' she said, after a moment's perusal of the top sheets. 'It's a copy of the documents for the sale of my house.' She sent him a curious glance, but Wakefield only shrugged.

She flicked through the contract and stopped at the next document. Company records this time, for Australis Holdings. She knew that name. Quickly she referred to the sale contract. Her house had been sold to Australis Holdings. She'd assumed it was a family trust.

Then, rapidly scanning the pages, she found what he wanted her to see. Her pulse stalled for a second before the blood rushed in her ears, the buzzing so loud she could barely hear Wakefield when he spoke again.

'Our friend Carlisle couldn't wait for you to come to him, could he? The sale to one of his companies was rushed through. Leaving you homeless. And vulnerable.'

Marina ignored him, frantically double-checking the papers in her trembling hands.

But it was true. Ronan *had* bought her home, insisting on an immediate settlement at the same time as he'd demanded that she move in here.

Her forehead puckered. He'd pretended he hadn't known about the sale. What had he to gain by doing this?

She delved further and came to the final document, sinking back wide-eyed as she read it.

According to this, Charles Wakefield had transferred ownership of Marina Enterprises two days ago. But the name Lucchesi appeared nowhere on the document. Instead, the new owner was Ronan Carlisle.

CHAPTER EIGHTEEN

PAIN sliced through Marina, so sharp and raw it held her motionless, afraid even to breathe. It stabbed deep, so real she could have sworn she felt bleeding inside.

Last night, as she'd lain in Ronan's arms, he'd already been the owner of her family firm.

The invisible knife twisted savagely.

He'd known then. He must have known. But he hadn't said anything.

Her body chilled to numbness as foreboding swept through her. If he'd known, why hadn't he told her?

'It's painful having one's illusions shattered.' The spurious sympathy in Wakefield's voice didn't have the power to annoy her now. She was too busy trying to grasp the meaning of the agreement before her. Yet she heard every word he said.

'I don't know what line Carlisle fed you,' he was saying, 'but he was out for his own gain. He'd had his eye on your little company for some time. My staff found out about his interest, so I decided to get it first.'

She looked up to see him watching her closely.

'I should have been more cautious,' he admitted with a casual shrug. 'I've made a few…unorthodox acquisitions lately that have become troublesome. Given Carlisle's continuing interest, I've sold this particular one to him. That's what he wanted all along.'

He shook his head and flashed his crocodile smile at her. She shuddered, helpless in the grip of dread.

'You thought *I* was greedy, sweetheart. But at least I was up-front. Carlisle wanted you *and* the company, but he didn't tell you that, did he? He scammed you into thinking he'd help you win back what you'd lost, when all the time he wanted it for himself. He was after the company and a bit of variety in his bed.'

His words sank into silence. Frantically she read and reread the pages. They spilled to her lap from nerveless fingers.

It couldn't be. She knew Ronan didn't love her. But he was a decent man. She'd trusted him.

'One last thing.' Through her blurred vision she saw Wakefield stand. 'Once your precious Ronan knows you've discovered what he's done, your tenure here will be over. He won't want you around, sulking about how he did you wrong.' He paused, then spoke again from the doorway.

'My advice is to get out before he throws you out. You may be decorative, but anyone can see you're not his usual type. I guarantee your novelty value has worn off now. If you have any pride left, you'll leave here instead of waiting to be chucked out.'

The words sank in, but Marina didn't respond, didn't move. There was a rushing, swirling sensation in her head, making her giddy, sucking the air from her lungs in shallow, desperate breaths.

It couldn't be. It couldn't. Not Ronan.

He'd cared for her. Hadn't he?

Tears swam in her eyes and she squeezed them shut. Had it all been a sham?

Ronan had wanted her, all right. He'd needed her to help with his scheme to strip Wakefield of his assets. There was no doubting the intensity of his fury as he'd spoken of what had happened to his sister, or his hatred for Wakefield.

But had he also been motivated by the desire to help Marina? Or had she been only a convenient dupe? After all, she'd never got round to asking for an agreement in writing that he'd pass the company over to her.

She'd been so gullible. So trusting. Even after what had happened to Seb. She should have known the Lucchesi family was out of its depth among the rich and powerful.

Her chest ached with a burning intensity as she fought to keep the tears at bay. It was a fruitless exercise. She felt them, hot and bitter, running down her cheeks and chin.

Ronan owed her no loyalty.

Could it be true? The question circled again and again in her shocked brain.

A novelty, Wakefield had said. Was that how Ronan had seen her? Had his passion, his wonderful, smoking-hot desire, merely been enthusiasm for something new? She wouldn't have thought it of Ronan, would have said it was impossible.

If it weren't for the papers Wakefield had left behind.

She swayed as another blast of pain rocked her. Had that been it? Had her makeover been some sort of sick joke?

She gasped and bent double, arms wrapped tight round her, as if she could stop the agony from welling inside her. Had Ronan been laughing at her all the time? Had he enjoyed taking the ugly duckling and pretending he had transformed it into a swan?

He couldn't be so cruel.

She'd never quite believed his compliments on how beautiful she looked. They'd been designed to boost her confidence; she knew that. But she'd hoped, had secretly clung to the idea, that she'd transformed enough to be appealing. Even a little.

She rocked back in her seat—and looked up to see Ronan in the doorway. His tie was askew, his hair rumpled. There was blood on his knuckles.

Absently Ronan cradled his hand. Who'd have thought Charlie Wakefield had such a hard jaw?

He relived his satisfaction at the memory of Wakefield's stunned face as he'd crashed to the ground. It had been small enough revenge for the devastation the bastard had inflicted on Cleo and on Marina, but it was a start.

Wakefield didn't look nearly so cocky now that his net value had plummeted by over fifty percent. Even with the help of his family contacts it would take him years of hard work to rebuild what he'd lost.

Now, *that* was satisfying.

Ronan smiled to himself as he walked into the sitting room, but pulled up short, horrified at what he saw.

Marina was there. Huddled in a corner of the sofa. She had her arms wrapped round herself and she was as pale as a wraith. He strode across the room. If Wakefield had hurt her…

He slammed to a stop within a few paces. Close enough to discern her flooded eyes, tear-streaked cheeks and full, trembling lower lip.

And the way she flinched as he reached out to her.

Something closed like a vice round his heart.

Scared—of him? The realisation was a punch to the gut, paralysing him where he stood.

'Marina.' His voice was hoarse. 'Don't look at me like that.'

She blinked and wiped her eyes with the back of her hand. The childish gesture made something twist inside him. He'd wanted to protect her, but somehow he'd failed her.

Why did she shrink from his outstretched hand?

'Whatever he said, don't believe it. Wakefield's a born liar. You know that.' She must understand that by now. She *knew* what an unprincipled shark Wakefield was. 'He'd say anything to make trouble between us.'

'Where is he?' she whispered, even her voice fragile.

'Gone.' He took a careful step nearer. 'Don't worry about him. Security's seeing him off the premises. He can't harm you.'

He was damned if he knew why she'd let Wakefield into the house. She'd promised not to see him alone again. If it hadn't been for Mrs Sinclair's urgent call, interrupting his meeting, he might not even have learned about Wakefield's visit. The thought of that creep alone with Marina made his blood boil. It was obvious he'd injured her somehow.

Then he noticed the papers, splayed across her knees and spilling down onto the floor.

'What are those, Marina? What are all the papers?' He kept his voice low and even, as he would with an injured animal that was scared of more pain. She'd had enough drama already with Wakefield, that was clear. His job now was to rectify the damage, even though it meant holding back from her, waiting to hear about it rather than tugging her straight into his arms.

Her dark eyes were huge and anguished in her pale face. 'Copies of commercial papers.' Her voice was colourless, tearing at his conscience. 'The sale of my house.' She paused and cleared her throat. 'The transfer of Marina Enterprises to you.'

Hell! No wonder she looked as pale as a ghost. She was in shock.

He could imagine the poisonous lies Wakefield had poured into her ears. The callous bastard would have been out for revenge this morning. He couldn't get retribution from Ronan, so he'd gone for a soft target—for Marina. How he must have enjoyed himself. He always had been a sadistic swine.

Ronan's fists clenched. He should have thrashed the bastard unconscious when he had the chance.

But now his priority was Marina. He'd never seen her like this. Even that first night, when she'd collapsed with nervous and physical exhaustion after confronting Wakefield. Then she'd been weak, unsteady, but filled with fighting determination. She'd stood up for herself with a courage that had grabbed at his heart.

But the fight had seeped out of her now. She looked defeated. Dejected. He couldn't stand it.

He reached out and took her hands in his. She tried to resist, to push him away as he sat on the sofa beside her, but he was having none of that. He faced her, knees pressed against her thigh, holding her clenched fists, ice-cold in his hands.

She scared the hell out of him.

'Tell me,' he demanded.

'He said you only ever wanted the company for yourself.' Her voice shook. 'That you tricked me...'

Ronan stared into her blind eyes, desperately searching for his vibrant, passionate Marina. This wasn't her. She was so passive.

'I don't want Marina Enterprises,' he said urgently. 'Let's get that straight right now. I've never sought to take it over, and I haven't schemed to get it for myself.'

Something flickered in her eyes. 'But Wakefield signed it over to you.'

'That was just another tactic of his.' Ronan squeezed her

hands, worried by their coldness. He should get her something for shock, but he couldn't leave her, even for a moment.

'Wakefield was lying.' Her eyes still had that awful blank look of pain and he hurried to explain. 'He must have planned this from the moment he realised he'd have to relinquish the company. By the time my legal people told me he was making the transfer to me, rather than you and your brother, I decided to go with it. Better to have the company safely away from him first. Then we could settle the rest later. That's what I've been doing today—organising a transfer to the Lucchesi family.'

She blinked, and he felt a tremor run through her.

'It's true,' he urged, desperate for her to believe him. 'Your brother Sebastian is at the meeting right now. You can call him.'

She shook her head. 'You didn't tell me,' she whispered.

'No.' His conscience smote him. If he'd been willing to take a risk, to trust Marina as she deserved, none of this would have happened.

His gaze dropped to her mouth. Her bottom lip was swollen where she'd bitten it. He wanted to lean across and kiss it better, pull her against him and keep her close.

'And you bought my house.' It wasn't a statement. It was an accusation.

He looked down to the papers strewn round her feet. How did he explain? His motives hadn't been at all pure. She'd think him manipulative, and she'd just been burned by a master manipulator. Would she judge him to be as bad as Wakefield? He'd wondered that himself, especially when he'd been unable to harness his libido enough to leave her alone while she came to grips with her grief and pain. Why should she see him as any different? That was the dread that woke him in a cold, terrified sweat far too often.

But he had to take that risk.

He took a deep breath and pulled her close, telling himself she needed the body warmth to counteract her shock. The pathetic truth was that he was desperate to have her safe in his arms. She held herself stiffly in his embrace, but she was there, warm and soft, where she belonged.

'Yes, I bought the house. You needed money fast. So I bought it. And I requested a quick settlement.'

She pulled back enough to see his face, and speared him with a look that demanded the truth. He was relieved to see there was a little more colour in her cheeks.

'Why?'

'I did it because I wanted you.' His voice was harsh. 'It's as simple as that.' He heard his own breathing, laboured and heavy in the throbbing silence. Felt the crash of his heart against his ribcage.

'By the time I'd taken you home from Wakefield's reception, by the time I'd put you to bed and walked out the door, I'd decided you were going to be mine.'

Marina gaped at him and he plunged on. He had nothing to lose now. 'That's why I insisted you play the part of my mistress. Because I wanted you close. I wanted you with *me*. But when I had you here in my home, in my bed, things changed. I realised I needed more.' His heart beat so loud now it was like a jackhammer, thudding through his body. 'I wanted...'

'You wanted?'

'To make you fall for me,' he admitted.

Silence. His pulse reverberated like thunder in his ears as he waited for her response. A haze of sweat dampened his skin as he felt real, gut-wrenching fear.

'I don't understand. Why would you want that? Was it because I was some sort of...novelty?' She didn't meet his eyes but looked down at his collar. He had to lean close to catch her words. 'Was it for a bit of fun, because I was different?'

'Novelty! Is that what he said? When I get my hands on that gutter trash I'll—'

'Forget Wakefield and answer my question.' Her whisper brought him up short.

'Oh, honey. You didn't believe that, did you? You couldn't have! Don't you know you're gorgeous? Don't you know I'd do anything to keep you with me?'

Huge, pain-shadowed eyes met his. 'All I know is that you lied to me.'

She'd stabbed him in the heart. And he deserved it. He knew it even as the pain lanced through him.

'You're right.' He heaved in some oxygen. He couldn't seem to catch his breath. 'I lied to you, Marina.'

'Why? Why would you want to hurt me?'

He laughed then, the sound bitter. He'd been worse that Wakefield. At least she'd known what to expect from him.

'I didn't want to hurt you, Marina. Believe me. I—' He swallowed hard and forced himself to continue. 'I wanted you to fall in love with me. Like I'd fallen for you.'

Silence throbbed between them, alive with the sound of his breathing, harsh and rapid. Expectant.

Her eyes looked huge, as if with shock.

Would she, could she, forgive him?

'Well, you managed that,' she murmured at last.

'What?' He'd seen her lips move, but... Had she really said it? 'What did you say?'

Her eyes held his, and in that single, glorious moment he knew. The weight of the last weeks, the horror of unaccustomed uncertainty, lifted from his shoulders, making him dizzy from relief. And around his chest the searing band of pain vanished as he took his first clear breath since he'd seen Wakefield, trying to escape out through the front gate.

'You heard me,' she said. Her lips curved in a tiny smile, and her eyes fell from his as if she were suddenly shy.

In one surge of movement he clasped her to him, close enough to imprint their bodies together. Nothing had ever felt so good. Not even their frantic, passionate lovemaking. For what could compare with knowing his love was reciprocated? And by such a woman. *His* magnificent, sultry, sexy, soon-to-be wife.

'I love you, Marina.' He paused and listened to the satisfying sound of it echo in the air. 'It's taken me long enough to admit it. I kept pretending to myself it was simply lust I felt. And the need to keep you safe. But I was wrong.'

He let his hands slide down over her, slowly caressing. 'And I was a coward. I didn't want to tell you until I was sure you needed me too.'

He leaned close and pressed a kiss on her jaw. Another on the tender spot just below her ear. She tasted like paradise. He circled her ear with his tongue and felt her shiver in his embrace.

He'd never get enough of her. Never.

'You scared the living daylights out of me when you talked about moving out.'

'I was trying to be independent,' she said in a muffled voice. 'You never told me how you felt.'

'That's because I was a damned idiot.' He smiled against her hair, inhaling her fresh, sexy scent. He revelled in the feel of her against him, returning his embrace, her hands stroking restlessly.

'Tell me,' he urged, determined to overcome that one last vestige of fear.

'You're so bossy.'

'Tell me,' he urged, lifting her face to his, 'or I won't kiss you.'

She was smiling now, with her whole face, a wide, wondrous grin that made his heart stutter.

'I love you. I thought that was pathetically obvious.' And then her lips were on his, demanding, persuading, clinging.

He fell into her as if she was his haven. She welcomed him as if she'd never let him go. Her lips were so soft, her mouth so deliciously seductive under his. Her luscious body pressed up against his, driving him inevitably out of his mind. Kissing Marina always short-circuited his brain.

His woman. Warm and wonderful and oh-so-right in his arms. His world began and ended with her.

'I knew from the first that you were mine,' he gasped minutes later, as he fought for breath. He didn't bother to mask the satisfaction in his tone, or the possessiveness of his touch as he sculpted her body with his hands.

'But I looked—'

'Gorgeous,' he whispered against her ear. 'Even in that godawful suit. Full of fire and passion. Standing up against that bully Wakefield as if you could take on the whole world to protect your family. It was no wonder I fell in love with you.'

'Really?' Even now there was doubt in her voice.

'Marina Lucchesi, you are one stunningly gorgeous woman.' He watched her eyes widen at the words. He hoped that this time she'd believe him. 'You're clever and capable and sexy as hell.'

'Yet I practically had to beg you to make love to me the first time.' She looked away, but he caught her chin and tilted her face so she couldn't avoid him.

'I was trying to do the honourable thing. I wanted you so badly it was killing me. But I knew you were hurting. You'd lost your father, your home, your whole future. You were injured and unsure of yourself. I had no right to force you into intimacy. You were a virgin, for God's sake!'

She shook her head. 'You didn't force me into anything, Ronan. It was my choice, my own free will.'

'And you'll stay? Of your own free will?' He had to hear her say it.

She nodded, a gentle smile curving her lips. 'I'll stay.'

'You're the only woman for me, Marina.' Her dark eyes held him spellbound as his pledge echoed between them.

'So you're after a long-term lover?' Her eyebrow arched inquisitively after a moment.

'Hell, no.' He pulled her tight against him. 'My mother and Cleo are flying over from Perth this weekend, to welcome you into the family. They're all agog to meet you. But I made them wait till I was sure of you.'

'Ah, so Marina Enterprises was going to be a bribe? To persuade me to marry you?'

His heart thudded again as he saw her sweet, teasing smile. He shook his head. 'No, that's already been signed, sealed and delivered. I admit I thought it would help my cause when I handed the documents over to you today as a surprise, at a nice, *intimate* lunch. But I was relying on my natural charm to convince you.'

He lowered his head to take her mouth again, but instead felt the press of her fingers against his lips.

'You've forgotten something,' she said. 'If you want a wife you need to ask me first. That's the traditional way.' There was a glint of laughter in her dark eyes. 'Maybe I'll need persuading.'

Immediately he bent and swept her up into his arms. He pulled her close against his heart, where she belonged. Then he turned and strode to the stairs.

'I'm counting on it,' he said with a grin.

HIS BOUGHT MISTRESS

BY
EMMA DARCY

HIS BOUGHT MISTRESS

BY

EMMA DARCY

Don't miss Emma Darcy's exciting new novel,
Maverick Plus, available in September 2009
from Mills & Boon Modern.

Initially a French/English teacher, **Emma Darcy** changed careers to computer programming before the happy demands of marriage and motherhood. Very much a people person, and always interested in relationships, she finds the world of romance fiction a thrilling one and the challenge of creating her own cast of characters very addictive.

CHAPTER ONE

ANGIE BLESSING did not feel particularly blessed on this fine summer Sunday morning. In fact, the bright sunshine was giving her a headache. Or maybe it was her relationship with Paul that was giving her the headache.

Here she was, sitting in his Mercedes convertible, being driven home to the apartment she shared with her best friend and business partner, Francine Morgan—her choice because she didn't want to go yacht-racing with Paul today—and instead of thinking how lucky she was to be the love interest in the life of one of Sydney's most eligible bachelors, she was thinking of Francine's current bible: *The Marriage Market After Thirty—Finding the Right Husband For You.*

For the past three years she'd been Paul Overton's *partner.*

No proposal of marriage.

The really troubling part was, if he got down on his knees right now and asked her to marry him, Angie wasn't sure she'd say yes.

'Don't forget we've got the fund-raising dinner next Friday night,' he tossed at her as he drove down her road at Cremorne, conveniently situated on his way to the Royal North Shore Yacht Club.

More politics, Angie thought. Just like the party last night. Everything with Paul was politics, making influential connections, building a network of powerful support that would back his ambition to go into parliament. His current career as a barrister had little to do with a love of the law. It was more a showcase for his rhetorical skills, a step towards what he really wanted.

'Angie…?' He threw a frown at her, impatient with her silence.

'Yes, Paul. It's marked in my calendar,' she said dutifully, hating the way she was little more than an ornament on his arm at such functions. 'And we have the ballet on Wednesday night,' she reminded him, relieved at being able to look forward to that date.

'I don't think I'll be able to go. The case I'm on this week needs a lot of preparation. Big trial, as you know, and the media will be covering it.'

Angie gritted her teeth. Ballet was *her* thing. But, of course, that wasn't important to his career. He could have worked on his case preparation today instead of yacht-racing, though naturally it wouldn't occur to Paul to give up one of his pleasures.

'Take Francine with you,' he suggested brightly.

'Right!' she bit out. No point in arguing. Waste of breath.

He pulled the Mercedes into the kerb outside her apartment block, engine idling, which meant he wasn't about to get out and open the passenger door for her. Angie wondered if the romance went out of every relationship after three years. Was being taken for granted the norm?

Paul beamed her a rueful smile. 'Hope the queasy stomach settles down soon.'

Her excuse for not spending today with him.

She returned the smile. 'Me, too.'

He wasn't going to kiss her. Couldn't afford to catch a tummy bug with the big trial on this week.

'You do look peaky,' he commented sympathetically. 'Look after yourself, Angie.'

He wasn't about to, she thought.

'I'll call you during the week,' he added.

Sure. To check I'm okay for Friday night when you need me again.

'Fine,' she said, struggling to rise above her jaundiced mind-set.

Paul was the most handsome man she'd ever met: tall, broad-shouldered, instantly impressive, dark wavy hair swept back from what she thought of as a noble forehead, riveting dark eyes that captivated with their sharp intelligence, a strong male face to complement his very male physique. He came from a wealthy family, was wealthy himself, and she could share a brilliant future with him if he ever got around to offering it.

'Have a nice day,' she forced out, then opened the door and swung herself out of the car.

She watched him drive off—the A-list man in his A-list car—and seriously wondered if Paul saw her as an A-list woman. She probably projected the right image: tall, long blond hair, slim enough to wear any clothes well, though her figure was too curvy for classic model proportions, good skin that didn't need make-up to cover blemishes, the kind of clear-boned face that always photographed well though she certainly didn't consider herself beautiful. Her eyes were her most attractive feature, probably because they were an unusual sage green.

When it came to self-presentation, she was good, having learnt that this art was an asset in her line of business. People who hired professional help from an interior design company had more confidence in a professional who was well groomed and colour co-ordinated herself. She definitely had the image Paul liked but did she have the right *substance* for him to consider her marriageable?

Was being a successful career woman enough?

No wealthy family in her background. No political pull there, either. Her parents were both artists with antigovernment attitudes, perfectly happy for their daughter to make her own choices in life, but staunchly into alternative society themselves. They were hardly the right people for Paul to have as in-laws, though Angie knew her parents would never thrust themselves into *his* limelight.

Besides, they lived so far away, right up the north coast at Byron Bay. They'd never actually been a fac-tor in her relationship with Paul, not like *his* parents who seemed to accept her. On the surface. But was she suitable as a lifetime partner? More importantly, did she want to be Paul Overton's lifetime partner?

It had once been a dazzling prospect.

Now, Angie wasn't so sure.

In fact, she was beginning to feel she might well have wasted three years on a rosy dream which was fast developing wilting edges. She headed into the apartment block, wondering if Francine had found her Mr. Right last night at the *Dinner for Six*—a group of thirty-something singles wanting to meet their match, this being her friend's latest dating ploy in hunting for a husband.

She found Francine sitting on their balcony over-looking the bay, Sunday newspapers spread on the table in front of her, a mug of coffee to hand, and the gloom of failure denying any interest in the lovely morning or anything else. She was still in her pyjamas. Her dark curly hair was an unbrushed tangle. Smudges of last night's mascara gave her grey eyes a bruised look. Slumped shoulders added to her air of dejection.

'Struck out again?' Angie asked sympathetically, stepping outside to join her friend.

'Too earnest. No spark,' came the listless reply.

The thirty-something men were probably as desperate to impress as Francine was, Angie thought. 'Maybe they'd be more relaxed on a second date.'

'Bor…ing.' Francine rolled her eyes at her. 'And they'd be all over me like a flash if I gave them a second chance. Hot to trot, all of them.'

'Well, you did look hot in that red dress last night.'

Positively stunning, Angie had thought, the fabric clinging to Francine's gym-toned body, plus some provocative cleavage showing due to the purchase of a new push-up bra. Her figure was petite but certainly very feminine. Pretty face. Gorgeous hair. Francine was a knockout when she set out to be aggressively attractive.

'I need to light a fire in the right guy when I meet him,' she expounded. 'That's what the book says. Stand out from the crowd. Be positive and memorable. Always look my best.'

'Not exactly practising that this morning,' Angie teased, trying to lighten her up. 'What if I'd walked in here with a friend of Paul's in tow?'

'So I would have blown it. I'm just having some down time. Besides, you're not supposed to be here. What happened to yacht-racing?'

She shrugged. 'I didn't feel like it.'

'Easy for some,' Francine muttered darkly, then slammed her hands on the table and rose to her feet. 'Okay. Clean myself up. Go to the gym. Spread myself around. I'm doing it.' Grim resolve was in her voice and on her face as she marched off towards the bathroom.

'You might need to relax more yourself.' The words tripped out before Angie could think better of them.

Francine wheeled on her, spitting mad. 'Don't give me advice! You've had your Mr. Right for so long you don't know how it is for me, Angie. Or what it's like out there on the dating scene. And I'm not settling for just anyone!'

'Neither you should,' Angie quickly agreed, not even sure that *settling* for Paul was an option. Her confidence in his rightness for her was also at an all-time low.

'All these years, building up our business, you said yourself I'm brilliant at marketing our design company,' Francine ran on heatedly.

'You are,' Angie acknowledged.

'I've even snagged the Fullbright contract for us.'

A plum contract, worth a lot of money to them.

'So I should be able to market myself and get the result I want,' Francine said decisively. 'That means I have to sell what my husband-to-be finds appealing. And let me tell you I'm not going to leave any stone unturned. I'm thirty years old and I want a husband and children in my future.'

Having delivered this firm declaration, Francine marched on to the bathroom.

They were *both* thirty years old, Angie thought, taking her friend's empty mug to the kitchen, intent

on brewing some fresh coffee for herself. They'd
spent their twenties establishing their business, working hard, climbing up in the world. The Fullbright
contract proved they'd reached the top level in their
field—being given the job of colour co-ordinating a
fabulous new block of luxury apartments situated
right on the harbour shoreline. That success should
be very sweet. And it was. But they were women,
too, and priorities definitely changed as the biological
clock started ticking.

Angie told herself she probably shouldn't be feeling so discontented with Paul. So what if the excitement and passion in their first year together had
waned! It probably did in every relationship, giving
way to a comfortable sense of being able to count on
each other. It was unrealistic to expect everything to
be perfect. Hadn't she accepted that maintaining
something workable demanded a fair amount of com-
promise?

Except Paul never compromised on anything.

She hadn't noticed this at first. Now she was probably noticing it too much. But if she broke off with
him…It was scary to think of herself being suddenly
single again, out there in the thirty-something dating
scene. Francine's total dedication to her mission
seemed far too extreme to her, yet…would she begin
to feel just as desperate, given no readily available
prospects?

Maybe she should count her blessings with Paul
instead of being critical.

Yet he had never once brought up the subject of
marriage.

Three years…

Was he ever going to?

Was she just a handy habit to him, one he'd shed when the time came to make a marriage that suited his ambitions?

The coffee percolator pinged, and she poured herself a mugful, then wandered back out to the balcony with it, her mind hopelessly riddled with doubts.

The newspapers did not provide the soothing distraction she needed. Angie tried focusing her thoughts on the Fullbright contract, planning how best to handle the scheduled meeting with Hugo Fullbright himself, scheduled for next Thursday morning. The billionaire property developer was bound to be demanding and she'd need to impress him with her answers. At least she was confident of achieving that.

Francine re-emerged, looking very bright and bouncy, dressed in spectacular lime green lycra shorts and a matching midriff top, ready for her trip to the gym. 'I've made up my mind,' she announced. 'I'm going to spread my net wider.'

'A new strategy?' Angie queried.

'I've spent eight months doing what the book recommends with only dud results. The thing to do now is grab attention big-time.'

'How?'

'I read about a really bold scheme in the newspaper. I get my photo scanned, blown up, and plastered on a billboard placed at a busy city intersection. Anyone interested can contact me on the Internet.'

Angie's jaw dropped in shock. 'A billboard!' she gasped.

'Major public exposure,' Francine rattled on, apparently uncaring about any negative outcomes. 'Should bring in a huge number of guys for me to choose from.'

'You're using your face and name on a public bill-board?' Angie was appalled. 'What about crackpots and perverts and...'

'Not my *real* name. More of a teaser which will be a password to reach me through a third party on the Net. I'll be protected, Angie.'

'But people will recognise your face.'

'So? No harm in being a celebrity. Probably do me a power of good.'

'Francine, what about our business associates? What are they going to think?'

'I don't care what they think. Business is business. We deliver what our clients want. Nothing wrong with me going after what *I* want.'

'But a billboard...it's so...so public!'

'Are you going to be ashamed of me?' Francine bored in belligerently.

'No! No, of course not. I'm just worried for you. What you might end up having to handle.'

'Let me worry about that. I'm simply giving you fair warning so you don't get a shock when the bill-board goes up. I'm off to the gym now.'

Cutting off any further argument.

Angie didn't like the idea one bit. It horrified her. On the other hand, she wasn't a go-getter type, not like Francine whose job it was to bring in the interior design contracts for Angie to work on. In any event, nothing she said was going to change her friend's mind, and it was probably better to stay silent on the highly sensitive issue of how to reel in Mr. Right.

Angie hoped Paul wouldn't see the billboard.

He'd be scathing about her friend's blatant self-publicity.

But it wasn't *his* life and he would never have

Francine's problems. Any amount of eager women would leap at the chance to be Paul Overton's Miss Right, no need for him to advertise what a prize he was. Angie decided she would stick loyally by Francine, regardless of the consequences of her scheme.

Three days later, the inevitable was announced. 'It will be up tomorrow,' Francine informed her as they settled in their seats at the ballet. Her eyes were dancing with excited anticipation.

'Up where?' Angie asked, trying her utmost to hold back any dampener on the happy sparkles.

'You'll see it on your way to the Fullbright meeting tomorrow.'

And see it she did the next morning.

No one crossing the Sydney Harbour Bridge by car, bus, train or foot could miss it. Angie almost drove into the back of the car in front of her. Not because she was agog at seeing Francine's face on the billboard. She'd been mentally prepared to see it somewhere.

The shock—and it was totally mind-blasting—was in seeing her own face on the billboard.

Hers!

And underneath it the caption—*Foxy Angel*!

CHAPTER TWO

HUGO FULLBRIGHT had a very good view of the billboard as the cars in front of his slowed to a crawl approaching the toll booths at the southern end of the bridge. It amused him to check out the passing parade of people brave enough to hang themselves out in public. Six new faces on it this morning. The blonde stirred his interest. *Foxy Angel.*

Few women looked that good. Probably a computer enhanced photograph. Undoubtedly she would prove a disappointment to the guys who leapt on her bandwagon. Logic insisted that something had to be wrong for *her* to need this medium to get a man. But she sure was a winner on the billboard.

Foxy Angel... Hugo grinned over the teaser. Great marketing. Intriguing suggestion of naughty but nice. Just the mix he liked himself. Except he didn't care for the *naughty* part to be inspired and driven by cocaine.

It had hit him like a brick when he'd found Chrissie snorting a line of it at the party last Saturday night. And her argument—'But, darling, sex is so much more fun when I'm on a high.'—was not what a man wanted to hear, as though the pleasure he gave didn't do enough for her.

Goodbye, Chrissie.

Hugo had no regrets over that decision. To his mind, people who depended on recreational drugs to *perform* weren't in control of themselves or anything

15

else. He didn't tolerate it in any of the top executives in his company and he wasn't about to tolerate it in the woman closest to him. Besides, illegal substances were illegal, bound to lead to messy situations.

Having passed over the bridge and beyond sight of the tantalising photo on the billboard, Hugo concentrated his mind on the fast approaching meeting with the colour co-ordinator for his new Pyrmont development. He'd purchased three old warehouses along the harbour front, then had them torn down to accommodate this project. Since he'd be putting million-dollar prices on each luxury apartment, he wanted a top class job done on their visual presentation.

It was important to impress that on the specialist he'd contracted, so best he did it personally, let the woman know he wasn't interested in any cost-cutting that might have a negative effect. A quality finish was essential. He was happy with the architectural design but *the finish* should be the icing on the cake.

Attention to detail—that was the key to success.

Nothing overlooked.

One of the ground floor apartments had been turned into a temporary business centre for on the job requirements and supervision. Hugo mentally approved the security system for the garage as he parked his car, and the exclusive access system to each apartment as he moved on to enter the company *office*. He greeted his people there, left instructions for Miss Blessing to be escorted to the meeting room, and for refreshments to be brought ten minutes after she arrived.

The meeting room had been set up at the far end of the open living area where a wall of glass allowed a spectacular view of the harbour and its ever-changing traffic. It comprised a rented lounge setting with a large square coffee table. Hugo didn't bother sitting down. He stood looking out, watching various boats going past—cruisers, yachts, ferries—glancing at his watch to check the time.

The woman was late. Five minutes. Ten minutes. Unpunctuality always niggled him. It disregarded the value of his time, invariably shortening his temper. When he finally heard the footsteps signalling her arrival, he had to school himself not to display impatience as he swung around to greet her.

In actual fact, any sense of impatience shot right out of his mind as recognition hit. The long blond hair was swinging naturally around her shoulders just as he'd imagined it could, the face was an exact replica, no computerised touch-up to make her features more attractive, no blemishes on that glowing skin, and the unusual green eyes were even more fascinating in real life...

Foxy Angel!

Not only living up to her photograph, but delivering the complete goods with stunning oomph!

Her figure was femme fatale class—lush curves where there should be lush curves, stunningly outlined by a citrine silk dress that shouted sensuality, and long shapely legs enhanced by sexy strappy highheels. High impact stuff. No doubt about it. Hugo felt a hot tingling in his groin, a charge of adrenalin shooting through his body, excitement fizzing in his brain.

It was fantastic luck that Chrissie was gone from his life, because this woman was walking into it, ringing bells that said he had to have her.

And she was available!

The trick was to win her before a horde of eager beavers jumped on the billboard bandwagon.

Angie was used to guys giving her the once-over but Hugo Fullbright's comprehensive head to foot appraisal felt more sexual than most and it bothered her. It bothered her even more that he made no attempt to switch to business meeting mode. And he looked unbelievably sexy himself, stunning blue eyes simmering with bedroom interest, a tantalising little smile that smacked of sensual satisfaction lurking on his mouth as he watched her walk towards him.

A wave of his hand dismissed her escort.

His focus did not deviate from Angie, and her heart gave an agitated skip as she realised Hugo Fullbright was probably a blitz operator in more than property development. Paul might be classical male but this guy was animal male in spades. And he radiated the kind of magnetic intensity Russell Crowe brought to his movies.

His thick black hair was cut short but it still had an untamed look about it. His skin was darkly tanned, suggesting he lived more under the sun than away from it. His body was encased in tailored sophistication—a beautiful grey suit that had a sheen of blue silk running through it—yet she had the sense of a strong, lithe physique, like that of a big jungle cat, wired to pounce.

It took all her willpower to step up to him, offer her hand, and make her vocal chords perform at a natural pitch. 'Mr. Fullbright, I'm Angie Blessing.'

'Angie…' He rolled her name off his tongue as though tasting it for honey. The vivid blue eyes twinkled with wicked teasing. 'Short for Angel?'

Her heart sank like a stone. He'd seen the billboard, connected her to it. 'No. Angela,' she answered sharply, desperate for some diversion. 'But everyone calls me Angie.'

'I think Angel suits you better,' he mused, holding on to her hand, his thumb fanning her skin, shooting heat into her bloodstream.

She felt her cheeks burning. Her mind was torn over what to do—ignore the allusion to the billboard or confront it? This was business. Business! It was wrong to get into anything personal.

'I do apologise for being late, Mr. Fullbright,' she rushed out.

'Hugo.' He smiled invitingly.

'I had an urgent call…'

'I imagine you'll be getting many urgent calls. I'm sure I'm not the only man who…*likes what he sees*.'

The direct reference to the words on the billboard—*If you like what you see, contact…*—was too pointed for Angie to dismiss. She took a deep breath and plunged straight into trying to clear the murky waters of this meeting.

'Mr. Fullbright…'

'Hugo,' he slid in, and started to lift her hand as though he intended to kiss it!

She snatched it out of his grasp, firmly claiming, 'A mistake was made!'

He moved his now empty hand into a lazily elegant gesture that requested more information. 'A mistake?'

'The person who composed that billboard used the wrong half of a photograph sent in by my friend,' she said heatedly, Francine's frantic excuse doing little to stop her blood from boiling on this issue.

'A friend,' Hugo Fullbright repeated mockingly,

not believing a word of it. Then he grinned. 'You don't have to hide behind a friend, Angie. I'm not in the least perturbed by your enterprising move. It cuts straight to the chase, doing away with any need for preliminary manoeuvres. I admire the sheer nerve of it.'

Angie realised that nothing she said was going to change his mind. The *friend* cover was too often used to insert distance from a personal interest. He'd seen her image on the billboard and any mistake seemed too improbable. Angie wondered if she could sue the billboard people for damages. Francine had promised to fix everything but Francine wasn't here right now and somehow Angie had to get this meeting on a business footing. It didn't matter what he *thought,* as long as he…

'I'm just letting you know you needn't be *foxy* about this,' he dropped into the silence, benevolently forgiving what he saw as pretence. 'In fact…'

'Mr. Fullbright,' she swiftly cut in.

'Please make it Hugo.' Charm on full blast, making her heart pitter-pat like a fluttering shuttlecock being batted around her chest.

'Hugo,' she conceded, taking another deep breath to calm herself down. 'I'm here on a professional basis.'

'So you are. Sorry for confusing the issue.' His smile was very white and patently apologetic, so why was she thinking of a wolf in sheep's clothing?

It was the animal thing again.

Male on the prowl.

All her instincts were picking it up and reacting to it, throwing her into a fluster because he was terribly attractive and the situation was making her feel more vulnerable than she should be. She'd been with Paul for three years and this man...she couldn't imagine this man without a woman in tow, married or otherwise.

'Though I can't help thinking how fortuitous this meeting is,' he ran on. 'Both of us...currently unattached...'

Had he read her mind? Those blue eyes were dynamite.

'...and I do, indeed, like what I see.'

It was a very pointed statement of personal interest and intent. He wanted her. Or, at least, wanted to try her out, see how she fitted with him.

And to Angie's intense embarrassment, she felt her body responding positively to it, telling her in no uncertain terms that she would like to have the experience of this man on a very personal level.

In spite of her attachment to Paul!

'Could we...' She swallowed hard to remove the weird constriction in her throat. 'Could we talk business now?' Her voice sounded slurred, husky, desperate, embarrassing her further.

A delaying tactic. A *foxy* tactic. His interpretation of this request danced through the amusement in his eyes. 'By all means tell me...what you want to tell me,' he invited, gesturing to the lounge setting. 'Would you like to sit down?'

'Yes. Thank you,' she jerked out, and hoped her suddenly tremulous legs would carry her to the leather sofa without any graceless teetering in her high-heeled sandals.

She made the move without mishap, deliberately choosing to seat herself in the centre of the sofa, delivering the hint for him to settle for an armchair, leaving her with enough personal space to feel comfortable. Which he did. Though it didn't lessen her physical awareness of him one bit. In fact, it was probably heightened, being able to see all of him, sitting with a relaxed waiting air, confident he would eventually get the outcome he wanted one way or another.

Angie fiercely concentrated on business, determined to stay professional. 'I don't know how hands-on you are on this project...' she started.

Disastrously.

Because he instantly inserted, 'My involvement in any project is never without a hands-on approach.' The quirky little smile had a double-edged kick as he added, 'You have my full attention, Angie.'

'Right!' She wished he wouldn't keep sucking the breath out of her. 'The concept I've decided upon for designing the colour co-ordination in these apartments...'

'I've already approved the concept.'

Oh great! Now he was pulling the mat out from under her professional feet. 'Then why am I here? What point is there to this meeting?' she demanded, losing her cool under the barrage of heat she felt coming from him.

His straight black eyebrows slanted in a kind of quizzical self-examination of his motives. 'Well, I'd have to say it's developed more points since I made the initial request.'

Since he saw her photo, advertising she was available!

Angie gritted her teeth, waiting for a *business* answer.

He grinned, aiming all his megawatt masculinity at

her. 'But the primary aim was simply to meet you and assess for myself if you will deliver what you promise.'

Her stomach curled. The only assessment going on in his eyes was centred on how much pleasure he might find in having her with him on a very personal level—whether she'd live up to whatever he thought she'd been advertising on the billboard!

'We have a contract,' she bit out. 'Ask anyone our company has dealt with. We have always honoured our contracts and delivered on schedule.'

'That has been checked, Angie,' he smoothly assured her. 'But even within the letter of the contract, some things can be fiddled and often are.'

Foxy.

Was that word going to haunt her on this job?

'What I want is a quality finish,' he continued. 'No cost cutting.'

'The prices we've quoted on materials are precise,' she shot in, emphatically adding, 'We have never compromised on quality. It wouldn't even occur to us to do so in this job. Our design company has a reputation to maintain.'

'And I willingly concede you do project a high-quality image, Angie.' Warm appreciation in his eyes. Too warm. 'It reinforces my feeling that I've made the right choice.'

His choice.

As though she had no say in it!

On the other hand, if he was talking about giving them the contract…best not to make any reply. Besides, her chest had tightened up again, rendering her breathless and speechless.

Hugo Fullbright smiled his white wolf smile. 'I just

wanted to impress on you that I don't believe in cutting costs when going after what I want.'

'Fine!' she choked out.

'So we now have an understanding of where we both stand,' he concluded.

'Yes.'

Point achieved, meeting over. Angie told herself to get up and take her leave. She uncrossed her ankles, planted her feet on the floor, ready to rise from the sofa…

'I'm flying to Tokyo tomorrow morning,' he tossed at her. 'Back Sunday night. What you might call a long weekend.'

Angie remained poised where she was, wondering what this had to do with her.

'A bit of business,' he explained offhandedly. 'I built a resort in Queensland for a Japanese consortium. They probably want to run other plans past me but primarily it's a hospitality trip—wining, dining, sightseeing.'

'Nice for you,' she commented, not knowing how else to respond.

'For you, too, Angie…' A wicked challenge sparkled in his eyes. '…if you'd like to come with me.'

Tokyo.

She'd never been to Japan.

And being whisked off there by him…

Shocked at these wayward thoughts—he was *wickedly* attractive—Angie pulled herself together and frantically tried to find an appropriate reply. Rejection in this situation was very tricky.

'Thank you. But I've never thought it a good idea to mix business with pleasure. It could develop into an awkward situation between us.'

'I would agree…if you worked directly for me. But you'll be working independently on this contract. Your own boss with absolute autonomy.' The white wolf smile flashed again. 'In fact, this trip may very well provide some beneficial business contacts for you and your design company.'

He was so smooth.

And appealing.

Even making business mixed with pleasure a plus instead of a minus.

Angie couldn't believe how tempted she was. Accepting such a proposition was tantamount to being gobbled up by this marauding man. It would be such a wild thing to do. Besides, there was Paul. The fund-raiser dinner on Friday night. Why hadn't she thought of that before?

'I'm sorry. I have other plans—commitments—this weekend.'

'Fair enough,' he accepted gracefully, though his eyes were weighing how serious her commitments might be.

Angie flushed with embarrassment as she remembered the billboard—the vast flood of replies Francine was expecting through the Internet. Was Hugo thinking she wanted to check them out before picking *him?*

Useless to state again that her photo was a mistake.

No way would he buy the friend excuse.

She pushed up from the sofa, too agitated to remain seated a moment longer. 'Thank you for your time. I hope you have a great trip to Tokyo,' she rattled out, forcing the offer of her hand to make a polite, *businesslike* farewell.

He stood up in all his overpowering maleness, making Angie quake inside. Instead of taking her hand, he reached inside his suit jacket and extracted a slim, gold card-holder. 'Let me give you my card.' He opened it and pressed all his contact details into her hand, smiling a sensual promise as he said, 'Should you change your mind about Tokyo…give me a call.'

'Yes. Thank you,' she babbled, and somehow managed to stretch her mouth into a bright smile. 'Goodbye.'

'Until next time,' he purred.

Jungle cat, just biding his time for another opportunity to pounce.

Angie could feel him watching her walk away from him. Every nerve in her body was tingling as though a field of highly charged electricity was emanating from him. His card was burning in her hand. She tried to think of Paul—Paul who might or might not marry her—but Hugo Fullbright and a trip to Tokyo with him were terrible distractions.

Of course she couldn't do it.

She wouldn't.

She wasn't the type of person to throw all caution to the winds, dump a man who had every reason to expect love and loyalty from her, and leap into a relationship with someone else.

It just wasn't right.

CHAPTER THREE

THE moment Angie stepped into their official office and showroom at the trendy end of Glebe Road, Francine leapt to her feet from behind her desk and was in full spout, frantically trying to appease the wrath she felt coming her way, the forerunner of it being the urgent call that had made Angie late for her meeting with Hugo Fullbright.

'I've been onto the billboard people. Told them you were threatening to sue for damages. They apologised profusely for the mistake, but they can't get your photo off and mine on until tomorrow. They'll print a public apology if you want, Angie. I know it's partly my fault for giving them the photo of the two of us, but it was the best one ever taken of me, and I swear it was clearly specified which half to use. I don't know why the technician got it wrong. But I'm terribly, terribly sorry that he did.'

Her wildly flapping hands moved into wringing. 'Did...ummh...Hugo Fullbright recognise you like you thought he might?' Her grimace imagined the worst but anxiously hoped for a let off.

Angie heaved a long loosening-up sigh, resigning herself to the fact that what was done was done. A mistake had been made and Francine had clearly worked hard at correcting the situation, so there was no point in carrying on about it.

'Yes, he did recognise me,' she answered, rolling her eyes to lighten the fraught mood. 'He had *Foxy*

Angel on his mind from the moment I walked into the meeting.' Which reminded her to ask, 'Why on earth did you pick that name? He related it straight to Angie.'

Francine scrunched up her shoulders as though defending herself from an imminent attack. 'I thought it would appeal to men's fantasies.'

'Well, it certainly did the trick,' Angie dryly informed her, though everything Hugo Fullbright had aimed at her had not felt like a fantasy at all. It had been very direct and highly disturbing.

'Were you…horribly embarrassed?'

'Yes, I was horribly embarrassed.' *And tempted.* Though best to put that out of her mind now. 'Hugo Fullbright didn't believe the billboard photo was a mistake. He said he admired my nerve and invited me to accompany him to Tokyo for a dirty weekend.'

If she put it in those terms, the temptation would go away. It was probably true, too, if he thought the billboard photo meant she'd do anything for a man.

Francine's jaw dropped.

Angie had to smile.

Tit for tat in the shock department.

'A pity it wasn't you at the meeting,' Angie ran on, needing to lighten up about what had happened. 'Hugo Fullbright is as handsome as the devil, as wealthy as they come, plus sex appeal in spades and currently unattached. You missed out on quite a catch!'

'Damn!' Shock collapsed into disappointment at the lost opportunity. 'All my meetings leading up to signing the contract were with the architect and he was seriously married with children. I never got to meet the boss man.'

'Francine…' Angie eyed her friend with deep exasperation. 'Can't you see there's a big down side to this scheme? Guys who might not take no for an answer. I was lucky that Hugo Fullbright was gentleman enough not to really come on to me.'

'I can handle it.' Francine's grey eyes flashed reckless determination. 'And let me tell you if Hugo Fullbright is all you say he is, I would have been off to Tokyo with him like a shot. You've got to seize the main chance, Angie, make it work for you. That's how it is out there. You've been safely ensconced with Paul so long, you've got blinkered eyes.'

'Paul…' Angie's inner tension geared up several notches at the reminder of her long-term relationship which could very well be in serious jeopardy. She should have been worrying about it instead of…

'He wouldn't have seen the billboard, Angie,' Francine offered in anxious hope. 'Not travelling from his apartment at Woolloomooloo to the law court at Darlinghurst.'

Angie shook her head. 'It doesn't have to be Paul. Can you really imagine that not one of his friends or colleagues, having known us as a couple for years…not one of them would have driven across the Sydney Harbour Bridge this morning without noticing the billboard and recognising *Foxy Angel* as me?'

'It *is* possible,' Francine argued. 'I mean…they wouldn't be expecting it to be you.'

'Hugo Fullbright took one look at me—one look—and had no trouble whatsoever in making the connection.'

'But anyone who knows you—really knows you—would think they're mistaken. You're so straight, Angie. It's not your kind of thing at all.'

Why did that suddenly make her feel she'd lived her life in a straitjacket, limiting her options instead of expanding her horizons?

Francine rushed into apology again. 'I'm sorry. Truly, truly, sorry. If it causes trouble with Paul, just lay all the blame on me, where it belongs, and I'll tell him so myself. I won't mind if he considers me a hopelessly ditzy woman who doesn't know which side is which.'

That wasn't going to help. Paul would be furious. Mistake or not, he'd find the whole photo thing offensive.

'Surely he's big enough to laugh it off,' Francine suggested tentatively.

More likely he'd drag it into the law court, demanding redress. Though that could turn into a distasteful circus. Possibly he would choose to laugh it off on the principle of least said, soonest mended.

'We'll cross that bridge when we come to it,' Angie said on a helpless sigh. Her own state of confusion about how she felt towards Paul—and Hugo Fullbright—was making her stomach churn.

'Right!' Francine clearly hoped for a reprieve on the Paul front. 'So…ummh…was there any business in the meeting with Hugo Fullbright?' she asked warily. 'I mean…this didn't have some negative effect, did it? The contract is watertight.'

'We have his full approval to go ahead with our concept.'

'Great!' Huge relief.

Angie wished she could feel relief. The next best thing was distraction. 'Let's get to work, Francine.'

They worked.

Every time the telephone rang, Francine pounced

on it, anxious to divert any possible trouble from Angie. At lunchtime she offered to go to the local delicatessen to buy them both salads, thus avoiding the chance that Angie might be accosted by some guy wanting *Foxy Angel* to fulfil his fantasies.

It was a very special salad—Thai beef with mango.

Angie's favourite.

Except her stomach was in no condition to appreciate it. She wondered if sushi would be easier to swallow, then wrenched her wayward mind off Tokyo and Hugo Fullbright and determinedly shoved lettuce leaves into her mouth.

The telephone rang.

Angie's stomach knotted up even further as she listened to Francine rattling out what had happened with the billboard, pulling out all stops to explain the mistake. It had to be Paul calling. And the way Francine was wilting was warning enough that he was not amused. Having exhausted all avenues of appeasement, she limply passed the receiver over, grimacing defeat.

'Paul...demanding to speak to you.'

Angie took a deep breath. 'Paul...'

'Our relationship is over!'

Just like that!

Not even a stay of judgement.

Angie was totally poleaxed, speechless.

'I can no longer afford to have you at my side,' he ranted on. 'I have been subjected to intolerable comments and sniggers from my colleagues all morning...'

'But...it's not my fault,' she managed to get out.

'Irrelevant!' he snapped. 'I do not intend to spend my time trying to explain away a mistake that no one will believe anyway. I've told people I severed our relationship last weekend and if you have any decency at all, you will back that up. If asked. The only saving grace from this mess is that I didn't go to the ballet with you last night. Goodbye, Angie.'

The line was disconnected before she could say another word.

The shock of this—this brutal dismissal from his life—stirred a turbulent anger that broke every restraint Angie would normally keep on her temper. She rose to her feet, marched over to Francine's desk and slammed the receiver down on the phone set, startling her friend into looking agog at her.

'What…what happened?' she asked nervously.

Angie ungritted her teeth and bit out, 'He dumped me.'

'He…' Francine swallowed hard. '…dumped you?'

'Three years together and he shoves me out in the cold, just like that!' Angie snapped her fingers viciously, growing more and more inflamed by the injustice of it all.

'I'll go and grovel to him, Angie. I'll…'

'Don't you dare!'

'But…'

'If Paul Overton came crawling to me on his hands and knees I wouldn't take him back,' Angie hurled at her, wheeling away and tramping around the office, working off a surge of violent energy and venting her ever-mounting outrage. 'It shows how much he cared about me. No love. No loyalty. No taking my side. Just wiping me off as though I was too tainted for him to touch anymore.'

She scissored a furious gesture at Francine who

was all galvanised attention. 'Even a criminal gets to have extenuating circumstances taken into consideration. And I'm innocent. Completely innocent.'

'You're right,' Francine gravely agreed. 'He doesn't deserve you.'

'He even backdated our separation to last weekend so he could save his precious pride in front of his precious colleagues, distancing himself from any action I've taken since then.'

'Mmmh…I wonder if he told them this was your revenge for being…'

'Francine!' Angie yelled in sheer exasperation.

It rattled her into trying to excuse her speculative mind-frame. 'I was just working it through…'

'I didn't do it, remember?'

'Completely and utterly innocent,' came the emphatic agreement. 'Uh…there's someone at the door, Angie,' she quickly added with the harried air of one wanting to grasp any distraction.

Angie swung to confront the intruder.

It was a florist delivery boy, carrying in a spectacular arrangement of exquisite orchids. He paused, glancing inquiringly from one to the other.

'Miss Angie Blessing?'

'That's me,' Angie snapped, eyeing him balefully. At this point in time, no male could be trusted.

'These are for you.'

'Fine. Thank you.'

She waved in the direction of her desk. He set the delivery down and scooted, undoubtedly aware that he'd blundered into an area mined with highly volatile sensibilities.

Angie glared at the gift.

Who would be sending her flowers?

Extremely expensive flowers.

There hadn't been time for Paul to start regretting his decision. If he ever did.

It was a very artistic arrangement, Japanese in style. This latter thought put a tingling in Angie's spine. It drove her over to the desk to unpin the attached note and read it.

A taste of Tokyo—Hugo.

The dark place in Angie's soul unfurled to a lovely blast of light. Hugo Fullbright didn't think she was too tainted to have at his side. He wanted her there. And he really valued her company. These perfect orchids had definitely cost him a small fortune.

'Right! I'm going!'

'Going where?' Francine asked in bewilderment.

'To Tokyo. With Hugo Fullbright.' She headed around the desk to get her handbag where she'd stowed his card.

Francine rocketed to her feet. 'Angie...Angie...just hang on a minute. This isn't a decision you should rush into.'

'Why not? You said yourself you'd go with him. Seize the main chance.' She found the card and held it triumphantly aloft as she moved to the telephone, abandoning all sense of caution on this wild plunge into a different future.

'It's not your style,' Francine argued frantically.

'And where did that get me? Dumped. Cast off. Devalued to nothing. This is the new me, Francine, and nothing you say is going to stop me.'

'But...'

'Not another word. I'm going.'

She snatched up the receiver and stabbed out the numbers printed on the card for Hugo Fullbright's

personal mobile telephone. Francine sank back onto
her chair, rested her elbows on the desk and covered
her face with her hands, emitting a low groan denot-
ing inescapable disaster. The buzzing call signal in
Angie's ear drowned out the mournful noise.

'Hugo Fullbright.' The name was rolled out in a
deep sexy voice.

Angie's stomach curled. She screwed it to the sticking point. 'It's Angie Blessing. I've changed my
mind.'

'A woman's prerogative,' he said charmingly.

'The flowers are truly lovely.'

'They reminded me of you. Beautiful, appealing,
with a fascinating hint of the exotic.'

Angie's pulse rate accelerated but she determinedly
kept her voice calm. 'Thank you.'

'Our flight to Tokyo leaves at ten-thirty tomorrow
morning,' he went on matter-of-factly. 'I'll have my
chauffeur call for you at nine.'

His chauffeur. That was one up on Paul. Not that
she cared about Paul anymore. Not one bit!

'Can you be ready by then?'

A reminder that she'd been late for their meeting
this morning. 'Yes,' she said firmly. 'I'm not normally unpunctual.'

'Good! Now I do need your home address.'

She gave it.

'I'm very glad you changed your mind, Angie.' He
was back to purring.

Her heart started hammering. She told herself that
having the very personal attention of a jungle cat
would certainly broaden her horizons, not to mention
tripping off to Tokyo. It was time to live dangerously.
And best not to let Hugo Fullbright know there was

any apprehension in her mind. He was thinking *Foxy Angel*—bold and enterprising.

'I look forward to seeing you tomorrow, Hugo,' she said, deciding that was a reasonably foxy reply.

'Until tomorrow.' The purr positively throbbed with pleasurable anticipation.

Angie quickly put the receiver down. 'Done!' she said, not allowing the slightest quiver of doubt to shake her resolution.

Francine dragged her hands down enough to look at her with huge, soulful eyes. 'Please...please... don't blame me.'

'What for? I'm grateful to you, Francine. You showed Paul up for what he was.'

'A skunk,' she said with feeling.

'Absolutely. You saved me from wasting more time on him, liberating me so I can take a step in a new direction.'

'But is this direction right for you, Angie?' she worried.

'Won't know until I'm in Tokyo.' She grinned at Francine as she collected her handbag, wanting to show there would be no hard feelings between them, whatever the outcome of this adventure with Hugo Fullbright.

'Angie, you shouldn't think of it as a dirty week-end,' Francine anxiously advised.

Seeing her friend's genuine concern, Angie paused to give her the real truth. 'I don't care, Francine. Hugo really got to me this morning—made me wish I wasn't with Paul. I want to take this chance with him. Come what may.'

'You're not flying off the rails because of what Paul's done?'

Angie took a deep breath and slowly shook her head as she examined her feelings with absolute honesty. 'I'm so mad at Paul because I'm angry with myself for staying with him for so long. I knew it wasn't right. And I knocked Hugo back this morning because of him. I knocked him back and I'm not going to knock him back again. Paul never really focused on me. Hugo…' The sheer magnetism of the man tugging on her—just the thought of being with him tugging on her. '…he's something else, Francine, something I want to be part of, and now that I'm free of any sense of loyalty to Paul, I'm seizing this chance!'

Angie grabbed the arrangement of beautiful, exotic orchids and sailed out of the office, determined on pursuing this course of action wherever it led. She was thirty years old with nothing to lose. Hugo Fullbright beckoned very brightly—the man himself, the trip to Tokyo, the flowers, the chauffeur…all making her feel this might very well be the trip of a lifetime.

She wanted to go with him.

And go she would.

CHAPTER FOUR

HUGO FULLBRIGHT put away his mobile phone and relaxed back into the plush leather seat of his Bentley, grinning from ear to ear, enjoying his triumph. 'I won, James,' he said to the man driving him to his next meeting. '*Foxy Angel* is mine.'

'Congratulations, sir. Though I had no doubt you would win, once you set your mind on it.'

Hugo laughed, brimming over with good humour. He had to hand it to James. As his household executive, the man was brilliant. Only twenty-seven when Hugo had hired him four years ago—a New Age butler trained to do whatever was required of him: chauffeuring his boss, shopping, doing household chores, cooking, serving meals, co-ordinating the social calendar, making travel arrangements.

All that on top of the traditional trimmings—the art of etiquette, protocol, wine appreciation. Not to mention also being equipped with computer skills and having experience in conflict resolution.

Certainly James Carter was one of his best acquisitions, highly efficient and wonderfully discreet. He made the perfect confidant for Hugo because he was privy to all his affairs, both business and personal, and could be trusted with anything. Of course, he was paid very well, as befitting a top executive, and to Hugo's mind, he was worth every cent of his six-figure annual salary, plus perks.

Life moved very smoothly with James handling all

the details. Hugo appreciated that. So what if the guy
was gay! Probably better that he was. James' mind
was definitely on his job. A man's man. One hundred
per cent. And like many gay guys, he had a great eye
for stylish clothes, a great eye for everything.

Hugo knew that his suitcase would be perfectly
packed ready for him to leave for Tokyo tomorrow
morning, and best of all, Angie Blessing was going
with him. 'You should see her in the flesh,' he said,
the pleasure of it rolling through his voice as he remembered the amazing physical impact she'd had this
morning. 'Well, you will see her.'

'Nine o'clock tomorrow morning,' James affirmed.
'I've written down the address.'

'Sex on legs…'

'You do seem to fancy legs, sir. All those models
you've dated.'

Hugo frowned. The comparison was wrong. 'Angie
Blessing is blessed with everything. Brains as well as
beauty,' he corrected.

In fact, she put Chrissie Dorrington so far in the
shade, on every count, he wished he'd met Angie long
before this.

'Sounds like you might have hit the jackpot, sir.'

He might very well have. He could hardly wait to
have his *Foxy Angel* to himself tomorrow. 'Thank you
for finding the right florist, James,' he said appreciatively.

'Did the trick, sir?'

'A timely piece of persuasion.'

'If I may say so, sir, your timing is always impeccable. It's a pleasure to work for you.'

'Thank you.'

James was pleased everything had turned out well. He absolutely adored working for Hugo Fullbright. Not only was his employer suitably wealthy—cost no object with anything to do with his private life—but he had a flamboyant personality, never stuffy or boring. There was always something *happening*. It made life interesting, exciting, challenging.

And he was generous. Not a mean bone in his body. Generous with praise, and best of all, generous in showing his appreciation financially. James knew there wasn't a butler in Sydney with a higher wage than his.

Some of the rather peevish older butlers did not consider Hugo Fullbright *a gentleman*. He was one of the new rich, a racy bachelor, not really respectable. A bunch of bloody snobs, James thought, probably eaten up with envy. For one thing, they had to drive around in black Daimlers or silver grey Rolls-Royces, some even in an ordinary Mercedes. *He* had charge of a brilliant red Bentley. Mega-dollars with panache! No one could beat that!

All the same, James did feel it was time for his employer, who was now thirty-eight, to get married and have children. It would round off his life. James' life, as well. He'd been trained to look after kids and since it was most unlikely he'd ever have any of his own, there was no doubt in his mind that Hugo Fullbright's children would be fun. Definitely entertaining little creatures. How could they not be?

It would be very interesting to meet *Foxy Angel* tomorrow. Miss Blessing surely had a flamboyant personality, as well, or she wouldn't have put herself up on that billboard. This could be the perfect match.

James started planning what he'd pack for Tokyo.

The new Ian Thorpe brand underpants—very sexy—the Armani suit for dinner engagements—smooth sophistication—the Calvin Klein jeans for sightseeing—brilliant for showing off a taut, cheeky butt—the Odini black leather battle-jacket—some women were kinky for leather...

Ah, yes! If Miss Blessing was *the one*...still, it wasn't up to him. He'd do his bit to aid the process, should she be good enough for his boss. The billboard act *was* a bit dodgy. He'd know better tomorrow.

CHAPTER FIVE

THE doorbell rang at precisely nine o'clock.

Angie was ready. At least she was ready to go. She wasn't sure she was ready for this new situation with Hugo Fullbright—there was a swarm of butterflies in her stomach—but she'd weather it somehow and hopefully come up smiling. Which reminded her to put a smile on her face as she opened the door, starting off as she meant to go on, all bright and breezy.

'Good morning,' she lilted, determined that it would be good.

A surprisingly young man in a smart grey chauffeur's uniform tipped his cap to her while his eyes made a swift appraisal of his boss's new woman. Angie tensed, wondering if she passed muster. While it was summer in Australia, it was winter in Japan, so she'd teamed fine black wool pants with a frayed edge cropped jacket in black chenille, the latter very form-fitting with a diagonal hook and eye opening down the front which left a hint of cleavage on show, but not too much. Looking *foxy* wasn't really her style.

The chauffeur apparently approved, beaming a cheery smile right back at her. 'Good morning to you, Miss Blessing. My name is James Carter, answering to James.' He gestured to her suitcase and carry-on bag over which she'd slung her faux-fur leopard print overcoat, deciding it was definitely appropriate for wearing in the company of a jungle cat. 'Ready for me to take?'

'Yes. Thank you, James.'

'If you don't mind my saying so, Miss Blessing, I do like Carla Zampatti clothes. Always that subtle touch of class,' he said as he set about collecting her luggage.

Angie was so amazed at having the designer of her outfit recognised she barely got out another, 'Thank you.'

It dawned on her that the chauffeur was gay, which amazed her even further. The very macho Hugo Fullbright with a gay chauffeur? Well, why not? If he could pick a woman from a billboard photo, the man clearly had eclectic tastes in the people he drew into his life.

She didn't have to say goodbye to Francine who had left for work half an hour ago, squeezing Angie's hands as she said, 'Please...if things go wrong...just don't blame me.'

Angie would have much preferred a cheerful 'Good luck!' She was nervous enough as it was about what she was doing.

James led her down to the street where a gleaming red Bentley stood waiting. A red Bentley with cream leather upholstery! This was travelling in a style Angie had never experienced before. It made her feel like royalty, sitting in the back seat of such a car. The smile on her face did not have to be forced one bit.

Magnificent flowers.

Magnificent car.

Would the man match up to them?

And if he did, could she keep him?

She would hate it if she discovered that dirty week-

ends were his style when it came to women, picking
them up and putting them down at his leisure, easy
come, easy go. If he gave one hint of that she would
not take the flight to Japan. She hoped it was an irresistible impulse on his part, as it was on hers.

'Will Mr. Fullbright be meeting me at the airport,
James?' she asked, once they were on their way.

'We'll be picking him up from the Regent Hotel,
Miss Blessing. He has a business breakfast there this
morning. It was scheduled a week ago,' came the
obliging information and explanation for his absence
from her side.

'Thank you.'

A very busy man. And this trip to Tokyo had a
business connection, as well. Angie wondered if he
had room in his life for a wife and children. Not so
far, and she judged him to be in his late thirties. Or
maybe he was divorced. A bad marriage record. She
needed to find out these things, though that kind of
thinking was probably leaping too far ahead.

They drove over the harbour bridge. Angie checked
the billboard, needing to know if her photo had been
removed. She breathed a huge sigh of relief when she
saw that Francine's image had replaced hers, then
barely smothered a groan as she read the new caption—*Hot Chocolate*. Francine would have men's
fantasies zooming!

Still, how could she criticise?

Foxy Angel had caught Hugo Fullbright's interest.
Though that was a double-edged sword. Angie didn't
know if he was genuinely attracted to her or caught
up in a fantasy that appealed to him.

James used the car phone to alert his boss to their
imminent arrival at the Regent Hotel. Running to

schedule was clearly an important issue to such a busy man. Every minute counted. In fact, as the Bentley pulled up at the main entrance to the hotel, Hugo Fullbright was making his exit. Perfect timing.

Angie barely had a minute to compose herself before James was holding the passenger door open, and the man she was committed to spending the next three days with swept into the car, filling it with a vibrant energy. He flashed his white wolf smile at her and her heart hopped, skipped and jumped all over the place.

'Hi!' he purred, his eyes gobbling her up.

Angie knew the Bentley was air-conditioned but it suddenly felt very hot in there. 'Hi to you, too,' she replied with as much aplomb as she could muster. He was also wearing all black, a superbly tailored suit, silk shirt, and no tie. She found her gaze glued to the bared little hollow at the base of his throat until he spoke again.

'You look ravishing.' He rolled the R and Angie couldn't help feeling it was like a drum-roll anticipating many hours of ravishment.

Her toes curled.

'I was trying for beautiful, appealing, and exotic,' she tossed back at him.

He laughed. It was a laugh of pure enjoyment and Angie thought this weekend might be a lot of fun with him, if she could just let her hair down and go with it. For a long time there hadn't been any real fun with Paul. It was well past time she enjoyed life again, though she hoped for much more than a quickly passing enjoyment with Hugo.

The Bentley was in motion again, carrying her off with this man on very possibly the adventure of a lifetime—one that might lead to a lifetime of adventure! Maybe that was a hopeless fantasy but Hugo Fullbright certainly inspired it.

'Did your business breakfast go well?' she asked, interested in how he spent his time.

'A group of investors wanting to be in on my next property development. I'll let them know.' He reached over and took her hand, his thumb lightly fanning her skin again, sending electric tingles up her arm. 'I want to forget business now and learn more about you.'

Changing rooms.

'Is that how you manage your life, Hugo?' Angie asked curiously. 'Switching from one room to another? No cross-overs?'

'I don't want to bore you,' he purred, giving her the full riveting focus of his bedroom blue eyes.

Which was very flattering, having all his attention concentrated on her. Angie didn't know why she felt it was a smoke haze designed to keep her distant from the man behind the sexy charm, but her instincts demanded she challenge him.

'You think I'm some dumb blonde to be buttered up for her bed-worthiness?'

A sound suspiciously like a snort of amusement came from the driver's seat.

'Now how could I think that, Angie, when I'm trusting you with a huge budget to deliver the perfect finish for my apartments?' Hugo smoothly challenged back. 'I merely thought we could both take time out from work for a while. Enjoy each other's company without business intruding.'

'Fine! Just so you know I want to learn more about you, too.' And she gave him a long penetrating look to emphasise her interest was not purely sexual, nor centred on her own desirability to him.

He grinned. 'Well, I'd have to say I'm already flattered by the removal of your photo from the billboard.'

Heat scorched her cheeks. She barely bit back the impulse to state the truth again, which, of course, was *the straight* thing to do. And where would that get her? The sure knowledge that he wouldn't believe her anyway held her tongue. Her mind frantically composed a *foxy* reply.

'It seemed the decent thing to do since I'm not available…until further notice.'

Which put him on trial, competing for her interest. Best for him not to think she'd wiped every other guy out because he'd stepped forward. She'd had quite enough of the male ego from Paul Overton. No way was she going to let Hugo Fullbright think he could take her for granted because he considered himself so great!

He weighed her reply, his dynamite eyes twinkling appreciation of it. 'A move I respect,' he said. 'Thank you for giving me pole position. I promise I'll do everything in my power to ensure you won't regret it.'

And the power was coming at her in huge swamping waves. Angie just managed to collect her wits enough to continue the conversation. 'Interesting that you should use a car-racing term…pole position…and here you are with a very sedate Bentley.'

His brows drew together in mock disappointment. 'You don't like this car?'

'I love it. I'm just wondering why you chose it.'

'Can't I love it, too?'

'I would have thought a red Ferrari more your style. Dashing, glamorous, powerful…'

Something dark flickered in his eyes. 'No, I'm not into sports cars.' His mouth tilted sardonically. 'I wouldn't want any woman to think I'm the kind of man who needs one to make him a desirable male.'

Intriguing that he was touchy on the point. 'So the Bentley is…a perverse choice?' Angie queried, trying to probe for more.

'No.' He shrugged. 'It's simply *my* choice. A positive liking, not a negative reaction to something else.'

'They say a car does reflect the character of the man who owns it,' she mused, thinking of Paul with his Mercedes sports convertible—an establishment car with macho appeal.

'Tell me what this car stands for to you?' Hugo inquired, amused by the idea of testing her theory.

Angie paused to think about it, intuitively knowing her answer would be important in his judgement of her. 'Firstly, it yells very solid wealth. But also seriously classy style. Not something transient. It's the kind of car you could own all your life without its ever going out of style or losing its impact. Yet the red says its owner is not conservative. It's a bold choice, probably expressing his nature. I also think it's a statement that he doesn't care what other people think. Yet the high respectability of the car reassures them he can be trusted to deliver the goods, whatever they are.'

He nodded thoughtfully. 'An interesting analysis.' His mouth quirked. 'So you think I'm bold.'

Considering his blitzkrieg approach to her— 'Very,' she said with feeling.

'And you like that?' His eyes were twinkling teasingly again.

Angie's chest tightened up. Thoughts of sharing a bed with him—being bold—whizzed around her mind. 'It's…different,' she finally choked out.

He lifted her hand to his lips and pressed a very sensual kiss on her palm, his eyes never leaving hers as he did it. *'Vive la difference,'* he murmured with that throbbing purr of anticipation in his voice humming along every nerve in Angie's body.

She didn't even notice the Bentley slowing to a halt.

'Airport, sir,' James announced from the front seat.

'So…we begin our journey together,' Hugo said, still with the eye-lock that pinned Angie to her decision, despite the reality of the situation rushing in on her.

James was out of the car, holding the door open for them to alight. Hugo did not release her hand. He swung himself out and drew Angie after him. She arrived on the pavement adjacent to the international departure entrance, completely breathless and acutely aware of the man holding her.

Was she ready to go with him…accepting everything it entailed?

Was she really?

This was the moment of truth.

She could cry off, ask James to drive her back home again or get a taxi, cut every personal connection to the man. It was a woman's prerogative to change her mind. She could still do it. How was it going to feel right if she was just giving in to…*lust?*

Hugo was having no trouble with it. But men didn't, did they? They just followed their natural animal instincts. It was only women who wanted more. And she did want more than just sex. He was an amazingly attractive, fascinating man. But if she turned away from him now, what were the chances he would pursue his current interest in her? He'd admired her sheer nerve in putting her face on a billboard! Wimping out of the weekend might completely wipe out his interest in her.

Hugo Fullbright was a bold man looking for a bold partner. She could regret being bold, but wouldn't she always regret not being bold? A man like him might only come her way once in a lifetime.

Seize the main chance!

She didn't realise she'd squeezed his hand until he shot her a quizzical glance. 'Nervous?'

'A bit!' she admitted. 'It's just hit me that I'm actually going to Tokyo with you.'

He flashed her a reassuring grin. 'I'll look after you, Angie. I've been there before. Don't worry about it.'

It wasn't the foreign country angle that was worrying her. However, she'd fretted away enough minutes for James to have acquired a luggage trolley and stacked everything ready to go. There it was in front of them, Hugo's bags and hers, about to be consigned to a Qantas jet that would fly them both to Japan.

Francine's advice slid into her mind—*You shouldn't think of it as a dirty weekend.*

'I won't,' she said decisively.

'Good!' Hugo approved, thinking she was answering him.

James handed Angie her coat and tipped his cap.

'I hope you have a splendid journey, Miss Blessing,' he said chirpily.

'Thank you.'

He turned to Hugo. 'And you, sir, all the best! I'll check with the airport for your landing time on Monday morning.'

'Do that, James,' he said dryly. 'You might also need to see a doctor about your nose.'

'My nose, sir?'

'I've never heard you snort before.'

'I do beg your pardon, sir.' He frowned apologetically. 'A temporary ailment. I'll see to it.'

'Try to get it fixed before Monday morning.'

'You can count on it, sir.'

'I'm sure I can. Thank you, James.'

The chauffeur actually clicked his heels before turning away to round the Bentley, heading back to his driver's seat.

Hugo was smiling in some private amusement as he took charge of the luggage trolley. 'Nice coat,' he remarked, nodding to the leopard faux-fur hanging over her arm.

'I thought you'd like it,' she said, resolutely banishing any quiver from her legs as she walked at his side into the departure hall.

'Is that another piece of character analysis?' he asked in teasing challenge.

She shot him a foxy glance. 'You remind me of a jungle cat.'

'Ah! Survival of the fittest?'

'Slightly more dangerous than that.'

He laughed, making Angie's mind fizz with what might very well be dangerous pleasure.

But she wouldn't worry about that anymore.

It was not going to be a dirty weekend.

She refused to even think it might be that for him. It was going to be a getting-to-know-you fun weekend.

Wild, probably irresponsible, but didn't every woman deserve to just let her hair down and go with the flow without worrying about consequences for just a little while? Angie reasoned she could be sane and straight again when she came home. Until then she'd ride along on Hugo Fullbright's wave and if he dumped her at the end of it…well, at least she wouldn't be wasting three years on him.

CHAPTER SIX

HUGO decided he should probably try to get some shut-eye himself. They were four hours into their nine-hour flight to Tokyo and it would inevitably be a late night with his Japanese hosts once they arrived. Angie was out like a light, stretched out comfortably on the almost horizontal bed set up by the handy controls on their first-class seats.

He smiled over her apology for her drowsiness—the champagne on boarding the plane, the wines accompanying a very fine lunch, not much rest last night. He didn't mind. Her uninhibited pleasure in travelling first-class, happily accepting everything offered, enjoying it, had made it a delight to be with her, and gave him cause to reflect that too many of his companions in recent years had been picky women, demanding special food and drinking only mineral water on flights.

Not that he'd minded that. It was sensible to drink water and faddy diets seemed to be all the rage these days, but it was infinitely more companionable to have a woman with him who shared his lust for every pleasure in life.

Maybe the difference came from Angie's background. As with himself, there'd been no family wealth behind her. She'd climbed her own ladder, just as he had. Her parents had been flower children, and even now lived in an alternative society community up near Byron Bay, selling their arts and crafts to tourists.

Career-wise she'd well and truly earned her success, having the guts to get out on her own and capitalise on her talent for design, not riding on the back of anyone else. No doubt there would have been years of tight budgeting. That had to give an extra edge to enjoying the best of everything now. It did for him.

His own parents had chosen to live up on the North Coast, too—Port Macquarie, where he'd built them a retirement home with every luxury he could provide. They were happy there, and he dropped in on them when he could. Their only current concern was he hadn't found a nice girl and settled down to produce grandchildren for them.

Could Angie be the *nice* girl?

Hugo was bemused by the thought. He really had no yen to settle down. He liked his life just the way it was. Besides, he didn't need a wife. James ran a household probably better than any woman could. And Hugo was never short of feminine company when he wanted it.

Although…there was the matter of quality versus quantity. There were certainly qualities in Angie Blessing that lifted her…but this was only the beginning of their relationship. Far too soon to make a judgement, especially when it came to marriage.

Even more especially when it came to having children, which was the biggest responsibility of all. Possibly he would want them someday, but that could wait. He had no biological clock ticking. Besides, he'd want to get married first, and basically, he didn't trust any woman enough to hand her that much power over his life.

Angie's remark about sports cars had reminded him of Paul Overton, his arch-rival at school. The guy had been born with everything—good looks, brains, strong athletic ability, *and* a silver spoon in his mouth, the son and heir of a very wealthy establishment family with connections in the top legal and political circles. But that wasn't enough for Paul. He had to be number one at everything and it had always rankled him when Hugo pipped him for some prize or other.

And there was definitely no accident about the revenge he'd taken for those slights to his overweening ego. Being given a Porsche on his eighteenth birthday had handed him the tool to snag Hugo's girlfriend, and he'd deliberately set out to do it. Right in front of him. With smug triumph.

The guy was a top barrister now, probably manoeuvring his way towards a seat in parliament. If he ever made it to Prime Minister, Hugo sure as hell wasn't going to vote for him. But Paul had inadvertently taught him a lesson about women. They were inevitably drawn to what looked like the higher prize. And these days, if the prize didn't live up to their expectations of happily married life, there was always the divorce settlement to look forward to.

No thanks.

He'd worked too hard, risked too much, won too many battles to hand over half the spoils to a woman who'd done nothing to contribute to them. He was quite happy to share them, as with Angie here and now, as long as he had the controlling hand.

Even with Angie, whom he found so very appealing on many levels…would she have come with him on this trip if he wasn't a top runner in the wealthy bachelor stakes? If he hadn't sent her flowers that few men could afford, reinforcing what was on offer? He'd certainly won her, but had he won her because the price was right?

Irrelevant really. He had her with him, which was what he'd wanted. And she hadn't done any running after him, actually backing off when he'd offered himself, certainly not leaping at the invitation. At least, she'd provided him with a challenge—quite a rare event—and while she'd opened up a lot about herself since they'd been in flight, there was still something cagey about her, keeping a reserve while testing him out, as though there were other things more important to her than his surface attributes.

Foxy Angel....

Could be a lot of fun while it lasted, Hugo thought with much pleasurable anticipation, and pressed the controls to lower his seat into the bed position. Best that he be well rested for tonight, too. He wanted to enjoy every aspect of Angie Blessing, and be in top form to do precisely that.

A feather-light touch on her cheek tingled into Angie's consciousness, followed by the purring sound of Hugo Fullbright's voice.

'Wake up, sleeping beauty.'

No dream.

Her heart kicked out of its slumberous rhythm. Her eyes flew open. He was right next to her, instantly taking her breath away with his white wolf smile.

'We're about ninety minutes from Tokyo…'

She'd slept for hours!

'…and light refreshments are being served. Probably

best you eat something before we land. It will be a late dinner tonight,' he warned.

Angie bolted upright, a flood of embarrassment heating her face. 'I'm so sorry. I thought I'd only doze for a while.'

'No problem.' His grin was positively wicked. 'Nice to know you don't snore.'

Which turned up her temperature even more. 'I'll go and tidy up. Back in a minute.' She grabbed her handbag and scooted away, needing time out to regain her composure, not to mention urgent repairs to her make-up.

The reminder that she'd be *sleeping* with him tonight had completely flustered her again. She'd put it out of her mind once they'd boarded the plane, determined to focus on having fun and enjoying Hugo's company. And he'd let her do that, not pushing anything *physical,* happy to indulge her in a getting to know you conversation. It had made her feel comfortable with him—as comfortable as she could be, given that he was a very sexy man and she was undeniably excited by him.

Those dynamite blue eyes twinkling at her, warmly appreciative, admiring, teasing, laughing…above all, really interested in her. It hadn't felt like just a flirtatious game, filling in time until he could pounce. It had felt…good. Very good.

Angie tried to wash the heat from her face with a thorough dousing of cold water. She was being silly, worrying about tonight. Hugo liked her. She could tell. And the liking was definitely mutual. Besides, if she wanted to say no, she was sure he would respect that. Her instincts told her he would turn away from forcing any woman to do what she didn't want.

A matter of pride.

Though he hadn't bragged about how clever he'd been in targeting the real estate market as a money-maker, starting off with buying and selling, building up funds so he could move into property development. She had virtually dragged the details out of him. His attitude had been more dismissive than proud.

Yet he was a self-made billionaire and Angie couldn't help but admire the enterprising way he'd achieved that. Nothing handed to him on a plate…unlike Paul. Though that was probably unfair. Paul wouldn't be where he was if he hadn't applied himself to using all his attributes very effectively. They were just different men, coming from different places.

Vive la différence…

She smiled over the phrase Hugo had used as she got out her make-up bag, needing to put on her best face for whatever was waiting for her in Tokyo.

It also made her feel good that Hugo hadn't looked down his nose at her parents' lifestyle or been critical of it in any way, musing that she must have had a free and happy childhood, allowed to pursue whatever interests she liked, no pressure to meet expectations.

He was the late and only child of more elderly parents, not pushy people either, but his achievements had given them a lot of pleasure and he liked doing things for them. Angie thought it was great that he'd built them a luxurious retirement home in the location of their choice. Definitely a loving son.

It was a warming thought to take back to her seat beside him, having restored her face to presentability and brushed her hair back into shape.

The cabin steward was hovering, waiting to serve the light refreshments. Her seat was upright again, the tray lifted out ready to be lowered. Angie quickly settled, apologising for the delay.

'There's no hurry. We have plenty of time,' Hugo soothed.

She flashed him a quick smile. He really was a nice man, though he was looking at her again as though he'd prefer to taste her rather than what the cabin steward was offering. It gave Angie goose bumps.

As soon as they were served, she opened up a conversation, desperately needing the distraction of talk to lessen the physical effect he had on her. 'Tell me about the people we're meeting tonight, Hugo. I'll probably need to practice their names so I'll get them right.'

He obliged her, describing the men and what positions they held, repeating their names until she'd memorised them and was pronouncing them correctly.

'Can you speak Japanese?' she asked, wondering if she was going to be a complete fish out of water at their dinner.

'Yes. I learnt it at school and have polished up my knowledge of it since then,' he answered matter-of-factly. 'But don't worry about a language barrier, Angie,' he hastened to add. 'Since we're their guests, they'll be speaking English.'

'Oh! Well, that's a relief.'

He laughed, his eyes caressing her with a warm approval that set her heart pitter-pattering. 'I'm glad you care enough to learn their names,' he remarked.

'It's only polite.'

'And good business.'

'I believe in being prepared.'

He cocked a wickedly challenging eyebrow at her. 'For everything?'

'I wasn't prepared for you,' she shot back at him.

He grinned. 'Taken by surprise. Jungle cats do that.'

Would he pounce before she could think? A primitive little thrill shocked her into wondering if she wanted that, wanted the responsibility of making the decision shifted off her shoulders. Her gaze dropped nervously to his hands. Somehow it reassured her that his fingernails were neatly manicured. He wouldn't be rough. Sleek and powerful. Her stomach contracted as she imagined him bringing those assets into play, but she wasn't sure if it was fear or excitement causing havoc with her inner muscles.

She forced her mind back onto safe ground. 'Since you can speak the language, would you please teach me the correct greeting and how to say thank you in Japanese?'

Again he obliged her, coaching her pronunciation as she practised the phrases, letting her become comfortable with the foreign words, amused by her satisfaction in being able to remember them and say them correctly. He made a light game of it, passing the time pleasantly until they landed at Narita Airport.

The business of disembarking and collecting their luggage made Angie very aware that she was now actually in Japan, with nothing familiar around her, and the only person who knew her here was Hugo Fullbright. It made her feel dependent on him, which was rather unsettling, but he smoothly took control of everything so she had nothing to worry about. Except how he might take control of her.

They were met by a smartly dressed chauffeur and Angie wondered why he was wearing white gloves, which stood out in stark contrast to his dark uniform. They were ushered to a gleaming black limousine. Along the top of the passenger seat was a spotless, and obviously freshly laundered white lace covering, precisely where heads might rest.

Angie looked curiously at it as she settled beside Hugo, prompting him to explain, 'The Japanese are big on hygiene. You'll find Tokyo a very clean city.'

Different culture, different customs, she thought, wondering what other surprises were in store for her.

Hugo took her hand, giving it a reassuring squeeze. 'You'll love it, Angie. Although it's too dark now for you to see, the overall impression of the city as you drive in is of a huge white metropolis. There aren't the masses of red roofs you see when flying over Sydney. Tokyo is the whitest city I've seen anywhere in the world.'

Of course he would notice that, being a property developer, Angie thought, but it was a fascinating fact to hoard in her mind, which was altogether too busy registering the sensations being stirred by his closeness to her, now that they were virtually alone together and he was holding her hand again.

Hugo continued to talk about features of the city as they were driven to their hotel, pointing out Disneyland as they passed it. She hadn't known there was one here. Nor had she known about the Tokyo Tower that was constructed similarly to the Eiffel Tower, only higher.

As a tour guide, Hugo added a great deal of interest to the trip, yet Angie was far more conscious of him as a man, and while he appeared perfectly relaxed, she sensed a simmering energy waiting for the right moment to burst into action.

Occasionally his gaze would drop to her mouth when she spoke back to him, watching the movement of her lips, as though imagining how they'd respond to his. There were flashes of dark intensity behind the sparkle in his eyes. The hand holding hers did not remain still, his fingers stroking, seemingly idly, yet to Angie's mind, with sensual purpose, stirring thoughts of how his touch would feel in other places. Sometimes he leaned closer to her, pointing something out, and the tantalising scent of some expensive male cologne accentuated his strong sexiness.

When they reached the Imperial Hotel, they were driven to the VIP entrance and met by a whole entourage of hotel management, everyone bowing to them, then taking charge of their luggage and escorting them along wide corridors, up in a classy elevator, right to the door of their suite and beyond it to ensure everything was to their satisfaction.

It was mind-boggling treatment to Angie. She'd imagined this kind of thing only happened to royalty or heads of state or famous celebrities. Was Hugo considered *a star* by the Japanese? She was certainly moving into a different stratosphere with him. This suite had to be at least presidential. The floral arrangements alone were stunning.

She was still trying to take it all in as Hugo chatted to their entourage and ushered them out, dealing smoothly with the situation as though he was born to it. Angie was way out of her depth, yet she couldn't deny it was an exhilarating experience to be given so much courtesy and respect. All because she was with *this man,* she reminded herself. It was enough to turn any woman's head.

As he walked back to where she stood, still dumb-struck by the extraordinary world she'd stepped into, Hugo gestured towards the bathroom and warned, 'We don't have a great deal of time before the call will come for us to be taken to dinner. Would you like to shower first?'

Angie nodded as a swarm of butterflies attacked her stomach again. Bathroom…naked…with him prowling outside in this very private suite.

'Let me take your coat.'

His hands were on the collar, drawing the coat off her shoulders, down her arms. He was standing so close, face to face, Angie's breath was helplessly trapped in her lungs. He tossed the coat on an arm-chair. Then his hands were sliding around her waist, his mouth smiling his wolf smile, his eyes sizzling now with sexual challenge.

'It feels I've been waiting a long time for this,' he purred, and Angie had a panicky moment at the thought of being devoured by him.

Yet as soon as his mouth claimed hers, she knew she'd been waiting for this, too, wanting to know how she'd feel when he kissed her, needing to know, hoping it would settle the questions that had been buzzing around in her mind. She slid her arms up around his neck, closed her eyes, let it happen, all her senses on extreme alert.

It didn't start with any marauding forcefulness, more a seductive tasting that charmed her into responding, sensual lips like velvet brushing hers and the electric tingling of his tongue gliding over them, inviting—inciting—her to meet it, to open up to him, to explore more.

A slow kiss, gathering an exciting momentum as Angie was drawn into a deeper, more intimate journey with him, and she felt the pressure of his hands, gathering her closer, bringing her into full body contact with him, gliding over her curves as though revelling in their soft femininity, loving it.

Somehow his touch gave her the sense of being intensely sexy, making her acutely aware that she certainly hadn't felt this desirable to Paul for a long time. Maybe it was simply the wild pleasure of finding this dangerous gamble with Hugo was stirring sensations that some primal need in her wanted in order to make the risk right. Angie's mind wasn't really clear on this as it was being bombarded by impressions of the hard, strong maleness of the man who was holding her, kissing her as though he was enthralled by what she was giving him.

Then all thought disintegrated as he kissed her a second time, her mouth totally engaged with his in an explosion of passion so invasive that her whole body yearned to be joined with his, and exulted in knowing he was similarly aroused, desire becoming a vibrant urgency that could not be ignored.

And to Angie's confusion afterwards, it was Hugo who backed away from it, not she. He moved gently, not abruptly, slowly lessening the white-hot ardour, disengaging himself, taking a deep breath. 'We don't have enough time, Angie,' he murmured, his voice uncharacteristically rough, strained. 'You'd better go and have your shower now.'

She went, though how her quivering legs carried her into the bathroom she didn't know. The image of

herself in the vanity mirror seemed like that of a
woman in a helpless daze. How could there be so
much incredibly strong feeling coursing through her?
She'd barely met Hugo Fullbright…and all her worry
about saying no to him…while here she was with her
whole body screaming yes.

Having managed to undress and cram her long hair
into a shower cap, Angie turned on a blast of water
and tried to wash herself back to normal. Conscious
of time being in short supply, she didn't linger under
the sobering spray, quickly drying herself and don-
ning the bathrobe supplied by the hotel. Cap off,
clothes scooped into her arms, and she was out of the
bathroom, calling to Hugo, 'It's all yours.'

He'd stripped down to his underpants!

Her gaze instantly veered away from them, though
she barely stopped herself from staring at the rest of
his bared physique—more definitively muscular than
Paul's, very powerful thighs, and smoothly tanned olive skin that gleamed as though it was polished. No
hair at all on his chest. Somehow she forced herself
to keep moving towards her suitcase which was set
on a luggage stand, ready for her to open.

'Thanks,' he said, flashing her an approving smile
for not holding them up too long as he headed for the
bathroom.

Angie dressed as fast as she could, her heart pumping overtime as she castigated herself for comparing
Hugo to Paul. Hugo Fullbright was his own man. Paul
was gone from her life. It was just difficult to wipe
three years out in what was little more than a day.
Even more difficult to come to terms with the fact
that she'd been intimate with one man last week and
was now about to plunge into intimacy with another.

But she hadn't really been happy with Paul, she frantically reasoned.

And Hugo was...special.

Incredibly special.

It didn't matter how soon it was and how fast it was happening, not to admit she wanted him was stupid. Better to be *straight* with herself—and him—than play some *foxy* game that would leave them both frustrated. Games weren't her style. Never had been.

Though whether this relationship would have any future in it or not, she had no idea. Francine would think she was mad not to suss that out first, and she probably was mad. Maybe she'd have second thoughts about it all before they returned to the hotel after dinner.

She'd chosen her Lisa Ho outfit for tonight— crushed velvet in shades of green; a Chinese style jacket with long fitted sleeves flaring at the wrist, and a long slim-line skirt that flared gracefully below her knees. Black high heels with sexy crossover ankle straps. She'd just seated herself at the well lit dressing table to attend to her grooming when Hugo emerged from the bathroom, a towel tucked around his hips.

Angie's heart was already galloping. It positively thundered as he stripped off and set about dressing. He was not acting in any exhibitionist way, just going naturally about the business of putting his clothes on, perfectly comfortable with having a woman in the room with him, chatting to her as though everything was absolutely normal.

She couldn't help thinking he was used to these circumstances. Inviting a woman away for a weekend was probably as familiar to him as it was unfamiliar for her to accept such a proposition. Which begged the question—was she just one of a queue that suited him far more than any permanent relationship would? An endless queue of women he found desirable at the time, but who'd always have a *use by* date?

Angie wasn't happy with that thought.

Yet it seemed to fit.

He wasn't married.

He'd never been married.

The telephone rang—notification that their car had arrived.

Angie quickly grabbed her small evening bag and stood up, ready to go. Hugo put down the telephone receiver and his gaze swept her from head to foot, before lingering on the row of buttons fastening the front of her jacket. *He* was now dressed in a superb pin-striped navy suit, looking both moody and magnificent.

'Will I do in this outfit?' she asked nervously, willing her legs to get steady so she could walk safely in these precarious shoes.

His face lightened up as he smiled with a touch of irony. 'You do…extremely well…in every sense.'

Her whole body flushed.

'I'd have to say the same of you,' she tripped out, trying to keep a level head.

He laughed. 'Then we clearly make a fine couple.'

And Angie carried that wonderfully intoxicating thought with her as they started out for their first night in Tokyo.

CHAPTER SEVEN

HUGO found it difficult to keep his mind focused on appreciating the hospitality of his hosts, let alone pursuing their subtle interest in future business. Tonight he was definitely not on top of the game. In fact, he was seriously distracted by Angie Blessing.

He couldn't remember the last time he'd been so excited by a woman. His usual control had slipped alarmingly when he'd kissed her. He'd actually struggled to assert it again, having to fight his reluctance to part from her, despite the tight schedule that demanded other action. And even now the provocative row of buttons down the front of her jacket was playing havoc with his concentration.

Ironically enough, his hosts were charmed by her, as well. Maybe it was an innate business sense coming to the fore, or simply a genuine interest in them and their country, but she delighted them with the very positive energy she brought to this meeting. Hugo mentioned the work Angie was doing on his latest project and they presented her with their business cards and respectfully requested hers. She was definitely quite a hit with them, doing herself proud. And him.

He could not have chosen a better partner—he frowned over that word—*companion* for this weekend. Why had he thought *partner*? Angie Blessing had been very accurate in naming herself *Foxy Angel*. She was demonstrating that right, left and centre—

clever and beautiful. It was okay to admire her, want her in his bed, but it would be stupid of him to lose his objectivity with this woman. Bad enough that he was currently sucked in to thinking about her all the time.

No doubt that would change soon, Hugo assured himself.

Anticipation was insidious.

Satisfaction would put his mind back in order.

Angie's mind was dancing waltzes with Hugo Fullbright. A bridal waltz featured very strongly. Pure fantasy at this point, but it buoyed her spirits enormously to mentally see them as a well-matched *couple,* fitting perfectly together.

In every sense.

Not just sexual!

This dinner party was turning out to be very much a pointer in that direction, much to Angie's relief and delight.

Their Japanese hosts seemed to like her, even giving her their business cards. Not that she expected anything to come of their taking hers, but it was a mark of respect, and best of all, Hugo had talked up her talent for interior design, making the point that she was very successful in her area of expertise—an accolade that made her a focus of interest, as well as him.

His ego had not demanded she simply be an ornament on his arm, though it was his business that had brought him to Tokyo. To Angie, it was an amazing thing for him to do. She tried to return the favour by being as congenial a guest as it was possible for her to be.

Which wasn't difficult. She was truly having a marvellous time—dining in a private room in this obviously high-class Japanese restaurant. The walls were made of the traditional paper screens, lending a unique ambience, and while they did sit on cushions on the floor, luckily there was a pit under the table to accommodate legs—a concession for Westerners?

They were served by wonderfully graceful Japanese ladies dressed in kimonos, and each course of what seemed like a never-ending banquet was artfully presented. Much of the food Angie didn't recognise but Hugo helpfully explained what it was whenever she looked mystified. She was happy to try all the different tastes. The seaweed soup was the only course she couldn't handle. Three mouthfuls and her eyes were begging Hugo to be released from eating more.

He grinned and lifted his little cup of sake, indicating she could leave the soup and appreciate the rice wine instead. The sake was surprisingly good and Angie had to caution herself not to drink too much of it. Her level of intoxication was already incredibly high, just being with this man who made her feel valued and appreciated and understood.

Of course, he did want her, as well.

There was no ignoring what was all too evident in the way he looked at her whenever there was a lull in the conversation. It was a wonder the buttons on her jacket didn't curl right out of their eyelet fastenings from the searing intent in those bedroom blue eyes. Angie could feel her breasts tingling with a tight swelling in response and knew she wouldn't try to stop him from undressing her once they were alone in their suite again. The very thought of it excited her.

His hands, his mouth, his body, the kind of person he was…everything about him excited her. She felt as though all her lucky stars were lining up to deliver the best that life had to offer tonight. No way in the world could she turn her back on it.

The time finally came for them to take leave of their hosts. Angie found herself babbling in a kind of wildly nervous exhilaration during the limousine ride back to the hotel. Hugo was not nearly so verbose, patiently listening to her gush of pleasure in the marvellous evening.

Patiently waiting.

Making no move to pounce.

Waiting…waiting…

The reality of what was about to happen didn't really hit Angie until they were on their way up to their hotel suite, the elevator doors closed, locking them into the small compartment, no one else with them, alone together. The feeling that she was now cornered rushed in on her, choking her into silence.

She needed Hugo to say something light to break her tension, to ease her into the next inevitable step, to somehow make her more comfortable with the idea of *sleeping* with him, but he didn't. The hand holding hers gripped more tightly, as though affirming she was caught—no escape. And the waiting was almost over. A matter of minutes…seconds…and he'd have her exactly where he wanted her.

The elevator doors opened onto their floor. Her feet were drawn into matching his steps while her heart thumped a rapid drum-roll and her mind whirled like a dervish, wildly trying to rationalise the choice she'd made.

Hugo hadn't forced her into anything.

She was here of her own free will.

Wanted to be with him.

All she needed was for him to kiss her again.

It would feel all right then.

He opened the door to their suite, placed a hand at the pit of her back, gently nudging her forward, a guiding hand, perfectly civilised, not the paw of a panther poised for the kill. And she was not walking into a dark, dangerous jungle. He switched the lights on for her to see she was once again in luxurious surroundings.

The curtains had been closed, blocking out the night view of the city. The door behind her was closed. Rather than look at the bed which loomed too largely in her mind, Angie fastened her gaze on the magnificent floral arrangement gracing the coffee table in the lounge area.

Her shoulders were rigid when Hugo lifted her coat from them, removing it for her. It was no more than a gentlemanly courtesy. He didn't try to make it more. She fiercely told herself to relax but her body had gone completely haywire as she felt the heat of his nearness to her, smelled the cologne he used.

'Have I assumed too much, Angie?'

The loaded question snapped her into swinging around to face him. He'd tossed her coat aside and was unbuttoning his suit coat, but his eyes stabbed straight into hers, probing like twin blue lasers.

'What…' It was barely a croak. Her mouth was so dry she had to work some moisture into it before she could get out the words. '…what do you mean?'

A mocking glint challenged her as he bluntly stated, 'You're frightened.'

'No, I'm not,' she shot back at him, instinctively denying any form of cowardice.

His coat joined hers on the dividing bench between the bedroom and living areas. His eyes derided her assertion as he began undoing his tie. 'I've been with too many women not to know how it is when they're willing…and eager…to go to bed with me.'

'Maybe that's the problem…too many women,' she defended hotly. And truthfully, as the thought of being only one in an ongoing queue burst into her mind again.

His mouth tilted ironically. 'I'm not in my teens, Angie. Neither are you,' he added, hitting the raw place Paul's dumping had left.

'So I should know the score?' she retorted with a bitter note he instantly picked up on, his eyes narrowing, weighing what was behind the response.

Her cheeks burned with guilt and shame. Hugo had every right to assume what he had and it was terribly wrong of her to give him a negative reaction because of Paul. She wasn't being fair.

'I'm not into keeping scores,' he said with a careless shrug. The tie was tossed on top of the coats. He flicked open the top buttons on his shirt, then started removing the cufflinks from his sleeves, dropping his gaze to the task in hand.

The cufflinks were black opals, rimmed with silver. Angie watched his fingers working them through the openings, savagely wishing she'd kept her mouth shut.

'Nor am I into bed-hopping,' he went on matter-of-factly. 'Every woman in my life has had my exclusive attention until such time as the relationship broke down...for whatever reason.'

'Why did your last relationship break down?' The question slipped out before she could clamp down on it, curiosity overriding discretion.

His gaze flicked up as he slid the cufflinks into his shirt pocket. His eyes mocked her need to know as though it shouldn't be important to her. But he did answer her in a sardonic fashion. 'I caught Chrissie snorting cocaine. I'm not into drugs, either. She'd lied to me about staying off them.'

Chrissie... Her mind latched onto the name, though it meant nothing to her. Just as Paul would mean nothing to Hugo. A new relationship should start with a clean slate. Why was she messing this up?

Hugo turned away from her, moving over to the bed. 'What about you, Angie?' he tossed back over his shoulder. 'Do you need an artificial high to unleash yourself sexually?'

Contempt in his voice.

For her or for Chrissie? Angie took a deep breath, needing to recapture his respect. 'No, I don't. Nor would I want to stay involved with someone who used drugs.'

'Glad to hear it. Makes people unreliable.'

He sat on the end of the bed and started removing his shoes and socks, not the least bit perturbed about her watching him undress. Weirdly enough, Angie didn't feel in any way threatened by it. His detached manner seemed to place her on some outer rim, having no influence at all on what he did. Yet she knew intuitively he was very aware of her presence and he was waiting again, waiting for her to give him something to work with.

The problem was she couldn't make herself move. Any physical approach felt like a horribly false step, like throwing herself at him, which he'd surely view cynically at this point. And she couldn't think straight enough to know what would be the right thing to say.

He tucked his socks in his shoes—a tidy man who obviously preferred a *tidy* life—and sat upright, the expression on his face suggesting he'd been struck by an idea that he found oddly titillating.

'Are you a virgin, Angie? Is that why you're so nervous?'

'No!' The denial exploded from her, throwing her into more anguished confusion over what she should do to correct the negative impressions she hadn't meant to give this man, especially when he was the most attractive man she'd ever met.

He cocked his head consideringly. 'Have you been…attacked by a man?'

She shook her head, mortified that he should judge her as sexually scarred by a bad experience.

He stood up, casually rolling his flapping sleeves up his strong muscular forearms as he strolled back towards her. 'Are you worried about protection?' he inquired, frowning over her frozen attitude. 'If that's the case…' He paused, waving to the far bedside table. '…I did bring a supply of condoms with me. You have no need to fear unwelcome consequences.'

'Thank you,' she choked out, feeling an absolute idiot for getting herself into such an emotional tangle when he was being perfectly civilised and looking after everything like the gentleman he clearly was.

A wry little smile sat provocatively on his lips as he slowly closed the distance between them and lifted his hand to stroke his knuckles gently down her burning cheek. 'I'd have to say this is not what I expected of *Foxy Angel*.'

She wanted to say—*Just kiss me*—but what came blurting out of her mouth was, 'I'm not *Foxy Angel*.'

It shocked him into a freeze on action. 'Pardon?'

'*Foxy Angel* is *Hot Chocolate*.'

He shook his head as though she wasn't making sense.

'On the billboard this morning.'

'It was a different photo. Different woman.'

'Yes. It was the photo that should have been used yesterday with the caption of *Foxy Angel*. Francine had to change the name to something else to avoid confusion.'

'Francine…' Again he shook his head, not taking it in.

'I tried to explain to you at our meeting that a mistake had been made. You didn't want to believe me. But the truth is that my friend had sent in a photo of the two of us and the technician had used the wrong half. Francine is the one who's marketing herself.'

'This is absurd,' he tersely muttered.

'Worse than absurd,' she retorted heatedly, and before Angie could think better of them, more damning words tripped out. '*You* took the wrong impression of me, and my partner of three years was so humiliated by the billboard he dumped me cold.'

The cloud of irritation and confusion instantly dissipated. The air suddenly sizzled with electric energy as dangerous bolts of lightning were hurled at her from Hugo's eyes. 'So what is this? Your revenge on men?'

Her heart contracted under the violent force of his

reaction. A convulsive shiver ran down her spine. But her mind rose to the challenge, sharp and clear.

'No. I came with you because I wanted to. Because I'm attracted to you. But I've never done anything like this before and…'

'And you got cold feet,' he finished for her, the frightening electricity instantly lessening.

'Yes,' she admitted, sighing with relief at his quick understanding. 'I'm sorry. I didn't mean to be such a fool…' She gestured her inner anguish. '…when it came to this.' Her eyes begged his forgiveness. 'I knew what you expected…'

Hugo's mind was spinning, fitting all the odd pieces into this new picture of Angie Blessing, realising everything about her made better sense now. 'It's okay,' he quickly soothed, playing for time, needing to get the action right when he moved in on her.

No question that he had to if he was to be certain of keeping her, and keeping her was now his prime objective. He wanted this woman and it was abundantly clear that he had to make his claim tonight. Letting her off the hook would only give her more time to doubt her decision to come with him, more time to think about the guy who'd dumped her, perhaps wanting him back, hoping he would reconsider and call her on Monday.

The attraction she'd admitted to was real.

There'd been ample proof of that in the way she'd responded to him before they'd gone out to dinner.

Hugo could barely quell the raging desire to blot the other guy out of her mind. Gently, gently, he told

himself. He'd never seduced a woman before—never
had to—but if he had to seduce Angie Blessing, he
would.

This woman was going to be his.

CHAPTER EIGHT

FRANCINE was right.

Dirty weekends weren't her style.

The relief at getting everything straight with Hugo was so enormous, Angie felt totally light-headed. Even her heart was skipping happily as though a terrible pressure had been lifted. Especially since Hugo had told her it was okay with him, accepting that he had been at fault, too, disbelieving her explanation of the mistake. Though she shouldn't have played up to the false identity. Any form of deception was wrong.

'I should have told you the truth before I accepted your invitation,' she said ruefully.

He smiled. Not his wolf smile. There was a warm caress in his eyes, making her feel better. 'I'll take that omission as a measure of your wanting to be with me,' he said, a hint of appeal taking the ego edge out of his statement.

'I did. I do,' she eagerly assured him.

'Then it's all good, Angie. Because if you had laid it out to me, I would still have pressed the invitation. *Foxy Angel* had its appeal but only because it was attached to you.'

She could feel herself glowing with pleasure.

It truly was okay.

Hugo was attracted to her, not some fantasy.

He tilted her chin, locking her gaze to the powerful intensity of his as he softly said, 'Believe me, the guy was a fool for letting you go. But I almost feel kindly towards him because he opened the door for me.'

His hand slid up over her cheek with a feather-light touch, the kind of reverent touch used in feeling something precious, wanting a tactile sense of what made it so special. Angie's breath caught in her throat and she stayed absolutely still, feeling thrilling little tingles spreading over her skin.

'And I now have enough time with you to show *I* value you,' he went on. 'Far more than he did.'

The purr of his voice was thrilling, too, not threatening at all. And what he was saying hit deep chords of truth. Paul hadn't valued her. He'd thrown her away like garbage, while Hugo treated her not only as an equal partner, but as a woman whose feelings really mattered to him.

'It's easy to get blinded by familiarity, Angie,' he murmured caringly. 'Not seeing what else there can be, only feeling safe with what you've known before. But I want you to look at me, feel how it is with me, give it a chance. Will you do that?'

'Yes...' She wanted to very much, was dying for him to kiss her as he had before.

He did.

Though so gently at first, it was even more tantalisingly sensual, giving her plenty of time to relax into the kiss, and Angie revelled in his obvious sensitivity to how she was reacting, responding. She understood he was exerting maximum control for her sake, wanting her to feel right with him, and this understanding removed any inhibition she might have had about moving closer to him, lifting her arms to wind them around his neck, inviting a deepening of the kiss, wanting to give as he was giving.

It was only fair.

Yet he seemed to shy away from trying to incite the passion he'd stirred before, his mouth leaving hers to graze around her face, planting warm little kisses on her temples and eyelids as his arms enclosed her in their embrace, one hand drawing its fingers slowly through her hair as though enjoying its silky flow around them.

'Everything about you feels good to me,' he murmured. 'Your hair...' He rubbed his cheek over it. '...your skin...' His lips trailed down her cheek to her ear which he explored very erotically with his tongue, arousing sensations that zinged along every nerve in Angie's body. '...the lovely soft curves of your body. All of you...beautiful,' he whispered, his breath as tingling as his tongue as he expelled warm air on a deeply satisfied sigh.

She couldn't even begin to catalogue his appeal to her. It was fast becoming totally overwhelming. Her mind was swimming in a marvellous sea of pleasure, revelling in his appreciation of her and loving his intense masculinity.

His fingers caressed the nape of her neck, slowly traced the line of her spine to the pit of her back. Then both his hands were gliding lower, gently cupping her bottom, subtly pressing her into a closer fit with him.

He was aroused.

Oddly enough, given her *cold feet,* it was not a chilling reminder that she was playing with fire, more a comforting reassurance that he really did desire the woman she was, a very warming reassurance that everything within her welcomed—more than welcomed when he kissed her again, not holding back this time, a long driving kiss that exploded into a passionate need to draw her into wanting all he could give her.

And Angie did want it.

It didn't matter that joining with this man might be premature, ill-considered, foolishly impulsive. She forgot all about being one of a queue. He was with her, wanting her, and she was wanting him right back, exulting in the fierce excitement he stirred, anticipation at fever-pitch, her whole body yearning for the ultimate experience of his.

'Angie...' His forehead was resting on hers, both of them gasping for breath. Her name carried a strained plea.

'Yes,' she answered, tilting her head back so he could see the unclouded need for him shining straight from her eyes.

A quick smile of relief, a sparkle of wild wicked joy. 'Is that giving me permission to undo the eight buttons that have been giving me hell all night?'

The lilting tease in his voice evoked a gurgle of laughter, erupting from her own relief and pleasure in him. 'You counted them?'

'Many times.'

He kept her lower body clamped to his, blatantly reinforcing her awareness of the desire she'd stirred, making her feel elated at her own sexual power over him as he lifted a hand to the top button, his fingers deftly releasing it from its loop.

'This one should have dissolved under the heat I subjected it to.'

The laughter welled up again.

Next button. 'Then this one should have popped open of its own accord, knowing it would get obliterated if it didn't.'

'Buttons are not sentient beings,' she said, feeling quite deliriously happy.

'But they do have two functions,' he carried on, attacking the rest. 'Opening and closing. And I didn't want you closed to me, Angie.'

Having unfastened the form-fitting bodice, his hand slid underneath it, around to the back clip of her bra, working it apart without the slightest fumble, demonstrating an expertise which might have given Angie pause for thought about that queue again, except for the swiftness of his warm palm cupping her naked breast, his fingers gently kneading its soft fullness, his thumb fanning her nipple into taut excitement, and the deep satisfaction purring through the 'Ah…' that throbbed from his throat, telling her how much he loved touching her like this.

For several moments she did nothing but revel in the way he was taking this new intimacy, the wonderful sense of his pleasure in it. Her breast seemed to swell into his hand, craving his caressing possession of it, greedy for all the exciting attention he was giving.

'Take off my shirt, Angie.' A gruff command, instantly followed by the compelling plea, 'I want to feel your touch.'

Yes pounded through her mind, though it was more a response to her own rampant desire to touch him. Her gaze swam to the row of buttons he'd left in place. Her hands lifted, eager to dispose of them, dispose of the shirt, too, bare his chest, shoulders, arms, letting her see, letting her feel the raw flood of his strong masculinity, absorbing it through her palms, skin against skin.

His breathing quickened as she glided her hands

over muscles that seemed incredibly smooth yet pulsing with a maleness which totally captivated the instinctive part of her that responded to beautiful strength in a man. And he was beautifully made. Perfect physique. It was exciting to feel the rapid rise and fall of his chest under her touch, knowing his heart had to be drumming in unison with hers.

His hand moved to her other breast, electrifying it into extreme sensitivity. 'Your jacket…get rid of it.' Hoarse need in the demand. His eyes were closed, a look of totally absorbed concentration on his face.

Exhilarated by how much he was into *feeling her,* Angie didn't hesitate, freeing herself of both jacket and bra, almost throwing herself against him as she flung her bared arms around his neck. And in the same instant he released her breast to wrap her in a crushing embrace, his mouth capturing hers, invading it with mind-blowing passion, possessing it with deep rhythmic surges, inciting a chaotic need that drove her into a frenzied response.

Waves of heat were swirling through her, crashing through her. He undid the zipper of her skirt, pushed it down over her hips—hips that wriggled their mindless consent, eager to feel closer to him. With seemingly effortless strength he lifted her out of the falling garment, scooping her off her feet and whirling her over to the bed, moving so fast Angie was still giddy from their wild kiss as he laid her down and completed the final stripping—her shoes, hose and panties—no asking permission now, just doing it with an efficient speed that screamed intense urgency, echoing the torment of coiled tension in her own body.

His eyes glittered over her, taking a searing satisfaction in her nakedness, and her heart suddenly quivered uncertainly over the rightness of what was happening here. Was it too soon? Had he cornered her into surrendering to his power? Her mind felt too shattered by raging need to think coherently.

He shed the last of his clothes, and it was as though the veneer of civilised sophistication—the gentleman image—was instantly shed, as well. He emerged from it like some primitive powerful warrior, his taut skin shimmering over muscles bristling with explosive energy, his magnificent maleness emanating a challenge that telegraphed he could and would stand up to anything, confident of battling any odds, vanquishing all opposition, winning through.

And the wolf smile was back.

Yet when he moved onto the bed, it was with the lithe prowling grace of a great jungle cat, inserting a knee between her legs, hovering over her on all fours, his head bent towards hers, his eyes blazing with the avid certainty that she was his to take as he willed…a mesmerising certainty that made every nerve in Angie's body quiver, whether in trepidation or anticipation she had no idea.

She wasn't ordinarily a submissive person. She'd always prided herself on being independent, capable of holding her own when dealing with life in general, yet she felt herself melting under the sheer dominance of this man, not wanting to fight for her own entity, yearning to merge with him, lose herself in him if that was how it was going to be.

Mine, he thought, revelling in the surge of savage triumph that energised every cell in his body, priming him to burn himself into Angie Blessing's consciousness, to put his brand on every part of her delectable femininity, use whatever means would bind her to him, take her as no man had ever taken her before.

Her eyes had a drowning look.

He felt a momentary twinge of conscience.

Dismissed it.

She'd said *yes.*

He swooped on her mouth and it said *yes,* too, her tongue as fiercely probing as his, engaging in an erotic tango that goaded him to do it now, appease the ache, fulfil the need. But that would be far too fast, not serving his purpose, and he forcefully controlled the raging temptation, tearing himself out of it, trailing hot sensuous kisses down her throat, savouring the wild gallop of her pulse-beat at the base of it.

He wanted to devour her, make her feel totally consumed by him. He moved lower, engulfing her breast with his mouth, drawing the sweet flesh deep, lashing the taut nipple with his tongue, sucking it into harder prominence, and he exulted in the convulsive arch of her body, the wild scrabble of fingers in his hair, digging, tugging, blindly urging the ravishment of her other breast. Which he did with a passion, feeding off her response, loving the vibrant taste of her, the headiest aphrodisiac he'd ever experienced.

He could hear her ragged breathing, the little moans that erupted from her throat, felt the tremors of excitement under her skin as his hand circled her stomach, his fingers threading through the tight silky curls below it, delving into the softly cushioned cleft at the apex of her thighs, caressing the slickly heated flesh, finding the most hidden places of pleasure, stroking them, feeling her inner muscles pulsing to his rhythmic touch, the hot spill of her excitement, the intense peaking of her clitoris.

He levered himself down, captured it with his mouth, moved his hands to cup her bottom, rocking her, thumbs pressing into the inner walls of the passage now yearning to welcome him. Not yet. Not yet. He drove her towards the sweet chaos of a tumultuous climax, feeling her exquisite tension spiralling higher, so high it lifted her body up to bow-string tautness.

He knew when it began to shatter, heard her cry out, exulted in her frenzied desire for him. Her hands plucked frantically at his head, his shoulders, her thighs quivering out of control, her body begging for his.

A wild energy charged through him as he surged over her, positioning them both for the entry she craved. He barely had sense enough to snatch up a condom from the bedside table and sheath himself with it before thrusting deep to settle the maelstrom of need, sharing her ecstatic satisfaction in the full penetration, feeling the ripples of her climax seizing him, squeezing, releasing, squeezing, releasing.

He held her thrashing head still and silenced her cries with a kiss meant to soothe and reassure and bring her into complete tune with him, waiting for more, wanting more, slowly tasting the promise of it, realising this was only a beginning of a sensual feast that could keep rolling on and on.

Her response was white hot at first, an almost anguished entreaty to finish it now, fast and fiercely, riding the storm of sensation he'd built to its ultimate limits, and Hugo was hard-pressed to hold on to his control, to calm her, enforcing a more conscious awareness of an intimacy that could be prolonged, that he was ruthlessly determined on prolonging so it would linger in her memory, obliterating every other memory of sexual connection she'd experienced before this.

No ghosts in this bed tonight.

Only him.

Taking absolute possession.

Angie could hardly believe Hugo was not choosing to ride the crest of her own turbulent pleasure, that he'd answered her need to feel him inside her, then stopped, as though it was enough for him to give *her* satisfaction.

Which couldn't be right.

Yet he made it feel right…the way he was kissing her…so caringly. It gave her the sense that he really treasured this gift of herself, and being so intimately joined with her was very special to him, too special not to pause over this first climactic sensation, deepening the delicious merge with a kiss that added immeasurably to how good she felt with this man.

Her inner chaos seemed to coalesce into a more intense awareness that circled around the strong core of his sexuality, anchoring her as she began to float on a warm sea of ecstasy. Her arms were strangely limp, but she managed to wrap them around him, wanting to hold all of him.

'Stay with me, Angie. Come with me,' he murmured.

The sensation of him starting to move inside her was marvellous, slowly, slowly leaving her to close tremulously behind him, retreating to the outer rim, then just as slowly pushing forward again so that her muscles clutched joyously at his re-entry, eager to have him sink as deeply as possible, wanting absolute possession of all he could give her.

He burrowed an arm under her hips, changed angles, teased, tantalised, delighted…exquisite pleasure peaking over and over again. Angie had never known anything like it…intoxicating, addictive, fantastic…her whole body keyed to feeling him, loving him, voluptuously revelling in this mind-blowing fusion.

Her legs wrapped around him, instinctively urging a faster rhythm. Her hands luxuriated in moving over him, feeling the tensile strength, wickedly wanting to test his control, make it break, draw him into the compelling overdrive that would end in his surrendering all his power to her. Somehow that was becoming more important than anything else…to take his mastery from him, make him lose himself in her, bring him to an equal place where the togetherness was truly the same.

She strained every nerve into focusing on making it happen, determined on exciting him to fever-pitch, caressing, pressing, goading with her hands, legs, kissing his shoulders, his neck, tasting him with her tongue. He laboured to catch his breath and she exulted in the tightening of his muscles, his thighs becoming rock-hard as need surged from them, forcing the more sensual rocking into a glorious primitive pounding, and she heard her own voice wildly crying *Yes…Yes…Yes…* to the beat of it.

Even more exhilarating was the animal roar that came from his throat when he finally rammed impossibly deep and spilled himself in great racking spasms, making her almost scream with the pleasure of rapturous release—her own and his, pulsating through both of them. A passionate possessiveness swept through Angie as he collapsed on top of her. She cupped his face, brought his mouth to hers, and sent her tongue deep in fierce ownership.

It seemed for a moment he was completely spent—or surprised. It gave Angie a brief, heady taste of being in control, seizing an initiative, but that quickly blurred as he responded, striking sweet chords of satisfaction before ending the kiss and carrying her with him as he rolled onto his back, tucking her head under his chin and holding her enveloped in his embrace.

Putting himself in charge again, she thought, smiling contentedly over being Hugo Fullbright's captive. There was no trepidation attached to it now. Her body was still thrumming with the pleasure he'd given. Or was it taken?

Didn't matter.

She wondered if this had just been normal sex for him. It certainly hadn't been for her—unmatched by anything in her previous experience. It might have been driven by sexual attraction but it had felt as though he was making love to her—if only physical love—brilliant, all-consuming physical love. Far from regretting her capitulation to it, Angie was intensely grateful to know how it could be with the right man.

The right man…

Had she fallen in love with Hugo Fullbright?

So soon? So quickly?

Or was she simply dazed by his expertise in making her *feel* loved?

And appreciated.

And valued.

He might make all the women he chose as his companions feel like this to begin with. What happened afterwards? How would it be tomorrow, the rest of the weekend, beyond that? For all she knew he was only intent on a *dirty weekend* with her! Though he had asked her to take a chance on him, give him time.

It was silly to start fretting over not being able to keep him in her life. That was out of her control. Hugo would undoubtedly do what he wanted to do, and whether that meant with her or without her only time would tell. Though not too much time. Not even if she loved him madly, was she going to spend three more years being dangled on the bait of a possible commitment.

If she was *right* for him…

'You're not relaxed anymore, Angie,' he said, one hand sliding into her hair, fingers seeking to read her mind. 'Tell me what you're thinking.'

She sighed away the edginess that had bitten into her contentment, then thought there was no point in not being open with him. He'd said quite plainly he didn't want her closed up. 'Just wondering how temporary I am for you.'

'Would you like not to be temporary?'

'Now there's a leading question, dodging right past mine.' She raised herself up to see if there was any hint of reservation in his eyes and was surprised to find amusement dancing at her. 'What's funny?' she demanded.

'You…thinking I might have had enough.' The wolf grin flashed out at her. 'Believe me, Angie, I'm already hungry for more of you, and if you'll excuse me while I go to the bathroom, I'll be very happy to come back and convince you of it.'

She hadn't actually been referring to sex, but he was rolling her onto the pillow next to him, extracting himself, heading for the bathroom to get rid of the protection he'd donned. The back view of him as he strode away from her was just as awesome as everything else about him. *Alpha Man,* Angie thought, and wondered why every woman in his past had failed to hold on to him. They must have wanted to. Did *she* have whatever it took to hold his interest beyond the bedroom? To become a lifetime partner?

Her gaze moved to the bedside table where a heap of condoms had spilled out of the packet he'd put there, ready for action. He hadn't asked her if she was on the pill, perhaps not prepared to risk her telling a lie about that, or simply protecting himself against any health issues. Did he always use them as a matter of habit? Did it indicate a freewheeling sex life?

He'd certainly come amply prepared for this weekend.

But given the *Foxy Angel* angle, and her unquestioning acceptance of his invitation, why wouldn't he?

What would Francine have done in this situation?

Seize the chance.

Angie took a deep breath and fiercely told herself to simply go with the flow until it didn't feel right. She had two more days with Hugo Fullbright—two days constantly in his company, in bed and out of it. By the time they landed in Sydney on Monday morning, she should know if there was a real chance of forging a relationship that would take them far beyond this weekend.

CHAPTER NINE

THE breakfast buffet in the Imperial Viking Room has to be seen to be believed,' Hugo had declared. 'And I'm *very* hungry this morning.'

So was Angie—so much energy expended last night, until sheer exhaustion had drawn them into a sleep. And again on waking up. If she wasn't in love with Hugo Fullbright, she was definitely in lust with him. He was an amazing sensualist with incredible stamina, and never in her life had Angie been made so aware of her body, which now tingled with excitement at simply a twinkling glance from this man.

Clearly he was very much into physical pleasures. Now food.

And he was right about the breakfast buffet. Hugo shepherded her around the incredible banquet laid out for people to serve themselves whatever took their fancy—every possible taste catered for: Asian, Continental, English, and all of it superbly presented to tempt appetites. Perfect fruit. Exotic pastries and croissants. Never had she seen such a wonderful selection of breakfast dishes.

'I'm going to be a pig,' Angie muttered as she kept loading a plate with irresistible goodies.

'Good! Saves me feeling guilty about indulging myself in front of you,' Hugo remarked.

She flashed him a curious look. 'Do you ever feel guilty about anything?'

He grinned. 'Rarely. Because I don't take what

isn't offered or paid for. And let me say that having you share my appetites is a joy I'd hate you to feel guilty about. Let's wallow in piggery together.'

She had to laugh.

Somehow he took any sense of sinfulness out of lusty greed, choosing to view their breakfast as an adventure into gourmet delights, encouraging her to sample far more than she would normally have done.

'Now we have to walk it off,' she told him when they finally gave up on trying anything more.

'I'll take you for a walk around the Ginza district.'

'What's there?'

'Shopping.' The blue eyes sparkled knowingly. 'The way to a woman's heart.'

It was true that most women loved shopping. And most men hated it. 'You don't have to indulge me. I'd rather we do something we'll both enjoy.'

'It's my pleasure to indulge you, Angie,' he happily assured her.

She *was* in love with him.

Absolutely drowning in beautiful feelings.

They left the Imperial Viking Room in high good humour, Angie more curious to see what the central shopping district in Tokyo offered than wanting to buy anything. She found the tour fascinating; with designer boutiques stocking clothes from all around the world, yet shops catering to distinctly Japanese culture, as well, like the one that stocked an astonishing array of umbrellas in every shade of every colour, some beautifully hand-painted or embroidered or featuring exquisite lace insertions.

'Women use them in summer to protect against the sun and heat. The streets of Tokyo are a mass of colourful umbrellas,' Hugo informed her.

'You mean like parasols?'

He nodded. 'Reduces the glare, too. Sunglasses aren't so popular here.'

'I'm not a big fan of sunglasses everywhere. Especially when people wear them indoors where there's no glare at all. It's a very irritating affectation.'

'Guarding their self-importance,' Hugo laughingly agreed.

Angie was glad he didn't seem to have any affectations, despite his VIP status. But his idea of indulging her hit a very wrong chord when he led her into a department store where the ground floor was completely taken up with displays of fabulous jewellery: gold, diamonds, pearls, every gemstone imaginable beautifully crafted into spectacular pieces.

Angie's gaze skimmed most of it in passing, recognising it was not in her affordable range, but she did stop to look at some fascinating costume jewellery, intricately worked necklaces that were exquisitely feminine and brilliantly eye-catching. They were designed like high-necked collars that sprayed out from the base of the throat, and one that was woven into a network of delicate little flowers particularly attracted Angie's eye.

It was displayed on a black plastic mould and she couldn't help touching it, thinking how wonderful it would look with her black strapless evening dress.

'Try it on,' Hugo urged, beckoning a salesgirl to help with it.

'I'm not wearing the right clothes,' Angie demurred, having donned a brown skivvy under her leopard print coat. However, she was tempted into asking how much the necklace cost in Australian currency.

The salesgirl whipped out a calculator, fingers darting over the buttons. She held it out for Angie to see the display box. Over twelve thousand dollars!

'Garnets,' the girl explained, seeing her customer's shock at the price.

'Thank you,' Angie replied, firmly shaking her head.

'Let me buy it for you,' Hugo chimed in.

Another shock which instantly gathered nasty overtones, making her query the kind of relationships he'd had throughout his long bachelorhood—mercenary women who'd jumped on him for everything? She wasn't like that and needed him to know it.

'No,' she said emphatically.

He frowned at her. 'It would be my pleasure to…'

'If you think this is the way to my heart, you couldn't be more wrong, Hugo.' A tide of scorching heat flooded into her cheeks. 'I'm not here to get what I can out of your large wallet. If that's what you're used to from other women, no wonder you don't trust what they feel for you.'

She'd gone too far.

Spoiling all the beautiful feelings between them.

Her stomach contracted in nervous apprehension as the blue eyes lost their bedroom simmer, sharpening into surgical knives that aimed at cutting through to the very heart she had steeled against *his pleasure* this time.

'What do you feel for me, Angie?' he asked very softly.

Too much. Too much, too soon, she thought, frightened to admit it when he'd just put her into the category of *bought* women. 'I was enjoying your company up until a moment ago,' she answered guardedly. 'And I'm sorry you made that offer. It puts me on a level I don't like.'

'Then please accept my apology,' he rolled straight back at her, his expression instantly changing to charming appeal. 'The offer was not meant to insult your sense of integrity. It was a selfish impulse on my part. I wanted to see you wearing the necklace. Wanted to see you taking pleasure in my gift.' His smile set her heart fluttering again. 'Will you forgive my self-indulgence?'

Confusion swirled in Angie's mind. Had she got it wrong, leaping to a false assumption about his attitude to previous relationships with women? He could certainly afford to indulge himself—the Bentley, travelling first-class everywhere, the best of everything. And she had accepted his invitation to share it all with him at no financial cost to herself.

Her pride might be leading her astray here. She wasn't used to being with a man like him. Nevertheless, she could not accept such an outrageously expensive gift on such short acquaintance, especially when that short acquaintance involved sharing his bed. It smacked of…sexual favours being paid for…and everything within her recoiled from being thought of in those terms.

'I'm sorry, too,' she said hesitantly, her hand lifting in an agitated gesture of appeasement. 'This just isn't…my scene.'

'Then let's get out of here.' He took possession of her hand and smoothly drew her into walking with him towards the exit. 'It's not far to the Sensoji

Temple—a must see in Tokyo. We could take in the
east garden of the Imperial Palace, as well.'

The tension in her chest eased as he resumed his
role of tour guide, coaxing her into chatting cheerfully
with him, erasing the awkwardness she felt over having made such a *personal* stand about the jewellery.

Even so questions lingered in her mind.

Did he really care about the person she was…what
she thought, what she felt? Or was he just a very deft
womaniser, well practised at pushing the right buttons
to win him the response he wanted? How much could
she trust in how he seemed to be?

Hugo worked hard at recovering the ground he'd
lost with Angie Blessing. Big mistake offering to buy
her the necklace, putting her right offside with him.
Her refusal to accept it from him had not been a ploy
to make her seem different to the women he'd dated
in recent years. She *was* different. No doubt about
that.

And he hated the doubt he'd put in her eyes.

Hated it with a passion.

Which surprised him.

Why did he care so much about her trusting him?
Certainly she'd got to him, harder and faster than he'd
ever been stirred before. Last night, and again this
morning, having her was more exhilarating—intoxicating—than…impossible to come up with even a
near comparison. She was pure sensual magic in bed.
And very, very appealing out of it.

The man who'd dumped her had to be an ego
creep. Giving her up over a technician's mistake was
so incredible to Hugo, it seemed only logical that the
guy would be grovelling for her forgiveness come

Monday. Which meant no more false steps between now and then, opening the door for a possible reconciliation. Angie Blessing was going to be his for as long as he wanted her, and at this point in time, Hugo wasn't putting any limit on the relationship he intended to set up with her.

The temple proved a good distraction from personal issues. The huge wooden Thunder Gate and the enormous red lantern welcoming people to the temple grounds immediately caught Angie's interest. All the activity in the main hall fascinated her: people buying fortunes and good luck charms, people praying or rubbing the billowing smoke from the bronze urn on themselves for its curative powers.

They wandered down to the colourful souvenir shops and Angie happily bought three beautiful fans, hand-painted in the Japanese artistic style: a sky blue one for her mother, a dramatic black one for Francine—currently named *Hot Chocolate* on the billboard—and a very delicate pink one for herself.

'Why the pink one for you?' Hugo asked, curious about her choice.

She laughed, a self-conscious flush blooming in her cheeks, her lovely green eyes seeming to question it herself. 'I guess all girls love pink, Hugo.'

'I thought that was little girls,' he countered, thinking her answer was evasive.

'Maybe it's genetic and it never really goes away, however grown up we think we are.'

'You're not feeling grown up today?' he teased, hooking her arm around his again as they walked on, wanting her as physically aware of him as he was of her, determined on reinforcing the strong sexual connection they had.

Her lashes fluttered at him in a sidelong glance. 'You must know you make me feel very much a woman.'

He grinned at the admission. 'You make me feel very much a man.'

She sighed. 'I don't think you need any help in that department.' They were passing a shop with a display of Samurai swords and she stopped to view the display. 'In fact, that's what you should buy for yourself, Hugo.'

'What would I do with a sword?' he quizzed. 'At least you can use a fan.'

'It would be a visual symbol of what you are.'

'A Samurai warrior?'

She met his amused look with deadly serious eyes. 'I think you were born a warrior. You've learnt to put a civilised cloak over it but my instincts tell me that's your true nature.'

Her instincts were sharper than he'd realised. He'd always thought of himself as a competitor, in any arena he chose, and the will to win, or at least put in his best possible effort to win was very strong in him. 'So you see me as a fighter,' he mused, wanting to probe her thoughts further.

'A bit more than that,' she answered dryly. 'A fighter fights. A warrior sets out to conquer, determined on making his way past anything that stands between him and his goal.'

Her pinpointing of the difference lit red alert signals in Hugo's mind. How had she got this far under his skin? Most women were blinded by surface things, seeing no further than his obvious assets. Why was Angie Blessing different? What made her different? Or had he somehow revealed more of himself to her than he had to anyone else?

He swiftly decided to turn her perspective into a positive score for him. With a wry little smile, he said, 'If you think this Samurai warrior is viewing you as his Geisha girl in Japan, you're wrong, Angie.'

'I'm not here just to pleasure you?' she lightly tossed at him, but he heard the testing behind the question.

He wrinkled his brow in mock dismay. 'I thought the pleasure was mutual. Don't tell me you've felt obligated to fall in with what I want.'

'Obligated...no. Though there is a certain... expectation...attached to generosity which is all one way and I'd prefer the scales to feel more balanced.' She paused, then delivered a punch line he was not expecting at all. 'So let me buy you a sword, Hugo.'

He held up a hand of protest. 'You wouldn't let me buy you the necklace.'

'Too much on top of this trip to Japan, which I did accept.'

She was still unsettled by the idea of his *buying* her. Best to clear this issue her way right now, or it might continue to niggle, regardless of what he said. 'Hmmm...why do I sense there'll be a sword hanging over my head if I don't agree?'

'Because you're a very perceptive person?' she suggested with a grin that knew she'd won this point.

'Then let me see how perceptive you are, Angie,' he challenged, making a game of it. 'Make it your choice of sword for me.'

'Now you're putting me on my mettle,' she quipped back.

He laughed and escorted her into the souvenir shop, not really caring what she chose. If she needed some symbol of equalising the situation, let her have it. The only tension he wanted between them was that wrought by sexual desire, waiting to be satisfied.

The Samurai wore two swords—one long, the other short. Angie selected a long one which also happened to be a Japanese Navy Officer's issue sword with the Navy arsenal mark of an Anchor stamped in it. Its scabbard was black lacquered wood, very handsome. The quoted price was over two thousand dollars— more expensive than all three fans together—and it surprised Hugo that Angie didn't quibble over the price, offering her credit card without hesitation.

Was she proving she was a woman of independent means? That it was important to her to be perceived as such by him? A woman who would not be swayed even by great wealth into doing anything she didn't want to do?

He'd been presented with more expensive gifts by other women, mostly clothes they fancied seeing on him, accessories that were blatant status symbols, or *objets d'art* they thought would look good in his house. None of them had carried any real personal meaning, neither for him nor the giver.

The sword was different.

And it made him feel uncomfortable.

It was impossible to gloss over it as though it was a nothing gift, irrelevant to what was happening between them. It was a very pertinent statement, both about Angie Blessing and himself. And Hugo had the strong sense that she was pulling him into a deeper place than he'd ever been before with a woman.

As they left the shop, he couldn't stop himself from asking, 'Why a Naval Officer's sword?'

Her eyes sparkled with her own satisfaction in the choice. 'Because I can see you as a swashbuckling pirate, too, going after all the booty you can get.'

'Do I get the fair maiden, as well?' tripped straight off his tongue. She was happy with him again. It was amazing how good that felt.

She laughed, completely relaxed with him now that he'd accepted *her* gift. 'Since you've carried her off on your ship, and she's already succumbed to…' Her eyes mischievously subjected him to a once-over. '…the physical pleasures you promised…'

'And delivered?' He arched his eyebrows in a rakish query.

'Mmmh….'

The sexily satisfied hum zinged into his bloodstream, arousing strong carnal urges.

'I'd say that was a given,' she concluded, and the happy grin on her face was completely uninhibited, no shadow of any reservations about being with him.

'Let's head back to the hotel,' he said, instantly quickening their pace from a slow stroll. 'I'm feeling hungry again.'

But not for food.

CHAPTER TEN

IT HAD been an absolutely brilliant weekend, Angie thought, wishing it didn't have to end. Though, of course, time inevitably marched on and here they were in the first-class lounge at Narita Airport, waiting for their flight back to Sydney to be called. Hugo caught her smothering a yawn and shot her a rueful smile.

'Have I worn you out?'

'No. Just happy tired.' She smiled back to prove it. 'Thank you for sharing Tokyo with me, Hugo. I've loved every minute of it.'

'You made it a pleasure, Angie,' he said warmly, his bedroom blue eyes sparkling at her, making her pulse skip yet again.

But it hadn't all been about sex, she assured herself. Yesterday afternoon they had left the hotel again to take in the amazing view of the city from the Tokyo Tower's observation platform, even being able to see as far as Mount Fuji, which had been covered by snow. Then they had visited the East Garden of the Imperial Palace and drank tea in the pavilion there...until the urge for more intimacy had them hurrying back to their suite.

He was such a fantastic lover he could trigger a flood of desire just with a look. Even when they were with his Japanese hosts last night, dining at a teppan-yaki bar on the top floor of a skyscraper overlooking the city lights, eating prawns flown in from Thailand, crayfish from Sydney, and the famous Japanese Kobe steak, she was sure their appetites had been highly stimulated by the physical pleasures they had just shared, not to mention the simmering anticipation of more to come once the evening was over.

Fabulous, addictive sex.

With the deep sense of loving running all through it.

Or was she fooling herself about that? Could such feeling not be mutual? Hugo hadn't said anything. But then, neither had she. Too much, too soon?

Angie knew she wouldn't have protested if Hugo had kept her in bed all day today. Nevertheless, she was glad he'd taken her on the harbour lunch cruise, showing her more of Tokyo, spending time just talking to her, giving her the sense that he really did care about the person she was, above and beyond their wonderful compatibility in bed.

'What do you plan to do tomorrow?' he asked.

'Come back to earth with a thump, I guess. Get back to work. Face up to real life again.'

He frowned, observing her sharply from narrowed eyes. 'This weekend hasn't felt real to you?'

'It might not have been anything extraordinary to you, Hugo, but to me…' She shook her head, amazed at all they'd done together in incredible harmony. '…it's like I've been on a magic carpet ride.'

'And you expect it all to disappear in a puff of smoke?' he quizzed half-mockingly.

She hoped not. Desperately hoped not. But maybe he was referring to the *Tokyo* experience. 'I'll always have the memory,' she assured him with a grateful smile.

'No regrets?'

Her heart sank. It sounded horribly like a cut-off line. Pride forced her to say, 'None. A marvellous experience in every respect.'

'Are you saying goodbye to me, Angie?'

Shocked into realising he was misinterpreting her comments, she immediately shot out, 'Why would I want to?'

'You're not seeing me as part of your *real life*,' he whipped back, a hard, cutting edge to his voice. 'And I'm very aware I've served as a distraction from that this weekend.'

Paul…

He was referring to her acceptance of his invitation because Paul had dumped her. The weird thing was, Hugo had literally wiped her partner of three years right out of her mind and it was another shock to be reminded of him.

'Tactically, it was the best move you could have made to put yourself out of reach for a few days,' Hugo went on. 'Let him stew over his incredibly stupid and rash decision. My bet is he'll call you at work tomorrow…'

'No, he won't! Paul burnt his boats by telling—'

'Paul? Paul who?'

'Overton.' The name tripped out under Hugo's driving pressure and Angie grimaced over the absurd situation that her ex-partner should be thought of as any kind of rival by the man who had so totally superseded him.

'Paul Overton.' Hugo drawled the name as though tasting it with all the relish of a warrior given a mission that was very much to his appetite.

'He's a barrister in the public eye and the billboard blotted my copybook beyond repair as far as he is concerned,' Angie rattled out, determined on setting the record absolutely straight so Hugo understood there was no contest involved. 'I do not expect a call from him tomorrow or any time in the future. Nor do I want one. He is out of my life,' she added emphatically, her eyes flashing defiance of any disbelief on Hugo's part.

Which was ridiculous, anyway.

How could he even think she would want any other man but him after all the intimacy they had shared? Yet he was looking at her with such burning intensity, Angie felt herself flushing, as though she was somehow at fault, not giving him enough assurance that she saw a future with him. On the other hand, *he* hadn't made any firm arrangement to see her again.

Why bring up Paul now? And ask her about no regrets? It certainly hadn't *felt* like a dirty weekend, but maybe she had coloured it far too rosily with her own feelings. For all she really *knew,* Hugo might like to spend his time off work focusing on a desirable woman, enjoying saturation sex. Everything he'd said and done could have been a tactical play to win what he wanted. Was he thinking she could take up with Paul again...no harm done?

Angie's stomach started clenching.

Deciding directness was called for she asked straight out, 'Are you about to say goodbye to me?'

His face relaxed into a wolfish grin. 'No. Definitely not. I want a lot more of you, Angie Blessing. A lot more. I'm nowhere near finished with you.'

His reply should have eased her inner tension but the words he'd used and the predatory gleam in his eyes set her mind into a panicky whirl.

Finished...

It implied an end.

When he'd had enough.

As with all the other women who'd been in his life? Did he walk away and leave them behind once his appetite for them had been satisfied? She was still new to him. How long would she last?

Stop it! she fiercely berated herself.

Hugo had asked her to give a relationship with him a chance. And she would. Because it would be self-defeating not to since she felt so much *was* right with him. But she also had to learn from her mistakes, not hang on beyond what was a reasonable time for a commitment to be made. Hugo was obviously still in lust with her, but love was what she wanted, the kind of love that nothing could shake or break.

Faith in each other.

Loyalty.

Emotional security.

Her mind and heart were gripped by these needs as she heard their flight being called. Both she and Hugo rose instantly from their armchairs, action providing relief from the tension of the past few minutes. They were about to say goodbye to Tokyo but not to each other, and possibly to reinforce his intent, Hugo tucked her arm possessively around his for the walk to the boarding tunnel.

'Believe me, I'm real,' he murmured in her ear as they set off together.

She flashed him a quick smile, acutely aware of the hard muscled solidity of his claim. 'What do you plan to do tomorrow?' she asked, wanting more than his magnetic sex appeal to make her feel right with him.

'Make damned sure you don't dismiss me as a dream,' he softly growled.

Angie laughed, a wild irrepressible happiness bubbling up again, chasing away the fears of being foolishly blind to where she might be going with this man. If he was leading her down a garden path, the garden was certainly worth looking at before she closed the gate on it.

Hugo was all the more determined to keep Angie Blessing in his life now. She was a prize, definitely a top quality prize for Paul Overton to have hung on to her for three years, despite her less than sterling silver family background.

And there was such a delicious irony in the situation!

Good old Paul's overweening ego had fumbled the catch and who was there to pick up the ball? None other than the hated rival who'd pipped him at the post so many times throughout their teen years that Paul had stooped to using his parents' wealth to rip Hugo's girlfriend off him.

Not this time, Hugo vowed.

In fact, he would take great pleasure in rubbing Paul Overton's nose in the fact that Angie had moved on to him, and there'd be no buying her back. Hugo could more than match anything the Overtons had to offer by way of wealth. He had the means to shower Angie with whatever her heart desired.

Though he'd have to be careful not to overstep the mark there. She took pride in being a lady of independent means. Nevertheless, wealth was a seductive tool and Hugo intended to wield the power it gave him. He certainly wasn't about to hand any advantage to Paul Overton, who'd undoubtedly come out fighting, once he was made aware that his loss was Hugo Fullbright's gain.

But he wouldn't win, not by hook or by crook.

And how sweet it would be to see him face this defeat!

Indeed, Hugo was brimming over with exhilaration at the thought of this future confrontation as he and Angie settled themselves in the plane and they were handed glasses of champagne. He clicked Angie's in a toast, his eyes flirting outrageously with hers, promising pleasures to come.

'To Tuesday night.'

She effected an arch look, though her whole body language telegraphed yes to whatever he wanted. 'What's happening on Tuesday night?'

'I think I can manage one night without having you at my side. I'll give you tomorrow to catch up on business and sleep, but come Tuesday…dinner at my place?'

No hesitation. Big smile. 'I'd like that.'

'I'll pick you up at seven.'

'Fine.'

She happily drank to the arrangement and Hugo was satisfied nothing would change her mind. Paul Overton's pride would not allow him to call her. Not until he knew who had taken his place in her life. Which he'd discover only when Hugo chose to reveal it…with maximum impact.

A public spotlight would be perfect.

Hugo made a mental note to get James doing all the undercover work on that. With his butler network it should be no problem for him to ascertain what would be a prime meeting place and do whatever was

required for Hugo and Angie to be present, parading
their relationship.

Of course, by the time that was put into action, it
would be too late for Paul to make a recovery.

Hugo was ruthlessly determined on ensuring it was
too late.

Far too late.

He was not about to give up this woman.

Not to anyone!

CHAPTER ELEVEN

AS THE Bentley crossed the Harbour Bridge, taking her home from the airport, Angie swivelled around in her seat to look out the back window and check the billboard. Amazing to think only a few days had passed since it had caused such a change in her life!

The photo of Francine—*Hot Chocolate*—was still on it, as it should be since her friend had paid for a full week's advertising. It was only Monday morning. Three full days of exposure so far, four more to go. Angie wondered if it had brought in any real possibilities for the outcome Francine wanted.

Hugo's gaze followed the line of hers. 'Your business partner,' he said, recalling what she'd told him.

'Yes. Francine Morgan.'

'Does *Hot Chocolate* really describe her?'

Angie grimaced. 'Probably *Foxy Angel* is more true to Francine's character but she couldn't use that after the mistake was made of putting my face with it instead of hers. I think, in her angst over the situation, she just went for something madly provocative.'

'Stirring the pot.'

'I just hope it doesn't backfire on her, landing her in big trouble. Francine is my best friend as well as the marketing force in our design company. We share the apartment, too.' Angie checked her watch. They had landed at six-thirty, but being first-class passengers, there'd been virtually no delay in the arrival procedures at the airport. It was only seven-thirty now. 'She'll still be at home.'

'Then I'll get to meet her.' Spoken with warm anticipation.

Angie glanced sharply at him, remembering he'd admired her friend's enterprising nature, though he'd attributed it to herself at the time. 'Francine may want to steal you from me,' she said wryly.

He laughed and squeezed her hand. 'No chance.'

Her heart tap-danced in pleasure, yet to Angie's mind, in the marriage market he was a prize that any woman would covet. Even fight over. 'You must know you're a very attractive package, Hugo.'

His eyes instantly lost their twinkle of amusement and acquired the searing intensity of twin blue lasers. 'I'm very much taken by you, Angie. Don't doubt that for a minute.'

It was good to hear.

Nevertheless, the plain truth was they'd basically spent an exclusive weekend together, no intrusion from their normal social circles, and most of the time dominated by the strong sexual chemistry between them. Angie couldn't help wondering how their relationship would fare, given the various pressures of their day to day lives, not to mention the judgements of people who were close to them.

She looked at the chauffeur in the driver's seat. James had greeted them cheerfully at the airport, welcoming them home. He appeared to have his attention completely focused on the road, but he was probably listening intently to whatever was going on in the back seat. He gave no indication of it, not by so much as the tiniest snort, but he had to be fitting her into the context of Hugo's previous women, making comparisons.

Would he favour her or work against her if he saw the relationship turning serious? He might not care to have any woman interfering with his running of Hugo's household. Why hadn't Hugo married before this?

He's been waiting for me, Angie told herself in a determined burst of positive thinking. It was what she wanted to believe, and when they arrived at her apartment and Hugo escorted her inside, briefly making the acquaintance of Francine before taking his leave, his manner definitely reflected that she—Angie Blessing—held prime position in his heart.

'Wow! What a sexy hunk! Those eyes…and he's obviously smitten with you, Angie,' was Francine's comment the moment Hugo had gone. 'No need to ask how the weekend went. I bet he's dynamite in bed.'

'It wasn't just sex,' Angie protested, flushing at the inference that nothing else mattered.

'Got to have the spark to start with,' came the knowing retort. 'And Hugo Fullbright is sparking on all cylinders! It's clear to me that you two are up and running, Angie. And good for you, I say! Even better for me.' She rolled her eyes in relief. 'Takes away my guilt over Paul. Who, I might add, has made no contact though he must have seen that *my* photo has gone up on the billboard, proving what we told him was true.'

'The truth was irrelevant,' Angie said dryly, drawing up the handles of her bags, ready to roll the luggage into her bedroom. 'Come and tell me how *Hot Chocolate* fared while I unpack.'

'Brilliant! I'm snowed under with responses,' Francine declared, pirouetting with glee as she danced ahead to open Angie's bedroom door for her. 'I've got bug eyes from reading them through on the computer this weekend.'

Angie shot her a look of concern. 'I thought the name you used might draw some gross stuff.'

Francine waved an airy hand. 'I've eliminated all those.' Her eyes twinkled with happy anticipation. 'Kept only the clever ones. And don't you worry. I'm vetting them very carefully. If they don't come up to my exacting standards…no meeting.'

'What precisely are your exacting standards?'

She grinned. 'Someone who works hard at winning me.'

Angie cocked a challenging eyebrow. 'There doesn't have to be a spark?'

'Oh that, too. Naturally I'm asking for photographs. After all, they have seen mine.'

'You think you can tell from a photograph?'

As Angie heaved her larger bag onto the bed, ready to unpack, Francine bounced around to the other side, wagging a confident finger. 'The eyes have it,' she asserted. 'Your Hugo has just demonstrated that. I look for sparkly, intelligent, wicked eyes.'

'Wicked?'

'Definitely wicked.'

'That might not be husband material,' Angie warned, once again reminded that Hugo was a long-time bachelor, though he had certainly gone all-out to win her. But what if winning was an end in itself?

'Well, at least I should have a lot of fun finding out,' Francine declared, totally undeterred from her mission for marriage.

Fun…or heartbreak?

Angie shook off the doubt.

Tomorrow night she'd be with Hugo again. Nothing was going to stop her—or Francine—from pursuing what seemed right for them.

Hugo focused his mind on what had to be done as James drove him home to Beauty Point on Middle Harbour. 'I want you to acquire two tickets for all the upcoming ballet performances, James,' he said, having decided that was top priority.

'Ballet, sir?' The astounded tone was comment enough on Hugo's previous lack of interest in that artistic area.

'It's never too late to try something new.' Especially with Angie, Hugo thought.

'Of course not, sir. One's experience can always be broadened.'

'Exactly. Have you seen a ballet, James?'

'Oh yes, sir. Never miss a performance. It's always quite splendid. I'm delighted to hear Miss Blessing enjoys it, too.'

Hugo noted the warm approval in his voice—definitely a recognition of top quality. No doubt this would facilitate James' co-operation in securing what was required.

'In fact, sir, I have prime seats already booked for the ballet season. No problem to give them to you for the…uh…duration.'

'Very kind, James, but the duration could be longer than such self-sacrifice could stand. See if you can book more.'

'As you wish, sir,' came the cheerful response.

Apparently the idea of a *long* relationship met his

approval, too. Hugo wondered how Angie had scored so many positive points in his butler's book. While James had invariably acted with faultless courtesy towards the women Hugo had brought home in the past, he usually remained extremely circumspect in any remarks about the relationships. Still, there was no time to reflect on this change right now. Instructions had to be given.

'When you unpack, you'll find a Samurai sword in my bag. I'll leave it to your good taste to find the best way of displaying it in my bedroom. Some place it can't be missed, James.'

'A sword, sir?' he repeated in some bemusement.

'A gift from Miss Blessing.'

'I will see that it's *prominently* displayed, sir.'

'Before tomorrow night.'

'Do I understand Miss Blessing will be…uh… joining you tomorrow night, sir?'

'I thought dinner on the patio. I trust you can organise something special, James. For eight o'clock?'

'Any dislikes I should know of, sir?'

'Only seaweed soup.'

'Ah! Splendid to have so much leeway in preparing culinary masterpieces. Fussy eaters are very restricting.'

'Please feel free to be as creative as you like,' Hugo drawled, amused by his butler's enthusiasm.

A sigh of pleasure. 'At last! A lady who will appreciate my training with gourmet food.'

'Let's not lose perspective here, James. I have always appreciated your skill in the kitchen.'

'Thank you, sir. I didn't mean to imply…'

'Fine! I also want flowers sent to Miss Blessing's

office today. Let her know I'm thinking of her. What do you suggest? She likes pink.'

'Then it has to be carnations and roses, sir. And lots of baby's breath for contrast.'

'Baby's breath?' Hugo wasn't sure he liked the sound of that.

'Tiny white flowers, sir. Very feminine.'

James sounded so smugly satisfied with the idea, Hugo let it go, telling himself the exotic Singapore orchids had certainly served their purpose. 'Okay. Get it done. The note should read…*Until tomorrow*.'

'That's all, sir?'

'It's enough, James. Sorry if that blights your romantic soul.'

'As you say, sir, best not to go overboard. Less can sometimes be…'

'When I want your advice on how to deal with a woman, I'll ask for it,' Hugo cut in dryly. 'In the meantime, I have another task for you. Do you know about the Overton family?'

'Old establishment posh people, Wallace and Winifred Overton?' was instantly rattled out. 'Son, Paul, heading for a Blue Ribbon seat in the Liberal Party?'

'The same. I want you to find out what parties or social events they'll be attending in the next month or so. Very discreetly, James. I'd prefer not to have them know I'm interested in meeting them.'

'With a view to business, sir?' Clearly his curiosity was piqued by this uncharacteristic interest in *posh people*.

Hugo was not inclined to explain. This was personal. Deeply personal. 'Just report back to me as

soon as you can. Anything to do with politics won't
suit, but a fashionable ball or a premiere…'

'A social occasion that you might naturally attend,'
James swiftly interpreted.

'Exactly.'

'And I should wangle you an invitation to it?'

'Two invitations. I shall be escorting Miss
Blessing.'

'Does Miss Blessing have an interest in the
Overton family, sir?'

Hugo grimaced at the linkage James had uncannily
seized upon. 'No, she hasn't,' he said emphatically,
though, in fact, Hugo felt a compelling need to have
that proven. It wasn't just winning over Paul. He
wanted to be certain there was no rebound effect running through Angie's attachment to himself. 'Nor do
I want this mentioned to her,' he added. Surprise gave
no room for pretence.

'Miss Blessing will simply be accompanying you,'
James smoothly interpreted.

'I want her at my side…yes!' he answered curtly,
finding himself somewhat discomfited by these questions.

Was he sure he wanted to do this?

Paul Overton wasn't part of his life anymore,
hadn't been for twenty years. Though he had been a
motivating force behind the desire to make big
money, to build up so much wealth that winning or
losing no longer depended on what could be given. It
came down to the man.

Who was the better man for Angie Blessing?

Because it was Paul she'd been with for the past
three years…Paul who had dumped her, not the other

way around…Hugo wanted him to fight to get her back. Fight and lose.

Then he would know beyond any shadow of a doubt that Angie was his.

Not by default.

Her choice.

Regardless of what Paul offered her.

And he'd offer her all he could because it was Hugo who'd taken her over and that could not be tolerated by Paul Overton.

What it came down to was Hugo wanted closure on that old battleground. And he especially wanted closure because Angie Blessing was involved.

The confrontation had to take place.

CHAPTER TWELVE

DINNER on the patio was going brilliantly. The balmy summer evening made being outdoors particularly pleasant and James congratulated himself on perfect stage management.

Of course, the location itself—overlooking the very creatively landscaped swimming pool right above Middle Harbour, plus the clear starlit sky—had its natural beauty, but the addition of strategically placed candles with subtle floral scents added to the romance of it all, and his table setting with the centrepiece of miniature pink roses was pure artistry.

Miss Blessing had obligingly worn pink, as James had anticipated she would after yesterday's gift of flowers—subliminal choice—and his boss was wearing the white clothes which had been laid out for him. They looked a very handsome couple. A fitting couple.

James found himself humming the wedding march as he worked away in the kitchen, loading the silver tray with the sweets course. Highly premature, he told himself, but all his instincts *were* picking up promising signs.

The weekend in Tokyo had clearly inspired desires that were far from quenched. One could say they were burning at furnace heat out there on the patio. And never before had James received such meticulous and far from the usual instructions about the continuation of an affair.

Ballet!

And not just flowers to be sent. Exotic Asian flowers last Thursday. *Pink* flowers on Monday. When had his boss ever taken note of a woman's favourite colour?

Then there was the Overton family element that also had to be connected to this new relationship. What could his boss possibly want from self-styled upper class snobs? Normally he'd avoid them like the plague. Total contempt for their values. Surely the only reason he would go out of his way to meet them was for the sake of Miss Blessing.

Whose photo, apparently, should not have been on that billboard. This circumstance certainly added to the fascinating scenario. James had actually thought it was rather a dodgy self-marketing stratagem, coming from a lady who shone with natural class. Nice to know his judgement had not been astray. On the other hand, there was no doubt that Miss Blessing did have a flair for taking bold initiatives...giving his boss a Samurai sword.

That cut to the quick.

Clever woman.

Yes, it could very well be that his boss had met his match.

James carried the tray out to the patio, benevolently observing the glow of contentment his dinner had raised, not to mention the holding of hands across the table and two faces happily absorbed in drinking in the sight of each other.

'My pièce de résistance,' he announced. 'Orange almond gateau with drunken apricots swimming in Cointreau. King Island cream on the side.'

'Oh! How blissfully sinful!' cried the lady, her

lovely green eyes lit with delight at this special offering.

James barely stopped himself from preening over
his gourmet masterpiece. He did so enjoy having his
talent appreciated. 'A pleasure to serve you, Miss
Blessing,' he crooned.

'I've never had such a wonderful meal!'

'Thank you.' James swiftly passed on the credit to
get the flow of appreciation moving in the right direction. 'Mr. Fullbright did request something extra
special for you. Without seaweed.'

She laughed and squeezed the hand holding hers.
James felt an emanation of hungry urgency coming
from his boss that had nothing whatsoever to do with
food.

'You have quite outdone yourself, James,' he said,
smoothly adding, 'Just leave this with us now. I think
we'll forgo coffee in favour of finishing the wine.'

Rampant desire barely held in check.

Clearly aphrodisiacs were not needed. However, no
harm in having replenishment on hand. A dish of the
Belgian chocolate truffles he'd purchased to serve
with the coffee could be put on the bedside table.

'Very well, sir.' He clicked his heels and bowed
stiffly from the hips. 'May I wish you both a very
good night.'

He loved doing that stuff. It was so deliciously
camp under the guise of proper formality. Though he
was tempted to swagger a little as he made his exit,
as his acute sense of hearing picked up Miss
Blessing's whispered words.

'Your butler, chauffeur—whatever he is to you—
is worth his weight in gold, Hugo.'

'Mmh…that's just about what he costs, too,' came the dry reply.

Worthy of my hire, James thought, sailing out to his kitchen with all the majestic aplomb of the Queen Mary 2. He'd laid the scene. It was up to his boss now to capitalise on it. And there had better not be just sex on the menu, because Miss Blessing—bless her marriageable heart!—had the stars of love in her eyes. Anyone could see that.

As Angie savoured the glorious taste of the sweets course, she felt as intoxicated as the drunken apricots. Though not from alcohol. She couldn't help thinking this was the kind of courtship dreams were made of—being magnificently wined and dined in an exclusive romantic setting, everything arranged for her pleasure. Life with Hugo had felt so extraordinary during the weekend in Tokyo. She hadn't really expected that sense of awe to continue, but here she was feeling unbelievably privileged again.

She loved his beautiful home. She loved everything about the man sitting opposite her. She even loved his butler. Best of all was the mounting evidence that Hugo was certainly not viewing this relationship lightly.

When the masses of pink roses and carnations had been delivered to the office yesterday, even Francine had commented, 'What we have here are serious flowers, Angie. You've definitely got him hooked.'

Angie had shaken her head. *Hooked* was the wrong word. Hugo Fullbright would never let himself be caught. He was the hunter, the jungle cat, the wolf, the warrior. If he took a partner, it was for his pleasure. The big question was, would she be a lasting pleasure?

The hope she was nursing had certainly received a big boost tonight with Hugo's announcement that he had acquired tickets for them for the rest of the ballet season. This had to mean he planned on their being together for months, at the very least. And he cared enough about *her* pleasure to open his mind to sharing her interest.

It wasn't just lust on his part. It couldn't be. Besides, she had to concede those feelings were mutual. The sizzling desire in his eyes had her body buzzing with excitement, and there was no denying she loved his touch. Simply holding hands was enough to set her mind racing towards—wanting— more intimate contact.

Having consumed most of the delicious gateau, Angie set down her spoon, smiling ruefully at Hugo. 'I'm so full I can't eat any more. Will James be terribly offended if I don't finish it?'

'No.' The vivid blue eyes glinted wickedly. 'He'll probably think I raced you off to bed before you could.'

'Is that what you usually do?' tripped off her tongue, instantly raising a tension she didn't want between them.

Making comparisons to previous relationships was an odious intrusion when she should simply be revelling in being the sole focus of his attention. Yet once the challenge was out, she realised the answer was important to her.

Did Hugo have seduction down to a fine art?

Was the aim to dazzle her into compliance with whatever he wanted?

He'd sat back in his chair, the sexual magnetism suddenly switched off as he looked at her with the weighing stillness of every sense alert, sifting through what was coming at him. Angie's pulse skipped into a panicky beat. The warm harmony she had been revelling in was gone, supplanted by this tense stand-off. Had she spoiled their evening together?

'Yes, it is what I usually do,' he stunned her by saying, his eyes locking onto hers with searing intensity. 'I won't deny I have a strong sex drive and I've never been involved with women who don't want to go to bed with me. On an evening such as this, the natural follow-up would be to seek and enjoy more physical pleasures. Do you find that wrong, Angie?'

'No.' It was reasonable. Perfectly reasonable. And she felt stupid and flustered by his logic. 'I just…wondered…'

'How special you are to me?' he finished softly.

Heat flooded up her throat and scorched her cheeks, but she bit the bullet and stated the truth as she saw it. 'I still feel I'm on your magic carpet ride. All this…' Her hands moved in an agitated gesture to encompass the luxuries he could and did provide. 'You could overwhelm any woman if you set your mind to it. And I do feel overwhelmed by the way you're treating me, but I don't know what's in your heart, Hugo.'

'My heart…' An ironic little smile tilted his mouth, softening the hard look of a keenly watchful predator, weighing up the most effective way to pounce.

It gave Angie's own heart a jolt when he surged to his feet, swiftly stepping around the table to seize her hands and draw her up from her chair.

'Feel it,' he commanded, pressing her open palm to the vibrant heat of his chest.

Her whole body seemed to be drumming at his closeness—the forceful contact, the compelling intensity of his eyes blazing into hers. Was she feeling his response to her or hers to him? Angie didn't know, was helpless to discern anything beyond the physical chaos he stirred in her.

'You hold it,' he fiercely declared. 'You're pounding through my bloodstream. I ache for you. I can't take another second of separation.'

His mouth swooped on hers, passionately plundering, obliterating all Angie's concerns with the sheer excitement that instantly coursed through her. A melting relief soothed her jagged nerve-ends as Hugo swept her into a crushing embrace. She wanted this. Needed it. Loved the feverish possessiveness of his hands renewing his knowledge of her every curve, fingers winding through her hair, holding her in bondage to him.

Hungry kisses.

Greedy kisses.

And the desire for more and more of him erupted like the hot lava of a volcano, a force of nature that was unstoppable.

'Come with me.' Gruff urgency.

He broke away, grabbed her hand, pulled her along with him.

Angie's legs seemed to float in the wake of his stride, weak and wobbly yet caught up in the flow of energy driving him. She was too dazed to question where he was taking her. He tugged. She followed. Strong purposeful fingers encompassed hers, transmitting a ruthlessly determined togetherness, no separation, feet marching to a place of his choosing. Into the house. The luxurious living room facing onto the patio was a blur. Down a wide corridor.

A bedroom.

It had to be his.

And he'd raced her there.

Her dizzy mind registered a strikingly minimalist room, just the bed dominating a huge space—a king-size bed with many pillows—and lamp tables on either side, a soft glow of light from them. The top bed-sheet was turned down, ready...*ready*...and there was a silver dish of chocolates...*seductive* chocolates...

'Look!'

The command meant nothing to her. She *was* looking, feeling a terrible jumble of emotions, telling herself that the *readiness* didn't matter. Whatever had gone on in this bedroom in the past didn't matter. Only what she and Hugo felt together mattered. Yet if it was no more than elemental chemistry...

'Not there!' Terse impatience.

He spun her around to face the wall opposite the bed. A huge plasma television screen was mounted on it, and below that a long, low chest storing what seemed like massive amounts of home theatre equipment. Obviously he could lie in bed and...

'You see?'

His pointing finger forced her gaze upwards, above the mind-blowing size of the television screen.

The Samurai sword!

Angie's heart kicked with a burst of wild exultation.

Hugo had not set her gift aside as a meaningless souvenir. He had been so impressed—so pleased—by her choice, the sword was now hung in a prime place for his private pleasure, mounted on brass brackets that made it a fixture, not something that could easily be moved, on or off display as it suited him.

'It's the last thing I see at night and the first thing I see in the morning,' he said, stepping behind her and wrapping his arms around her waist, drawing her back against him. He lowered his head beside hers, purring into her ear. 'It's like having you speak to me, Angie. Does that tell you how special you are?'

'Yes.' The word spilled from a gush of a delight in the wonderful knowledge that she had touched him deeply. This was not a superficial attraction. Not for her. Not for him.

His hands slid up and cupped her breasts and the pleasure of his touch swelled through her on a blissful wave of happiness. She leaned back into the powerful cradle of his thighs, wanting to feel his arousal, wanting him to know it felt right for her.

He grazed soft kisses over the one bared shoulder of the silky top she wore—a warm, sensuous, tasting that made her quiver with anticipation. 'I want to make love to you, Angie,' he murmured. 'I want to sink myself so far into you that we're indivisible. I want...'

'Yes...yes...' she cried, not needing to hear any more, wanting what he wanted.

But he did not race into it.

'Don't move,' he growled. 'Let me show you how special you are. Look at the sword, Angie. Look at it...and feel how I feel about you.'

She looked at it, stared at it, remembering what she'd said about him being a warrior, determined on getting past anything that stood in his way...and he slowly removed her clothes, caressing them from her

flesh, his hands sliding, stroking, palms gently rubbing her nipples into pleasure-tortured peaks, fingers
finding the moist heat he'd excited, using it to drive
her awareness of her own sexuality even higher. And
his mouth trailed kisses everywhere, a hot suction that
was incredibly erotic, a gentle licking that was intensely sensual.

The sword…an anchor engraved on its handle.

Was Hugo the man who would anchor her life?

Always be there for her?

She had the sense of being completely taken over
by him, territory he was marking as his own, and she
stood there, so enthralled by what he was doing to
her that passively letting it happen didn't seem wrong.
She didn't know if he was taking or giving. Somehow
that was irrelevant. She felt…*loved.*

And when he finally moved her onto the bed, a
mass of tremulous need crying out for him, the image
of the sword was still swimming in her mind, and as
the strong thrust of him slid deeply inside her, she
saw herself as made to receive him, a perfect fit, like
the black lacquered scabbard encasing the steel of the
man, holding the heart of the warrior.

True or not…it was what Angie felt.

No memory of Paul Overton flitted through her
consciousness.

And the women in Hugo's past…no substance to
them. None at all.

The only reality was *their* union.

CHAPTER THIRTEEN

WOULD she spend the coming weekend with him?

Angie's mind was still dancing with *yes* to that question—*yes, yes, yes* to anything at all with Hugo—as she raced into her apartment to get ready for work the next morning. Francine accosted her before she reached her bedroom, taking in her bright eyes and flushed cheeks, not to mention the happy grin.

'So...Take Two went off with flying colours,' she concluded.

'And Take Three is already on the drawing board,' Angie literally sang.

'Well, I've had some luck, too,' Francine drawled smugly, stopping Angie in her tracks.

She looked expectantly at her friend, hoping that somehow *Hot Chocolate* had produced some magic for her.

'You'll never guess.' Francine laughed, shaking her head as though even she thought it was a miracle. 'I got an e-mail last night from the boy next door.'

'What boy next door?' There were no eligible guys in this block of apartments.

'From the old days. When we were kids in our home town before I moved to Sydney. Tim did an engineering course at Newcastle so our lives kind of diverged and we lost track of each other.'

'He saw your photo on the billboard?'

'Uh-huh. Then wrote to ask if it was me. Gave me his e-mail address in case it was. We've been chatting on the Net half the night, catching up and feeling out where we are now.'

'So where is he?'

Francine grinned. '*Not* married. And we're meeting for lunch today.'

'For the spark test?'

It had been Francine's prime requisite for starting a relationship, yet she wasn't dressed in her sexy *out there* best. She was wearing a yellow linen shift dress, more classy than sexy, though the colour did stand out enough to say *look at me,* stating a confidence in herself which Francine never lacked.

'You know, I haven't even thought about that,' she replied in a bemused tone. 'I like Tim. Always did. We were buddies in our teens though...' She grimaced. '...he never asked me out or anything. Never asked any girl out. He always had part-time jobs to help out with his family. Big family. Not much money.'

'Then you're just looking to renew a friendship?' That didn't exactly jell with this degree of pleasure.

She shrugged. 'Who knows? Tim was always a bit of an enigma. Most of the kids considered him a nerdy type but he wasn't really. He was just too smart for his own good. It's not popular, having stand-out brains, always questioning how things work. But you could have a really good conversation with him, not just slick boy-girl talk.' She heaved a happy sigh. 'I'm *so* looking forward to having that kind of company again.'

Without the strain of always trying to sell her attributes, Angie thought. Which answered the question of why Francine wasn't doing her power-play. However, she was in such a good mood, Angie hoped the meeting would work out well for her. With *a spark* happening, as well. Francine deserved a really good guy, one who truly appreciated the person she was. Though it was still a worry that the billboard photograph was the means of reforging this contact.

'This Tim…what's his full name?' Angie asked, a warning on the tip of her tongue.

'Tim Haley.' Francine rolled out the name as though it tasted like a sweet, heady wine.

Angie instantly checked herself from possibly striking a sour note. It had been a long time since their teens. *Hot Chocolate* might have provoked some sexual fantasy Tim Haley was now pursuing, taking the advantage of previous acquaintance. However, if this was so, Francine would find out soon enough.

Angie smiled. 'Reminds me of Halley's Comet. Zooming into your life out of the blue. I wish you all the best with him.'

Francine laughed. 'Thanks, Angie. At least I know he genuinely likes me.'

Genuine liking…

Yes, it was all important in a lasting relationship, and Angie thought about that on and off all morning as she worked beside Francine in their Glebe Road office. The materials they'd priced for the Pyrmont apartment block had to be ordered, contractors lined up to do the painting and tiling. It was difficult to focus her mind on the job when it kept returning to what she had with Hugo.

Strong sexual attraction was such a powerful distraction to really knowing how deeply the liking went. In that respect, an old-fashioned courtship was probably a much better proving ground. Would Hugo have pursued an involvement with her if she hadn't gone with him to Tokyo?

Impossible to ever know that now.

She had plunged headlong into this relationship and now she had to cope with having moved way out of her comfort zone.

So far there was nothing not to like about Hugo and she was fairly sure he thought the same of her. They enjoyed each other's company…just talking together. Though how much was he actually listening to her? Weren't his eyes always simmering with what he wanted to *do* with her?

Making love…

Angie had no doubt about the physical loving.

Apart from that, she did have the certainty that she'd touched something in Hugo's heart with the gift of the Samurai sword. He was also willing to take her to the ballet. Both of which proved he listened to what she said. Cared about what she said.

And their work sort of dovetailed, with Hugo being the driving force behind building new places and her colour co-ordination expertise making them even more attractive. This provided a common interest, making them compatible on more than one level.

It was probably foolish, worrying about sex being a dominant factor in their relationship. If the spark wasn't there, nothing would have happened between them. In fact, she'd be wallowing in depression from being so summarily dumped by Paul, hating him, hating herself for ever having thought she loved a man who could wipe her off for something she hadn't even done.

Three years…

How long did it take to really *know* a person?

Maybe never.

The thought slid into Angie's mind... *We colour them in how we want them to be.*

Yet instincts played a part, too, she quickly amended. Her instincts had been questioning Paul's *rightness* for her before last Thursday, and they were definitely signalling a great deal of *rightness* with Hugo.

All the same, after Francine left for her lunch date with Tim Haley, Angie found herself on tenterhooks, waiting to hear the outcome of their meeting, wanting to know if 'the spark' meant more than liking. The two didn't necessarily go hand in hand and her friend could be in for big disillusionment if Tim came onto her hard.

It was a very long lunch. When Francine finally returned to the office, she walked in as though floating on Cloud Nine, the dreamy smile on her face telegraphing that friendship had definitely turned into something else.

'Well?' Angie prompted impatiently.

The dreamy smile turned into a sparkling grin. 'I think I've found the man I'm going to marry. And what's more, I think he's got the same idea in mind.'

'From one meeting?' It seemed too incredible.

She laughed in a giddy fashion. 'Even I can hardly believe it.' She threw up her hands in a helplessly airy gesture. 'There I was, explaining about the billboard, trying to find a marriageable guy because I just wasn't meeting anyone I fancied as a possible husband, and Tim asked straight out if I could I see him in the frame.'

'And could you?'

Francine nodded as she hitched herself onto

Angie's desk to confide all to her. 'I was hoping he might be interested if I toned myself down a bit. Not hit him full on. But it was he who knocked me out.'

'Big improvement on the past?'

'Just…a lot more impact. Grown up. Filled out. And the way he looked at me…'

'Wicked?' Angie quickly slid in, since *intelligence* was not in question.

Again Francine laughed, her own eyes twinkling with happy anticipation. 'Lurking behind warm and cosy, I think. Waiting for the green light.'

'Did you give it to him?'

'Not straight up green but certainly a very encouraging amber.'

'You're truly attracted to him?'

'I sure am!' came the delighted reply. 'It turns out that he patented an invention of his in the U.S. and made pots of money from it, and he's so confident now…'

'So he can well afford a wife and family,' Angie said, mentally ticking off Francine's requirements.

'No problem.'

'Then why amber? Why not green?' Angie queried, not understanding why Francine hadn't seized her chance.

'I didn't want Tim to think I was considering him for marriage out of sheer desperation. Like I'd grab him just because he was putting himself on the line. He's special. And I want to feel special to him.'

Yes.

Hugo had made her feel very special last night.

And he was special, too. Incredibly special.

'Besides…' A determined look settled on Francine's bright face. '…I still want my husband to win me. Show me I'm truly *the one* for him. Convince me of it.'

Angie nodded. 'Passion,' she murmured, her heart lightening with the certainty of Hugo's passion for her.

'Deep and abiding,' Francine said with considerable passion herself, making Angie realise how very serious her friend was about Tim Haley.

'He did give you reason to believe he might have serious intentions and wanted to pursue them with you?' she pressed worriedly.

'No question.' She lightened up, bubbling with excitement again. 'I tell you, Angie, I was so flabbergasted, I had to keep on testing if he was real or not. He said, like me, he's ready for marriage and wants to have a family. When he saw my photo on the billboard he started remembering what a good connection we'd had as kids, and our chatting last night, and again today, demonstrated a level of easy communication he'd never had the pleasure of with any other woman. Tim thought that was an extremely good basis for marriage.'

'Smart man,' Angie couldn't help commenting.

'I told you he was smart.' Francine grinned. 'And I do love smart.'

Hugo was smart, too, picking up on her needs, answering them, but had the thought of marriage even vaguely crossed his mind? Did she answer *his* needs?

'I've invited Tim to dinner with us tomorrow night.'

'Us?'

Francine slanted her a wise look. 'I can control what happens in our own home. You can be the chaperone, Angie. Make it proper and respectable. I want Tim to court me.'

Courting…not plunging into an intimacy that over-whelmed every other consideration. In fact, Angie realised she wasn't in control of anything with Hugo. He just kept sweeping her away…

'If he's truly serious, it won't put him off,' Francine ran on. 'Besides, I don't want him to think I'm after his money and what it can buy. If he comes to our place, it won't cost him anything, and the apart-ment will show him I've done well for myself, too.'

Angie frowned…shades of Tokyo with Hugo pre-pared to buy her the necklace. That had been bad. Bad, bad, bad.

'You're sure this marriage frame is not just a ploy to pull you in?' she asked, worrying if they were both giving their trust to men who were on different paths to the one she and Francine wanted them to take.

'Tim wouldn't do that to me.' With a very direct look that burned with conviction, Francine added, 'I know him, Angie. Long-time knowing. People don't change their character. I think his success in business has given him the confidence to go after what he wants and he figures the timing is now right for us.'

Long-time knowing.

Angie wished she had that with Hugo. Though it hadn't served her well with Paul, had it? Three years to find out what came first with him. Though that wasn't entirely true. She had known Paul always came first for Paul. She just hadn't wanted to see how little *she* meant to him.

It was different with Hugo. Completely different, she fiercely told herself.

Francine hugged herself exultantly as she waltzed

from Angie's desk over to her own, then flopped into her chair, arms opening out to encompass a whole new world. 'Just think! Last Thursday, life was the absolute pits! Six days later and our prospects are looking bright! You've got Hugo and I've got Tim. Happy days ahead!'

It sounded good.

It was good.

Angie vowed to give up negative thinking right now. Just because she hadn't known Hugo very long didn't mean she couldn't be blissfully happy with him. As she had been last night. And this morning. And was sure to be next weekend, too. They were on a journey together. There was no solid reason to think this journey wouldn't have a happy end.

CHAPTER FOURTEEN

THE State Governor's black tie dinner and charity auction…

Angie eyed her reflection in the full length mirror on the door of her clothes cupboard…hair up in an elegant style, make-up as good as she could do it, around her neck the gold pendant necklace on which hung a pseudo emerald—costume jewellery she'd bought to go with the black strapless evening dress, earrings to match—and the dress itself, so perfect for her it had been impossible to find anything better.

The only problem was she'd worn it before.

With Paul.

Which made it feel…somewhat tainted…with memories she didn't want.

And Paul was bound to be at *this* function. Angie had known it the moment Hugo had mentioned he'd bought a swag of tickets for it, saying it was a very worthy cause, raising money for a new children's hospital. At a thousand dollars a ticket, he'd put out a lot of money, booking a table for ten, inviting his closest business associates and their wives along, Francine and Tim included especially for Angie, making a party of it.

Hugo's obvious pleasure in his plan, and the expense already incurred, had made it impossible for her to say she didn't want to go. If she'd tried to explain it was because of Paul, it would have been like a negation of what she felt with Hugo. He might have thought she still cared about Paul Overton and she didn't.

The truth was, she just didn't want a night with Hugo spoiled by any show of Paul's contempt for her. The brutal call he'd made to dump her demonstrated an attitude he would undoubtedly carry through in public. Pride alone would demand it of him.

His parents, friends and associates would be there, as well, all of whom probably regarded her as something of a tart because of the billboard photo. And Paul wouldn't have told them the truth about that. Oh no! It would have messed up *his* story of what had happened.

Maybe she should tell Hugo…warn him there might be some unpleasantness. But if he then thought she still cared about Paul…

No!

Best that she try to shut the whole horrible business out of her mind. Concentrate on Hugo and how great their relationship still was, even more intimate after three months of being together in most of their free time from work. She would not let Paul's presence spoil anything, not even her pleasure in this dress. It looked great on her. In fact, this was as good as she could look…for Hugo.

'Anything wrong, sir?' James asked.

Hugo instantly smoothed out the frown James had observed in the rear-vision mirror. 'No. Where are we?' he asked, glancing out the side window of the Bentley.

'Almost at Miss Blessing's apartment. Five minutes away. We're on time.'

'Good!'

Angie was always ready on time, another thing he liked about her. He hated being kept waiting. Only at their very first meeting…and that was because of the shock of seeing her photo on the billboard instead of Francine's, probably worry about Paul Overton's reaction to it, too.

'The State Governor's dinner… I did get it right, sir? Meeting your requirements?' James asked a trifle anxiously.

'Perfectly,' Hugo assured him. 'Thank you, James.'

No way could he not go through with it now. He hadn't liked Angie's reaction to attending the special charity function…going all quiet, probably realising instantly it was the kind of event the Overtons would attend. She shouldn't have cared. With him at her side, she should have been happy with the opportunity to defy whatever they thought.

The hell of it was, he still felt uneasy about it.

He would win over any machinations Paul Overton came up with to take Angie away from him tonight.

Of course he would win.

That wasn't the point anymore. The problem was…Hugo suspected he'd made a bad move where Angie was concerned and he didn't know why it was bad. Tonight should be a triumph for her. Why wasn't she feeling that? Given everything they'd shared over the past three months, nothing the Overtons could do should touch her.

The Bentley came to a halt. Hugo picked up the jewellery box, determined on getting Angie to wear his gift. He hoped it would make her feel better about appearing at his side tonight, lift her spirits, give her joy.

'Good luck, sir,' James tossed at him as he alighted from the car.

Hugo didn't answer.

Luck had nothing to do with tonight.

If he was the right man for Angie, nothing should touch what they had together.

The doorbell rang.

Angie grabbed her evening bag, took a deep breath, told herself she had nothing to worry about, and went to open the door to the man she truly did love with all her heart. He looked breathtakingly handsome in his formal black dinner suit and his smile instantly sent a rush of warmth through her.

'Is Francine gone?' he asked.

'Yes. Tim picked her up half an hour ago. He wanted to take her somewhere else first.'

'May I come in for a minute?'

She nodded, slightly mystified by the request. Though his eyes sent their ever-exciting message of wanting to make love with her, a minute wasn't long enough and they were all dressed up and ready to go. Nevertheless, once inside with the door closed, he took her hand and drew her into her bedroom with such an air of purpose, her stomach started to quiver.

'Hugo…' she began to protest, then fell silent, mystified even further by the box he set on the bed.

'Face the mirror,' he commanded, moving her to do so and positioning himself behind her. His hands lifted to the catch of her necklace. 'This looks lovely on you, Angie,' he purred, 'but I want to see you wearing something else.'

He whipped the pendant away, opened the box, and Angie was stunned to see him lifting out the necklace she had admired in Tokyo. 'You bought it?' she gasped as he hung the exquisite collar of garnet flowers around her neck.

'Over the telephone when we got back to the hotel.' He flashed his wolf grin. 'While you were in the bathroom. I arranged for it to be delivered to the reception desk for me to collect before we left.'

'I told you not to.'

'You bought me the sword, Angie.'

'But…' She touched the fabulous piece of jewellery, loving it, yet feeling confused about Hugo's motives.

'No buts. I've kept it for you until now so you can't have any doubt about its being a true gift, without any strings attached. There's no reason for you not to accept it,' he stated unequivocally, making it a churlish act to even quibble about it.

Angie sighed, surrendering to his forcefulness, telling herself this was solid proof of how much Hugo cared about her, buying this gift and holding on to it until he felt the timing was right. 'Thank you. It's beautiful,' she whispered, choked up by a flood of mixed emotions. A ring on her finger was what she really wanted from him. To hide her inner turmoil she busied herself taking off the pseudo emerald earrings. 'I can't wear these with it.'

'Put these on.' He held out a matching set for the necklace, long tiers of the exquisite garnet flowers, almost like miniature chandeliers, probably costing as much as the necklace.

Her fingers fumbled over putting them on. At last they were fastened in her lobes and the effect with the accompanying elaborate collar was mesmerising…dramatic, exotic, an abundance of richness that dazzled the eye.

'You look magnificent,' Hugo declared, his eyes burning possessively at her reflection in the mirror.

Angie found her voice with difficulty, but the image facing her demanded she ask the question. 'Is this why you wanted to take me to a formal function? An occasion fit for the gift?'

Something savage flickered in his eyes. 'The gift is worthy of you,' he growled, then bent his head and kissed her bare shoulder, hotly, as though he wanted to brand her as his. But a necklace, however magnificent, didn't do that, Angie thought. Only a ring did. And the ring didn't have to be anywhere near as extravagant as this gift.

'Now we can go,' Hugo murmured, meeting her gaze in the mirror again with a look of searing satisfaction.

Angie nodded and smiled, though she wasn't smiling inside. She felt distressingly tense as Hugo tucked her arm around his to escort her out to the Bentley.

James was standing to attention by the open passenger door, waiting to see them seated. He flashed Angie an appreciative once-over. 'May I say you look splendid, Miss Blessing!' Warm approval and admiration were beamed at her.

'Thanks to Hugo,' tripped off her tongue, touching the necklace nervously as the thought slid through her mind that the fabulous showpiece jewellery had turned her into an ornament on his arm tonight.

It was not a happy thought.

Shades of being with Paul.

Angie fiercely told herself Hugo wasn't Paul. He was nothing like Paul. And she was not going to let

her experience with Paul Overton twist up her feelings for Hugo.

The boss has made a big mistake with that lavish
jewellery, James thought, covertly observing his passengers as he drove them towards Government House.
The lady was not impressed with it. She kept touching
it as though it was an uncomfortable cross to bear,
not a glorious pleasure to wear.

She wasn't like the other women who'd traipsed
through his boss's life. Couldn't he see that? He was
going to stuff up this relationship if he didn't realise
he had real gold in his hands. And James was nursing
quite a few doubts about the purpose of this charity
function that the Overton family would be attending.

A few subtle questions in the right places had elic-
ited the information that Angie Blessing had been
Paul Overton's partner for three years, the relationship breaking up just before the billboard incident. So
what was the boss up to? Proving he was the better
man? Loading the lady with flamboyant jewellery to
show that she was his?

This was not a good scenario.

James had bad vibes about it.

Very bad.

As he drove into the grounds of the Governor's
official residence, he hoped his boss was right on his
toes tonight, because James figured some very fancy
footwork would be needed to come out of this situation the winner.

Angie had been to Government House before. With
Paul. Tonight it was to be drinks on the terrace first,
then dinner and the charity auction in the function

room. As James drove the Bentley into the grounds, she saw a string quartet playing on the terrace overlooking the gardens and a good smattering of people already there, enjoying the ambience of the evening. She wished there was a crowd. The jewellery she was wearing was so highly noticeable, she would have felt less on show in a crowd.

But, of course, they were arriving at the stated time on the tickets. Hugo had no patience with unpunctuality. He considered being fashionably late an affectation that was plain bad manners.

There would inevitably *be* a crowd, Angie assured herself. This was definitely a top A-list function. Everyone who was anyone would come, some to be seen, others to prove how wealthy they were, movers and shakers.

It was a relief to see Francine and Tim strolling up from the gardens. Angie needed her friend's support tonight. Not even the secure warmth of Hugo's hand holding hers could settle her nerves.

Francine spotted the Bentley and waved. The flamboyant red car undoubtedly stood out like a beacon in the cavalcade of black limousines arriving. Red…garnets…did Hugo want her to stand out, too? Showing her off…*his* woman? She had to stop thinking like this. It wasn't fair. It wasn't right.

There were ushers lined up to open car doors, saving the time it would take a chauffeur to do it. The moment James brought the Bentley to a halt, the back door was opened and Hugo was out, helping Angie to emerge beside him, tucking her arm around his again. *Curtain up,* she thought, and hated herself for thinking it. There was nothing wrong with Hugo feeling proud of her. She should be glad he was.

Francine and Tim were waiting for them on the edge of the terrace. Angie noted her friend was glowing with happy excitement, almost jiggling with it beside Tim who wore the air of a man enjoying sweet success.

Francine's sparkling eyes rounded in astonishment at seeing the spectacular jewellery that had replaced Angie's far more modest choice. 'Wow!' she breathed, her gaze darting to Hugo and back to Angie with a raising of eyebrows.

Angie nodded, acutely conscious of the elaborate earrings swinging back and forth.

'That's some gift, Hugo,' Francine said in an awed tone.

'Angie carries it off beautifully,' he purred with pride.

'That she does,' Tim agreed, grinning away, his confidence in himself and Francine's attachment to him not the least bit dented by Hugo's extravagant giving.

He thrust out his hand in manly greeting and Hugo had to detach himself from Angie to take it. Francine skipped around Tim and thrust out her hand for Angie to see. 'Look! Look!' she cried, positively bubbling with excitement.

A diamond ring!

A beautiful big sparkling solitaire firmly planted on the third finger of her left hand!

An engagement ring—marriage proposed and agreed upon!

A stab of envy sliced through Angie so fast, shame drove her into babbling every congratulatory expression she could think of, hugging Francine, hugging Tim, forcing herself to be happy for them because she was. She truly was. Especially for Francine who had finally found the kind of husband she'd wanted. And the love shining from both of them left no doubt about how they viewed their future together. Absolute commitment.

For them this was a night to remember.

For Angie…her friend's happy situation underlined her darkest thoughts about tonight.

She wasn't Hugo's bride to be.

The jewellery he'd placed around her neck made her feel like a high-priced tart.

She wanted to feel good about it.

But she didn't.

Couldn't.

It felt the same as it had in Tokyo…the kind of thing Hugo habitually did for his women. It didn't mark her as anyone special to him. It said she was just another one in a queue who would eventually pass out of his life. Regardless of the three months they'd been together, nothing had really changed for him.

Though maybe she was wrong.

Angie fiercely hoped she was.

CHAPTER FIFTEEN

As soon as the Master of Ceremonies requested guests move into Government House, ready for dinner which would soon be served, Hugo wasted no time leading his party inside to the function room. They were ushered to their table and he designated the seating, ensuring for himself a clear view of the people streaming in for the business end of the charity evening. Angie, of course, was placed beside him.

He had not spotted the Overtons in the crowd outside and he had not tried searching for them. The mood of his own group of guests had been very convivial, celebrating the happy news of Francine's and Tim's engagement, and he'd wanted to keep it that way, especially since he'd sensed Angie's tension easing as bright repartee flowed back and forth, evoking merry laughter.

Besides, he felt no urge to hurry the confrontation he'd wanted. In fact, he was in two minds whether to push it or not. Mostly he wanted Angie to feel happy with him, happy to be at *his* side.

Waiters served champagne. Appreciative comments were made about the table settings, the floral decorations, the chairs being dressed in pastel blue and pink covers, a reminder that this function was to benefit children. Hugo kept a watchful eye on the people being ushered to their tables.

He saw Paul's parents come in with a relatively senior party, their haughty demeanour instantly striking old memories of them looking down on his parents as not worth knowing, and being vexed with him whenever he snatched some glory from their son. Though they had deigned to congratulate him. With thinned lips.

It occurred to Hugo that Paul had been born to live up to their expectations, bred to an arrogant belief that he should be the winner. But that didn't excuse some of the tactics he'd used to be the winner. The self-styled noble Overtons did not have nobility in their hearts. They simply had a mean view of others.

Angie didn't notice them. She was busily chatting to his guests, being a charming hostess, very good at drawing people out about themselves. Which was another thing he liked about her, not so full of herself that she always had to be the focus of attention. She even took an interest in James' life, not treating him as just a super servant on the sidelines. No meanness in her heart.

How the hell had she been fooled by Paul into staying with him for three years?

That really niggled at Hugo.

Especially since Paul had dumped her, not the other way around. As it should have been. How could she not have seen, during all that time, what an egomaniac he was?

At least she knew it now.

But something about Paul Overton still affected her and Hugo needed to know what it was.

Focusing all her attention on the company at the table and forcing herself to make bright conversation had served to lift Angie's spirits. She was determined on making this a fun night for Francine, setting her own inner angst aside. They were all here to enjoy themselves and she was not going to be a spoilsport.

The champagne helped.

Though she almost choked on it when Francine, who was sitting beside her, leaned over and whispered, 'Paul has just come in.'

Angie swallowed hard and flicked her friend a derisive look. 'I'm not interested.'

'Neither you should be,' Francine fervently agreed. 'But I've got to say the woman on his arm isn't a patch on you, Angie. Big come down.'

'His choice,' Angie answered flippantly.

'And Hugo leaves him for dead.'

In every way, Angie fervently confirmed to herself. It didn't matter that he hadn't yet offered her an engagement ring. The jewellery was a special gift, bought months ago to please her when the time was right. Hugo went out of his way to please her, which surely meant she was special to him. She just wished this gift had been presented to her on some other occasion.

She smiled at Francine, then directed a question at Tim, not wanting to even look at Paul. Though Francine's comment about his new woman piqued her curiosity enough to take a quick glance towards the entrance to the function room.

Recognition was instant—Stephanie Barton, daughter of one of the leading lights in the Liberal Party, one of the best political connections Paul could make. Well, the grass certainly wasn't growing under Paul's ambition, she thought cynically, and her set course of ignoring him was suddenly made much easier.

His view of her was totally irrelevant. In fact, he

could look at her with as much contempt as he liked. He was the one who deserved contempt, trading himself for political advantage.

Hugo watched Paul scan the room, budding politician in action. He was not paying any attention to the woman hanging on to his arm. Not a beautiful woman like Angie. Not even a pretty woman, although she had certainly worked hard on effecting a stylish appearance. Hugo decided she had to be a well-connected woman—silver spoon matching up to silver spoon.

As Paul's gaze roved around, picking out notable people, nodding and smiling when he received some acknowledgment, Hugo rather relished the shock that would hit him when he caught sight of his old rival. It had been a long time, but the animosity on Paul's side would undoubtedly still be there. On his own side? Only the problem with Angie's feelings weighed heavily. That had to be resolved.

The moment of recognition came.

A visible jolt and double take, his mouth thinning in displeasure as he visually locked horns with Hugo, silently challenging the effrontery of *his* presence in a place where he didn't belong. Except money was the only requisite here, and his contemptuous grimace revealed he knew Hugo was now loaded with it.

The contempt did it.

Irresistible impulse took over.

Hugo leaned back in his chair and stretched his own arm around the back of Angie's chair, deliberately drawing Paul's attention to her, ramming home how big a loser he was, despite the silver spoon cramping his mouth. Angie should have been treated

as a queen, which was what she was—so far above
other women she was right off the scale. And for Paul
to have dumped her...well, let him at least acknowledge her worth now!

The moment he saw Angie, his whole face tightened up. He stared, then jerked his head forward, jaw
clenched with determination not to look again. At either of them. Especially the two of them together.

His party was ushered to a nearby table and since
all the tables were round, he could and did manoeuvre
the placings so that he sat with his back turned to
Hugo and Angie—an act of disdain, but Hugo wasn't
fooled by it. Paul didn't want to face what he'd just
seen. He had no weapons to fight it.

Unless Angie gave him an opening.

Hugo swiftly tuned in on what was happening at
his table. Tim was explaining one of his inventions
to the rest of the party and Angie was turned to him
in listening mode. She seemed more relaxed now and
Hugo relaxed himself, reasoning that if Angie had
been disturbed at the thought of meeting Paul again,
she would have kept a watchful eye out for his arrival
herself, and clearly she hadn't.

Or was determined not to.

In which case, there was still a problem.

The dinner served was of the finest, most expensive
foods, all beautifully presented and accompanied by
a selection of wines chosen to complement each
course. Francine raved about everything but Angie
found it difficult to eat. She was still too conscious
of the elaborate collar around her neck. It felt as
though it was choking her.

A children's choir came in to entertain with traditional Australian songs, starting with *Waltzing Matilda* and finishing with a rousing rendition of *I Still Call Australia Home*. Angie turned around in her chair to face and applaud them. She caught sight of Paul's mother staring at her from the table closest to the stage. Or rather staring at the jewellery Angie was wearing. Then her gaze flicked up and she raised her nose in a sniff of dismissal before looking away.

Fine! Angie thought savagely. I didn't want you as a mother-in-law, anyway!

Yet she found her gaze skimming around the tables for Paul and found Stephanie Barton seated almost parallel with her on the other side of the room. The man next to her faced away from where Angie was but it was Paul all right. Had he seen her and deliberately chosen to keep his back turned to her?

That was fine, too, Angie decided.

Ignoring each other was the best way through this function.

But the garnet collar felt tighter than ever.

It was a relief when the sweets course was taken away and the auction started. Tim bid for and eventually won a walk-on part in a movie which was about to be shot in Sydney.

'I didn't know you wanted to be in movies,' Francine quizzed when he was triumphant.

'It's for you,' he answered, grinning from ear to ear. 'I couldn't afford to take you to the movies when we were kids. Now I'm going to have the pleasure of seeing you in one.'

They all laughed and Angie thought how nice Tim was, and how lucky Francine was to feel free and happy about accepting any expensive gift from him.

He wasn't buying her. He loved her. And the proof of that was on Francine's finger.

Coffee and petit fours were served as the auction continued at a wild pace, an amazing variety of goodies up for grabs. Huge interest was stirred amongst the men when Steve Waugh's autographed bat was offered. The recently retired cricket captain had been named 'Australian of The Year' and had reached the status of legendary hero amongst the sport's fans.

The bidding for the personal bat was fast and furious. Hugo joined in. Angie couldn't help noticing Paul did, too. Hugo's jump bid to ten thousand dollars seemed to be the clincher for him, but as the auctioneer wound up the sale, Paul suddenly called, 'Fifteen,' opening it up again.

'Twenty,' Hugo called, without so much as blinking an eyelid.

A hushed silence as everyone waited for a possible counter-bid. Paul didn't look around to see who had beaten him. He faced the auctioneer and raised his hand, drawing the attention of the whole room to himself as he called, 'Thirty,' in a terse, determined voice.

The auctioneer raised his eyebrows at Hugo, 'Do we have a contest, sir?' he asked, clearly wanting to whip one up. 'It's for a very good cause and this bat hit a century for Steve Waugh.'

'Then a century it is,' Hugo drawled. 'I bid one hundred thousand dollars.'

It evoked a huge burst of applause.

When it finally died down, the auctioneer gestured to Paul and whimsically asked, 'A double century, sir?'

Paul forced a laugh and waved the offer away, conceding defeat.

'That's very generous of you, Hugo,' Angie said warmly, impressed that he had contributed so much for a children's hospital.

He swung around to her, his eyes glittering with the savage satisfaction of a warrior who has swept all before him, his mouth curling with a deep primeval pleasure in his victory. 'To the children, the spoils of war,' he said.

'War?' Angie didn't understand.

'Cricket might be a sport but it's also a battle. A fight to the finish,' he explained.

'Well, you sure hit that other bidder right out of the playing field,' Tim said appreciatively.

'What you might call a deep six,' Hugo agreed with his wolf grin.

The other men at the table chimed in with good-humoured comments involving cricket terms which clearly amused them. Not ever having been a cricket fan, the repartee was completely lost on Angie. Francine, as well, who suggested they slip off to the ladies' powder room.

'Paul was livid at losing,' Francine whispered as soon as they were out of earshot of their party. 'I bet he was deliberately bidding against Hugo because of you.'

Angie glanced at Paul's table before she could stop herself. Stephanie Barton was staring venomously at her and even as their eyes caught, she said something to Paul, and from the nasty twist of her mouth Angie assumed it was some jealous snipe. Paul, however did not look around and Angie quickly turned her own gaze away.

'More likely he wanted to make a charitable

splash,' she muttered to Francine. 'He'd be angry at being frustrated, having decided what to bid on.'

'Well, I'm glad he's not having a happy night,' Francine shot back with smug satisfaction. 'Serves him right for being such a stupid snob as to dump you because...'

'That's water under the bridge,' Angie sliced in.

'True. And Hugo is much more giving.' She heaved a happy sigh. 'I do love generous men.'

Generous, yes, but what of the motive behind the generosity?

Angie didn't voice that thought. It touched too closely on the current ache in her heart—an ache that grew heavier as she refreshed her make-up in the powder room and the ornate jewellery from Japan mocked her dream of a forever love with Hugo.

Self-indulgence...that was what he'd called his impulse to buy it for her in the first place. He was still indulging himself with her. He'd wanted the pleasure of seeing her wear his gift and she'd let him have his way. He'd won her compliance. Won it all along. And maybe winning was what it was all about with him. Like with Steve Waugh's bat—decide on something—get it!

Interesting question...what was he going to do with the cricket bat, now that he had it? Angie resolved to ask him when she returned to their table. However, she and Francine were no sooner out of the powder room, than they were waylaid by a furiously determined Paul Overton.

'I want a word with you, Angie. A private word.' He grabbed her arm. 'Out on the terrace.'

'Let go of me,' she cried, angered at his arrogant presumption. 'I have nothing to say to you, Paul.'

'Well, I have a hell of a lot to say to you,' he seethed, the hand on her arm a steel clamp as he started pulling her away with him.

'If you don't let Angie go, I'll get her guy to come,' Francine threatened. 'You don't want a scene, Paul,' she added sarcastically.

'By all means get Fullbright,' Paul snarled at her, carelessly revealing knowledge of his name. 'While I tell Angie the truth about my old school buddy.'

'What?' Shock weakened Angie's resistance to Paul's dragging her outside with him. Her feet automatically moved to keep up with him.

'You're just a pawn in his game,' he shot at her, his eyes glittering with the need to shoot more than her down. He dropped a scathing look at the necklace as he jeered, 'Dressing you up like a queen to checkmate me.'

'You have nothing to do with us,' she protested, though a host of frightening doubts were clanging through her brain.

'I have *everything* to do with him parading you here tonight,' Paul grated out viciously.

Was that true?

They were outside, away from everyone else. The auction was still continuing in the function room— the auction that had provided a battle between Hugo and Paul, with Hugo bidding an enormous sum...to be charitable or to thwart a rival?

It had been a gorgeous Indian summer day but the night air was crisp now, bringing goose bumps to Angie's skin. Or was it the chill of a truth she didn't want to believe? She told herself Paul was an egomaniac and he was reading the situation wrongly, hating being publicly beaten, taking his anger out on her.

'This is absurd!' she insisted. 'Hugo was interested in me before he ever knew I'd had a relationship with you.'

'Sure about that?' Paul whipped back at her.

'Yes, I am,' she retorted heatedly.

'How soon did he learn about me?'

The quick insidious question stirred more emotional turbulence. She'd given Paul's name to Hugo at Narita Airport, at the end of their *dirty weekend*. But he'd bought the jewellery before that, on the Saturday, she reasoned feverishly, so he'd meant to continue their affair. Hugo's interest in her could not hinge on Paul.

'It doesn't matter,' she muttered, firmly shaking her head.

'You think it's not relevant?' Paul mocked. 'When you told him about me, did he mention we knew each other?'

No, he hadn't. Not a word. 'School was a long time ago, Paul,' she argued, not wanting to concede any substance to the point being made.

'Some things you don't forget.'

'Like what?' she demanded.

He told her.

About the intense rivalry between them.

About the chip on Hugo's shoulder because he hadn't been born to a life of privilege.

About the girl who'd dumped Hugo for Paul.

He fired bullets at her so fast, Angie was reeling from the impact of them. She could see the influence they might have had in forming Hugo's ambition, motivations…and they hammered home the point…*some things you don't forget.*

But there was one big flaw in Paul's scenario and she leapt on it. 'But *you* dumped *me*. Why would Hugo want your discard?' she flung at him.

'Good question.'

The drawled words startled them both into swinging around.

Hugo strolled forward to join them. He appeared completely relaxed, supremely confident, yet Angie sensed the powerhouse of energy coiled within, ready to be unleashed. It played havoc with her nerves which were already torn to shreds under Paul's very personal attack on her position in Hugo's life. She didn't want to be a bone of contention between them, yet all her instincts quivered with the sense that it was true. Terribly true.

It was a dangerous smile Hugo bestowed on Paul, and the airy gesture he made as he closed in on them had a mesmerising sleight-of-hand about it. 'The answer is...I want Angie because she is beautiful...inside and out. Nothing at all to do with you, Paul. Though I do wonder that you were such a fool as to let her go.'

Paul's jaw clenched. Sheer hatred burned in his eyes. 'Not such a fool that I didn't finally see she was no more than a cheap whore who'd sell herself to the highest bidder,' he bit out in icy contempt.

Angie gasped at the painful insult, her hand instantly lifting to her throat, wishing she could tear off the damning necklace.

'You're welcome to her, Fullbright,' Paul jeered.

'Always the sore loser,' Hugo mocked silkily. 'Do choose your weapons more carefully. You wouldn't want that vote-winning smile rearranged.'

Paul's shoulders stiffened, bristling with the aggression stirred. 'I didn't lose anything worth having,' he snapped.

'No? Then why drag Angie out here? Why do your venomous best to destroy her trust in my feelings for her?'

'Feelings?' He snorted derisively. 'I was doing Angie a favour, letting her know she'd been used by you.'

'How benevolent! Strange how I never noticed that trait in your character. Much more in keeping that you'd badmouth me so I'd lose, too.'

'You kept her in the dark, Fullbright. That speaks for itself.'

'Or does it say you were simply not a relevant factor?'

'Angie's not stupid. She can put it together.'

'I'm sure she can…from the way you treated her.'

'Still got your debating skills, I see.'

'Sharp as ever.'

'But not sharp enough to pass the real test, Fullbright.' A glint of triumph accompanied this challenge.

Angie had been sidelined as a spectator to the contest being waged, but suddenly she found herself the target of Paul's *test*. 'If you hadn't cheapened yourself on a public billboard, I would have married you, Angie,' he threw at her. 'If you think Fullbright's *feelings* for you will lead to marriage, think again. He'll never take you as his wife and you know why?'

She stared at him, feeling all the vicious vibes being aimed at both of them.

'Because I had you first,' he flung down, then

swung on his heel and strode off with the arrogant air of having finished with people who were beneath him.

Which left Angie and Hugo alone together—an undeniable statement hanging between them.

She had given herself to Paul first.

CHAPTER SIXTEEN

SOILED goods…

It was an old-fashioned phrase, out of step with life as it was lived now, yet it slid into Angie's mind and set up camp there, burning into her soul.

'Are you okay, Angie?' Hugo asked, his laser blue eyes probing hers for possible problems.

She looked blankly at him, feeling herself moving a long distance away from this whole situation, detaching herself from the entangled relationships with Hugo and Paul, standing alone. Chillingly alone.

'You can't believe I'd be influenced by what Paul is,' he said in a tone of disgust. 'But if you need to talk about it…'

'No!' The word exploded from her need to be done with the mess she had been drawn into. 'I want…' *to finish this right here and now.* Yet wouldn't Paul feel some filthy triumph if she left the scene before the night was over? Not only that, her disappearance would worry Francine, cast a shadow on her friend's happy night. She lifted her chin with a heightened sense of holding herself together and said very crisply, 'I want to return to our table. We've been missing too long already.'

'Fine! Let's go then.'

He clearly interpreted her reply as a positive decision towards him, smiling his relief and pleasure in it as he offered his arm. She took it, merely as a prop to present the right picture so Francine would be pleased that she had sent Hugo to the rescue. And Paul would not have the satisfaction of knowing how deeply she had been hurt.

Oddly enough, the physical link to Hugo had lost all its sexual power. There was ice in her veins, not one trickle of heat getting through from the contact with him. She hated being a trophy woman. Once this evening was over and they were in the privacy of the Bentley, she would stop being one, and never, never again fall into that horribly demeaning trap.

Hugo was delighted that Angie was dismissing the confrontation with Paul as not worth any further consideration. Sour grapes on Paul's part. Which, of course, it was. Clearly her mind was satisfied that her former lover did not impinge on their relationship in any way whatsoever and she was well rid of him.

Closure had definitely been effected.

Though as they reentered Government House, Hugo noted Angie's cheeks were flushed and she was holding her head so high it smacked of proud defiance, which told him she had been stung by Paul's personal insults to her. Perhaps badly stung. And his previous doubts about whether he was making the right moves came crashing back.

What had he achieved tonight?

Yes, it had felt good to outbid Paul in the auction, though that wasn't particularly important to him. He'd meant to bid for something anyway, giving to a charity that would benefit children.

And it had felt good, seeing Paul's reaction to finding Angie attached to him now.

Being the winner always felt good.

But at what cost if Angie was hurt by it?

Out there on the terrace, he had felt savagely satisfied that Paul's behaviour had stripped any wool
from Angie's eyes where her ex-lover was concerned,
but now he had the strong and highly disturbing sense
that it had not righted the wrong he'd been feeling.

Far from it!

Paul's last childish shot of the night—*I had her
first*—started some deep soul-searching which Hugo
pursued relentlessly while he played out the charade
of continuing a bright happy party at his table.

Had he been driven to arrange this encounter because he needed affirmation from Angie that she truly
felt he was the better man? Right from the beginning
he'd felt possessive of her. Finding out she'd been
with Paul for three years…and it hadn't been *her* decision to break the relationship…had definitely struck
him hard.

Not the sexual aspect of it. That didn't matter a
damn. After their first night together in Tokyo, he'd
had no doubt he and Angie were so sexually attuned
to each other, the kind of physical intimacy they
shared was something uniquely special to them. That
had never been a problem.

It was the long attachment to Paul that had niggled.

Would she have married him if the billboard mistake hadn't happened?

Hugo's gut twisted at that thought.

But she knew better now, he told himself. Tonight
Paul had surely obliterated any lingering sense of being robbed of a good future with him. She couldn't
possibly regret losing him now. He'd demonstrated
beyond any doubt what a mean-spirited bastard he
was.

All the same, Hugo was acutely conscious that

Angie was not turning to him with a renewed flow of positive feeling. She was focusing almost exclusively on the others at the table, barely acknowledging his contributions to the conversation, not touching him and not welcoming any touch from him, actually detaching herself from contact with him. Not obviously. Under the guise of turning her attention to someone else or making a gesture that seemed perfectly natural.

It made Hugo increasingly tense. He craved action, a resolution to whatever was distancing Angie from him. As the auction drew to a close, he took out his mobile phone and sent a text message to James, ordering the car up, ready for a quick departure. He suffered through the wind-up speech by the M.C., applauded the end of it, then rose from his chair, thanking his guests for their company, wishing Francine and Tim well again, and taking his leave of them, ruefully announcing his work schedule demanded an early night.

Angie was quickly on her feet without any assistance from him, but she did submit to having her arm placed around his for the walk out of the function room. Again she held her head high and despite the many admiring and envious glances she drew as they made their exit, her gaze remained steadfastly forward, acknowledging nothing.

The Bentley was waiting.

James sprang to attention the moment he saw them, opening the passenger door with his usual flourish. 'Did you have a good evening, sir?' he asked as Angie stepped into the car and settled on the far side of the back seat.

Hugo handed him the cricket bat. 'Belonged to Steve Waugh. Take care of it, will you, James?'

'A prize, indeed, sir,' James enthused.

Not the one he most wanted, Hugo thought darkly as he moved in beside Angie who sat with her hands firmly in her lap, her gaze averted from him, not the slightest bend in her towards the intimacy they had so recently shared.

Hugo waited until the Bentley was on its way out of the Royal Botanic Gardens before he broke what he felt was highly negative silence. 'I'm sorry about what happened with Paul tonight,' he started gently, hoping she would unburden the hurt she felt so he could deal with it.

'Are you, Hugo?' she answered in a flat, disinterested tone.

He frowned, sensing one hell of a chasm had opened up between them.

Then she turned her head and looked directly at him, her green eyes as cold as a winter ocean. 'You planned it. Please don't insult my intelligence by denying it. You planned how this evening would play out.'

'No. Not how it did,' he quickly corrected her.

'You knew Paul would be there, just as I knew he'd be there,' she said with certainty.

'You could have said something if you didn't want to risk a social meeting with him,' he countered.

A mocking eyebrow was raised. 'Avoiding him would have given him an importance he no longer had to me.'

'Sure about that, Angie? I sensed you didn't want to see him and I readily confess I didn't like the feeling that…'

'It was bound to be unpleasant if we met,' she cut in crisply. 'That was my only concern. But you must

have known that, Hugo. With your old history with
Paul, you must have known he'd force a meeting...and you deliberately led me into it.'

The accusation sat very uncomfortably. Hugo
didn't have a ready reply to it.

'But *I* didn't matter, did I?' she continued. 'It was
between you and him. I was just the means to...'

'No!' he asserted vehemently. 'You do matter.
Very much. And I'm deeply sorry Paul subjected you
to...'

'The truth?'

'I doubt Paul Overton has spoken the truth in his
whole damned life! As for *his* version of my history
with him, I'm sure that was twisted to suit the purpose
of undermining what we have together.'

His aggressive outburst didn't stir one ripple in her
icy composure. She simply sat looking at him, apparently weighing the strength of what he'd claimed.
Then very quietly she asked, 'What do we have,
Hugo?'

'You know what we have,' he shot back at her. 'A
great rapport. We enjoy each other's company. Every
time we're together it's good.'

Her mouth twisted in bitter irony. 'Good enough to
think of marrying me?'

Marriage!

Hugo shook his head in furious frustration at how
poisonous Paul's barbs had been.

'Well, at least you're honest about that,' Angie
commented wryly, misinterpreting his reaction.

'For God's sake, Angie!' he protested. 'I needed to
get your hangover from Paul out of the way first.'

'*My* hangover!'

She didn't believe him. The scorn in her eyes

goaded him into saying, 'We've only been together three months. Let's be reasonable here. You were content to be with Paul for three years without getting a proposal from him.'

Big mistake.

Huge mistake!

Incredibly stupid to compare the two relationships!

Her face instantly closed up on him and she sat facing forward again. Her hands lifted and one by one, removed the earrings from her lobes, dropping them onto her lap.

'What are you doing?' he demanded in exasperation at her apparent choice not to argue with him.

No answer.

It was all too obvious what she was doing.

She removed the necklace, too, then gathered the jewellery together and placed it on the seat space between them. 'I don't want this, Hugo. I did tell you not to buy it,' she flatly stated.

'It suited you. It looked great on you,' he asserted, feeling a totally uncharacteristic welling of panic at this clear-cut indication she was cutting him off. 'There's no reason for you not to keep it,' he insisted heatedly.

She flicked him a derisive look. 'It makes me feel like a high-priced whore.'

Paul again!

'You know you're not one, Angie!' he threw at her furiously.

'Yes. I know,' she said dully, her head turning towards the side window, away from him.

'Then why are you letting Paul Overton colour my gift to you?'

'He didn't. I felt it when you put it on me tonight,

Hugo,' she answered, speaking to the night outside, the darkness seeping into her mind, shutting him out.

'You gave me the Samurai sword,' he fiercely argued. 'Why can't I give you a gift without you thinking…'

'The sword wasn't for public show,' she cut in wearily.

How could he make her understand? He had wanted her to wear his gift tonight to show how much *he* valued the woman Paul had rejected, to make her feel like a queen compared to other women. For her to know that this was how he thought, and feel it, especially when she saw Paul again.

'I would have broken up with Paul if he hadn't leapt in first,' she said, and slowly, slowly, turned her gaze back to his. 'You see, I finally realised I was a trophy woman to him, not someone he really loved for who I am…the person inside. I guess I was dazzled by other things about him but I did finally see…' Her mouth twisted. '…and I have no intention of spending the next three years being your trophy woman, Hugo.'

'That's not what you are to me,' he swiftly denied.

Rank disbelief in her eyes.

He threw out his hands in appeal. 'I swear to you, Angie…'

She recoiled away from him. 'Don't! The contest is over. You won whatever points you wanted to make. Just let me go now, Hugo.'

'No. I don't want to lose you.'

'You have already.'

He sought desperately for words to hold on to her. His mind seized on what she'd said about Paul not loving the person she was. He did. He very much did.

She *was* beautiful, inside and out. In a wildly emotional burst, he offered that truth.

'Angie, I love you.'

She flinched as though he'd hit her. 'Do you say that to all your women?' she flashed at him with acid scepticism.

'I've never said it to any other woman. You're the only one,' he declared with more passion than he'd ever felt before. 'The only one,' he repeated to hammer home how uniquely special she was to him.

He knew Angie had never been with him for the ride he could supply. His wealth truly was irrelevant to her. She was not out to get anything from him except his respect. And the love she deserved. He had to make her see she had both his respect and love.

Before he could find the words to convince her of it she tore her gaze from the blaze of need in his, jerking her head forward. Her throat moved in a convulsive swallow. She spoke with husky conviction. 'This is only about winning. It's all been about winning. A man who loves me would not have put me in that firing line tonight, knowing Paul as you did.'

'Knowing Paul as I did…' God damn the man and the baggage they both carried because of him! '…I hated the thought of you still feeling something for him, Angie. And yes, I wanted to win over him tonight,' he confessed, desperate to set things right. 'I wanted to be certain you're now mine.'

'I'm not a possession,' she flung at him, her cheeks burning scarlet. 'I chose to go with you. Be with you. I told you so before I ever went to bed with you, Hugo.'

But he'd seduced her into his bed. He'd done it very deliberately. Because he'd wanted her. And he'd used sex to tie her to him ever since. But sex wasn't going to work tonight. She'd hate him, despise him, if he tried it.

He told himself to calm down, reason through the important points he needed to make. He was fighting for his life here—*his life with Angie*—and suddenly he knew that was what he wanted more than anything else, and if he didn't make it happen, he'd face a terrible emptiness in all the years to come.

'I do love you, Angie,' he repeated quietly. 'I just didn't like how Paul had belittled you over the billboard photo and tonight I wanted to punch him out with how magnificent you truly are. I didn't plan for you to get hurt. I wanted you to feel proud that you were with me. The truth is…you're the woman I want to spend my life with, not a trophy for show. If you'll do me the honour of marrying me…'

'Don't!' Tears welled into her eyes, and once again she jerked her head away.

'I mean it, Angie,' he pressed, harnessing every bit of persuasive power he had to bring into play.

She shook her head. 'This is still…about winning,' she choked out.

'Yes, it is. Winning you as my wife.'

'It's the wrong time. The wrong time,' she repeated in a kind of frenzied denial.

'Then I'll wait for the right time.'

She looked at him with eyes swimming in pain. 'How can I believe you? Paul threw this challenge at you, Hugo. Paul…' She bit her lips and looked away again.

'Do you imagine I'd let him dictate how I spend the rest of my life, Angie?'

Her fingers plucked at the skirt of her dress, agitatedly folding the fabric. 'This is too much for me. Too much...' Her whole body suddenly jerked forward in alarm. 'James, this is my street,' she cried. 'You've just driven past my apartment block. Stop!'

'Missed the parking spot. Thought I'd just drive around the block, Miss Blessing,' James hastily explained.

'Please...back up!' she begged.

'Sir?'

'Stop and back up, James.'

While he appreciated James' ploy to give him more time, Hugo knew force would only alienate Angie further. Besides, she was right. It *was* the wrong time to make anything stick. He could only hope he'd made strong inroads on the barriers she was still holding on to.

The Bentley was reversed and brought to a halt. James alighted to open the passenger door. Angie rushed out an anxious little speech. 'I don't want you to accompany me to my door, Hugo. I need to be alone now.'

He nodded, not wanting her to be afraid of him, but his eyes locked onto hers with all the searing intensity of his need to convince her of his sincerity. 'Please think about what I've said, Angie. Think about us and how good it's been. And how much more we could have together. Promise me you'll do that.'

The passenger door was opened.

She didn't promise.

She bolted.

'James, see Miss Blessing safely to her door,' he quickly commanded.

'Yes, sir.'

He waited, the need to rein in all his aggressive instincts reducing him to a mass of seething tension. As soon as James had resettled himself in the driver's seat, Hugo asked, 'Did she say anything to you?'

'Miss Blessing thanked me for my many kindnesses, sir.'

'That doesn't sound good.'

'No, sir. Sounded like goodbye to me.'

'I have to win her back, James.'

'Yes, sir. Shall I drive you home now, sir?'

'Might as well. Breaking down her apartment door won't do it.'

'No, sir.'

The Bentley purred into moving on.

Hugo concentrated on coming up with a positive plan of action. 'Flowers tomorrow. Red roses for love. Masses of red roses delivered to her office, James.'

Throat clearing from the driver's seat. 'If I may be so bold, sir, I don't think flowers will do the trick this time. Not even red roses.'

'It's a start,' Hugo argued.

'Yes, sir. Shouldn't hurt,' came the heavily considered reply.

'But it's not enough to swing a change of opinion. I know that, James. You don't need to tell me.'

'No, sir.'

'I have to back them up with something else. Something big. Utterly convincing.' A sense of urgency gripped him. Failure to break this impasse with Angie in double quick time could mean losing her.

'Are you asking me for a suggestion, sir?' came the somewhat dubious question from the front seat.

'If you've got one, James, give it to me,' Hugo bit out.

More throat clearing. 'Please forgive me for…uh… overhearing what was…uh…most certainly a private conversation…'

'Oh, get on with it, James,' Hugo broke in impatiently. 'This is no time for sensibility or sensitivity. I have a crisis on my hands.'

'Right, sir. Well, it seemed to me, Miss Blessing felt you'd made a public show of her for…umh… self-serving reasons, and you'll need to somehow counterbalance that.'

'A show. A public show.'

Hugo seized on the thought, an idea blooming in his mind so fast, it zapped into the mental zone of *perfect move*. There'd been times in his life where he knew intuitively that all the pieces pointed to taking one single winning action—an exhilarating recognition of *rightness*. And when he'd followed through, it had worked for him. Worked brilliantly.

'I've got it, James!' he declared.

'You have, sir?'

'And I'll see to this myself. Push it through. Bribe, coerce…whatever it takes.'

'If I can be of any assistance, sir…'

'What I'm going to do is…'

And he outlined the plan.

Once again, James felt proud and privileged to be in the employ of Hugo Fullbright. Not only did he have the perspicacity to see Miss Blessing as the perfect wife for him, his plan to win her hand in marriage had that marvellous touch of flamboyance that made him such a pleasure to work for.

It was to be hoped—very sincerely hoped—that it would produce the right result.

CHAPTER SEVENTEEN

ANGIE barely slept. The mental and emotional turmoil revolving around everything that had happened with Hugo and Paul gave her no peace. It was impossible to sort out what she should do—give Hugo another chance or end a relationship that felt hopelessly entangled with motives which made her shudder with wretched misery.

She dragged herself out of bed the next morning, red-eyed from bouts of weeping and so fatigued that the idea of facing a day at the office with a happy Francine, fresh from a night of loving with Tim, made her heart quail. But it had to be done. Best that she did occupy herself with work. She'd probably go mad if she fretted any more over whether Hugo truly loved her or not.

The marriage proposal after what Paul had said…it had felt so wrong, so terribly, terribly wrong…how could she believe anything that came out of Hugo's mouth now?

She pushed the whole mess to the back of her mind and determinedly kept it there, even when Francine sailed into the office one hour late and poured out all her excitement and pleasure in Tim's proposal once again, raving about how *perfect* he was for her, how well he understood her, how sweet and generous he was, etc etc etc.

Angie agreed with her, managing as many smiles as she could, feeling sick about not having understood anything about Hugo, except his drive to win. Fortunately, she had a meeting with a contractor after lunch, giving her a break from Francine's blissful contentment. *Unfortunately,* it was at the Pyrmont apartment complex where she was assailed by memories of her first meeting with Hugo.

He hadn't known about Paul then—impossible to doubt that his desire for her company had been genuine. During the whole Tokyo weekend it had definitely been genuine.

Could he be sincere about loving her? Nothing to do with ensuring he didn't lose before he wanted to? These past three months had been so good, everything feeling *right* between them. Even when he'd taken her to the new ballet performance, he'd enjoyed it with her, finding the dancing quite fascinating. And erotic, he'd told her wickedly. Definitely interested in sharing this pleasure with her.

What if he truly didn't want to lose her at all?

What if the marriage proposal was genuine, too?

But he shouldn't have done it last night!

It still felt hopelessly wrong.

At four o'clock Angie returned to the office and winced at seeing a huge arrangement of red roses sitting on her desk. 'You'll have to move Tim's roses somewhere else, Francine,' she tossed at her friend. 'I need the work space.'

'They're for you!' The announcement came with a delighted grin. 'I think Tim's plunge into a marriage proposal has fired up Hugo. Red roses for love, Angie.'

Her heart fluttered nervously, wanting to believe, fearful of believing. Her agitated mind reasoned it was nothing for Hugo to order up flowers. James had probably done it for him. But *red* roses was definitely a first from him.

'There's a note for you,' Angie brightly informed her.

Angie set her briefcase down beside her desk and settled in her chair, needing to feel calmer before reading the attached note. She opened it gingerly. The note was actually hand-written in Hugo's strong scrawl, not some anonymous printing from a florist.

> *I do love you.*
> *I want us to spend the rest of our lives together.*
> *Please don't turn your back on what we have together, Angie.*
> *I'll contact you tomorrow.*
>
> > *Hugo*

Tomorrow… Angie drew a deep breath. She had another day to think about it. Not that she was getting anywhere much with her thinking.

'What does he say?' Francine asked eagerly.

Angie shrugged. 'Just that he'll call me tomorrow.'

'He adores you, Angie. Every time he looks at you, it's like he wants to eat you up.'

'That's sex, Francine, not love,' she said with some asperity.

'Oh, yeah? Well let me tell you, when I told him last night about Paul waylaying us and taking you off, he charged out like a bull to get you back with him. That's not sex. That's love.'

Or reclaiming his possession, Angie thought. Francine was rosy-eyed about everything right now. Nevertheless, Angie was reminded that the sense of intimacy she had known with Hugo had extended far beyond the bedroom. If it hadn't been for the too-extravagant gift of jewellery and the nasty encounter with Paul last night, would she be doubting a declaration of love by Hugo?

Wasn't it her own insecurity about the previous women in his life—all of them *temporary* attachments—that had made her see the gift as so much less than a ring of lifelong commitment?

And after all, their relationship *was* only of three months' standing. Three very intense months. But it was still a far cry from Francine's and Tim's situation, the two of them having known each other all through their childhood and teens. It was quite reasonable that Hugo hadn't seriously considered marriage...until she'd challenged him on it in the car last night.

She'd forced the issue.

He'd risen to it.

Why couldn't she accept that it was right for him?

Was she going to let Paul take from her what she most dearly wanted?

If only she could believe Hugo would have asked her to marry him, anyway.

She stared at the note.

He didn't mention marriage...just living together. But he did say...*for the rest of their lives.* And this note wasn't written in the heat of the moment. Hugo had had all night to think about what he wanted.

Tomorrow, Angie thought. *I'll see what happens tomorrow and take it from there.*

Thursday morning...

Angie felt more refreshed, having gone to bed early and slept like a log. Francine had also crashed out at home, and since neither of them had separate plans for today, they both travelled to work in Francine's car. They were in the usual tight stream of traffic crossing the Sydney Harbour Bridge when Francine remarked, 'Change of billboard today. Let's check out who's on it.'

'You don't need to check out anyone anymore,' Angie dryly reminded her.

'I have sympathy for the hopefuls.'

'Well, keep at least half an eye on the traffic as the billboard comes into view.'

She didn't.

She put her foot on the brake and stopped dead, causing mayhem and much honking of horns behind them. And Angie was too shocked to say a word. She didn't even hear the fracas around them. Her stunned gaze was fastened on the one mind-boggling, heart-squeezing photo of a man covering the entire billboard...

Hugo!

A much larger than life Hugo with a bunch of red roses resting in the crook of one arm, his other hand held palm out, offering a small opened box lined with white satin, and nestling in the middle of it, a blindingly gorgeous ring—an emerald with diamonds all around it.

Text was flashing with a kind of spectacular urgency.

Angie—will you marry me?

'Now that...is some proposal!' Francine muttered breathlessly.

Someone rapped on her window and an angry face yelled. 'Have you got trouble, lady? You're holding everyone up.'

Francine rolled down the window and yelled back, 'Have you got no romance in your soul?'

'What?'

'Look at the billboard!' She pointed. 'That's my friend's fiancé up there. Or he soon will be. Right, Angie?'

'Right,' Angie replied faintly.

'You can't get a more public commitment than that,' Francine told her stunned critic.

No, you can't, Angie thought dazedly, and wasn't the slightest bit aware of the rest of the journey to their Glebe office.

Where the red Bentley stood parked at the kerb.

'Stop!' she cried to Francine, totally unprepared for facing Hugo here and now.

Francine brought her car to a screeching halt, causing more mayhem to the traffic behind them on Glebe Road. 'Better get out, Angie,' she advised. 'Guess you won't be working today.'

'I don't know. I don't know,' Angie babbled nervously.

'Out you go and say yes. That's all you have to do. I have no doubt Hugo will take it from there. He's one hell of a go-getter,' Francine said admiringly. 'And all the best to both of you!'

'Thanks, Francine,' Angie mumbled and made herself move, alighting from the car to a blast of honking horns.

Francine stepped on the accelerator, shot forward, braked again as her car came level with the Bentley, honked her horn to draw the notice of the chauffeur, then carried on to drive around to the parking area in the back lane behind the office building.

Angie's suddenly tremulous legs managed to carry

her from the street to the sidewalk. Her heart was galloping as she saw James alight from the driver's side of the Bentley, resplendent in his chauffeur's uniform. He raised a hand to her in a salute of acknowledgment, rounded the gleaming red car, and opened the passenger door on the sidewalk side. He stood at attention beside it, his usual stately dignity slightly sabotaged by the hint of a smile lurking on his lips.

Angie paused to take a deep calming breath and unscramble the assault of wild thoughts in her mind. Was Hugo in the car? Or had James been ordered to take her somewhere to meet him? In which case, should she go or stay? It was a bit presumptuous of Hugo to send his man to collect her when she hadn't even said *yes*.

'*Please* step in, Miss Blessing,' James urged, a slight frown replacing the slight smile. His dignity even cracked so far as to beckon her forward.

Well, it wasn't fair to upset James, Angie reasoned. Besides, it was absurd to play hard to get at this point, when Hugo had well and truly put himself on the line for her. 'I'm coming,' she announced to James, giving him a grin as assurance that all was well.

He actually grinned back!

Which lightened Angie's heart immeasurably as she hurried to oblige him. James definitely approved of her marrying his boss, which should make for a happy household. She dived into the Bentley and straight into another heart-fluttering situation.

Hugo *was* in the car, sitting on the far side of the back seat. 'I've been waiting for you, Angie,' he purred at her as she flopped down beside him, his bedroom blue eyes sizzling with wicked intent. 'Waiting all my life for you to join me.'

'Oh!' was the only sound that came out of her mouth. Her dizzy mind registered that Hugo had just voiced exactly what she'd wished to hear from him. *Exactly!*

James closed the door, locking her in with the man who was fast proving to be the man of her dreams.

'Will you marry me?' he asked, wasting no time in pressing the critical question.

Angie looked askance at him but her heart was dancing, performing cartwheels. 'I'd have to love you first, Hugo.'

His mouth quirked into a very sensual smile. 'I think I love you enough for both of us. Why not give it a chance?'

She laughed. She couldn't help it. A cocktail of happiness was bubbling through her. 'Well, since I love you to distraction, I might just do that.'

'Then you will marry me.'

'Yes. Yes, I will.'

'I need your left hand.'

She gave it to him.

He immediately produced the ring that had glittered so enticingly on the billboard and slid it onto her third finger. 'Perfect fit!' he declared smugly.

'How did you guess?'

'Angie, there is nothing about your body that I don't know intimately. There's nothing about your heart that I don't know intimately. If you'll just let me fully into your mind…'

'I think if you kissed me…'

He did.

And the magic of knowing Hugo really, truly loved

her, and meant to love her all his life, made it the most special kiss of all, making them both sigh with satisfaction when it ended.

Some heavy throat-clearing from the driver's seat signalled that James was ensconced there, ready to drive off. 'To the airport now, sir?'

'Yes. Straight to the airport.' The furred edge of Hugo's voice was very sexy.

'May I be the first to congratulate both of you on your forthcoming nuptials, sir?' James said somewhat pompously, returning to form now that everything was satisfactorily settled.

'You may. Thank you, James.'

'Thank you, James,' Angie warmly chimed in, then turned quizzically to Hugo, 'Why the airport?'

'It's time for meetings with parents. We'll fly to Port Macquarie for mine to drool over you, then on to Byron Bay for yours to look me over. Or we can do it the other way around if you prefer.'

'All in one day?'

'I thought today and tomorrow with one set of parents and the weekend with the other. Enough time for everyone to get to know each other.'

It was a wonderful idea, but...I can't wear the same clothes for four days, Hugo. Can we go home first...?'

'No time. The flight is scheduled.' He gave her his wolf grin. 'You can give me the pleasure of buying whatever you need. That has to be allowable for my future wife!'

Staking out his territory, Angie thought, and laughed, moving to cuddle up to him, blissfully content for Hugo to indulge any pleasure he liked as long as it was with her. 'My warrior!' she murmured happily.

'At your service,' he said just as happily.

Angie sighed. 'Fighting for me from a billboard in full view of everyone crossing the Sydney Harbour Bridge is a story I'm going to relish telling our children.'

'And grandchildren,' he said with equal relish. 'Worth the price,' he added. 'Worth any price to have you, Angie. I just feel the luckiest man on earth to have found you.'

Amen to that, James thought.

The boss sure had a prize in Angie Blessing. And the pitter-patter of tiny feet was clearly on the drawing board. James felt he could now look forward to a fascinating new phase in his life.